THE WRITING ON THE WALL

HEARTS
OF THE
CHILDREN

VOL. 1

THE WRITING ON THE WALL

A NOVEL BY

DEAN HUGHES

DESERET
BOOK

SALT LAKE CITY, UTAH

First printing in hardbound 2001.
First printing in paperbound 2009.

Library of Congress Cataloging-in-Publication Data

Hughes, Dean, 1943–
   The writing on the wall / Dean Hughes
     p.   cm. — (Hearts of the children; v.1)
   Includes bibliographical references.
   ISBN-10: 1-57008-725-3 (hardbound: alk. paper)
   ISBN-13: 978-1-60641-172-8 (paperbound)
   1. Mormon families—Fiction. 2. Salt Lake City (Utah)—Fiction. I. Title.
PS3558.U36 W75 2001
813'.54—dc21   2001004151

Printed in the United States of America
R. R. Donnelley and Sons, Crawfordsville, IN

10 9 8 7 6 5 4 3 2 1

For David and Shauna Weight

PREFACE

*H**earts of the Children* is a "sequel series." It tells the story of the
Alexander and Bea Thomas family during the 1960s and '70s.
Many readers will already know the Thomases from my earlier
five-volume *Children of the Promise* series, which was set in the era of
World War II. These new books will feature the next generation, the
coming-of-age period for the children born toward the end, or just after
the end, of the war. I have tried to write *Hearts of the Children* so that it
can stand alone, with new stories about a new generation.

I am often asked whether any of the Thomases are based on actual
people. The answer is no; they are all fictional. I place them in history,
and I try to be accurate about the events and places where they live, but
they exist only in my head, and I hope, by now, in the heads—and maybe
the hearts—of the readers.

Fiction has its power. Perceptions and emotions of imaginary characters can be understood more completely than we ever understand each
other, and those perceptions can recreate a feel for history in a way that is
rare in a history book. But careless fiction can also distort. That's why I
include many perspectives. I try to create characters who differ in their
views and values, and by doing so, bring a realistic complexity to the time
I'm writing about.

I try to disturb history as little as possible, and yet historical fiction
always starts with a basic distortion: invented characters are dropped into
the stream of real events. In *The Writing on the Wall*, for instance, Gene
Thomas plays for East High in a football game on October 26, 1962. He is
the quarterback. The fact is, no one named Gene Thomas was going to

East High that year. But East did play Olympus High that night, and the final score really was 21 to 13, as I report. The perfect pass Gene throws is fictional, and that's a distortion, but I have kept the score right, and East actually did reach the semi-final game in the state championships that year, just as it happens in my novel.

Where I can, I use real names. President Blythe Gardner really was the mission president in the South German Mission in 1964 (I know; I was there), and President John Fetzer did take over for him that summer. But there was no Elder Bentz or Elder Johns. And by the way, my friend Jim Backman really was student-body president at East High in 1961–62, but, of course, he didn't turn over the presidency to the fictional Gene Thomas. (Had he done so, the students at East might have been quite confused.)

One of my interests in this new series is the way that the influence of a generation, or of a specific married couple, extends to its children, and then, to their children. But that means I have many characters in these books. I feature one of the children—actually the oldest, in each case— from four second-generation families, so that four cousins become the main characters. You may find it confusing to keep track of all their brothers and sisters. To help out, I am including, at the end of this preface, a family chart to show the entire Thomas family as it exists at the beginning of the series.

I don't use footnotes mainly because most of my history is general background rather than specific historical events, but I do want to suggest some books that make for interesting reading on the era of these novels. When I began the research for this series, I thought I wouldn't need to work very hard this time, since I graduated from high school in 1961 and know the time period. But memories are slippery, and any individual sees only a tiny portion of a "time." It has turned out that I've had to read a great deal.

Some books I found useful as general introductions to the issues and events of the era are: *Grand Expectations: The United States, 1945–1974*, by James T. Patterson (Oxford University Press, 1996); *The Sixties: From Memory to History*, ed. David Farber (University of North Carolina Press, 1994); *The Best and the Brightest*, by David Halberstam (Fawcett, 1969); and *How We Got Here: The 70's*, by David Frum (Basic Books, 1970). David Halberstam's book about the fifties is also a helpful introduction to the decades that follow: *The Fifties* (Fawcett, 1993). Jon Margolis has also written a really informative book on 1964: *The Last Innocent Year: America in 1964, the Beginning of the "Sixties"* (HarperCollins, 1999). Certain biographies are also helpful: *President Kennedy: Profile of Power*, by Richard Reeves (Simon and Schuster, 1993) and *Flawed Giant: Lyndon Johnson and His Times, 1961–1973*, by Robert Dallek (Oxford, 1998). And for coverage of JFK's funeral, *Jackie after Jack: Portrait of a Lady*, by Christopher Anderson (Warner, 1998), was most helpful.

On the subject of the civil rights movement, my favorite book was *Walking with the Wind: A Memoir of the Movement*, by John Lewis (Harcourt, Brace, 1998). Along with the Lewis book, Taylor Branch's two monumental works on Martin Luther King Jr., are seminal: *Parting of the Waters: America in the King Years, 1954–63* (Simon and Schuster, 1988) and *Pillar of Fire: America in the King Years, 1963–65* (Simon and Schuster, 1998). Also important is another David Halberstam book: *The Children* (Fawcett, 1999). Two books about Mississippi in the summer of 1964 were especially useful to me, both with the title *Freedom Summer*, one a memoir by Sally Belfrage (University of Virginia, 1965), and the other a history by Doug McAdam (Oxford, 1988).

In trying to learn about the German Democratic Republic, especially as experienced by members of The Church of Jesus Christ of Latter-day Saints, I am indebted to Regina Schreiber and her son Oliver, who lived in the country. I interviewed them, and they were also willing to read my manuscript and make suggestions. I also read *Behind the Iron Curtain: Recollections of Latter-day Saints in East Germany, 1945–1989*, by Garold N.

and Norma S. Davis (BYU Studies, 2000); *The Rise and Fall of the German Democratic Republic, 1945–1990*, by Mike Dennis (Pearson, 2000); and *The German Democratic Republic from the Sixties to the Seventies*, by Karl W. Deutsch (Harvard, 1970).

Books that especially portray the student movement of the sixties are *My Generation*, by Michael Gross (HarperCollins, 2000); *The Sixties: Years of Hope, Days of Rage*, by Todd Gitlin (Bantam, 1987); *All You Need Is Love: The Peace Corps and the Spirit of the 1960s*, by Elizabeth Cobbs Hoffman (Harvard, 1998); and *Deep in Our Hearts: Nine White Women in the Freedom Movement* (University of Georgia, 2000). And I found the best resource on the origins of the Vietnam War to be *Vietnam: A History*, by Stanley Karnow (Viking, 1993).

I should perhaps remind the reader that some of these books are like the sixties themselves, not only intense but also profane.

World War II was a trying time, but most people love to read about it. After all, good triumphed, we feel, and people joined arm in arm to win the victory. It wasn't really quite that simple, but it seems so, and we like to think of it that way. But the sixties and seventies were times when families were torn apart and people tended to split into factions. It's not an easy time to write about. But through it all, Latter-day Saints found their way, and families survived. I'm interested in this other kind of test for the Thomases, and perhaps in reading about the time, we can better understand our own families and where we are now, long after that time, living with many of its effects.

One of the most difficult issues for me was deciding what word to use for African Americans. *Negro* was standard at the time, and so I used it, along with the common term *colored*. That's historical. But what is also historical is the word *nigger*, and I used it with hesitation. I thought of calling it profanity and excluding it, just as I do other profane language, but in certain scenes, I feel it's the word that expresses the time and the anger that went with it, and so I have used it. I don't want to pass it to any more generations, but I think everyone needs to remember how some Americans once thought and acted. I wish to thank Darius A. Gray, who reviewed my use of black dialect and made some helpful corrections.

My schedule was tight this year. It took all my time to do the research and get a book written. It helped to take a leave of absence from BYU, but I had little time to ask my usual friends and family to read the manuscript. My wife, Kathy, did, as always, and she helped me focus the story in outline form as well as after some drafts. Most helpful to me were Emily Watts, director of the Bookcraft imprint at Deseret Book, and editor Jack Lyon. I always get lost somewhere along the way, and then I need editors to help me see where I am.

This book is dedicated to Dave and Shauna Weight. They have been friends to Kathy and me for thirty-four years. But the word *friend* hardly expresses the closeness we feel to them. We have gone through life together, sharing all our joys and challenges. What I appreciate most from them is that they believed in my writing long before most people even noticed it, have read most of my manuscripts over the years, and along with advice, have always given me hope that what I was doing had value.

D. Alexander and Beatrice (Bea) Thomas Family
(1961)

Alexander (Alex) [b.1916] [m. Anna Stoltz, 1944]
    Eugene (Gene) [b. 1945]
    Joseph (Joey) [b. 1947]
    Sharon [b. 1949]
    Kurt [b.1951]
    Kenneth (Kenny) [b. 1956]
    Pamela (Pammy) [b. 1958]

Barbara (Bobbi) [b. 1919] [m. Richard Hammond, 1946]
    Diane [b. 1948]
    Margaret (Maggie) [b. 1953]

Walter (Wally) [b. 1921] [m. Lorraine Gardner, 1946]
    Kathleen (Kathy) [b. 1946]
    Wayne [b. 1948]
    Douglas [b. 1951]
    Glenda [b. 1955]
    Shauna [b. 1959]

Eugene (Gene) [1925–1944]

LaRue [b. 1929]

Beverly [b. 1931] [m. Roger Larsen, 1953]
    Victoria (Vickie) [1954]
    Julia [b. 1955]
    Alexander [b. 1957]
    Suzanne [b. 1959]

CHAPTER 1

Gene Thomas drove his own car home from Sunday School, got there ahead of his family, and was happy to find that no one had bothered to lock the back door. He was tempted to go straight to the TV room, but instead he hurried upstairs to his bedroom to change clothes. The Yankees were playing on television that afternoon, but Gene didn't want to watch the game in his suit and tie. He would have to dress up again to go back to sacrament meeting, but he still preferred his Levi's for the hours in between. He sat down on his bed, pulled his penny loafers off, and then reached over and switched on his radio. At the moment, Ricky Nelson was singing, and Gene joined in. "Hello, Mary Lou, good-bye heart. Sweet Mary Lou, I'm so in love with you." He pretended to play a guitar riff, cocking his left arm and strumming the air with his other hand.

Gene had worn his summer suit to church that morning, and he knew how easily the polished cotton wrinkled, so he took the time to hang it up. He had become conscious of his clothes lately. It wasn't lost on him that the girls in his ward paid more attention than usual when he wore that suit. He had a good tan, and with his hair sun-bleached to pale blond, the tan suit was definitely the right touch. He had worked to get his hair right that morning too. He kept it short, just long enough to part. It was the "Beta" look that all the coolest guys at the University of Utah were wearing these days.

Gene had turned sixteen in June of that year, 1961, and gotten his driver's license a few days later. He had made good money all summer working for his Uncle Wally at his Rambler dealership. Mostly Gene washed cars and cleaned up around the place, but at times the sales manager had let him help customers, and he had actually closed a couple of deals. The commissions on those sales had added greatly to the dollar-twenty-five an hour income he normally got, and more important, it had given him enough cash to make a down payment on his own car. It was a two-tone red and white '54 "Vickie"—a Ford Crown Victoria—that Uncle Wally had let him have for $300. He had fixed it up with a new set of moon hubcaps and white rolled and pleated Naugahyde seat covers, and he had kept those seats occupied with lots of East High girls. He had told his friend Jeff Richards, a guy he played football with, that his goal was to date every good-looking girl in the school *once*—just to be sure he had enough information to start round two. He figured that on the second time around he could be a little more selective.

He had his Levi's on and was pulling an old knit shirt over his head when a disk jockey began to read the news: "In Berlin, early this morning, East German officials took action to stop the flow of refugees to the west. In a major crackdown, workers, protected by armed guards, began sinking posts into city streets and stringing barbed wire."

Gene sat down on his bed and turned the volume on his radio a little higher.

"Reports from West Berlin indicate that a rush is on, many East Germans risking their lives to flee to the West before all escape routes are cut off. At the Brandenburg Gate, West Berliners pelted East German police with rocks and bottles before East Germans responded with a water cannon, driving back the demonstrators. Thousands of hopeful refugees, fearing the closure, have been filling the city in recent days, and now tensions are high. Russian tanks are lined up at several points along the border."

Gene had heard his father predict that something like this might be coming, but that didn't relieve his fear. What if someone started to shoot? How long would it be after that before missiles were flying?

"Soviet leader Nikita Khrushchev earlier this summer gave Western nations six months to withdraw from Berlin, in the center of Communist-held East Germany. President Kennedy and other Western leaders have insisted, however, that they have no intention of leaving. President Kennedy, spending the weekend at his Hyannis Port retreat, has issued no public statement, but an anonymous source close to the president was quoted as saying, 'This is a very touchy situation. We're staring World War III straight in the face, and the last thing we need is heated rhetoric. Perhaps the closing was inevitable; it may serve to calm tensions once the crisis has passed.'"

If it passed. But Gene was also thinking about the other matter—the concern his mother would have. He had heard her and the other kids come in while he was changing his clothes. He jogged down the hallway in his stocking feet and called, "Mom, where are you?"

Anna's door opened. She had already taken off her church clothes and slipped on a cotton dress. "What is it?" she asked.

"The East Germans are closing off the border in Berlin. I heard it on the radio."

"Oh no." Anna's hands leaped to her face. "I *knew* this would happen. I tried to tell them."

"Maybe they can still get out. Maybe the government will—"

But Anna had begun to cry. "I'll never see Peter again. I never will."

She leaned toward Gene, and he took her in his arms. She let her head rest against his shoulder, and in a moment he could feel the heat of her tears through his shirt.

"Maybe it's not as bad as it sounds, Mom. Maybe this will quiet down, and then you can at least go see him."

Gene had only met his Uncle Peter once—at least when he was old enough to remember. Peter had come to Salt Lake after World War II but then had decided to go back to Germany. He had gotten married, but he and his wife, Katrina, had chosen to move to the Russian Zone, where

Katrina's mother had a farm. Anna and Peter's parents, who still lived in Salt Lake, had tried to convince Peter to return to America, especially after the Communists had tightened their control, but Katrina had not wanted to leave her mother, and Peter had always said that things were not so bad as everyone in the west claimed. Maybe he would regret his decision now.

Anna patted Gene on the back, and then she stepped away from him. She wiped the tears from her cheeks with the palm of her hand. "I've got to go see my parents before they hear it on the radio," she said. "This could kill my mother. It's the only thing she has hoped for since she got so sick, to see Peter and his children one more time."

Gene usually didn't think of his mother as German, rarely noticed any accent, but he heard it now in the word "radio," with a softer "r" than usual, and even more in the name "Peter," pronounced, as always, "payter," but now with more emphasis on the first syllable. Gene had heard the story about his mother and her family, their flight from the Gestapo, Peter's nightmare experiences in the German army after failing to escape with the others, but it was all just that—a story. Now the meaning of his mother's past—her separation from her brother—seemed to sink in. "Are you going to be okay?" he asked.

"How would you feel if you knew you would never see Joey again? Joey's so much like Peter was at that age. He looks just like him." Joey had recently turned fourteen, but he looked younger. He had innocent brown eyes and an almost constant, wide smile.

Mom was crying again, and Gene suddenly felt angry. Governments had no right to lock their people up, to take away their freedom. What kind of system was it that couldn't operate without building walls around its country?

"Do you want me to find Dad?"

"No. He has meetings. And there's nothing he can do." Anna smiled. Her eyelashes were wet. "I'm all right. I just hate so much to tell Mama and Papa." She took a step away, then stopped and looked back. "Keep an eye on the kids, will you? Remind the boys it's the Sabbath. You know how upset your dad gets when he comes home and finds them playing football."

"Or watching baseball on TV. He doesn't like that, either."

"I know. And he's probably right."

Gene smiled at her. She was never quite as strict as Dad. Gene admired his father more than any other man he knew, but there was always something a little frightening about him, as though he were a giant in the house—and he expected Gene to stand just as tall.

Gene walked back to his room and grabbed an old pair of Converse high-tops, which he carried with him downstairs to the family room. His family had moved to this house—an elegant, two-story place on Harvard Avenue—just two years before. It was a house that Gene's dad, Alex Thomas, had had his eye on for years—partly because it reminded him of the house he had grown up in, and partly because it was in the East High area, where he had gone to school and where he wanted his children to go. What Gene loved was the cozy family room at the back of the house, with lots of windows that looked out on a well-manicured backyard. His dad had worked with his parents and his brother Wally in some of the family businesses—real-estate and land-development operations—at one time, but for years now he had been a building contractor. He had started out building homes, but his company had expanded into commercial properties and had taken on some big projects. Gene knew his father had made a lot of money, and he had spent plenty modernizing the old house, but Dad wasn't a socialite. He was a Church leader—a member of his stake presidency—and a community and state leader. He had been serving in the state legislature for several years, first in the House, and now in the state Senate.

Gene watched the baseball game, the second of a doubleheader, the Yankees playing the Washington Senators. Roger Maris and Mickey

Mantle had each hit home runs in the first game, and Maris got another one in the game Gene watched. That meant the two were tied, with forty-five homers each, and both had a great chance to beat Babe Ruth's record of sixty in one season. Gene wanted to see Mantle—his hero— break the record. He hated to think that Maris might be the one to do it.

Still, Gene didn't watch the game all that closely. His brothers and sisters all showed up, and they wanted to know why Mom had been cry-ing. Joey and twelve-year-old Sharon—even Kurt, who was ten—knew about their cousins in Germany and understood something about the troubles with Russia. But Kenny, who was not yet five, and little Pammy, at three, were only worried about Mom.

Gene didn't know how to explain things to the little ones, but he tried to sound confident. He hoped the world didn't scare them too much—even though it was scaring him more than he liked to admit. What if war did break out? He would have to be a man about it, to stand up and fight the way his father had during World War II. But in the back of his mind was the image of mushroom clouds he had seen on TV from test sites in Nevada. How could anyone fight against those?

Kathy Thomas was sitting on a lawn chair in her backyard. Sunday dinner was over, but her father, Wally—Bishop Thomas—hadn't man-aged to get home in time to eat with the others. He always tried to make it, but with five hungry kids it was hard for Mom to hold off very long. Kathy's dad had been bishop for two or three years—Kathy couldn't remember exactly—and was the sweetest man anyone knew, but that meant that all the ward members wanted to share their problems with him. He always started Sunday with a schedule, but it evaporated virtu-ally every week.

Kathy was reading, but she had actually gone outside to catch a little sun. All summer she had been doing volunteer work as a candy striper at the LDS Hospital. That had kept her busy, and her voice and piano practice had also kept her inside. But it was August 13 now, and school wasn't far away. She didn't want to start her ninth-grade classes at Hillside Junior High still ghastly white. It was bad enough that she was so tall and skinny. A cloud cover had gradually moved across the sky, but Kathy didn't care all that much. The truth was, she didn't really like sitting in the sun. She had dark hair, like her father's, but her skin was more like her mom's— fair and easy to burn. Besides, the clouds took away the glare that had forced her to squint to see the pages of her book.

Reading was Kathy's passion, and she liked all kinds of books. She loved novels, biographies, even history, and she kept up with issues and read about trends in American society: civil rights, poverty, the arms buildup. Her dad teased her that she was the only fourteen-year-old girl in America who had read *A Nation of Sheep*, by William J. Lederer, the best-selling nonfiction book in the country that summer. But Kathy's mom was a member of the Book of the Month Club and had received a copy automatically. Lorraine hadn't found time to read it, but Kathy had gotten interested and read it cover to cover. She had told her parents that she was "changed forever." Lederer accused the American people of neglecting their democratic duty by being so uninformed. The government made decisions in secret, based on false premises, but the people, out of apathy, didn't speak up. Kathy had made up her mind; she wasn't going to be like that.

Kathy knew the kind of person she *did* want to be. Her idol was her Aunt LaRue, who was an economics professor at Smith College in Massachusetts. Aunt LaRue knew *everything*, and she *cared*. Kathy would talk for hours with her whenever she was home. The woman was not just smart; she was also beautiful and classy and funny and shockingly independent. Kathy wanted to be every one of those things. She was so sick of junior-high boys, who were shorter than her, dumber than her, and annoying—whether she liked to admit it or not—because they were so unaware of her. She longed to be grown up and on her own, like Aunt LaRue, but she also longed to be as beautiful. For that she held out little hope, however.

Today Kathy was reading a new book by Harper Lee, *To Kill a Mockingbird*. She knew something about conditions in the South; her Grandpa Thomas had served as a mission president in the southern states during the early fifties. He and Grandma Bea had told her painful stories about the things they had seen. But Harper Lee's novel had made her much more aware of—and indignant about—the injustice Negroes suffered. She found herself longing to be like Atticus, someone who stood up for right no matter what it might cost her personally. Sometimes she was embarrassed that her family lived in such a fancy new house on Country Club Drive. It just seemed wrong to her that some people had so much while others had nothing.

Kathy was lost in the story when she heard the whoosh of a storm door. She looked up. Lorraine, her mother, stepped halfway out the back door and said, "Kathy, I just heard something on the radio that really worries me. The East Germans are sealing off East Berlin."

Kathy let her book drop. "They're really doing it? I didn't think they'd dare."

"The American troops haven't tried to stop them. Maybe there won't be a fight." But Lorraine was gripping her hands into fists. Kathy knew her mother feared war more than anything—because of her memories of World War II.

"Are you okay, Mom?"

"Sure. But it feels so much like Pearl Harbor day, all over. And it could be worse this time." She slipped her hands into her apron pockets and looked down. "I'm also thinking about Anna. Her brother's fenced in now."

"Did you call her?"

"Not yet. I guess I'd better. I just hate to be the one to let her know."

"Maybe she's heard by now."

Lorraine nodded, hesitated as though considering, and then stepped back through the door. Kathy heard the gush of the door-closer again, then watched the metal door settle into place. She thought of soldiers face to face in Berlin. What if one man pulled a trigger? She got up and walked inside, went to the family room off the kitchen and dining area, and turned on the TV. Her mom was in the kitchen, holding the phone to her ear, dialing.

Kathy waited for the television set to warm up, but when it did, a baseball game was on. She turned the sound down a little and switched the knob to another channel. She tried all three stations but found nothing about Berlin. She walked in and sat at the little counter that separated the family room from the kitchen, and she listened to her mother.

"Things can change, Gene. This might be temporary, while they're trying to clamp down." Lorraine hesitated, listened, agreed with something Gene said. Then she turned toward Kathy. "Gene wants to talk to you," she said. She held out the phone in Kathy's direction.

Kathy slipped off the stool and walked to her mother. "Did Aunt Anna know about it?" she asked.

"Yes. She went to tell her parents, and they were terribly upset. She's spending the afternoon with them."

Kathy took the phone. "Hello. Gene?"

"Did you hear the news?" he asked.

"Yes. It makes me sick."

"I wonder what Hans is thinking."

"Their government probably feeds them a lot of lies."

"I wish we'd take on the Russians, Kathy. I wish we'd just fight this war right now. It's going to come sooner or later anyway."

Kathy couldn't believe Gene. "Oh, sure," she said, "that's just what we need. Nuclear war."

"Let 'em fire away. We've got as many ICBMs as they do."

Kathy took a long breath. She had been interested to know that Gene was worried about Hans, his cousin, but she didn't need this. "Gene, they have enough missiles to *destroy* us. And we have enough to do the same to them. I don't think it's a question of who is *more* destroyed. When we're all dead, we're all dead." She was standing by the light-colored "blond" kitchen cabinets. She turned now, leaned back against them, let the cord slip over her shoulder.

Lorraine had walked into the family room, and now she was trying what Kathy had tried, to check the TV for news. She glanced up at Kathy, and her look said, "Don't get into another argument with your cousin."

Kathy made a decision to say nothing more. But Gene said, "I don't know who'll fire what, but I wish I could stop those guys. The world needs to stand up to the Commies before it's too late—just like we finally did with Hitler."

Kathy hesitated, glanced at her mother, and then decided to allow herself one last comment before she dropped the subject. "What is it with *boys?* You all say you want to go on missions, but you'd *much* rather be out shooting somebody."

"We're not the ones starting the trouble, Kathy. It's the Communists who keep trying to force their system down people's throats."

"What do you think we do? We go into poor countries, hire the peasants, pay them next to nothing, and then bring all the profits back to America." This was all part of Kathy's newfound knowledge about what was *really* going on—the things the government didn't tell people.

There was silence on the other end of the phone for a moment, and Kathy knew she had won a little victory. She looked away from her mother and said to Gene, "I would hope that a *good* Mormon would want to solve problems *without* going to war."

"Hey, the Book of Mormon is full of righteous wars. Sometimes you have to fight. Look at Captain Moroni. That guy didn't back down to *anybody*. He's *my* hero." He laughed. "Right up there next to Mickey Mantle."

Now it was Kathy who was silent for a moment, and she hated that, because she knew what Gene was thinking—that he had won round two and they were even. "I thought to be *your* hero, a guy had to wear nothing but Gant shirts and Corbin slacks," she said.

"Hey, if Moroni came back today, that's *exactly* what he would wear. With Adler socks."

"Oh, brother."

Kathy was tempted to throw some more punches, but Mom was saying, "Kathy, that's enough." So Kathy held up her hand to acknowledge her mother's demand, and she said nothing more. The sun had just come out from behind the clouds, and the family room suddenly filled with light. Kathy told herself she would go back outside to her chair, her book, and get some more sun. She knew she did have to stop getting so upset with people, the way she did so often lately, and she had to calm down about what was happening in Berlin. There was not one thing she could do about it.

"Look, Kathy," Gene said. "Let me just say two more things. First, I don't *want* to fight a war. I'm just saying that the Russians might not give us a choice, and the longer the thing gets put off the worse position we might be in. And second, and this is the really important point"—but now he laughed again—"you're my very favorite cousin. I like you, even though you're just a kid, and you're almost always wrong."

"Shut up. Okay?" Lorraine was staring at Kathy, looking shocked. Kathy said, in a nicer voice, "But really, Gene, aren't you scared?"

"Sure I'm scared. But I'll do what I have to do."

There was so much drama in his tone that Kathy wanted to gag. "I love you, Gene," she said. "But it would be nice if you were right about something, even just once."

"Yeah. Grandpa, Dad, and me—three generations. We're all wrong. And one little girl just happens to know *everything*."

But that burned. Kathy couldn't joke about that kind of remark, and she was suddenly too mad to know what to say. When Gene said, "Hey, I'm just kidding you," she didn't buy it.

Kathy said very little after that, and she got off the phone, but when she did, she was furious. "What is it about people who think they're such good Christians?" she asked her mom. "Why are they always so ready to start wars? Sometimes I think Gandhi was the only man who ever understood what Christ was talking about—and he wasn't even a Christian."

But Mom said, "Calm down, Kathy. You don't sound very Christian yourself right now."

That finished Kathy. She walked back outside. But she was too angry to read, so she lay back on her lawn chair and thought up a dozen arguments, all to answer Gene and all these other Utahns who liked to use the Book of Mormon to prove that war was such a fine thing—no matter what God happened to think about it. Kathy's father had been in World War II, had been a POW for three and a half years. Her Uncle Alex and Uncle Richard had been in the war, too. They rarely spoke of it now, but never once had she heard them say anything but how horrible it was. Why couldn't people trust that? Why were they so quick to look for new chances to make a mess of the world? World War II had ended with atomic weapons, but this next war might *begin* that way—and what would be left? Kathy thought of Berlin again, thought of tanks facing each other across a silly line someone had drawn on a map, and she imagined the soldiers on both sides just itching to get started. What was wrong with people?

But her anger faded as she thought of the reality the world was facing. It could all be over—this war—in a matter of minutes. She found herself glancing at the sky, wondering. Everyone said that northern Utah would be a target if the missiles were ever launched. She wondered what it would be like, if it ever happened.

∼⚬∼

On Sunday morning Hans Stoltz had gotten up at the last minute, as usual. He dressed quickly and put on his white shirt and tie—but no coat. He knew it would be hot, and the walk was rather long to church. In the winter the family usually took a streetcar, but money was always tight, so the walk to church was worth it, at least as far as Hans's parents—Peter and Katrina—were concerned. Hans was tired from staying up too late the night before—not that he had done anything very important. He had done homework most of the evening—mainly because his father didn't think he should study on the Sabbath—and then he had listened to the family radio and read a little. The Stoltzes had a television set, but television in the German Democratic Republic—the GDR—was hardly worth watching, and his father had never put up an antenna to receive West German television. Some people did that even though it was illegal.

Hans felt almost numb as he plodded alongside his father on their way to priesthood meeting. His mother and seven-year-old sister, Inga, would come a little later for Sunday School. Hans had some friends he liked to see at church, but the man who taught his deacons quorum was a tiresome old fellow who repeated himself a thousand times, giving more or less the same lesson every week. Church manuals and teaching materials were not easy to come by in the GDR, and some of the teachers were better than others at inventing their own lessons. Sunday school was a little better, but nothing Hans actually looked forward to. At thirteen, he was one of the youngest in a class that included most of the young people in the Schwerin branch. He was a smart boy—even if he didn't always study as hard as he might have—but at church, he rarely said much of anything.

Outside the church, on the *Schlossgarten Allee*, Brother Wohler and

Brother Kastaler were standing close, leaning toward each other as though exchanging secrets, both seeming to talk at the same time. As the Stoltzes approached, the men turned. "Have you heard the news, Peter?" Brother Kastaler asked.

"What news?"

"The government has done it. They've closed the border in Berlin."

Hans felt something like pain strike his chest. He had told his father, told him so many times: They had to get out before it was too late. Now it *was* too late.

"What do you mean 'closed'?" Peter asked. "How can they close off a whole city?"

"Barbed wire—strung clear across. They're going to build a high wall, all the way through Berlin."

"What about the people who live on one side and work on the other?"

"No more," Brother Wohler said. "You should have heard the announcement. It's all for our own prosperity and well-being—and to keep the imperialist enemy from attacking. Do they expect us to believe that?" But such sarcasm required some bravery in this country. Brother Wohler was a man in his sixties. He had fought in World War II, on the eastern front, had a terrible scar across his ear and neck. He had lost the hearing in his left ear, the sight in his eye. There was something almost frightening in the way he stared now, with that one good eye.

"What did the Americans do—just let them get away with this?" Peter asked.

"They didn't do a thing. Not so far," Brother Kasteler said. "I doubt they will. Khrushchev has them all shaking over there—scared to death he'll fire his missiles."

Peter put his hands on his hips, looked at the pavement, and stood that way for some time. Finally, he said, "We were losing all our best people—the best trained, best educated."

But to Hans this sounded like an excuse for the government. It was what his father always did—explain everything away. Hans didn't want to hear any more of this. He walked on inside. But even in the chapel, the talk was the same. Every man there, every boy, was talking in hushed tones, but Hans wondered whether any of them were as sick as he was. He had wanted so long to get out of this country, had pleaded with his father to leave while they still could. Now it was too late—too late to have a life, it seemed. He had always longed to live in Utah, where his grandparents and his cousins lived so well.

Hans didn't say a word in either meeting that morning. His friends wanted to talk about Berlin, but he didn't have the heart. After Sunday School he avoided his family, as he often did, and headed outside to begin the walk home by himself. But as he was leaving the building, he saw some of his friends gathered on the street.

"It might be a good thing, really," Walter Kleiner was saying. "We can't move ahead in this country until people stop running off."

Hans heard the strained tone, however, and he thought that Walter was only trying to put a good face on something that he knew was wrong. It was the tone he heard so often from young people: a certain embarrassment, combined with a will to believe, or maybe a feeling that a person was better off to claim belief.

Hans stopped. "Yes, it's a fine thing, Walter. Most of the best nations lock up their people and place armed guards on their borders. It's a great sign of love our government wants to show us."

Walter walked away from the other boys, took Hans by the arm, and turned him away. He whispered, "Hans, don't say this. It's a very big mistake to speak this way. You know that." It was what Hans's father always told him, that the Secret Police—known as the *Stasi*—infiltrated every organization, including the Church. It was never safe to be so open, anywhere.

"We're forced to stay. And then we're forced to say we like the idea. What a wonderful country we have. So much freedom."

"Hans, you must not do this. It's bad enough that people know we go to church. If we speak this way, we'll pay the price."

"I'll speak however I wish," Hans said, and he walked away. But as he walked home, he began to regret his honesty. Walter wasn't likely to repeat what he had said, but Hans knew he couldn't say such things to anyone else. By the time he reached his apartment house, a weary fatalism had replaced his anger. This was nothing new, he told himself; he had always been trapped. This last step made little difference.

So Hans hid away in his room. When the rest of his family came in, he stayed where he was. He didn't want to talk about any of this. He lay on his bed and tried to think what kind of future he could expect now. He was in his eighth year of school, and he had always believed that he would be admitted to the advanced high school—*Oberschule*—where the students were on track to enter universities. More often than not, religious people were rejected for college entrance, so Hans understood that to have a better future than his father, he would have to watch his tongue, show himself to be cooperative.

All Hans wanted was something to look forward to. If he missed his chance to attend a university, he could easily end up shuffling papers in some dreary office all his life—just as his father did. Or he could be placed in some trade, like his mother. She worked at a sewing machine all day, in a large factory, reproducing the same pattern over and over for months at a time. Sometimes he thought he wanted to be an architect, and he also thought of becoming a scientific researcher. Whatever he did, he wanted some level of prestige, some status in the world, and something interesting to do. He knew he was smart, and he wanted to prove it. He told himself often that he had to start giving more effort in school, and then everything would be all right. But all this was searching for a compensation. What he had really wanted for as long as he could remember—

since his father had first told him about the homes his relatives had in Salt Lake City, the cars they drove—was to emigrate, get out of this dismal country and live where he could be happy. He didn't want to give up on the idea that that was possible.

After a time, Hans's mother called him to dinner. Peter spent the time at the table trying to justify everything, make it seem all right. "It makes no difference to us," he told Hans. "We weren't planning to leave the country anyway."

"No. We certainly were not," Hans told him.

Peter set down his knife and fork. He looked at Hans for a long time before he said, "And what does that mean?"

"You said it yourself. We weren't planning to leave. I was merely agreeing with you."

"But you think we should have had such plans?"

"You know what I think. We should have left a long time ago."

Hans was eating his boiled potatoes. His mother had cooked a tiny roast of pork—divided the one pound she had been able to buy, with meat in such short supply, in order to make two meals of it. Hans's portion had hardly made a mouthful, so he was filling himself with potatoes, with red cabbage. It was what they ate with so many of their meals. What he didn't want, to go with all this blandness, was another fight with his father.

"Hans, look at me."

Hans looked up. His father was like a mirror, reflecting his own face back at him. They had the same loose brown hair, the same dark eyes. They looked like their Grandfather Stoltz, mother always said; they were built strong, not tall, but both seemed young for their age, their faces almost delicate.

"You have to start thinking about all of us—not just yourself. There are higher purposes in life sometimes. It does no good to dream of America all the time."

"What higher purpose?" Hans asked, and now his anger was returning.

"We're the ones who must keep the Church going in this country. If all the Saints leave, what happens to the gospel in this land? Our duty is to do missionary work in quiet ways, support the members, continue what the missionaries started here long ago. It's taken a long time to establish a branch here. Do you remember how hard we worked to build our chapel?"

Hans wasn't going to have this conversation again. It was all such nonsense. What did it matter whether the Church existed in Schwerin? The membership could grow in countries that didn't make things so difficult. And in any case, there were other Mormons who could keep things going here, if that's all that mattered.

"My mother needs us here, Hans," Katrina said. "It would have been so hard for her, had we decided to leave."

But *Oma* had two sons. Wasn't that enough for her?

"Hans, why can't you at least try to understand?" Peter asked.

Little blonde Inga was sitting across the table from Hans. She was tiny for her age, but she had a surprisingly deep, strong voice. "He does try, Papa," she said.

Hans didn't know what she meant exactly, except that it was her way of supporting him. Hans was touched by that. He knew how much she hated these arguments, and so he tried to calm things a little. "I'm fine. Don't worry about it. As you said, this new barrier is nothing new. We've been fenced in for a long time."

But Hans heard the gloom in his own voice, and he knew what that had done to everyone else. No one spoke for quite some time. Hans felt the oppressive closeness in the little kitchen, hardly big enough for the four of them to sit around the table, felt the tiresome heat in the room. At night, Hans kept his bedroom window wide open, but that only seemed to let in the humidity without moving the air. He had heard about America, where people bought air conditioners and put them in their windows, slept in comfort, and he had heard all about Utah, where the humidity was low and the mountain air cooled at night. All his life he had imagined himself there with his grandparents, among his cousins who were so wealthy. He had worked hard at his English so that he could attend an American university, could have the same chance to succeed that his cousins had. Sometimes his parents had talked of it, but in the end, his father had always come back to the same idea: they had to stay and serve the Church.

"Hans," his father finally said, "when life is over, the only thing we'll care about is the work we did for the Kingdom. Nothing else means very much. That's what I keep trying to help you understand."

"But, Papa, our relatives in America have good lives. Why do we have to give up so much? Don't you want to see your mother before she dies? Don't you want to see your father and your sister?"

Peter looked down at the table for a long time. When he finally spoke, his voice was little more than a whisper. "Of course I do. But son, we're needed here. When I've asked God, that's the answer I've always received."

Hans felt his frustration building again. "Maybe God talks to you, but he's never told me anything like that. He's never told me anything at all. So maybe I'll do something on my own. Maybe I'll do what I choose."

"And what would that be, Hans?"

"If I can find a way to get out, then I'll go. Maybe not yet. But sooner or later."

"And how would you do that?"

"I don't know. There must be ways."

"Hans, you're thirteen years old. Don't act like you know everything. You'll understand more as you grow up. For now, just trust me. I'm your father."

But Hans was tired of listening to a father who thought he got his opinions directly from God. Hans would get his chance someday, and then he would make his own decisions.

CHAPTER 2

Diane Hammond loved "Gram"—her great-grandmother Thomas—but she was nervous about looking after her for an evening. Diane had heard from Grandma Bea that Gram couldn't live much longer, that her heart was giving out. It scared Diane to think of being there when that finally happened. Still, it was a little hard to believe. Great-Grandpa Thomas had died when Diane was little, and she couldn't remember him very well, but Gram had always been livelier than anyone else she knew. It hardly seemed possible that someone so energetic and fun could stop living.

Diane's parents, Richard and Bobbi, had decided to take Grandpa and Grandma Thomas out to dinner. Bobbi was worried that Bea spent so many hours with Gram that she hardly ever got out of the house. So Bobbi had called one night and said, "We're taking you out to dinner. Diane said she would be happy to sit with Grandma while we're gone."

Bobbi had actually seemed surprised that her mother had accepted the invitation, but by the time the Hammonds arrived on a cool Friday evening in October, Grandma Bea was obviously worried. She talked to Diane about all of Gram's medicines, and what to do if she began to have trouble breathing. "We won't be gone all that long," she said. "I thought we'd go over to the Harman's here in Sugar House. It's not like some of these fancy places that think they have to take all night to bring your meal." Still, Grandma had looked up the restaurant's phone number and written it on a little pad, which she had set by the phone.

"Everything will be fine," Diane told Grandma Bea.

"I know. But you know me. I have to fuss about things." She laughed at herself, and then she gave Diane another hug, for no particular reason, and said, "Come on up. I'll go with you." Grandma climbed the steps, Diane behind her, with Mom and Dad and Maggie following. Gram was now staying in the room that had once been Bobbi's, and later, Aunt LaRue's. "Mom," Grandma said, as she opened the bedroom door, "Diane's here. Remember what I told you? She's going to sit with you."

"Bea, for heaven's sake," Gram said. "I'm not senile. You just told me ten minutes ago. Do you think I've forgotten already?"

Bea laughed. "Well . . . you do forget sometimes."

"Yes, and so do you."

"I *am* getting senile. No question about that."

But Bobbi was walking toward the bed by then, and Gram was stretching out a hand to her. "It's *so* good to see you, Bobbi," she said. "Why don't you come down more often?"

Bobbi bent and kissed her on the cheek. "Tell the truth, Grandma. It's not me you want to see. You still have a crush on Richard."

Gram smiled. "That's right," she said. "Come here, you handsome lout. Give me a smacker."

Richard laughed, and he did step closer and kiss her.

"I still wish I'd found you before Bobbi did," Gram said.

"As I recall, your husband was still alive then," Richard said. "That might not have worked out very well."

"Oh, well, I could have put a little arsenic in his soup and gotten rid of him."

Gram always joked with Dad this way, and Diane liked to hear it, but she didn't like what she was seeing tonight. Gram had gone downhill a great deal in the three weeks since Diane had seen her last. She looked transparent, as though her skin were thinning. She had lost more weight, too. Her face was all bones. There was also something sour in the air, like bad breath; Diane hoped it wasn't coming from Gram.

Diane slipped in front of her mother. "Hi, Gram," she said. When she kissed Gram on the cheek she was surprised at how dry her skin felt.

"Diane, I can't believe what's happened to you lately," Gram said. "You've turned into a woman. You look older than your cousin Kathy. How old are you now?"

Gram *was* forgetting things. She had told Diane the same thing the last time she was here. "Thirteen," Diane said.

"Good heavens." She looked at Bobbi. "You'd better hide her away for a few years. The boys are going to be circling your house like packs of wolves."

"You don't have to tell me, Grandma. It's starting to happen already."

Gram turned her head on the pillow and looked at Diane. "I was a gorgeous girl myself, you know. When I went to a church dance, every boy in the ward wanted to have a turn with me."

"I believe that," Diane said.

"I can still turn heads when I walk into a room." She spoke with her old flair, but then she added, more quietly, "At least I could until lately."

"I know that, Gram. I've watched you do it lots of times."

"It's because I'm the only one in this family who knows how to dress. Poor Bea has no taste for anything but brown and gray."

"What about my new black dress?"

"Black! I'm going to leave you all my pretty dresses: red and turquoise and purple, and all the rest. I'm just afraid that the minute they haul me out of here, stiff as a board, you'll give all my things to the Deseret Industries." Gram looked at Diane. "Di, honey, if I were you, I'd grab up some of those things. You're going to be tall enough to wear them. Bea's too stubby."

"That's the truth," Bea said. "But someone has to take over the job of flashy old woman in the family. Maybe I'll have some of those dresses altered."

"Now that I'd like to see," Gram said, but by then she was looking at

Maggie, who had stayed back all this time. Gram motioned to her, raising her thin arm barely off the blue comforter that was spread over her. "Come here, sweetheart," she said. "You don't have to kiss me, if I scare you. I know how ugly I am now."

Maggie didn't say a word for a moment but continued to stand at the foot of the bed. "Go ahead. Kiss Gram," Bobbi said.

Maggie slipped along the bed and gave her great-grandmother a little peck on the cheek. "Hi, Gram," she said softly, and the affection in her voice touched Diane. Maggie was a sweet girl, only eight. Diane suspected she *was* frightened. She had surely never seen anyone change so drastically. Gram was ninety-four, and she *should* have looked this old long ago—but she never had. She had always seemed as bright as the colors she wore, and she had never gone anywhere without makeup. Now all this white, this bluing of her skin, was hard to look at. Gram's dark hair— dyed, of course—was growing out now, an inch of white showing against her scalp.

"How old are you now, sweetheart?" Gram asked.

"Eight."

"Have you been baptized yet?"

"Yup."

"When?"

"Last February, when it was my birthday."

"Why wasn't I there?" Gram looked up at Bea, for the first time seeming confused.

"You weren't feeling well enough."

"I do forget things, don't I? It makes me so mad." But suddenly her eyes widened, and her voice was much louder when she said, "All right, everyone go away now. I'm wearing out, and I want to talk to Diane for a while before I get *too* tired."

"All right," Bea said. "We're just going down to Harman's for a chicken dinner. We won't be very long."

"Don't worry. If I die while you're gone, Diane can just wrap me up in a sheet and call the undertaker."

"Grandma!" Bobbi said. "What a thing to say. We'll hear no more of that."

"What I really want to do is go out dancing one last time. I want to drop dead at Rainbow Rendevu, right there on the dance floor, with a good band playing and me in a bright red dress."

Grandpa Thomas had stepped into the room. "Maybe it wouldn't kill you to go dancing, Mom," he said. "It might be the best thing in the world. Get that red dress on and I'll take you. But there's no Rainbow Rendevu. It's called the Terrace now."

"Not a chance. If I'm going, I want Richard to take me."

"You'd be awfully disappointed," Richard said. "I'm not a very good dancer—not good enough for you anyway."

"No one is. But at least you're good-looking. Al, here, he's getting too old and ugly."

Diane didn't know how old her Grandpa was. Maybe seventy. But he had always looked about the same. His hair was still dark, with only a little gray around his ears. But something about him had always scared Diane a little. He could be funny—even if he did tease a little too much—but he wasn't someone Diane had ever felt really close to. For one thing, he usually wanted to know how Diane's last report card had been, and that wasn't something she was always proud to tell him.

It was Grandma Bea whom Diane loved the most. Since Diane had been a tiny girl she had liked coming to Grandma's house, especially to stay overnight. Grandma would make cookies with her, play dolls, and talk until late at night. Grandpa would read his paper, watch the news, and sometimes chat with Diane a little, but he didn't know how to say anything truly personal. Still, he liked to dig out the old sleds from the garage and take the grandkids up into the foothills, where they could take rides down into Parley's Ravine. Or in the summer he would gather all the family at his and Grandma's cabin in Emigration Canyon. He would take the kids out to fish in the stream and patiently keep all the hooks baited, or he would borrow his neighbors' horses for the grandchildren to take turns riding. Diane loved him; she merely felt more comfortable with her grandma.

When everyone finally cleared out, including Maggie, who decided she wanted to go downstairs and watch television, Gram said, "Well, Di, this may be our last chance to have a good talk. I'd better give you some of my wisdom."

"Gram, are you really so sick?" Diane brought a chair to the side of the bed and sat down.

"Oh, honey, I joke too much. But I am dying. I don't feel so awful as all that, but my doctor says I have congestive heart failure. Fluids build up in my lungs, and I can't breathe so well. It's just old age, and there's nothing I can do about it. But I don't suppose I'll last a lot longer."

"I'll miss you, Gram." Diane was surprised at how suddenly her tears came when she spoke the words, but she was even more surprised to see her Gram's eyes fill up too. Gram had never been one to show much emotion.

She reached out and took Diane's hand. "And I'll miss everyone here. I've *loved* this world. I'm not sure all those purified spirits on the other side are going to take to me. I just hope they have turquoise over there, and red. I look terrible in white."

"Gramp is there. Remember that."

"I know." She wiped the tears from her cheeks with her thin fingers. "It will be nice to see him." Her eyes drifted away from Diane's. "I just hope all this stuff we believe turns out to be true. What if I get over there and they tell me I should have been a Catholic or a Buddhist or something? Or worse yet, a Baptist. Baptists don't even believe in dancing."

"You'll dance, Gram. Even if they have to change the rules. You'll talk them into it."

Gram laughed again. But then she said, more seriously than Diane would have expected, "But what if none of it's real? What if we just die, and everything is dark, and they stick these old bones in a hole in the ground? What if that's the end of it? That's what scares me the most."

Diane didn't want Gram to talk that way. The thought was so awful. "You know what's true, Gram. You know you'll have Gramp, and you'll have all of us with you again someday."

"Do you *know* that's true, Di?"

"I do, Gram."

"Good. That makes me feel better. You're much closer to God than I probably ever was. I've always noticed that about you."

Diane couldn't imagine that. She didn't feel righteous. She just knew what she believed.

Gram was quiet for a time after that. Diane wondered what she was thinking. Was she imagining death, wondering what it might be like? But as usual, Gram came out with something Diane didn't expect. "I want to tell you a secret—even though I probably shouldn't."

"What?"

"Your mother was always my favorite of all my grandkids. I tried to love everyone the same, but I loved Bobbi the most. She's got that same quality you have—like she knows God personally—but she's also kind of like me. She doesn't have such a smart mouth as I do, but she's *feisty*. She doesn't let anyone tell her what's what—not even these men in our family who think they have all the answers."

"I'm not like that, Gram. Mom always tries to get me interested in the things she likes—good literature and everything—but I don't like stuff like that. Most of the time, I'd rather watch TV than read a book."

Gram let her eyes go shut for a moment. But then she said, seriously, "That's okay, Di. We don't all have to be the same. But I'm just telling you that you can learn something from your mother. Women need to stand up for themselves, and a lot of them don't."

"What I hope for is a good husband who'll be really nice to me. And some nice kids. I don't like arguing with people."

"I understand that. But men have to know they can't run over you. They just tromp along, straight ahead, if you don't step up in front of them once in a while. It's just the way they are."

"I'll tell you the boy I could fall in love with—if he weren't my cousin."

"Gene, I suppose."

"Yup."

"I know what you mean. But the boy acts a little too big for his britches sometimes."

Diane laughed. "Not really. He's just confident. I like him."

"Well, sure. I do too. More than you can imagine. You'll never know what he meant to us when he was born, Diane. He was our replacement for his Uncle Gene, the boy we lost in the war. And he was born in England, away from us, when we wanted him with us so much. We don't love him more than the rest of you—honest we don't—but he has a special place. He was the first of your generation, and he came at a time when everything had been so horrible."

"I know. Mom's talked to me about all that. He's special to me too." She laughed. "But maybe it's just because he's so good-looking."

"He is that. But honey, you're beautiful, and you came to us as such a blessing too. After your mother lost her first baby, we all worried that she couldn't carry a baby full-term. We were all so happy the day you were born."

"Mom says it was kind of the same when she had Maggie."

"That's because she lost two more, after you. I'm sure you know that."

"She still wishes she could have a son. Dad does too."

"I know. But she's blessed to have the two of you."

Gram took some long, slow breaths and grimaced a little, and for the first time Diane could see that she was in pain. "Are you okay, Gram?" she asked.

"Oh . . . I'm getting by. I'll take some medicine before too long." But she let her eyes go shut again, breathing rather noisily.

Diane let her rest. She leaned back in her chair. She thought how much this room had changed from the way she remembered it. Grandma Bea had taken down the old wallpaper and painted the walls a soft beige color. She had also taken down the frilly curtains and put up some simple white ones. It didn't seem like "Mom's room" anymore, but Diane tried to picture her mother, as a teenager, growing up in this family, this house. Mom had told her about the apple tree outside that Grandpa had finally cut down because it had gotten so old and rotten. Mom always said that she liked the apples when they were green. She climbed up after them even though Grandpa always told her not to eat them that way. Diane wondered what her mother was like then. Even back then, had she been so different from Diane? Mom could be funny, but she was never silly, never just crazy the way Gram was, the way Diane liked to be.

"I know Mom's glad she could have me," Diane said absently, almost to herself, "but I think she wishes I was more like her. Here she is, trying to finish her doctorate, like it's the most important thing in the world, and I'm not even sure I want to go to college."

"Sorry, honey. That won't be one of your options. In this family, you go to college—if for no other reason, at least to make a good catch—get a husband who's going somewhere."

"I know. I'll probably go. When I do, though, I want to go down to the BYU. My mom and dad will probably want me to stay home and go to Weber, but I don't want to go where they both teach. Everyone would want to know why I wasn't as smart as they are."

"It might be good for you to get away, honey. But don't marry one of those really drippy Mormons down there—one of those returned missionaries who thinks he has to read the scriptures eight hours a day."

Her eyes came open and she smiled. "Find a guy who's got some *zip* in him."

Diane laughed. "Okay. I'll remember that."

But already Gram's eyes had gone shut again, and her voice was more distant when she said, "Di, tell me what's going on in the world. I don't hear things now."

"I'm not sure. I don't watch the news a lot. I know there's some kind of trouble in Berlin. That's still going on, I guess."

Gram laughed, and that made her cough. "Oh, Diane, the world could blow up one of these days, the way things are in Berlin, and you're talking about 'some kind of trouble.' The Russians keep testing A-bombs, and Khrushchev keeps threatening to use them. Sometimes I wonder if I'll live long enough to die. But let's not talk about that. I can't stand to think of it. Tell me what else is happening. Are those sit-ins still going on, down in the south?"

"You mean, what the colored people were doing?"

"Yes."

"I think so. I know some people were riding on a bus somewhere, and it got burned up. But that was a while back."

"Honey, those were the Freedom Riders. That was *months* ago. You need to catch up if you're going to pass any news along to me."

"I hate the news, Gram. It's boring."

"Honey, the news is life. Don't tell me *life* is boring."

"I didn't say that *my* life is boring. That's what *I* care about."

"So what's going on in your life, then?"

"Mom paid me this summer to watch Maggie, so I made enough money to buy a lot of really cool clothes."

"Now we're talking. What did you get?"

"Well, this sweater I'm wearing, for one thing."

Gram turned her head a little and squinted. "I like those big roll collars, and I love that color." The sweater was bright yellow. "What kind of skirt do you have on?"

"No skirt. I've got stretch pants on, with stirrups that go under my feet. They're really in style right now."

"*Stretch* pants? What do you mean?"

"Well—you know—they fit kind of . . . tight."

"You don't wear those to school, do you?"

"No. We can't wear pants to school. But I wore them to a matinee dance—you know, right after school—and Jay McGill, this friend of mine, told me the boys were all watching me when I was out there dancing."

"I would think so! You girls don't leave much to the imagination these days. When I was young, we might have worn slacks once in a while, but only at picnics or something like that, and they weren't these that show so much. Are you sure that's such a good idea?"

"All the girls wear them." She leaned closer. "At least, when *I* wear them, I look good. You should see some of the girls. They look awful."

Gram was laughing now, and she waved a finger at Diane as if to say, "You naughty girl." But then she said, "Well, in my day, we wore pretty things. We looked like *girls*."

"I think the guys at my school know I'm a girl." Diane winked.

She and Gram both laughed. "No doubt," Gram said. "But honey, don't give boys the wrong idea. If you look like you're trying to advertise your *assets*, you can attract the wrong kind. You're a sweet girl, not a little floozy."

"Everyone knows that too. I don't kiss boys. I've never even been out on a date."

"Why? Because your parents won't let you?"

"Well . . . yeah. But still, everyone knows I go to church, and I don't do anything bad."

"That's good to hear."

But Gram's breath was coming with more difficulty, her wheezing a little more pronounced. "Gram, I'm worried about you. You don't sound very good."

"I know. But if I take more medicine now, I'll just go to sleep. And I don't want to do that. Not yet. Tell me what else you bought to wear this fall. Any dresses?"

"I got a new church dress. It's pink with a really full skirt. But at school we wear mostly skirts and blouses—like maybe a plaid skirt and a pastel blouse."

"What about the church dances?"

"I go to those. Some of the stakes have dances on Saturday nights. A lot of kids around Ogden go up to the Highland Ward or out to North Ogden. But we don't dress really fancy. Just skirts. I'd wear capri pants, but they have rules against that. We can't have rock 'n roll music either. Some kids complain, but I think it's right. I mean, it is church. I don't think we should be dancing to Bobby Darin or Chubby Checker, or someone like that."

"But you don't know what it's like to *really* dress up and go dancing in a beautiful ballroom with a wonderful band. You have no idea how glamorous that is."

"We have proms. When I'm in high school, I can go to those."

"I know. But there's no music worth dancing to even when you do have a nice dance. Everything has just . . . *changed* too much. I don't know why we can't keep the best things and change all the bad ones. But it all seems to work the other way around. Everything happens in a car now. I hate these silly drive-in restaurants. You don't go to drive-in movies, do you?"

"Sure I do. It's fun, Gram. My girlfriend's sister is sixteen, so she drives us. And it's neat, because you can wear whatever you want, and you can take a lot of popcorn and stuff. We stay for a double feature, so we're there for *hours*. We even go in the winter. They have heaters you can put in your car."

"But we used to go to such *beautiful* theaters."

"We do that. I came down to the Villa and saw that Cinerama show. That was okay, but at the drive-in we can walk around for a while before the show starts—and see who's there. Maybe flirt with some guys."

"The movies aren't worth seeing, though, are they?"

"Some are. I saw some *good* ones this summer—'The Guns of Navarone' and 'The Parent Trap.' Those were both *really* good. And Sandra Dee, in the 'Tammy' movies. Those shows really slay me."

"Slay you?"

"You know. That just means they're really cool."

Gram was laughing again. "Oh, sweetheart, I keep forgetting how young you are."

"Gram, I just don't see why life can't be fun. I think Mom wants me to be serious about *everything*. But you're not that way. You know how to have a good time."

Gram nodded, rocking her head forward, still against the pillow. "Honey, I've had more fun in this life than anyone else I know—certainly much more than your great-grandpa ever did—and I don't regret anything. But don't sell your mother short. She's a deeper person than I am. More thoughtful. I could have used a lot more of that in my life."

"But like you said, we don't all have to be the same."

Gram turned her head and focused intently on Diane. "Of course. But don't sell *yourself* short either. Sometimes a girl can be *too* pretty. She starts to think looks are the only thing that matters in life. Maybe you want to be a Relief Society president instead of a professor. That's just fine. But don't act like some silly little thing who can't think for herself."

"Gram, I just want to be a mom. What's wrong with that?"

"Not one thing. That's what I was. But even there, you can stand up for yourself. Step up next to your husband. You don't have to walk behind him. There's been too much of that for too long. You may be the mother, but you're not the maid, and you're not the washwoman. It took me a long time before I figured that out. And maybe that's why I put too much of my energy into things that didn't really matter. I want you to know who you are from the beginning." She made a little nod again. "Will you do that?"

"I will."

Gram smiled, but weakly. "You go ahead and be like me. But honey, learn something from your mother, too. Let those boys know you've got something in your head. There's more to life than having a pretty shape—although you and I were both blessed in that regard."

Diane laughed, but she had begun to cry again, and she wasn't sure why. "Okay, Gram," she said. "I'll remember."

"Good. Now I'd better take that pill."

"Are you in a lot of pain?"

"I've had worse—much worse. What you don't know about life yet is that there's a lot more pain than anything else. That's why you have to laugh. A woman can't wait until the pain stops to enjoy herself. If she did, she'd never have any fun at all."

"Okay. I'll remember that too."

Gram took her medicine then, and before long she was asleep. Diane sat and watched her, and she wondered whether life would really be that way—wondered what pains she might have to deal with.

After a time, Diane walked to the chest of drawers where Gram had set out some of her pictures. There was one of Gram in her beautiful wedding dress, her black curls hanging around her lovely face. There was another picture of her in a fancy blue gown, dancing with a man in a tuxedo—like a performer. There was nothing but joy in her face, and that's how Diane wanted to remember her.

Three weeks later Gram died in her sleep. The family gathered for her funeral, said lots of nice things, even joked about Gram's humor and all her eccentricities. But Diane knew what she would always remember: this last talk, when the two of them had been alone, and the things Gram had told her.

CHAPTER 3

It was Christmas Day, 1961, and the Thomases were all together. Even Aunt LaRue had come from Massachusetts. Grandma Bea had set out a total of twenty-eight places, using the dining-room table with all its leaves, the kitchen table, and three card tables in the living room and entry. She'd had to send Al off to the ward house to borrow folding chairs, but she wanted a real sit-down dinner. That was part of Christmas afternoon, she kept telling everyone, and Gene agreed. It was what he remembered all the way back to when he was a little boy. He had watched the family grow, with new cousins almost every year—the number now up to seventeen. Most of the families hadn't had babies lately, and Aunt LaRue was still not married, but Aunt Beverly and Uncle Roger had been married eight years, with four children in the first six years. His other grandparents, the Stoltzes, usually came too, since they had no other family in Salt Lake, but this year Frieda had not been well enough to come, and Heinrich hadn't wanted to come without her.

It was a huge dinner, and Gene stuffed himself far beyond "full." He knew he needed to let the food settle before he could sample all the kinds of pie, so he lay down on the living room floor. It was a cold day and cloudy, with snow flurries—at least enough to call the day a "white Christmas." Still, Uncle Alex and Uncle Richard had taken a bunch of the kids outside to play basketball in front of the old garage out back— just to let them "get the wiggles out" for a while. The house was quieter than it had been, and Gene was half asleep when he heard someone sit down on the couch nearby. "How come you're not out there playing basketball?"

Gene opened his eyes to see Kathy. She looked cute in her red plaid jumper. She had a new haircut, too, short and turned under, just below her ears. But the truth was, even though Gene really liked her, she was not the sort of girl he would have asked out—even if she hadn't been his cousin. She wore dark, plastic-rimmed glasses that made her look studious, and she was shaped like a stick. "I've had enough basketball lately to last me for a while," Gene said. He had been working out with the East High team nonstop since football season had ended.

"Are you on the varsity team?"

"Girl, you've got to keep up. I've started every game so far this season. Don't you read the sports page?" Gene laughed. He knew that sports meant absolutely nothing to Kathy. "But I don't dare go out there and play with my dad and Uncle Richard. They try to show me up."

"They try to prove they aren't old. My dad turned forty last summer. He hates that, but he probably knows he can't keep up with you."

"Hey, that's not true. Uncle Wally plays sometimes, and he plays hard—especially on defense. I get hammered every time I play with those guys."

"Why are they like that? They're all such nice men, but they go out there to play a little ball and suddenly it's like they're at *war*."

"Maybe that's where they learned to compete like that."

"I don't think so. They never make a big deal out of the war."

Gene had let his eyes gradually go shut again, but he opened them now and turned his head a little to look at Kathy. She was leaning back on the couch; he couldn't see her face. "I've tried and tried to get my dad to tell me how he won his medals," he said. "When people introduce him at his political speeches, they always say, 'Alex Thomas, decorated war hero,' or something like that, but all he'll tell me is that other guys deserved the medals more than he did."

What Gene didn't say was that he was proud of his dad for that. The man always seemed at least two cuts above anyone else he had ever known. He had accomplished so much already in his life, but it just wasn't in him to praise himself.

"Well, anyway," Kathy said, "maybe I'll come and see you play sometime. A friend of mine told me you're going to be the big star of every sport. But I guess that wouldn't happen if you went to Highland High—where there are so many *great* athletes." She, of course, would be going to Highland the following year.

Gene laughed. "Yeah, right. I could be Billy 'The Hill' McGill, Merlin Olsen, and Jay Sylvester all wrapped into one, and you wouldn't admit it."

"Who are they?"

"Never mind."

"So is it true? Are you the star of every team?"

"Not really. I'm not that great at baseball."

Kathy leaned forward and looked down at him. "So what does that mean? You *are* that great at everything else?"

He put his hands behind his head and smiled. "I'll just say this. I'll be the starting quarterback next year—as a junior. And football isn't my best sport. I'm better at basketball."

"My friend said you're the fastest runner in town."

"Not really. A couple of colored guys at West High are faster than me. I'll have to start eating more fried chicken and watermelon, I guess, and see if I can't catch them this year."

"Gene! That's not funny. Why do you say things like that?"

Gene rolled his eyes. He never knew what might bother Kathy. What was wrong with saying colored guys liked fried chicken and watermelon? Everyone knew they did. "Hey, I told you they're fast—faster than me. I just hope I can gain on them this year."

"You're just like your dad and your uncles. You aren't happy unless you win everything."

"We're Thomases. We've got a tradition to keep up."

"Thomases and Snows," Kathy said, in a deep, hollow voice,

obviously intended to imitate her grandpa's. "When you're out there crossing the plains, boys, and the snow is twelve feet deep, your oxen are lost, and you're suffering with smallpox and diphtheria and whooping cough—all at the same time—and you haven't eaten anything but boiled leather for six weeks, just remember . . . ta-da! . . . you're a Thomas and a Snow. You can do *anything*."

Gene had started laughing halfway through her little recitation and was roaring by the end, but he rolled over on his side and propped his elbow under him, his head in his hand. "Hey," he said, "Grandpa may get a little carried away with some of that stuff, but I believe all of it. When I'm on the basketball court, getting worn down in the fourth quarter, sometimes I tell myself, 'You're a Thomas. Buckle down, man. You can still win this game.'"

"Oh, brother. That sounds like the stuff those stupid cheerleaders yell."

"What's wrong with cheerleaders?"

"I've never met one who had a brain. They think life's all about being *bubbly*."

"Hey, wait a minute." Gene pointed a finger at Kathy. "Didn't you try out for cheerleader last year?"

"No."

"Yes, you did. You told me you did."

"No, I didn't. I told you I might. But I didn't do it."

"But you wanted to be one. I remember you said that."

Gene was amazed to see how embarrassed Kathy was. Her cheeks and ears had turned pink, and she wouldn't look at him. "That was a long time ago. I don't know why I even thought about doing something like that."

"It was before you started this thing about being so brainy—the kid with all the answers."

"I don't claim that."

"Maybe not. But you read *Time* magazine, and you think *it* has all truth."

"I do not. I read all kinds of things."

"You read way too much. You should have gone out for cheerleader."

"Why? They don't *choose* girls who look like me."

Actually, Gene knew that was true. Kathy was probably too gawky to be a cheerleader. But he suddenly felt sorry for her, and he thought he knew why she had started playing up all the brainy stuff. She was way too young to be so serious. "Well," he said, "you wouldn't want to be a cheerleader when you get to Highland, not with East beating you all the time."

"And my cousin the *star* at East."

"I didn't say I was the star."

"But you are. You're a *Thomas*. You've got everything. You'll be just like your dad. You'll graduate from college with honors, make a ton of money, and probably become the governor."

"Governor? Why not president?"

Kathy leaned her head back and laughed. "Oh, brother," she said.

"Come on. I'm just kidding. It's what you expect me to say." Gene was well aware that his cousins all thought he was cocky. But he knew something about himself they didn't understand: He *had* to do well. He wasn't going to let his father down.

Gene glanced up to see Diane walk into the living room. She had been blessed with her father's silvery blue eyes and her mother's fair hair.

"So what are you two laughing about over here?" Diane asked. She was wearing a bright red shirt with a button-down collar—a Gant, probably—and white culottes.

"It's too annoying to repeat," Kathy said. "Gene thinks he's the great gift to the world."

"That's what I think he is, too," Diane said. She dropped down next to Gene and patted his cheek. "It's so tragic that we're cousins. You're the only boy I've ever loved, and yet . . . you'll never be mine."

Gene sat up, moved back a little, and crossed his legs, so he could look at both girls. "I just told Kathy I wanted to be president of the United States," he told Diane. "Tell me what's so bad about that?"

"I think you have to start shaving first," Diane said. She and Kathy laughed.

"Hey, I do. Dad bought me a Norelco Speed Shaver for Christmas. I'm going to start using it twice a month, whether I need it or not."

"Be careful. Don't hurt that delicate skin," Kathy said.

But Diane was already saying, "I think you *could* be president some day. All the women would vote for you."

Kathy took hold of her throat and pretended to gag. Gene smiled at that, but he decided to avoid her for the moment. "What do you want to do with your life, Diane?" he asked.

"You mean, like, what do I want to be when I grow up?"

"Yeah."

"I don't know. A grown-up, I guess."

Kathy obviously liked that. She laughed in that strange way of hers. Her voice was fairly mellow, almost low, but when she laughed, it would break off at some point and suddenly shoot high. "That's more than Gene will ever be." She kicked him with the toe of her pointy shoe.

"No, come on, I'm serious," Gene said. "What do you two want to be?"

The girls were on either side of him, looking down, Diane on the floor and Kathy still on the couch. Gene reached back with both hands to prop himself up.

"You go first, Gene," Diane said. "Do you *really* think you could be president?"

"Why not?" But Gene didn't dare admit how serious he was about that, how much the thought played a role in his decisions, how often he imagined himself rising up the ladder, office by office. "Don't you think we ought to dream big? President Kennedy wants to land a man on the moon this decade. No one makes fun of him for that."

"But what would you do first—before you ran for president?" Diane asked, and Gene liked her tone, as though she believed that he could actually do it.

"Well . . . follow what my dad's done. Go to law school, maybe even get involved in one of the family businesses. But the main thing is, I want to go into politics, the same as him—you know, start at the state level and work my way up. Dad's been talking about running for Congress someday. Maybe I would do that, first, and then try to become the first Mormon president."

"Maybe *I'll* run against you," Kathy said. "I'll be the first *woman* president."

"Oh, sure. I can just see that happening."

Some of the younger kids were running about, making a ruckus, and then one of them, little Pam, began to cry. Gene saw his mother step from the kitchen, Aunt LaRue with her. Anna picked up Pammy and hugged her, and then the two women sat down at the dining-room table, obviously continuing a conversation.

"Just wait and see," Kathy said. "I'm going to do something important with my life."

Gene nodded. "Okay. Like what? What's *important?*"

"Changing a lot of things."

"What, for instance?"

"I don't see why some people have *everything,* and other people have to live in poverty."

Gene sat up straighter and folded his arms. "Maybe some people *work* for what they get. And maybe others are too lazy."

"Come on, Gene. What have you worked for? Our dads have money, but where did they get their start? Mostly from Grandpa. Some people don't have rich parents to get them started."

Gene and Kathy had had this argument a dozen times, and Gene was tired of it. Kathy always cried about poor people, but she would never admit how many people cheated to get welfare or sat around and took checks from the government instead of trying to make something of themselves. Still, he knew better than to get into an all-out debate with Kathy. She read more than he did, knew more about the issues. "So anyway," he said, "you're telling us that your main goal is to get rid of poverty. Is that right?"

She paid no attention to his sarcasm. "Not by myself. But people have to start figuring out how we can make things a lot more fair in this country."

"I agree with that," Diane said. Gene knew Diane was only trying to sound smart—and serious—like Kathy.

"So what do *you* want to do?" Gene asked Diane. "Really."

Diane smiled. She flipped her head, the way she often did, and her long hair cascaded back over her shoulder. "I don't know. Just . . . you know . . . be happy."

"What will make you happy?"

"I'm not going to say. Kathy will make fun of me."

"No I won't." Kathy ducked her head. "Why do you say that?"

"I know what you think of me."

"Diane! No you don't. I'm *jealous* of you, more than anything. If I looked like you, I wouldn't do anything but sit around and look in the mirror all day."

"That's what you think I do, too."

"No, I don't. You're so used to being pretty, you don't even worry about it."

Gene could see the color come into Diane's face. He liked that. "Hey! Back to the subject," he said. "Just say what you want to do with your life. Do you want to be a model?"

"No. But I don't know what I want to do." Diane smiled. "The only

thing I ever think about is finding some guy who looks like James Dean
. . . really handsome but—"

"You mean, dead?"

"No. Like he looked when he was alive. He was really cute but a little
bit bad. You know what I mean? I want him to be good, and in the
Church and everything, but sort of dangerous at the same time."

Kathy had begun to laugh.

"See, I told you—"

"No, no. I'm sorry," Kathy said. "I'm not laughing at you. It's every
girl's dream. Anne—in *Anne of Green Gables*—says she wants a boy who's
good but one who's *capable* of being bad and chooses not to be. Something
like that."

"Yeah. That's it. That's exactly right."

"So who isn't capable of being bad?" Gene asked.

"*You!*" both girls said at the same time.

"Hey, what a rotten thing to say."

"I know," Kathy said. "It's the nastiest thing I've ever said about you.
But it's true."

"But we love you anyway," Diane said.

Gene was a little put down by all this, and he found himself wondering about his image. Did he really come across as such a sweetheart? He
didn't think anyone who had ever played football with him—or *against*
him—would say so. "Well, I'll tell you what," he finally said. "I want us to
check back with each other someday and see how we all did with our
goals."

"In other words, when you're president, you want to tell us that we
never should have made fun of you," Kathy said.

That was exactly what Gene had been thinking, but he didn't admit
it. "All I'm saying is, let's check back, say in ten years, and then twenty
and thirty, and just see. I want to find out if you've changed the world,
Kathy. And I'll want to know if you found that guy, Diane."

"That's not my only dream."

"Okay. Then go on record. What else do you want?"

"Well . . . I don't know," Diane said. "Sometimes I think about being a singer and making records and stuff like that. But I'm probably not good enough. I don't have to have my mind made up about everything yet, do I?"

"No. Of course not," Kathy said. "You're thirteen, for crying out loud. This is just Gene's way of saying that he's really going to do something and we're not. He wants to rub it in all of our lives."

Sometimes Kathy's tongue was too sharp. Gene was suddenly irritated. "Come on. It'll just be fun. It'll keep us on track so we don't forget what our goals are." He looked at Diane. "So if you have some other things you want to do, admit it. I've made a fool of myself by saying I want to be president."

Diane shrugged. "I just want to marry a good guy and have a nice family. That's all I know for sure."

"Hey, that's what we all want," Gene said. "And if we do that, we can all feel successful."

But he glanced at Kathy, and she didn't seem to agree.

"I won't be satisfied if I don't make a difference in some way."

"Well, okay," Gene said, "I do think family comes first, but I guess that's what I'm feeling, too. I want to do some good in the world."

"Okay, then, on Christmas day, 1971, we'll do our first progress check," Kathy said. "If Diane shows up with a guy who looks just like James Dean, we'll know she won."

"No winners. No losers," Gene said. "It's just for fun." But Gene was thinking that he would be twenty-six by then. Maybe that was too young to run for office, but he wanted to show he was making steps. He knew that he wanted to be student-body president at East, just like his dad, and serve a mission. By twenty-six he ought to be out of law school, married, and on his way to a good career. And by 1981 he wanted Kathy to eat a few of her words.

"Let's get to the important stuff," Diane said. "What did you guys get for Christmas—besides a shaver you don't need?"

Gene held up his arm. "An Elgin watch," he said, "with twenty-three jewels. And some new Head skis."

"I got a portable stereo for my room," Kathy said, "and a bunch of records. Ray Conniff, Four Freshmen. And some jazz I like. Dave Brubeck. Lionel Hampton." She looked at Diane. "What did you get?"

"Clothes. I picked it all out myself, at Castleton's. My mom would never know what to buy for me."

Gene looked up to see Aunt LaRue heading their way. "How come you older kids are so lazy?" she asked, her voice seeming louder than necessary. "You should be out playing ball."

"I don't see *you* out there," Kathy said.

LaRue smiled, her fists on her hips. "I'm your old-maid aunt—too old to play basketball."

"You're the prettiest old-maid aunt in the world," Gene said.

LaRue laughed, and then she sat on the floor, next to Diane. "We *are* a good-looking bunch, we Thomases, aren't we?" she said, and she laughed.

"Here we go again," Kathy said. "We're not only supposed to be tough as nails; we have to be good-looking too."

"The truth is," LaRue said, "Diane looks like her dad, Gene looks so much like his mother that he'd make a beautiful girl, and Kathy, you look like Lorraine. I don't see much Thomas in any of you. I think the Lord perfected the Thomas look when he made me, and after that, he couldn't think of any way to improve on his work."

"Grandpa thinks you could be improved a little," Kathy said.

"Not my looks. He just wants me to shut my mouth more often. I'm the bad child—the one who went off to the East and got my head filled up with apostate ideas."

The fact was, and Gene knew it, that was not so far from what Grandpa did think. Aunt LaRue had gone to the East right out of high school and had stayed. She had gone to Radcliffe and then gotten her Ph.D. from Columbia. She was thirty-two now, hadn't married, and joked all the time that no one would ever have her. She claimed that she went to church every Sunday, but Gene sometimes wondered what church it was.

"I don't think you have apostate ideas," Kathy said. "I think you're the most sensible person in the family—except maybe for Aunt Bobbi."

"Yes. But Bobbi's a . . . may I whisper the word? . . . *Democrat*." And then, in a louder voice—in fact, way too loud—she added, "Diane hasn't had a proper Thomas upbringing."

"That's why we live in Ogden," Diane said. "Grandpa can pretend he doesn't know us."

"I heard what Kathy was saying a little while ago," LaRue said. "It sounded like dangerous talk to me. As I understand it, we're supposed to *hate* the poor. Call them lazy bums. I'm pretty sure that's in the scriptures somewhere."

"You're a couple of bleeding hearts," Gene said. He only meant it as a joke, but he saw something serious in LaRue's eyes, and he knew he was going to take a pounding.

"Listen, Gene, people *do* need to work for what they get. But right now the playing field isn't even, and that's a metaphor an athlete like you ought to understand."

"Look, I don't want to get into a—"

"Do you know what's going on in Albany, Georgia?"

Gene had heard something on the TV news about Negroes being arrested, but he wasn't about to claim he knew much about it. "Not exactly," he said.

"Negroes are being thrown in jail, and you know why? Because they wanted to use the same waiting rooms that white people use at the bus station. And they had the nerve to think they ought to be able to *vote*. Martin Luther King was thrown in jail for protesting. No one ought to do *that* in America. Gene, don't talk to me about working hard and getting ahead. When people in our own country aren't allowed the most basic rights, when their kids can't get a decent education, how are they supposed to compete?"

"Hey, what do you think I am?" Gene said. "Everyone ought to be able to vote—or sit where they want to in a bus station. I've never said they shouldn't."

"But it's just a southern problem—right? Not something you or I have to worry about?"

"Things happen like that in Salt Lake, too," Kathy said. "Some of the movie theaters still send Negroes up to the balcony so they won't sit next to any white people. Negroes aren't allowed on most of the dance floors or swimming pools, and they can't stay in the Hotel Utah or the Newhouse. They can't even sit down to eat at most of the restaurants around Salt Lake."

"When the Freedom Riders went south," LaRue said, "they got beaten up, got their bus burned. And who got thrown in jail? The Freedom Riders, not the ones who beat up on them."

Suddenly a voice boomed from the dining room. "Well, now, that's not the whole story."

Grandpa Thomas had come out of his back office at some point, probably because he had heard LaRue. His voice had sounded like a divine warning, and it frightened Gene. But he looked at Aunt LaRue, and he saw resolution, not fear, in her eyes.

At that moment the front door flew open and all the kids came charging in from outside, followed by their fathers. "Let's have some pie," Alex said. "We're ready now."

A gust of cold air blew through the living room, and the noise of all the kids echoed from the front entry. Grandpa walked into the living room. LaRue stood, then turned and faced her dad. "So what's the *whole* story?" she asked, and her tone was challenging, almost hostile—something Gene had never heard from one of his relatives, not directed at Grandpa.

"Those Freedom Riders drove that bus into the south with one purpose in mind. They wanted to get beaten up. They provoked everything that happened to them."

"Come on, Dad. That's like saying America provoked Hitler by sending troops to Europe."

"There's nothing even similar about that."

"Dad, Negroes are doing nothing more than sitting at lunch counters, sitting up front in buses. They're saying, 'We have rights. We're not going to be treated like subhumans.'"

"That's fine. I don't blame them for feeling that way. But something that took hundreds of years to create can't be changed overnight."

Grandma Bea had stepped out of the kitchen, probably to ask everyone about the pie, but now she said, "LaRue, you haven't lived in the South the way we have. You don't know how deep those feelings go. If you force change too fast, it's the Negroes themselves who will suffer."

"That's exactly right," Grandpa said. "The white southerners will only get their backs up, and the Ku Klux Klan will go after Negroes with a vengeance."

The room had become quiet. Even the little children had stopped to see what was happening. Grandma had sounded rather conciliatory, but Grandpa's big voice was fierce.

"Well, let's see," LaRue said in a considered voice, "I think I follow your logic. The Mormons in Jackson County, Missouri, were the cause of all the problems. They had the nerve to think they could move in and live there. They should have said, 'Whatever you think, you lovely mob leaders. We don't want to cause trouble. We'll just look for another place to live.'"

"No! That's not what I'm saying. Negroes have every right to the things they want. But some of these men—like this King fellow—are getting things riled up on purpose. They know very well that they're going to get their people killed. But they do it anyway, just to force the issue."

"People die in a war."

"So that's *your* logic. Sacrifice some of these poor young students so ol' Martin Luther King can look like a big shot."

Alex stepped over, next to his father. "LaRue, Dad's got a point. Don't you agree that some of the Negro leaders are grabbing for headlines while the students pay the price?" His tone was careful, as though he wanted, more than anything, to calm things down.

"Reverend King has been beaten up, jailed, stabbed, had his house bombed, and he's been humiliated by redneck white sheriffs and judges," LaRue said. "He's paid the price right along with the rest."

"I know. But Dad's just trying to say—"

"I know *exactly* what he's trying to say. Don't make any waves. Let things go along the way they always have. Who cares about a bunch of Negroes anyway?"

Gene felt sick. He had never heard an argument like this in his family. He hated the way Grandpa looked, so angry. But what he hated worse was the way Aunt LaRue was willing to gamble away Christmas, ruin everything just to make a point. There were always problems in the world, but people didn't have to get so angry about them.

And then Kathy made things worse, which didn't surprise Gene. She stood up next to Aunt LaRue and said, "I have a Negro friend. She wants to go to the South if they do freedom rides again. She doesn't care if she gets thrown in jail. She's willing to do that so people will start to understand how bad things are. And no leader is making her do it. You can't say that all the students are being pushed into the battle. It's something they believe in themselves."

"But she has no business going down there," Grandpa said. "Southerners will do just fine when people let them solve their own problems. Northerners should stay out of it."

"And Negroes should wait for white people to decide that their children deserve decent schools. Is that the idea?" LaRue asked. "How long should they wait? *Another* century?"

"Dad isn't saying that," Uncle Alex said. "But he's been down there and—"

"You two are so hypocritical. I can't believe it."

"Hypocritical?" Grandpa said, and to Gene's surprise, he seemed knocked off his pegs a little. He started to speak, then hesitated.

"Admit it, Dad. You're prejudiced," LaRue hissed at him. "You don't like Martin Luther King because he's an uppity colored man. You don't *really* care about Negroes. They're not even human enough to have the priesthood."

Gene was stunned. No one moved. All the children were staring at Aunt LaRue. The aunts had come out of the kitchen, were standing stiff. Grandpa was taking long breaths. "For heaven's sake, LaRue," Alex said, "what a thing to say."

"God decides who receives the priesthood, LaRue," Grandpa said. "That isn't—"

"Are you sure? You show me one scripture, *anywhere*, that says that God thinks more highly of some of his children than he does the rest."

"So you think you know more than the prophet. Is that it?"

"No. But I think members of the Church have to think for themselves and not let bad doctrine creep in."

"Oh, come on. Don't call yourself a member. You don't even sound like one of us."

Somewhere in the background, Aunt Bobbi said, "Dad, don't say that. That isn't fair."

But LaRue was saying, "One of *us?* Do you mean the family or the Church?"

"Both, really."

"Well, fine. It's time I got out of here. I think I'll try to get an early flight back to Boston." She headed for the door.

Kathy ran after her, and so did Grandma Bea. And outside, Gene could hear a heated conversation—not the words but the sound of the voices. After a time Alex walked out, and then finally, even Grandpa. The voices gradually softened, but Gene had the feeling the damage had been done. He got up and sat on the couch, numb. Everyone in the room—the whole family—looked the same way.

Uncle Wally finally said, "LaRue gets so mad, she says things I know she doesn't mean."

But Bobbi was quick to say, "Maybe so. But Dad had no right to say something like that to her."

Gene wondered what was happening. He felt as though the family were ripping in half.

CHAPTER 4

Kathy was glad that the weather had turned warm—even though she knew it wouldn't last. It was late February, 1962, but the last couple of days had felt almost like spring. Lorraine had asked Kathy to stop by Douglas's school on her way home from the junior high and to walk home with him. Until recently, Douglas had usually walked with the kids in the neighborhood, but he was about to turn ten, and the boys his age were growing less patient about looking out for him. He had a way of dawdling, stopping to pick up rocks or to pet dogs. And he was always asking questions. "What's that?" he would stop and ask, pointing to some smudge on the sidewalk. So Lorraine came by for Douglas most days—except today, when she had a meeting of her Bay View Club to attend.

Douglas had gotten sick when he was a baby, had suffered through an extremely high fever. The doctor had told Wally and Lorraine, even then, that he might be "slow," but Kathy had come to hate that word. To most people it simply meant "stupid," and Douglas wasn't that. He struggled to learn, but in his own way he was a perceptive kid. He seemed to have a sixth sense for comprehending what people were feeling, and he responded accordingly—always the first in the family to offer sympathy. When his little sisters, Glenda and Shauna, got upset, he would hold them and stroke their hair. They loved him more than anyone. And Kathy felt the same way. He was the loveliest person Kathy knew, so guileless and so satisfied with life.

Kathy knew what she wanted to do today. Douglas had been cooped up for a long time this winter. It was a perfect day to let him take his time.

She would let him wander where he wanted. She had homework, and she couldn't take *too* long, but she knew she would make him happy when she told him they were going to stay outside for a while.

Kathy didn't find Douglas by the front door, where he usually waited, and that worried her a little. She walked inside and down the hall toward his classroom. She hadn't gone far, however, before she heard him. She knew the way he cried: the gentle, plaintive sound he made, as though he were pleading. She started to run, but she still couldn't see him, and then she heard another voice, the thick voice of a boy who sounded large before she ever saw him. "What's the matter, you little boob? Lost your mother?"

"Don't!" Kathy shouted, before she turned the corner and saw them down the hallway. There were three boys, not just the big one, and one of them was saying, "Suck your thumb, Dougie. Come on, let's see you suck your thumb."

Douglas still did that sometimes, and yet he understood that it was something his mother, his teachers, didn't want him to do. He tried so hard not to—Kathy watched him fight the impulse even when he was tired or upset. Why couldn't these boys understand something like that? "Leave him alone!" she shouted, and the boys all turned at once. They moved away from Douglas, drifting to the sides of the hallway. "You boys are going to the principal's office with me," she said. She grabbed for the big boy, caught him by the sleeve. He was wearing a quilted parka, and she almost pulled it off him before she got a good grasp on his arm. The others darted around her and stopped. "Come back here. You're going to the office with me."

"I can't. I've got to go," one of the boys muttered, and then both turned and hurried away, trotting but looking back. "Come on, Craig," one of them said.

But Kathy still had hold of his arm and had now grabbed onto his shoulder as well. "Don't try it," she said. "I know your name now."

"I didn't do anything."

Kathy let go of him with one hand and reached for Douglas. She took him under her arm and pulled him to her. He seemed such a little boy compared to these big fifth-graders, and she knew how easily his feelings could be hurt. "It's okay," she said. "Did you think I wasn't coming?"

"Uh-huh," he said, and she wasn't sure what he meant by that. He was sniffing, trying hard not to cry.

"Come on. We're going to get this stopped. I won't let these boys bother you again."

She began to walk, tugging Craig along, who was still saying, "I have to get home. My mom says to come home right after school." The sound echoed, hollow in the empty hallway. Kathy remembered the smell of the place—the oil the janitors used to treat the old wooden floors.

"Don't worry. You have a good excuse today, Craig. You can tell your mother that you had to stay after school and make fun of Douglas. She'll be very proud of you, I'm sure."

When Kathy reached the office door, she recognized the secretary who sat in the outer office. She was the same woman who had been there forever, since Kathy had been in elementary school and long before—Mrs. Sanders. She had a phone to her ear, but Kathy had some momentum going now, and she couldn't stop herself. "I need to see Mr. Bischoff," she said, and still pulling Craig, she headed for the door.

"Just a minute," Mrs. Sanders was saying, but Kathy kept right on going. She opened the door and looked in to see Mr. Bischoff at his desk, some papers in front of him. He looked up and gave his horn-rim glasses a shove with his finger.

"I need to talk to you," she said.

Mr. Bischoff nodded, but he looked a little out of breath, as though all the sudden action had been a bit too much for him. He had manned this same desk forever, growing stout and gray in the process. Kathy was annoyed by the sight of him. Too many bad feelings from her own years at the school were coming back to her. But she also felt the old fear, the sense of his importance. Some of her confidence was slipping away.

"This boy—and two others—were teasing my little brother, making him cry. Can't you stop that from happening?" Kathy saw Mr. Bischoff stiffen, and she already knew he wasn't going to listen. He was put off by her tone of voice, which had sounded much more forceful than she had intended. "Douglas is the kindest boy in the world." She pulled him close to her again. "He would never hurt anyone. It's not right for these bullies to hurt his feelings. It's been happening more and more lately."

Still, the man didn't speak. He looked at Craig and then back at Kathy, seeming to take the time to consider what he wanted to do. He had always moved this way—and people called her *brother* slow? But Kathy waited. She wasn't going to lose her temper the way she sometimes did. That wouldn't help Douglas at all.

"What about this, young man?" Mr. Bischoff asked. "Were you bothering this boy?"

"We were just joking," Craig said, his voice meek for the first time, even shaky.

"They were making fun of him," Kathy said. "They weren't just *joking*."

"Is that right, young man?" Craig didn't answer, but Mr. Bischoff said, "Well, now, that's not the right thing to do, is it?"

"No."

"You're not going to do it anymore, are you?"

"No."

Mr. Bischoff looked back at Kathy and gave a little nod, and that seemed to be the end of the matter. Kathy almost let go. But she took a breath and said, carefully, "Couldn't you call his parents? His name is Craig. I don't know the other boys' names, but Craig certainly knows."

Mr. Bischoff sat with his elbows on his desk, looking through those heavy glasses. "I'll call your parents and we'll talk about this. We'll decide what needs to be done." He looked at Craig. "Young man, you run on home now. And don't let me hear about any more of this."

Craig slipped away immediately, without a word, and Douglas said, "It's okay, Kathy. Don't be mad."

Kathy knew how Douglas thought. He hated upsets more than anything. The teasing was over, and what he didn't like now was Kathy's voice. He could hear the anger, however controlled she tried to keep it. "Douglas, go out by Mrs. Sanders. Sit down on one of the chairs. I'll be right out."

"Okay." He walked out and Kathy shut the door. "Mr. Bischoff," she said softly, "wouldn't it be good to find out who those other boys were?"

There were chairs in front of Mr. Bischoff's desk, but he didn't ask her to sit down. "I may do that," he said. "But that's not up to you. First, I want to talk to your parents."

"Mr. Bischoff, this has been happening a lot. If you could go into the hallway after school, or before, I think you would—"

"You have no idea how busy I am, Miss. I can't monitor the halls. But I'll—"

"You don't even know my name," she said. Her voice was measured but irate, and she couldn't seem to help it. "You never did know me. You don't know any of the kids."

Mr. Bischoff stood up, his wooden chair rolling back from under him, the springs squeaking. "You are *not* going to talk to me that way. I don't let our pupils do that, and I'm certainly not going to let you."

"It's about time *someone* told you the truth. You don't love these kids. You don't even care about them."

"Leave my office right now. Your parents are going to hear about this."

Kathy had spent most of her fury in that one burst, and she really was sorry she had gotten the man's back up. She didn't want her brother to be abandoned out of resentment for her behavior. "Mr. Bischoff, I'm sorry. I don't mean to be disrespectful. But what would it hurt to get to know the kids a little . . . and look after them?"

"This isn't a nursery school, and I don't have time to go wandering around the school 'getting acquainted' with every child. There's a lot of work in keeping this place going."

Kathy couldn't imagine what it was the man did all day, but she wasn't going to get anywhere by asking. "Well, anyway . . . could you at least talk to the teachers, or something?"

"I told you already. We'll do what we can. Now please leave."

Kathy gave up. She walked out and shut the door behind her. She took Douglas's hand and already, as she walked out the front door, she was berating herself for flying off the handle and making things worse for Douglas. She took her time walking home, let Douglas meander, play in some water in a gutter, and then toss a stick to Sister Ingebretzen's dog. He laughed each time the big Labrador loped back to him, but when he looked up at Kathy, saw that she wasn't laughing, he said, "Don't be sad. Okay?"

He was a perfect-looking kid, with a "bulldog" haircut and freckles scattered over his face. "I'm not sad," she said. "Are you okay?"

"Yes." But more as an observation than a complaint, he added, "Those boys don't like me."

Kathy dropped to one knee and hugged him. "Oh, Douglas, I love you," she said. "So many people do."

"I know."

But Kathy was angry again. She had to push her parents. They were just too nice to someone like Bischoff. He would call and pretend to care about Douglas, and Dad would tell him that he appreciated the help, and that would be the end of it. Someone needed to step up and *do* something, not just talk nice about it.

As Kathy and Douglas worked their way home, Kathy kept watching the sky. She loved the deep blue, the sun. A few days before, an astronaut named John Glenn had been the first American to orbit the earth. All of America was proud to be catching up with the Russians. Kathy liked the idea of it too, but what did it matter, really? If humans could figure out a way to go into space and spin around the globe, why couldn't they figure out a way to solve the problems down on the ground? She was a lot more excited about the new Peace Corps Kennedy was starting than she was about the space program. What bothered her was that she wasn't allowed to do her part right now. Everyone seemed to agree about one thing: she was too young to be listened to, or even to be taken seriously.

∽

That night when Wally got home, Kathy could see immediately that he was upset with her. He didn't say so, didn't even bring up the subject, but she knew that Bischoff had called, and she knew that Dad was going to have one of his "talks" with her.

Kathy decided she wasn't going to do it that way; sometimes her dad's patience almost drove her crazy, even when he was directing it toward her. "Dad, I know Mr. Bischoff called this afternoon," she said, "and I know exactly what he told you."

Wally was standing in the kitchen, where he had just run himself a glass of water, and Kathy was sitting in a big chair in the family room. She placed her geography textbook across her lap and waited to see how her father would react.

Dad drank his water, mostly in one long draft, and then he walked into the family room and sat down on the couch across from Kathy. Mom had bought new furniture for the room recently—all "Early American." The couch was brightly flowered, mostly in reds. "Just a minute," he said. "I asked your mother to come in. I wanted us all to talk about this together."

"Look, Dad, I know I made a mess of things today, but that man made me *so* mad."

Wally smiled. "I told him not to feel bad—that you didn't think very highly of me either."

It bothered Kathy to think that her dad probably had said that. It turned everything into a pleasant little joke. But it also concerned her to think that her dad really thought that. She thought her dad was the best man she had ever known.

Lorraine came down the hallway from her bedroom, where she had gone to change the dress she had worn to her meeting. She had on a straight skirt and one of her older oxford-cloth shirts, but it was neatly pressed, and Kathy wondered, as she often did, why her mother had to look so perfect all the time. She attended the Bay View Women's Club every month and came home talking about the interesting speakers or the book she had discussed with "the ladies." She even helped raise money for certain good causes, but she never seemed to look for bigger worlds to conquer. She was going to start dinner now, and even though she was home late—she would probably resort to sandwiches or canned soup—she would apologize about it, and she would cover the table with a nicely ironed tablecloth. Kathy never understood why all that was necessary.

"Lorraine, Mr. Bischoff called me," Wally began. Dad was still wearing his white shirt from work, but he had taken off his tie. He had always been slender, still was, but he had started to bulge around his belt line, which Kathy rather liked. He sat now, with his elbows on his knees. He waited until Mom sat down next to him. "Apparently, this afternoon—"

"Let me tell it," Kathy said. "Hear my version before you make your minds up."

"Actually, that's what I was going to do," Dad said. Kathy was sure that was true. Dad had this bishop's style of listening, then asking his kids to draw their own conclusions about their behavior. Kathy had rarely seen him angry, and even then he had kept himself under control. Sometimes she admired that, but at other times—in certain moods—she found it hard to take.

"I found Douglas in the hallway this afternoon, crying, and these three big boys were calling him a boob. It made me furious. I grabbed one of the kids and marched him into the office. But you know how Bischoff is. The only thing he cared about was that I had interrupted his *paperwork*. He wouldn't listen to me, and that just got me all the madder. I told him off a little—told him that he didn't care enough about the kids."

Wally chuckled. "He didn't tell me that part. You shouldn't incriminate yourself."

But Mom wasn't smiling. "Kathy, how could you say something like that to him?"

"Well, the one reason that comes to mind is that it's true."

"Kathy, he's the principal, and you're fifteen. You can't treat him like that."

"No. You're right, Mom. It's a lot better to let the kids work Douglas over. Above all, I should be *nice* to the man—no matter what a lousy principal he is."

"Kathy, don't speak in extremes. He's not *that* bad."

"Mom, the guy—"

"Wait. Wait," Dad said. He held his hands up. "Let's not get mad at *each other* over this. We can talk this out."

Kathy shut her book and dropped it on the floor. She slumped in her chair and folded her arms. She would accept the reprimands so they could get to the real point of the conversation.

But Dad said, "Mr. Bischoff *was* annoyed with Kathy. In fact, he wanted to talk more about that than he did about Douglas. And that got me just a little upset. I tried to pin him down about what these boys had done, and he didn't seem to know. He has no idea whether Douglas has been putting up with this stuff all along, or whether it was just a one-time thing."

"Douglas has been telling me that the boys at school don't like him," Mom said. "But that's all I can get out of him."

"You should have heard them, Mom," Kathy said. "You know how hard Douglas tries not to suck his thumb. But they were telling him, 'Go ahead, suck your thumb, *Dougie.*' It was just so cruel."

"I told Mr. Bischoff we'd go over to the school tomorrow," Dad said. "We're going to meet with his teacher and find out what she knows about it. But Kathy, a school can only do so much. Douglas will probably always have to put up with a certain amount of that kind of stuff."

"Why?" Kathy sat up straight. "Some things are just plain *wrong.*"

"Yes, they are. But who can stop all the bad things from happening?"

"Those kids need to be punished. All the kids at that school need to be warned." But Kathy knew that kids were going to be kids, and they were nasty little creatures sometimes. She just didn't want to admit that the adults around Douglas were powerless to protect him.

"Maybe we could put the boys in jail," Wally said. "What do you think, twenty-five to life? Or maybe straight to the electric chair?" He laughed. "Oh, sorry, you're the kid who doesn't believe in capital punishment."

"Shut up," Kathy said, actually joking, but her voice not showing it.

She got the predictable response from Mom. "Kathy! Don't speak to your dad that way."

Kathy shut her eyes and drew in all the breath she could. She didn't think she had to tell her mother that she had been kidding.

"Okay, let's start over," Wally said. "First, we *are* going to meet with the principal and Mrs. Carlysle tomorrow, and trust me, I am going to be firm about this. I do think the school can try harder to look out for Douglas."

"That's the irony in all this," Lorraine said. "I've been upset with the school all year. Half the time his teacher just sticks Douglas aside and lets him color. Here I am, trying to urge them to do something, and trying to be diplomatic about it, and Kathy, you come along and get them defensive. Now we're probably worse off than we were."

Kathy's anger was back. "Mom, you call it *diplomatic*. I call it being *nice*." She pronounced the word sweetly, stretched. "Whatever you call it, it's just *accepting* what they do."

"I've been taught that you can catch more flies with honey than you can with vinegar."

"And maybe you can catch even more with a gallon of gasoline and a match, Mom. Maybe sometimes you have to stand up for what's right—and not sugarcoat everything."

"All right now, Kathy, that's enough," Dad said. And Kathy knew. She could say almost anything to her dad and he would chalk it up to Kathy's temper, but if she got smart with her mother, Dad wouldn't hear it. "I appreciate how much you care about your little brother. But people can deal with each other in a civil way. If you spoke to Mr. Bischoff the way you just did to your mother, I don't blame him for being upset. I told him that I would have you call him and apologize. I think that's the first step in—"

"No."

"Kathy, I didn't ask you what you thought of the idea. It's something you're going to do. It's a lesson you have to learn. I don't mind that you have strong opinions, but you have to learn to work with people. It takes some give and take—being frank but respectful. You can do that. Tomorrow afternoon, after you get home from school, I want you to call him and tell him you're sorry for the things you said."

"No."

"Kathy, I—"

"I'm not sorry. I'm not going to lie."

"I want you to *be* sorry. I want you to think about the disrespect you showed—which, by the way, is not so different from what those boys were doing to Douglas—and I want you to ask God what he thinks of the way you acted. I'll give you three days, but not longer, and then I want you to talk to the man, take responsibility for your part of what went wrong."

"You can wait three centuries if you want, but I'm not going to apologize to that man. I think you and Mom ought to apologize to Douglas."

"Now you have two more people to apologize to, and I'm going to expect that, too."

Strangely, Kathy knew that, knew she was wrong to speak this way to her parents, and even knew that she would, sooner or later, tell them so, but the force of her position, her argument, was still too strong in her mind. "What I believe is that too many people are trying to be nice to each other, and not speaking the truth, and because of that, all kinds of things are wrong in our world. People *need* to offend sometimes."

"Don't start sounding like your Aunt LaRue," Lorraine said.

Kathy was livid. "Why not? I admire her more than anyone in this family. She *cares*." She started away, but her dad grabbed her, spun her around, and then, of all things, took her in his arms. And Kathy did what she didn't want to do. She began to cry. She clung to her dad and sobbed, and then she said it, already. "I'm sorry. I just get so angry."

"I know. And we love all that fire in you."

Mom put her arms around both Kathy and her husband, grasped them both tight, but she said, "Just learn to control the fire a little, honey. That's all we ask."

But the words only stung. Kathy wasn't mad now, but she was frustrated. Weren't there times when it was okay to be right and not back down? How could she apologize to that man?

And yet, she would do it. She knew she would. She couldn't think how she could stand to say the words, but for her dad, she would do it.

CHAPTER 5

Hans Stoltz's anger had been simmering all afternoon, but it was his father's indifference that had finally pushed him to the boiling point. He stood in the living room of their little apartment and faced Peter. "You aren't even listening to me," he said. "If what he says is right, I won't even be admitted to *Oberschule*."

"And why didn't you worry about that when I told you to spend more time studying?"

Hans didn't want to answer that. He stepped away and dropped down on the couch. He couldn't stand to think of all his friends going on to the upper school while he received vocational training. It was humiliating.

"Hans, I know Mormons who have been admitted to *Oberschule*. Some have even gotten into universities."

"But *Direktor* Schreiter told me that being a Mormon made things worse for me. It lowered my chances."

Peter sat down next to Hans. His voice softened. "Hans, didn't he say that your grades were the biggest problem?"

"He said I was 'marginal,' and my membership in a 'sect' would only make things worse." That was true, but Hans knew very well that when the school director had called him to his office that cold February afternoon, his purpose had been primarily to discuss his last set of grades, which had been his worst ever.

"But you still have a few months to improve. Wasn't that what he was telling you?"

That was exactly what the director had said, but Hans had been embarrassed by the man's insinuation that intelligent young people should know enough to reject religion. Why couldn't his parents understand what they were putting him through? They were the ones who made such a point of going to church every week.

"Hans, you act as though you haven't always known this," Peter said. "You know I've been held back in my career, that I haven't been advanced the way Party members are. That's one of the realities for religious people—or anyone who refuses to join the SED." The SED was the *Sozialistische Einheitspartei Deutschlands*—the "unity party"—the dominating political party in the GDR. It modeled itself on the socialist agenda of the Soviet government and was dependent on Russian support.

"Don't talk to me about realities," Hans shouted. He stood up. "I'm the one who told you last year that we had to get out of this country before it was too late. And you stayed."

Hans started away, heading for his room, but, his mother, Katrina, appeared at the kitchen door with Inga peeking around her. "What's this all about?" she asked.

Hans stopped. Peter stood up and turned toward her. "Hans was called in by *Direktor* Schreiter today. He warned Hans that he's close to the line, that he might not be admitted to *Oberschule*. But now Hans wants to put all the blame on the Church."

Hans hated that summary of things. It wasn't fair. He had admitted already that he hadn't studied the way he should have, but it was the Church that could make the difference. "We shouldn't have to worry about things like this," Hans said. "We could have left before they put up that stupid wall."

In these small apartments sound carried easily into other rooms. Hans saw his father cringe, then place his finger over his lips, but Hans *wanted* to scream. He wanted all the neighbors to know what fools his parents were.

"Hans, stop this," Katrina said. "You only think of all the gold glittering in America. But there are problems there, too. You can be as happy as you want to be, wherever you live."

"You can be a Mormon there, and no one *punishes* you for it."

Peter was shaking his head, obviously disgusted. "I keep trying to tell you, Hans," he said, quietly, "there are things more important than career or money—or anything else. In the long run, we'll be blessed for staying."

Hans took a long breath. His father always came up with something of that sort, always made some claim that couldn't be proven. It was unfair. "Papa," Hans said, "I have no future. Maybe that's not important to you, but it's *everything* to me."

"Then you should have thought of it when you were letting your studies slide. You're a smart boy, but you think you can get by without doing any work."

Hans headed for the door again. Maybe his father was right, but it was cruel for him to care so little, to rub it in that way.

Katrina hurried after him and grabbed his arm. "Oh, Son, don't make it sound worse than it is. Do your best the rest of the school year. That's probably all *Direktor* Schreiter wants—to see you work harder and prove yourself. He knows how bright you are."

"And then what? Even if I qualify for the upper school, will I get into a university? My friends will all have good jobs, be important people, and I'll be *nothing*."

"Hans, is our life so bad as that? We have wonderful friends in the Church; we share so much with them. What more do we want?" She hesitated, and when Hans didn't reply, she asked, "Would you want to give up the Church?"

"Maybe I would." It was nothing Hans had considered, nothing he had been allowed to consider. But he wondered now. Maybe he would choose to go his own way. He didn't like what he was seeing in his parents' faces, however—nor his little sister's. So he asked the other question, whispered it: "Why don't we leave the GDR? Some people are still getting out."

"Hans," Peter said even softer, stepping closer, "you know how dangerous it is even to speak of such a thing. If we tried and failed, I could go to prison. Your mother, too."

"Then you stay. I'm going."

"Don't start talking nonsense again. There's no way for a boy to find his way out. I know people who hired professionals to help them get papers—went through a lot of money doing it. And they ended up in jail, not in West Germany."

"Hans, you have to trust in the Lord," Katrina said. "You'll have opportunities in your life. Maybe in the Church. Or the government might change its attitude in time. It's hard to say. But the Lord loves you, and what he cares most about is your spirit, not your worldly success."

That was only another way of saying the same thing: Expect nothing out of life. Enter some miserable job and never advance. There were boys in Hans's class not half as smart as he was, and they would end up much better off. It wasn't right.

Hans hadn't realized that Inga had come so close, but now she was leaning against him, reaching her arms around his legs. "It'll be all right, Hans," she said. He patted her head, trying to comfort her. He told himself that he had to go, had to get out of the GDR, but even as he thought it, he knew that if he ever did, it was little Inga he would miss the most.

On Sunday, after sacrament meeting, while Hans's parents were visiting with some of the other branch members, Hans took his friend Berndt Kerner aside, to the back of the chapel. "I think you're right—what you said to me before. We have no chance if we stay here. We ought to leave."

"Would you dare try my plan?"

The boys had discussed all this before, but only as a kind of fantasy, not as something Hans had believed he would really do. Berndt was older, sixteen, and was especially disillusioned with the GDR. He was actually more devoted to the Church than Hans, but therefore more aware of what it would mean to be known all his life as a Mormon. A close friend of his had emigrated with his family to Utah, back in 1959, and now he often wrote to Berndt about the good life he enjoyed in Salt Lake City. Berndt had made up his mind that he was going to get there somehow. He had thought through all the possibilities and believed that the fenced borders were almost impossible to cross, and an attempt on the Berlin Wall was suicide. But it was harder for border police to keep people away from the Baltic Sea. That was the way he planned to get out.

During the summer, Berndt and his family had spent their vacation on the Baltic. They had visited Boltenhagen, seen the beautiful beaches where high-ranking government officials spent their holidays. Berndt had walked along the shoreline and studied the border guards, out in patrol boats. He felt that if he could push away at night, he could get past them and paddle his way out beyond the GDR-controlled water into the ship-ping lanes. Then he could hail a freighter from another land—some Danish or Swedish ship, perhaps. If he could get to a Western country, he could figure out a way to get to America. He had experimented, using an air mattress to give him buoyancy without raising him too high out of the water the way a raft or rowboat would. He had also located a spot where an outcropping of rock extended to the water and hid a quiet little cove. He figured he could hide away there and then launch himself at night without much danger of being spotted.

"It's a good plan. I think it will work," Hans said. "I want to try it."

Berndt stepped into the last pew and sat down. He motioned for Hans to sit next to him, and then he whispered, "Do you mean it? We'd have to leave our families—maybe forever."

Hans nodded. He didn't like to say it quite so flatly, but he was angry at his father—even his mother—for the way they made his needs sound so unimportant. "When my dad was about your age, back during the war," Hans said, "his family tried to get out of Germany. Everyone else got across, but he was stopped. He was on his own quite a while, and he was in the war. He told me he learned more from that experience than he has from anything else in his life. I think it would be the same for me."

"Sooner or later, we all go out on our own. And lots of people are separated from their families. Look how it is for all of us now. My parents both have relatives in the West that they'll never see again." Berndt was a serious boy, and confident. He was tall, with a solid chest, and his brown eyes, his even gaze, always seemed trustworthy to Hans.

Hans wasn't quite so sure of himself, but every time he thought of *not* trying an escape, he faced the worst option of all: giving up all hope for a better future. "Yes, it's the same in our family."

"So is this your decision, then? You've made up your mind?" Berndt pulled loose the knot on his tie and undid his top button. As he did, he glanced around, as though to be certain that no one was listening to them.

"Yes. Let's go," Hans said. "Right away."

"No, no. We have to think this through, get everything together without drawing any attention to ourselves. The Baltic is too cold this time of year anyway. We'll have to wait until summer—or close to it. Maybe we could go in May."

"All right. It doesn't matter to me." But actually, Hans was disappointed. He had looked forward to leaving his schoolwork behind, all the pressure he felt from his parents and *Direktor* Schreiter. Now, with the date set so far away, he would have to study more than he had in the past just to calm everyone. Lots of questions were also coming to him now. "If we got to Denmark, or somewhere like that, how would we get to America?"

"Would your relatives in Utah help you?"

"Certainly. As soon as we're out we could send a telegram to my Aunt Anna. Her husband is rich. She would send money to us."

"My friends over there will also help us. I'm pretty sure of that."

"I have a cousin in Salt Lake. He's your age. He just wrote to me that he owns his own car now. He says that a person can go to a university if he chooses; the government has nothing to say about it."

"Could you live with your aunt and uncle when you first get there?"

"Yes. Of course. They have a house as big as a cathedral. And she speaks like a native. She could help us improve our English. My uncle owns a business, and so does his brother. They could give us jobs, no question."

Berndt put his hand on Hans's shoulder. "That's perfect, Hans. We'll go in May."

"Lots of people have gotten out, Berndt. We can do it." Hans loved the sound of his own words, but he felt a fluttering sensation in his stomach and chest. The idea was exciting, but it was also terrifying, no matter what he admitted to Berndt.

For the next three months, Berndt and Hans planned. They couldn't spend too much time together and draw attention to themselves, but they talked at church, or they met after school. Hans had no money and no way to get any, but Berndt had been saving for some time—mostly just from odd jobs he had done for people. He didn't have much, but he was able to set aside enough to buy another air mattress. The boys decided they didn't need much money: enough for train fare to Boltenhagen, food for a couple of days, and telegrams to America when they made it out of the country. They would gamble everything on getting to a passing freighter and trust in the help of the sailors aboard. Who would pass up a couple of boys out in the sea like that?

Hans found the waiting time worse than he expected. He wished that he could have made the decision and then left immediately, but now, every day, he thought of his parents, how much he would miss them, how bad they would feel. And he couldn't look at his little sister without feeling guilty. He did study hard, however, partly to occupy his mind but mostly to prove himself to *Direktor* Schreiter and his father. Once he left, he knew he might never see his parents again, and he wanted at least to leave in good standing. After he reached his Aunt Anna and his grandparents in Salt Lake, he would keep in touch with his parents all the time, just the way Aunt Anna did. That way, they might not feel so bad—especially if he did great things with his life.

That's what he told himself constantly. And almost every day, he backed out, at least for a time. He would decide he just couldn't do it, and he would try to think what he was going to tell Berndt. But every time he reached that point, he would think of spending the rest of his life in the GDR rather than in America, where he could become a wealthy man like his uncles and cousins, and the loss of his dream was always too much for him.

It was late May, 1962, on a Saturday night, when the boys finally made their departure. They had picked the day so that after their school classes on Saturday morning they would have until Monday morning before their absence from school would be noticed. Both left notes to their parents—hid them away so they wouldn't be found immediately. Hans wrote to his parents that he was sorry. He told them that when he was doing well in America, he would try to send some help to them. He told Inga not to miss him. Someday he would see her again if there was any way he could. He cried as he wrote the words, and once again he almost backed out. But he knew he couldn't let Berndt down, not after all they had gone through together to get ready.

Hans knew he couldn't slip out of the apartment without his mother hearing, so he asked to stay a night at Berndt's apartment, and Berndt got permission to stay at Hans's. They met at the Schwerin train station, both in dark clothes and each carrying a small satchel that contained their air mattresses and little else. They bought their tickets and rode the train to Boltenhagen. Their plan was to spend the evening and the following day watching the patrol boats, learning their routine, and checking out the cove that Berndt had identified as their launching place.

The boys didn't have enough money to rent a room, and they didn't want to stay for long around the train station, where they might be questioned, so they strolled through the town and then out to the beach. Hans had never seen such a beautiful place: the sand was perfect, and the water deep blue in the evening light. He and Berndt watched a big white ferry, probably launched from Kiel or somewhere in West Germany, on its way to Sweden. They longed to be on that ship, or to walk along the beach westward, on across the border, only a few kilometers away. But they knew there was no easy escape. They would have to take their chances with their air mattresses. For now, they found a protected spot by some cliffs, and they tried to sleep on the sand. The night cooled drastically, however, and neither boy could get much rest. When morning finally came, they spent some of their money on rolls and a bit of cheese, and then they found the cove Berndt remembered. They watched for patrol boats and tried to chart a schedule, although they soon learned that the boats avoided a predictable pattern.

Hans would have given almost anything to give all this up and go home. He knew that his family and Berndt's were at church, and both would be aware that their sons were missing. What would they do? Would they start searching? Probably not. Both families would have a pretty good idea of what was going on, even before they found the notes, and they would know better than to notify the police. Hans was dreadfully homesick already, and he was almost sure he had made a mistake. He kept thinking too of getting caught, of spending years in prison, but he didn't say that, didn't want to be the one who acted the coward. Berndt had grown silent, his face pale, his eyes fixed, but he didn't suggest calling things off, either.

As the boys had often discussed in their planning, they did have one great challenge. At this time of year, this far north, the sun would stay up much of the night and reappear early. In some ways, that was good. They could leave in the cover of darkness, paddle hard to get far enough out, and be able to see ships early. What they didn't know, and what worried them, was how long it would take to make it out beyond the patrolled water. If the sun came up before they had made it that far, they could be spotted. On the other hand, if they left too soon, they were also vulnerable. They only had a narrow window of time, and they couldn't make a mistake.

It was a nervous time. They were able to sleep a little better in the afternoon warmth, but Hans never stayed asleep long, and the sun seemed to sit in one place, refusing to sink toward the horizon. Hans knew that Berndt, in his silence, was doubting this whole idea, the same as Hans was, but neither said so, and they continued to wait. When twilight finally came, they blew up their air mattresses. They planned to swim with their clothes on, even though the weight might cause them problems. They hoped their dark clothes might help to hide them, but they also thought they might be warmer. They had wanted to buy wet suits, but neither could afford one. What they couldn't take with them were their shoes, nor could they leave any trace of themselves, so they dug holes in the sand and buried the shoes.

And then they waited again.

By the time night was coming on, Hans was shaking all over. He had never been so frightened, never more sure that he was making a mistake. But still he didn't say it, and as the boys walked out into the quiet water and lay on their air mattresses, he was praying constantly—even though he hadn't done so all day. He had been afraid of the answer he might get if he had asked the Lord whether he should go through with this—but he prayed now, for help. The water was chilling, which, of course, didn't surprise him. He was sure the energy it would take to make the swim would heat him up. What scared him was the darkness. There was no moonlight, only the faint afterglow from the sun, and an overcast sky hid all but the brightest of stars. He hadn't thought enough about the difficulty of managing the air mattress when he couldn't see the water he was swimming in.

In the smooth water of the cove the boys made rapid progress, but then the waves began to strike them. In the darkness, the waves seemed to come out of nowhere, and at times it was all Hans could do to stay on the mattress, let alone paddle ahead. When he stopped stroking, he felt that he was being pushed back toward the shore. He was soon clinging with one arm, paddling with the other, then switching arms. But that wasn't enough. He kept trying to find his balance and stroke with both arms, but the motion was awkward, and he felt at every moment that he was about to roll over, to lose his grip on the mattress in the rough water. He was a fair swimmer, but he didn't know whether he could fight his way back to the cove without support under him.

Hans knew he had to keep working hard, but he hadn't realized how quickly his arms would tire. Berndt was stronger than he was, and it wasn't long before Hans lost track of him. "Berndt," he called. "Where are you?"

"Here, here," was all Berndt managed to say, and Hans could detect something close to panic in his voice.

Berndt was ahead, however, and above all, Hans couldn't stand the thought of losing contact with him. He drove his arms harder, seemed to find a better motion, and made up some of the gap. He could catch a glimpse of flailing arms now and again.

Hans was moving better, feeling a bit more confident, when a wave struck him from the side, turning him over. He caught the air mattress just in time, hugged it to his chest, kept the roll going, and came back up on top. But he had gulped sea water, filling up his nose. He coughed, clung, felt a sense that he had fallen farther behind. He searched for Berndt, called out again, but got no answer that he could hear. For just a moment he thought of turning back, but his greater fear was to be out there alone. He began to drive his arms hard again, felt that he was moving forward, but he no longer knew for sure which direction the cove had been. What he knew was that he was moving against the waves.

Then, suddenly, he seemed to break through a barrier. The water smoothed considerably, and the sound of the waves quieted. Berndt had told him that they had to cross a sandbar, and that things would not be so difficult after that. In his panic, he hadn't thought of any of that. "Berndt!" he called. "Where are you?"

"The water is better out here. We'll be all right."

"But I can't see you."

"Just keep coming. I'll wait."

Hans took a few strokes and then spotted Berndt. He kept pumping hard and caught up. "That was rougher than I expected—worse than last summer," Berndt said. "We're all right now. Let's just work as hard as we can and get out there fast. Don't ever yell out as loudly as you did back there."

"Okay. I can see better now. I was lost there for a minute."

The boys stayed closer now, side by side, and they stroked steadily and hard. Berndt was stronger, but he was heavier. Hans managed to stay up with him pretty well, but he wondered how long they would have to do this. The current was stronger than either of them had expected, and there was really no telling how far out they were. Hans had glanced around at times but had seen no lights, no sign of any sort of patrol boats, but he wasn't entirely sure he and Berndt were still moving out from the beach, toward the ship routes. Would they get to some point where they could rest and wait, not have to fight the current that kept throwing them back toward the shore?

Hans kept pushing until his arms were so tired that he hardly knew whether he was getting anything from his strokes. But he couldn't stop trying. At least he could see that Berndt's strokes were slowing too.

"Let's take turns resting," Berndt finally called to him. "Grab my air mattress. I'll stroke for a while. Then you do the same for me."

They tried that for a time, and it certainly helped. What Hans didn't know was whether they were actually getting anywhere. For all he knew, they were still very far from where they needed to be. Each time he rested, he felt the cold more deeply too, as though it were working its way into his bones, his core. But Berndt told him, "We're doing all right. I've kept my eye on a star. I know we're going in the right direction."

Hans hadn't thought of that, was embarrassed that he hadn't. "How much farther?"

"I don't know. We just have to keep moving ahead—until the sun comes up. Then we'll be able to see exactly where we are."

"That's hours." Hans didn't know whether he could last so long. His lungs were burning now, and his shoulders ached so bad that it was hard to keep stroking.

"I know. We'll keep taking turns. We'll be okay."

Hans liked Berndt's confidence. He felt a little better. He only wondered how long the night would last. But he kept taking his turn, and sometimes both boys rested at the same time for a minute or two. What Hans could feel was that the current was not so swift as it had been closer to shore. They weren't drifting very rapidly when they stopped stroking, and it felt as though they were moving ahead at a better pace when they did stroke. He was beginning to feel that they were going to make it, but he also wondered how long he could stand the vicious cold. They would have been better off under the water than on top, in the breeze.

Hans was taking a turn, letting Berndt rest, and swimming as strongly as he could, when he glanced to his right and saw lights. "Boat!" he called to Berndt.

"Stop swimming. Don't speak again. Let it go by."

The boat was coming straight at them, not fast but steady. A search-light kept swinging back and forth, randomly. Hans was sure the men on the boat hadn't spotted them; this was merely a patrol, working its way through the controlled water. But it was coming closer. Berndt finally whispered, "Turn back. Swim, but not hard. Don't lift your arms high."

Hans understood. He stroked with one arm until the mattress turned around, and then he started swimming, using a sidestroke, trying not to make a splash. But the boat was coming ever closer, the light swinging toward them at times. He could hear the motor buzzing, and he heard a voice, someone laughing. He and Berndt would be all right, he kept telling himself, but the boat wasn't going by. It was still bearing down on them, as though it were guided. The boys should have swum ahead, not back, Hans realized.

"Stop stroking," Berndt gasped, and Hans understood. The boat was so close now, their only hope was that it would slip on by, and no one would see them.

Hans clung to the air mattress with both arms locked around it. He tucked his face down against the rubber, and he waited. The buzz of the motor was becoming a roar, and the light slid by close a couple of times. And then finally, the boat was almost on them. It cut through the water, past their feet, and for a moment Hans thought they would be safe. But then the wake struck, and Hans was thrown over. He clung tight, held his breath, rolled in the water. For a time the sound of the water in his ears, the crazy motion, left him feeling that he was tumbling to the bottom of the sea. But then he popped out, rolled again on the surface, and finally came up right, bobbing wildly in what was left of the wake. The patrol boat was moving away, still on a line.

But where was Berndt?

Hans swung around, looking in all directions. For a few long seconds, he was sure Berndt had drowned, and then he heard a voice in the dark. "Hans, help me. Here. Here."

Hans stroked toward the sound and spotted him splashing in the water. He had cut most of the distance between them when he saw Berndt's head and arms slip under the water. Hans felt the despair, but he kept driving his arms, and suddenly something grabbed his air mattress, pulled it on its side. Hans tumbled sideways and struck Berndt's shoulder, and the two were tangled together for a few seconds, both clinging to the mattress. Hans fought to keep hold, to grab Berndt and to hold on to anything he could grasp. The confusion subsided in a moment, and suddenly everything was quiet. There they were, side by side, clutching each other and holding on to the mattress.

"What happened to your air mattress?"

"I don't know. I got thrown off. It's out there in the dark somewhere."

"Can we find it?"

"I don't know. I doubt it."

"Can we stay out here?"

This time there was a long pause. And then Berndt said, "No. We'd better go back."

Nothing else had to be said. It was what Hans had hoped Berndt would say. Hans thought of nothing but his desire to have the beach under his feet again. He let Berndt choose the direction, but both stayed in the water, pulled the air mattress under their chests, and then stroked with their feet.

The air mattress was awkward now, but the current was with them, and it was good to use legs instead of arms. What was shocking, however, was how little time it took to make it back to the shore. They had never been very far out. Maybe they had really had no hope of reaching the shipping lanes. All Hans knew was that when he stumbled onto the beach, then dropped onto his chest in the sand, he was relieved to be alive.

Hans took long, deep breaths, felt himself shaking all over, but gradually felt some strength coming back. He had lain in the sand for several minutes when he finally asked the question: "What are we going to do?"

"Let's find the cove—and rest for a while."

"Do you want to try it again?"

"No. We'd better go home. They didn't see us out there. We'll be all right."

"We don't have any money."

"I have a little. But we might be better off to catch a freight train, if we can, and not get caught in a train station. We're a mess. Someone would want to ask us a lot of questions."

Hans agreed, but then he looked away. He had started to cry, without exactly knowing why. He was exhausted, scared, and cold—but relieved too. He did want to go home.

CHAPTER 6

Hans and Berndt were standing in an alley, waiting. They had made it back to Schwerin, but nothing had been as easy as they had hoped. They had managed to dig up their shoes after several tries, but the shoes were now uncomfortable, wet and full of sand. Their clothes had gradually dried, but they looked disheveled and dirty. It was not good to be seen on the streets, where local police might stop them. How would they explain their wandering about, far from home on a school day? What kinds of questions would they have to answer? They had enough money to take the train, but they didn't dare walk into the station and try to buy tickets.

So they had hid out all day Monday, spending most of their time in the cove where they had first gone into the water. Both boys managed to sleep much of the day, and then, when night finally came, they looked for a chance to jump a freight train. But too many guards were near the train station. They had to walk well out of town, make a wild run to catch onto a train, and then climb on top of a car and ride in the open air. What they worried about then was the danger of getting caught in the Schwerin train yard. So they jumped off when the train slowed, but much too soon, as it turned out, and they had to tramp through a dark, damp wooded area until they found their way into the streets of Schwerin. Here again, they had a problem. Local police—*Vopos*, the people called them—walked the streets at night. Hans and Berndt had to get back to their own apartments, but they couldn't be spotted.

They worked their way slowly through town, using side streets and shadows, but they were still several streets from home when the sun started to rise. Now they were stuck in an alley, held up by a policeman standing on a nearby street corner with a rifle slung over his shoulder. "If he happens to walk down this way, he'll spot us," Berndt said.

"Maybe we should walk out, like nothing is wrong."

"It's still too early. If he stops us, what do we say we're doing?"

Hans glanced around. They could retreat through the alley, but that meant heading back toward another busy street they had been happy to get past. There could easily be a policeman back that way, too.

"Here he comes." Berndt had been peeking out, but now he ducked back in, and the two hurried back through the alley. "Down here," Berndt whispered, and they ducked into a stairway that led to the basement door of an apartment house.

Hans was glad for the cover. He doubted that the policeman would come down the alley, but the thought had hardly passed through his mind before Berndt said, "He's coming this way."

Hans jumped down the steps and tried the door, but it was locked. And so the two pressed their backs to the side of the stairway. If the policeman walked by, he might not see them, but if he chose to look down the stairs, they were definitely caught.

The footsteps were coming quickly now, and Hans could only think that the man had seen Berndt looking out and was now hurrying after them. And then the steps stopped. Hans held his breath and tried to squeeze tighter against the wall, but he didn't know, maybe the policeman was already bending over the railing, looking down at them. At any second he expected a voice, a command. But then he heard a trickle of water. It continued steadily for quite some time, hesitated, then came again in a short burst. Hans couldn't help but smile.

But he still might come this way. Hans heard some fumbling as the policeman apparently leaned his rifle against the wall and buttoned up his pants. Then the footsteps resumed, this time moving away. Berndt waited until the sound was gone before he said, "I'm glad he didn't get any on us. He wasn't that far away."

Hans grinned. "I know." But then he asked, "What do we do now? He's probably gone back to his corner."

"We'll have to wait—until it's fully light and people start moving about on the streets. But we have to have a story—in case we're stopped."

"We'll say we had football practice, early."

"We wouldn't play in these clothes—especially these shoes."

"What else can we say?"

Berndt didn't answer, and Hans knew he was thinking. "We're helping our grandparents," he said after a time. "Early in the morning, before school. We're cousins. Our grandparents are repairing their house, tearing out an old porch that was falling down."

"They'll ask for the address. That's how the police operate. They check out everything."

"I know. But what else can we say?"

"Maybe the football story is still better."

"They'll ask who our coach is, what team we play for."

It was true. Police, in a certain mood, would sometimes let things go by and not say much. But if they were suspicious, they would interrogate people, even take them in for questioning about minor infractions—or no infraction.

"Whatever we say, we say with confidence, and we laugh a little. If he starts to ask us questions, we're in trouble, no matter what we say. So when we do walk out, we have to act like we have no worries at all."

Hans nodded, but he wasn't sure he could do that. And what he hated even more, for the moment, was waiting in this stairway. He had the feeling that someone could come along at any moment and he and Berndt would look like burglars.

But the boys waited most of an hour and no one came into the alley. Finally, Berndt said, "Let's go. Let's just head home by the shortest route and hope for the best." He climbed the stairs and then strode away. Hans had to hurry to catch up. They came out of the alley walking at a normal pace, Berndt swinging his arms. "So how are we doing so far?" he asked.

"What?"

"Just talk. Act normal."

"What about the policeman? Was he on the corner?"

"I didn't look." They had turned the opposite direction and were heading to the next corner, away from the policeman. When they reached the corner, they crossed the street. Now they could see that the policeman was gone.

And so they continued down the sidewalk, still walking fast, still making up things to say. They put some streets behind them rather rapidly and were approaching their own neighborhood when they saw a policeman walking down the sidewalk toward them. "Okay, be natural," Berndt said. "Say hello to him, but if he says anything, let me do the talking."

Hans nodded, but he made up his mind not to speak at all. His voice would give him away, he feared.

"*Guten Morgen*," Berndt said as the policeman approached. Hans nodded.

"What are you boys doing, so early in the morning?" The question seemed friendly, not suspicious.

"Trying to find my dog. We took him for a walk and he got away from us."

"What? Your own dog won't come to you?"

"We just got him—from my uncle. I think he misses his home."

Berndt had stopped by now. The policeman was still smiling, not seeming concerned, but Hans could hardly breathe. "What kind of dog is it?"

"A *Schäferhund*," Berndt said. "A pretty, dark one. But he's just a puppy, really. We can't seem to get him trained. He makes messes all over the place. My mother doesn't like him much." Berndt laughed, and then he was moving again.

"Wait a moment."

Hans stopped and stood stiff. He tried to smile, like Berndt, but he couldn't do it.

"Are you boys brothers?"

But that couldn't be. They looked nothing alike.

"No, no. Just friends."

"And what's wrong with you, boy?" He pointed to Hans. "You look scared enough to wet your pants."

"I'm about ready to. I need to get home." Hans laughed as naturally as he could.

The policeman laughed too, and the boys turned to leave. "Wait, wait. Tell me your names. In case we find your dog." But no policeman would worry about returning a dog. He was being a policeman now.

"Berndt Kerner."

Hans had wondered whether they should tell the truth, but he followed Berndt's lead. "Hans Stoltz," he said.

"And where do you live?"

The boys gave their correct addresses. Hans felt almost sick as he watched the man write all the information in a little notebook he had pulled from an inside pocket of his uniform coat.

The boys finally walked away, and once they were well down the street, Hans finally asked, "Are we in trouble?"

"I don't know. I think he might have believed us. That was good, how you answered."

"I didn't mean to look scared. I tried not to."

"I know." He walked for a time before he said, "We'll probably be all right."

Hans wondered whether Berndt believed what he had said. Too many things had gone wrong. But now Hans had begun to think about his next problem: returning home. He wanted to be there now, wanted to feel safe, but he also hated to face everyone, especially his little sister. He felt guilty that he had been so willing to leave.

When Hans reached the apartment, he found the front door locked. He rang the doorbell and waited until he heard his father on the speaker. "*Ja?*"

"It's Hans."

"Oh, Hans. Good. Come in." Hans heard the buzzer and pushed against the door, which swung open. He hiked up the stairs and at the second landing saw his father in a white shirt with no tie. His suspenders were hanging around his hips. "I'm sorry, Papa," was all Hans could think to say.

Peter motioned for him to step in, so Hans walked by him without so much as a touch, and his father followed. "What were you thinking, Hans?" he heard from behind, but the tone wasn't angry, and when Hans turned around, he saw tears in his father's eyes. "What's happened? Why did you come back?"

"We couldn't make it."

"How did you try to get out?"

"On the Baltic. We tried to swim on air mattresses, out to the ship lanes."

"Were you seen? Can anyone trace you back here?"

"I'm not sure. I don't think so."

"Hans, why?"

"You know why."

For several seconds they looked at each other, and then, finally, Peter stepped forward and took Hans in his arms. "Oh, Son, we've been so worried."

Hans heard the kitchen door open, and he pulled away from his father and turned around. His mother was clearly taken by surprise, but she hurried to Hans. "Oh, you came back. You came back." She wrapped her arms around him.

By then, Inga had heard her mother, and she burst through the door. "Hans!" she squealed, and ran to him. Hans took her in one arm, his mother in the other, and he was surprised at how relieved, how happy he was to be there now, to feel safe.

"Everyone be quiet," Dad was whispering. "We can't let the neighbors hear this fuss. We have to act as though nothing has happened."

Hans stepped away from his mother, but Inga still clung to him. "Did anyone call from my school?" he asked.

"No, thank goodness," Katrina said. "But what could I have told them if they had?"

"I'm sorry, Mama. I really am." Hans was finally feeling the relief, the warmth, and tears had filled his eyes.

Katrina took him in her arms again. "I'm so glad you're back," she said. "Have you eaten anything?"

"Not since yesterday."

So everyone went to the kitchen, and Hans told them the story. But he said nothing of the policeman who had stopped them. He didn't want them to worry.

"You'd better get ready and go back to school today. We'll write you an excuse. We'll say you were sick yesterday. But don't make me lie for you again, Hans."

So Hans cleaned up and had breakfast, and then he walked to school. He was exhausted from all he had gone through, but everything seemed fine at school. He pretended a bit of hoarseness, but no one seemed to pay any attention. No questions were asked. By the end of the day, Hans was almost sure he was all right.

But then, on Wednesday morning, when Hans walked into his European History class, his teacher called him to her desk. "The *Direktor* wants to see you," she said. "Please go directly to his office."

Hans nodded, his voice suddenly gone, and he walked from the room. He thought of running, of heading for the front door. But he knew he couldn't do that, and his feet kept carrying him to Schreiter's office. When he presented himself before the school secretary, she was a little too quick to say, "Yes, I know. Please go in now."

Hans stepped inside the office, saw his director behind his big wooden desk. Another man—a sturdy fellow in a brown suit—was sitting at the side of the desk in a wooden chair. "You wanted to see me?" Hans asked, his voice sounding much too tight.

"Yes. Bring a chair. Sit down."

Hans was nodding again. He took another good look at the other man, someone he had never seen before. He was a colorless man with a flat face and no expression. "Thank you," he said. He carried a chair toward the desk, set it several steps away, and sat down.

"You missed school on Monday. Is that correct?" *Direktor* Schreiter asked.

"Yes. I was sick."

"What was wrong?"

"Just a sick stomach."

"You've recovered nicely, it would seem."

"Yes. I'm doing fine now." But he knew how nervous he sounded, knew that he was making things worse.

Direktor Schreiter was a strange, distant man. He was bald on top, and the gray hair above his ears stuck out like wings, giving him an odd, almost wild look. Hans would often go a month or two without seeing the man, but the *Direktor* knew every one of his students by name.

"This is *Herr* Meyer. He wants to speak with you."

Meyer didn't rise, didn't offer his hand, so Hans didn't either. But he saw the dismal expression in the man's stare, his gray eyes, and he knew this couldn't be good.

"Young man, were you stopped by a policeman yesterday morning, here in town?"

"Yes, I was."

"And you were with a boy named Kerner. Is this not true?"

"Yes."

"You said that you were searching for a dog?"

"Yes."

"Tell me this. Why were your clothes so wrinkled and soiled?"

Hans tried, desperately, to think of an answer. But the pause was a mistake and he knew it. Finally, awkwardly, he said, "They were my old clothes, that's all. We went out to walk Berndt's dog."

"He has no dog."

Hans didn't know whether Meyer had talked to Berndt, didn't know what he might have said. "His uncle gave it to him, but it got away. Hasn't he found it yet?"

But these questions made no sense. How could Meyer make such a fuss out of this? Did he know where they had been?

"We don't believe you were walking a dog. Tell me the truth now, and it will be better for you."

"What do you think we were doing?"

"You tell me. Did you leave Schwerin during the weekend?"

Hans tried to sound firm, but he couldn't bring himself to look the man directly in the eyes. "No."

"You can't wander about this country, two boys on a school day, without being noticed. We have many contacts. You went to Boltenhagen, didn't you? You bought train tickets here in Schwerin, and traveled to the sea."

Hans didn't answer. The man knew. What had Berndt admitted?

Meyer was leaning forward now, his eyes more alive, the speed of his speech picking up. "Kerner was sick on the same day you were."

—— 87 ——

Hans took a breath and answered slowly, just to break the pace. "I didn't know that."

Meyer shifted, leaned back in his chair, and didn't speak for a time. But this was all a game. The man knew the truth.

"Young man, do you know who I am?"

"You must be with the *Stasi*."

"That's not a respectful title."

"*Staatssicherheitsdient*, then." This was the official name of the Secret Police.

"Yes. You are exactly correct. You must know that we work with local police. We receive reports of strange behaviors. We add things up. We know that you and Kerner took the train to Boltenhagen. We know you came back Tuesday morning, your clothes full of sand. We can draw a conclusion from that."

But they didn't have proof. And Hans wasn't about to give them anything more. "We made a little holiday. That's all. We took a day off from school. We shouldn't have done it, I know—and we won't do it again."

Meyer nodded, almost respectfully. Hans had turned out to be more formidable than Meyer had expected, but clearly he didn't mind the challenge. "You're lying, young man. You know you are. I'm giving you a chance to make it easier on yourself—by confessing."

Hans didn't respond. Maybe he was doomed, but he wasn't playing into this man's hands.

"What do you think of people who try to leave our country, Stoltz? Maybe you think a fellow ought to be able to leave if he chooses. Some feel that way, you know?"

"You should interrogate those who feel that way, then. Not me."

"So you don't think it's wrong to punish those who try to leave?"

"If everyone were to leave, what sort of country would we have? That's how I look at it."

"Clever answers, young man. Very clever. But this cleverness is not wise. It's getting you into deeper trouble. There will be no pity for such an arrogant young person, I can assure you." He hesitated, and then he said, "Can you tell me why you haven't joined the Free German Youth?"

Hans had had enough. "That's my choice, *Herr* Meyer. If I would rather not join, that's up to me. That's the kind of freedom we have in this country, and I'm thankful for it."

"This is enough," Meyer finally growled, and he pointed a stiff finger at Hans. "We know that you and Kerner are Mormons, and we know that you have no love for the Socialist state. We also know that you tried to leave this country. You *will* pay for that. We will meet with your parents next, and we will decide your fate. But give up all hope for the future, young man. You can expect nothing but very hard work, no matter how *clever* you think you are."

Hans didn't respond. He knew better. But he also saw his own future clearly before him, and he knew that he was looking at a wall.

CHAPTER 7

The closing dance was one of the last events in the '61–'62 school year. It followed a carnival out on the football field behind East High, with lots of food and game booths. During the dance the student-body president for the following year would be announced. Everyone kept telling Gene that he had won—no question—and the truth was, he was pretty sure that was right, but of course, he didn't say that. "Well, I don't know. Tim ran a really good campaign," he would say, and then he would enjoy all the denials.

"You're the most popular guy in the whole school," Sondra Hebdon told him while they danced together. "No one had a chance, running against you."

"Are you sure people don't think I'm just a dumb football player?"

"Oh, *no*. Not at all. You get really good grades, too." She had nestled a little closer to him. "Please, please, call me this summer," she whispered. She turned her head just enough to breathe against his neck. He even thought he felt her lips touch his ear. What crossed his mind was that he might be wise to stay away from her. Brother Craythorn, his seminary teacher, always told the guys not to put themselves in a position where they might be in danger of making a mistake, and Gene had a suspicion this could be one of those cases.

He took a different kind of chance, however, when he asked Marsha Wimmer to dance. He had had the feeling for quite some time that she didn't like him all that much, and that bothered him. It wasn't that she was beautiful. She had rather ordinary hair—dark, cut fairly short—and a slim figure that demanded no special attention. But she was attractive in some way that Gene wasn't sure he understood. She had a nice smile—when she showed it—with pretty round lips, but she was more serious than most girls, didn't giggle, didn't show off. Her eyes were hazel, with a little sunburst of gold on the inner circle of the iris, and her skin had a rich, natural tone. He had realized a while back that she was one of the few people he knew who looked best close-up.

She didn't hesitate when he asked her to dance, but when he placed his hand on her back, he felt resistance. She only stayed a couple of inches farther away than he liked, but he could feel that steady pressure on his hand, as though she were saying, "*I'll* decide how close we dance."

Gene decided he didn't care. He glanced around to see who else was standing at the end of the gym, where most of the girls had congregated. Gene could see at least half a dozen girls he still wanted to dance with.

"Well, Gene," Marsha said, "I noticed that you were spreading yourself around today, but I never thought you would get to me."

"What do you mean, 'spreading myself around'? It's a stag dance."

Gene watched Marsha. He could see a subtle, barely perceptible smile, but she didn't say anything. "*What?*" he said.

"What do you mean, 'What?'"

"You're laughing at me."

"Laughing? How could anyone laugh at Gene Thomas, our new student-body president—every East girl's dreamboat?"

"Just answer. What was that crack about spreading myself around?"

She pulled back a little more, throwing his step off—his rather awkward little fox-trot that he never felt much confidence in. The record playing was "Johnny Angel," which Gene liked, but he wasn't sure he was hitting the rhythm just right.

"Okay. Tell me the truth," Marsha said. "Didn't you say to yourself when you got here, 'On the day I get elected, I'd better be friendly to *everyone*'?"

"Not at all. I'm always friendly."

"And you didn't say, 'I guess I'd better dance with a lot of different girls'?"

She had him now, and they both knew it. He could feel his ears getting warm, and he knew that he was getting red blotches on his neck, the way he always did when he was embarrassed. That was the worst thing about having such a light complexion. "Why would that be so bad, if I had thought that? Not that I'm saying I've won. But maybe it is the right thing to do."

"Why?"

"I don't know. It's just—"

"It's just good politics. The right image."

Gene was wondering what was so bad about that, but he wasn't going to ask. Marsha would certainly make fun of him again. So he just danced, deciding he would only stay with her through this one record. What he wished now was that he had asked her to dance to something faster. He wasn't much at the Mashed Potato, but he liked to do the Twist—and that would have kept them far enough apart not to talk much.

"I voted for you."

Now he was the one pulling away to have a better look. "Really?"

The little smile was back. "The lesser of two evils."

He stopped completely. "Hey!"

"Well, you may be a politician, but you're a nice guy underneath it all. Tim is just a manipulator." Gene was still trying to decide how deeply he had been cut, when she added, "But then, this whole idea of having a student-body president is silly in the first place."

"Why?"

"What can you do, really? The principal and the faculty make all the real decisions."

Gene had decided to get out of this one. The truth was, he had taken a hard look at what a student-body president did, and he had reached pretty much the same conclusion: that it didn't matter all that much who won.

"Answer this. Honestly. Did you *believe* what you said in that talk you gave at the campaign assembly?"

"Sure. What did I say that wasn't true?"

"All those promises about 'improving communications'—you meant all that?"

Suddenly Gene was smiling at himself. "That's what you say in a speech like that. Maybe I can't solve a lot of problems, but . . ."

"But what?"

The record ended and Gene stopped dancing. Marsha stepped back and let go of his hand, but they stood facing one another. "I don't know. We plan dances and assemblies and stuff like that. There's a certain amount of communication, I guess."

Marsha began to laugh, and Gene felt stupid. Still, she looked good, her teeth bright against her pretty skin. "Gene, you're finally being honest. I think we're communicating better."

"No, I think you've buried me alive, and now you're standing on my grave, laughing."

"I'm sorry."

"No, you're not."

"I know. But at least I like you better now. At least you know that speech didn't mean anything. I'd hate to think that you felt good about that stuff."

She was wearing a white, short-sleeved blouse and a green, sleeveless sweater. Her eyes were picking up the color from the sweater. He really did like the way she looked, but that didn't soften what she was saying. "So what are you all about, Marsha? Do you just take potshots at people, or is there something else you like to do?"

He was surprised at how much composure she lost, how quickly her eyes disengaged.

"You're on the debate team, aren't you?" he asked.

"I was this year. I won't be next year."

"Why not?"

Her eyes went shut for a moment, as though she didn't want to answer. But finally she said, "Debate is all about arguing, not about trying to understand anything."

"But it's good, isn't it? You know, to explain things and be persuasive—stuff like that?"

"Sure. But you argue for one side and then switch over to the other. If I believe something, I don't want to argue on the opposite side."

Gene nodded. He had actually thought the same thing. But he liked having her on the defensive for once. "So what are you going to do next year—just stand on the sidelines and knock everything everybody else is doing?"

He was grinning, and she seemed to like the challenge. She smiled back. "No. I'm going to be editor of *Pencilings.*" That was the school literary magazine.

"Are you a good writer?"

"Not all that good. But I like to write."

"Who's the best writer in the school?"

By now the music was playing again: Joey Dee and the Starliters were singing "The Peppermint Twist." "I don't know," Marsha said. "Probably Bryant Gibbs."

"He's gotten weird lately, don't you think?"

"Guys like you would think so. Maybe he's a little different, but he—"

"That's what I meant."

"No. I happen to think *different* is good. You think it's bad. Bryant is a sweet boy, but he walks up and down the halls like a lost soul. I'm almost his only friend."

"I talk to him sometimes. I've known him since kindergarten."

"I know. He's told me that. But you wouldn't have lunch with him, or—"

"Sure I would."

"You eat with the in-crowd, Gene."

"I eat with my friends—guys I play ball with."

"Well, spread yourself around a little, President. You might learn a lot about the school."

"That's a good point. I'm going to start doing that."

"So I guess you *do* think you're going to win."

He was stopped. She had him again. And yet, strangely, what crossed his mind was that he might want to take her out sometime. He couldn't imagine why. "I think I'm in over my head with you," he said.

"*Clearly.*" She smiled. "Does that mean I get delivered to the sidelines, and you dance with another one of your admirers?"

That *was* what it had meant, but now Gene was trapped again. "I'll tell you what. I'll let you decide."

"Okay. I want to dance with you every dance. And I want to have hold of your arm when they announce that you're president. I want you to turn to me with an amazed expression on your face and say, 'I can't believe it. I won.' And then I'll hug you and tell you that you're wonderful."

Gene was grinning by then and letting his head nod to the insistent beat of the music. "How about—instead—we dance what's left of this record . . . and then call it a day?"

"Sounds even better."

But she still had one more surprise for him. She danced the twist very well, got into it much more than he ever thought she would. She made his own reserved little, mostly-arm-movement version look rather dainty. And in a fitted skirt, she looked pretty good—even if she was awfully thin.

When the dance ended, Gene was relieved to "deliver her to the sidelines." But she told him, "Okay, now it's time to find the perfect girl. The announcement will be coming soon, and you need to have a girl with you who knows how to do everything just right. But don't you dare wonder what I think of the whole show."

He rolled his eyes and tried to think of a reply but finally just turned and walked away.

∞

Gene didn't know exactly when the big announcement would come, and it was actually mere coincidence that he was dancing at the time with Linda Lancaster, one of the cheerleaders—and certainly one of the cutest girls in the school. He had taken her out once, sometime in the winter, but they certainly didn't have anything "going." Still, she joined the circle around the microphone as the current president, Jim Backman, announced the winners, and she clung to his arm as though they had been going steady for years. Gene turned to her when he heard his name announced, nodded, and smiled, but he didn't act surprised. And when Linda began jumping up and down, he was suddenly self-conscious. He wondered where Marsha was. All afternoon he had practiced his little acceptance speech, going over and over the words he wanted to say, but suddenly the sentiments seemed wrong, and he found himself, when he stepped to the microphone, stumbling rather badly. "I just want to thank everyone," he said. But he didn't say how "overwhelmed" he was, the way he had planned. And he couldn't bring himself to say anything about all the things he wanted to accomplish. So he merely said, "It's going to be hard to fill Jim's shoes. He's done a great job. But I'll do the best I can." And then he repeated himself: "So thanks for voting for me."

No one seemed to notice how awkward that had been. His friends collected around him and told him what a great president he would be. He couldn't think how to deliver Linda anywhere, with her fingers clasping his arm so tight. They didn't dance a lot, not with everyone crowding around Gene, talking about the "great senior year" they were going to have, but Gene was almost relieved not to dance. Linda had a way of pressing in on him during the slow dances, and he didn't know how to stop her. It's not that he exactly minded her being crushed against him that way, but he was worried about what she was trying to establish between them.

When the dance ended, however, she was still on his arm, and when he said, "Well, let's see, did you come with—," she quickly said, "Oh, that's all right."

Gene understood the implication. The two walked out to his car, and Gene tried to create a little more space, but when they got into his "Vickie," she slid toward him as though he were downhill and the seats were lubricated. "Gene, I'm just so happy for you," she told him. "I've known you'd be our president since we were all in seventh grade. You're the neatest guy in our whole school. I'll bet we'll all brag some day, just to be able to say we knew you."

"Well, I don't know," Gene mumbled. "You know, like anyone, I have dreams. But—"

"Tell me what they are."

Gene had started the car. He pulled his arm loose long enough to shift into reverse, and he backed out of his parking space. But as soon as he shifted, she had him again. "I want to go on a mission, and go to college, and then we'll just have to see. Sometimes I think about going into . . ." But the word "politics" stuck in his throat. "Well, law school, probably."

"What about professional sports? You could do that, too."

"Oh, no. I'm not *that* good."

"Yes, you are. Everyone says so."

"Really, I don't think I'll even play ball in college. My dad thinks it's more important to buckle down and really study. Sports take a lot of time. They can hurt your grades."

"You know, I think you're right. You've got bigger things in mind, don't you? I think you should be an astronaut—maybe be the first one to land on the moon." She squeezed a little tighter. "Wouldn't that be cool?"

Once Gene had tried to catch a cat for a neighbor. The cat had run at first, but when he had grabbed at it and gotten hold of its tail, it had spun around and clamped onto his arm with all its claws. It had been all he could do to strip the thing off. That's about how he felt now. "So what do you want to do?" he asked—to change the subject.

"I don't care. We could—"

"No. I meant, after you graduate."

"You mean, what are my dreams?"

"Yeah."

"Oh, Gene, I can't tell you." She laughed and actually pulled away from him a little. "I told Janalee, but she's my closest friend. I could never tell you."

"You probably want to dance in a chorus line, down in Las Vegas. That's my guess."

"*Gene!*" She slapped his shoulder. "What a thing to say!"

Gene was laughing. What he had hoped was that he might divert her from whatever it was she had in mind—since he thought he knew what that was.

"No, I really do have things I want out of life. They're the kinds of things a girl starts thinking about when she gets a little older and starts realizing what really matters. You know, when she thinks about the family she'd like to have, and things like that."

"Now I know."

"What?"

"You want to marry Jerry Lee Lewis. Or is he still married to his cousin?"

Linda slapped his shoulder again. "Would you stop it?"

"Okay, okay."

"When I get married, I want someone who's just really, really special—someone I can marry forever and know what a really *wonderful* guy he is."

Gene found himself pressing down on the gas pedal a little harder. "Well, that's good," he said. "I'm sure you'll find him, too."

"I've found him, Gene. I just hope he finds me."

That was enough. Gene began to talk about the weather, and he drove straight to Linda's house. When he got there, he hopped out immediately, even though he pulled her with him partway out the door before she unleashed him. And when he got her to the porch, he stayed back at least two yards, thanked her quickly, and almost ran to the car.

Gene parked his car in the driveway, at home, and went inside. It wasn't all that late. He thought he might get on the phone and invite a few friends over. It was a rare weekend when he didn't have some kids over to listen to music on the new hi-fi, with stereophonic sound, or to watch scary movies on late-night television. One of the nice things about the house, besides the neighborhood, was the well-groomed backyard where Gene staged parties or got his friends involved in croquet matches. He loved it all. His parents were the coolest among all his friends' families, his Mom so pretty and fun, his dad so "important," or whatever it was kids thought of him. Gene couldn't think of a better life. But he was a little off his game tonight, and he knew it. Once he had escaped Linda, his mind had turned back to Marsha and the things she had said.

When he went inside, he found his mom and dad watching Jack Paar on the *The Tonight Show*. Gene tried to look as unhappy as possible as he approached them, but his dad laughed and said, "Don't show us any long faces. We know you won."

"Who told you?"

"I've had three phone calls, actually," Anna said. "Just people calling to congratulate you. Even the bishop called. I guess his daughter came home and told him all about it."

"Now I can't pull your leg."

Dad was beaming. "I'm thrilled for you, Son. I had a great time with that job. It's a family tradition now. The only thing I worry about is whether you can sing 'Dat Ol' Man River.'"

"Yeah, I'm worried about that myself." It was an East High tradition for the outgoing president to perform the song at the final assembly each year, and Gene knew he wasn't much of a singer.

Gene sat down on the big leather recliner across from the couch, where his dad and mom were sitting next to each other. "Let me ask you something, Dad. Is there any way to turn the job into something really meaningful?"

Alex smiled. He was wearing an old pair of khakis and a plaid button-down. Gene knew that he still liked to think of himself as a cool dresser. "Well, it depends on how you look at it. It's mainly a party chairman kind of thing, isn't it?"

"Yeah. I guess. But I was wondering whether it's the kind of thing where a guy could make some changes—you know, try to make some real improvements at the school." He found himself looking down. His parents both had their shoes off, and Gene noticed that his dad had a little hole in the toe of one of his white socks. For some reason, that delighted Gene.

"Like what? What do you want to improve?"

"I'm not sure. But I think I ought to improve something."

Anna and Alex both laughed.

"I know. That sounds stupid. But I'm just wondering whether it couldn't be a job where you look into what's happening at the school and try to see what needs to be done . . . and then straighten some things out."

"Sure," Dad said. "I thought you had some things like that in mind when you ran."

"Well . . . I sort of said I did." He smiled at his own admission. "But mostly, I just said we needed better communication . . . you know, the stuff people always say."

Kurt poked his head into the family room. He was wearing his old tan pajamas that were way too short in the legs now.

"Why are you still up?" Anna asked.

"Did you win, Gene?" he asked.

"No. I lost."

"No, you didn't. You're smiling."

"I'm a good sport."

"You won, didn't you?"

"Yeah."

"Good. I knew you would."

"Thanks, Kurt," Gene said, and he was touched. The kid really did look up to him. Gene could always feel that. He was something of a Gene look-alike, too.

"All right. Now get to bed," Alex said.

Kurt rolled his eyes, but he didn't argue. He headed back to his bedroom.

But Alex hadn't lost his train of thought. "Gene, before I start a campaign, I try to look into all the issues that I think are important. Too many times, when I first ran for office, I got caught in situations where I didn't know what I was talking about."

"Alex, it was only a school election," Anna said. "It's mostly a popularity contest."

"Every election is a popularity contest. But if you make a lot of empty promises, you pay for it. All those speeches are on record, and someone will bring up the things you haven't done."

"But Dad, I was only—"

"I know. It's a one-time deal, and no one really holds you accountable. But this won't be your last election. I know what your goals are. You were blessed to look like your mother, and that's going to take you a long way, but you need to be on top of the issues, too."

"Yeah. That's what I've been thinking. I want to make an appointment with the principal, so we can talk everything over."

"What would you do about Cuba?"

"What do you mean?"

"Do you know what's going on down there?"

"I just know about that Castro guy, with the beard."

"What about him?"

"He's kind of a wild man, isn't he? A Communist and everything."

"Gene, you need to know what's happening in Cuba. Kennedy didn't know enough, and that's why the Bay of Pigs invasion was a disaster. That whole thing will be connected with his name when he runs again, no matter what else he does. And he still has his hands full with Castro. The guy is all tied up with the Russians now, and there he is, sitting right off our shores."

Gene nodded, but he didn't understand what his dad was saying.

"Kennedy is telling the Russians he's going to start testing A-bombs above ground again. Do you think he ought to?"

"Sure. Those guys keep doing it."

"But you're a Utahn. Do we want those tests going on so close to us?"

"They don't hurt anything."

"Are you sure of that?"

"That's what they say."

"Well, *they* had better be right."

Gene nodded, but he was confused. "So you think I ought to know more about that kind of stuff?"

"Of course you should."

"Why? What's that got to do with being student-body president?"

"Nothing. But it's got everything to do with the future of this world. You don't just jump into politics one day and *then* start to think about the issues."

"You sound like Marsha Wimmer."

"Who's that?"

"Never mind."

Gene got up and walked upstairs to his room. He had expected this to be a much better day than it had turned out to be.

CHAPTER 8

The hike to Ben Lomond Peak, north of Ogden, was supposed to be the grand climax to the week at Camp Lamoni, but Diane wasn't convinced. She had made the hike once before, and to her it was mostly just long and hot. The camp was early this year, late June, but the day would eventually be very warm. Diane knew that the view from the top would be pretty enough, but she would lots rather have slept in late and relaxed around the camp all morning. Actually, if she had her real wish, she would take a vacation to California with these same girls and hang out on the beach all day. She loved being with her friends, and the camp was actually pretty nice, with decent showers and good bunks, but still, it was a little too far from civilization for Diane.

All the same, she was on the mountain, and not really in a bad mood. She and her friends were making the best of it—mostly making fun of the "majesty and inspiration" that Sister Riley had promised them. The woman was nice, but she saw something spiritual in virtually everything, and she was always telling the girls what a wonderful time they were having. To Sister Riley, girls' camp was like a religion in and of itself. She was up before the girls each morning, her hair already brushed, and she would laugh about the rattlesnake that crawled across her path while she was out "enjoying nature."

Diane and two of her friends, Janet Torgeson and Becky Burton, had decided it was time to take a breather. They were perched on a little outcrop of rock that ran along the trail. Most of the girls were far ahead of them. "I don't know if I can take too much more of this inspiration," Janet said. "Maybe we could turn around here and just *tell* Sister Riley we made it to the top."

"Not a chance," Diane said. "She's already up there. She's making a list and checking it twice."

"I'll tell her I have cramps and you two had to take me back."

Diane and Becky laughed, and then Becky said, in a falsetto voice, "'Oh, Janet, you must remember the pioneer sisters who bore their babies along the trail . . . who continued on, pulling their children in a handcart . . . who sang hymns as they *wended* their way to the West.'"

"Yeah, well," Janet said, "I'll bet some of those pioneer ladies did plenty of *grumbling* while they were *wending*." Janet was a large girl—"big-boned," Diane's mother always called her, but the bones were padded a little more than Janet wanted them to be. The climb was tough for her. Her brown bangs were matted and sticking to her forehead, and her old sweatshirt was wet around the neck.

Becky, on the other hand, had long legs and not an extra pound anywhere. The climb was nothing to her; she just didn't like it. But then, that was Becky. There was always something "naughty *and* nice" about her. She was pretty, with deep red hair and freckles, and she was straight as an arrow when it came to doing all the things she had been taught in church, but just beneath the surface was a hint of rebelliousness that Diane loved. Diane was more careful by nature, but she seemed to find the nerve to let herself go a little when she was with Becky.

Diane got up, turned, and looked toward the peak. "We're way more than halfway, don't you think?"

"I thought we were," Janet said, "but I swear, someone keeps moving the peak back."

Maybe Diane was still looking up when she took her first step. Later, she couldn't remember exactly what happened. She only knew that she tripped. And then she was falling down a steep little incline. She didn't roll far, didn't even bang herself up all that much, but as she tried to catch herself with her right hand, she heard the snap. It didn't really hurt, but as she was still rolling, she was saying to herself, "It's broken. My wrist is broken."

She came to a stop against a little thicket of oak brush and lay there for a few seconds. By then Becky had bounded down and had hold of her. "Are you all right?"

"I broke my wrist," Diane said. "Now I don't have to hike to the top."

But she didn't laugh, and neither did Becky. "Are you sure?"

Diane sat up, then raised her arm. She could see how bent the bone was, and the pain was seeping up her arm. But what alarmed her most was the look she saw on Becky's face. The girl had turned white, her freckles seeming more like blotches. "Oh, Diane, it *is* broken," she said.

Janet had finally made it down the little slope. "What should we do?" she asked.

"I'm getting sick," Diane said, and she remembered something about shock, something she had learned at MIA. For the first time she was scared. She didn't know whether she could walk all the way down. There were men somewhere, brethren from the stake who took the hike with the girls just in case something like this happened. She wondered how to find one of them.

"A couple of guys were coming up last," Becky said. "If we start hiking down, we'll meet them. Are you feeling like you might pass out?"

The suggestion seemed to make Diane's head spin, but she said, "No. I'm all right. I'll start walking. But go ahead of me and try to find someone."

"Yeah. You go," Janet said. "I'll walk with Diane."

Becky was back to the trail in four long strides, and then she began to trot. "I'll be back as soon as I can," she called back. "If you can't keep going, sit and wait."

But Diane could only think of getting back to camp, and then away from this stupid place. She wanted to be home, in her own bed, with everything all right. The pain was bad now, radiating through her elbow, numbing her hand. Still, she held the arm against her middle, grasping it with the other hand, and she made her way up to the trail, Janet holding her, helping her, and then the two started down the trail, taking careful steps.

"How bad does it hurt?" Janet asked her.

"Bad," was all Diane could stand to say, but with the word, the pain seemed to take on another level. She stopped for a moment, breathed deeply, and tried to think what she could do. But sitting down would only prolong everything; she would rather keep going.

She had walked for ten minutes or so when she heard Becky call. Diane looked ahead to see her coming back up the trail. "A guy down there has a horse. He's going to take you out."

Diane was glad for that; she wasn't sure she could walk much longer, but she also wondered how long this ordeal would have to last. Riding the horse would jostle her arm, too.

Still, she kept walking. She didn't know how far away the horse was, but every step, now, took her closer to someone who could stop the pain.

As it turned out, the man on the horse, Brother Redmond, was pretty well prepared. He had a first-aid kit in his saddlebag, and he had a piece of cloth large enough to make a sling. Getting the arm in the sling almost pushed Diane into that faint she had been trying to avoid, but once the cloth held the arm firmly, steadily, the pain diminished a little. And once the big fellow got her up on the horse, held her tight around the waist, she liked the relative speed at which they could move. The trail seemed even longer than it had, hiking up, but something had happened in her head. She felt distant, half asleep, and the pain was almost disconnected. Brother Redmond kept saying, "You just hang on, little girl; you'll be fine." And then, back at camp, he loaded Diane into his pickup truck, got a sister to go along, and drove very carefully until he hit paved road. Once he did, he took off hard, and Diane loved to see the trees whiz by.

It was a long ride, down through Ogden Canyon, then along Harrison Boulevard to the Dee Hospital, but Sister Hickcox kept telling her, "They'll be able to give you something once we get there, honey. They'll get the pain stopped." And that was all Diane cared about now.

When Brother Redmond pulled the truck into the emergency entrance, he jumped out and trotted to the other side of the truck and helped Sister Hickcox down. Then he held onto Diane as she stepped out of the truck. By then, a young man in a white coat was standing nearby. "What have we got?" he asked.

"This beautiful little girl fell, up on Ben Lomond, and I think she's broke her wrist. She's hurting pretty bad."

"All right. Let's get her in a wheelchair. You need to come in and fill out some papers for us."

"Well, I'll let this sister here do that, if it's all right."

By then, Diane wasn't hearing much, caring much. She sat in the wheelchair and let herself be pushed away. But she kept thinking that Brother Redmond had called her beautiful. Not just pretty but *beautiful*. She liked that. What a nice man he was.

The doctor was young and *very* good-looking. He was like the doctors on *General Hospital*, all polished and sparkling, with good cheekbones. He touched Diane, and the pain went away—for a moment. But then he took the sling off and moved her arm until Diane was panting, even whimpering. "I'm sorry," he said, in a voice so mellow that she was sorry too—sorry that she had given him concern. But he had a nurse give Diane a shot, which stung, but which soon sent her flying. She remembered little after that. At some point she slept and probably would have much longer if Sister Hickcox hadn't awakened her. "Honey, I'm sorry," she said, "but I can't find your mother. Can you think where I might be able to locate her?"

Diane was in something of a daze. "I don't know," she said, but she actually did. So she made the effort to say, "She's probably in Salt Lake.

At the U." She glanced around and realized she was still in the same little curtained-off emergency area. She felt the cast on her arm, the pressure, but she didn't have the energy to raise it enough to see what it looked like.

"How would I get hold of her?"

"She's probably in the library."

Diane was waking more all the time. She saw Sister Hickcox nod, but she also saw a certain sternness in the acceptance, and Diane could almost guess what she was thinking.

"She's trying to get her dissertation finished," Diane said. "She's worked on it for a long time, but she's pushing hard right now—to get it wrapped up."

Again, the nod. But this time Sister Hickcox asked, "What does she need a doctorate for?"

"She teaches classes at Weber. I think they pay her more if she has her degree." But that was just something to say. Diane knew that her mom was never motivated by money.

"Well, she's a smart woman. A lot smarter than me." Mrs. Hickcox was older than Bobbi, maybe in her late forties, or even fifty. She lived in the same ward, which was just a little north of the Weber College upper campus. She always looked frumpy to Diane, with "old lady" clothes. At camp all week she had worn big, full-legged slacks, never jeans, and never the capri pants that girls—and some of the leaders—liked to wear.

Diane had heard the censure in Sister Hickcox's voice. It was a tone she picked up often when women spoke of her mother. They called her "smart" almost as an accusation, as though she were showing off to be so educated. But Diane wasn't going to deal with that. "You could maybe call my dad," she said.

"He's at work, isn't he?"

"Yes. But I don't think he's in a class right now. It might be easier to find him than Mom, and he's closer. Call the Psychology Department at Weber."

"I don't like to bother a man when he's at work—not if we can find your mother."

"It's okay. Dad won't mind."

"Well . . . all right. I'll see what I can do."

She was gone for a time, and Diane drifted again, not really asleep but unattached. She could still feel the weight of the cast, and she wondered what would change because of it, what she might have to miss, but also what fun she might have. Maybe some guys would stop at the hospital to see her. She hoped the doctor didn't send her home too soon. She wanted to stay for at least a day or two. Some of her girlfriends could sneak food into her room. She had sneaked in a couple of corn dogs and a root beer to Becky when she had had her appendix taken out.

When Sister Hickcox came back, she said, "I'm at a loss about what to do. I can't get hold of either one of your parents. Down at the University of Utah, they knew who she was, there in the English Department, and they said they'd try to find her, but over at Weber, the secretary said your dad might also be at the U."

"Yeah. He might be. He's working on some research, and Weber's library doesn't amount to much."

"Well . . . they're busy people. I can see that. I guess I can stay here a while yet."

"You don't need to. I'm fine."

"The doctor's apt to release you before long. *Someone's* got to get you home." She brushed her hand over her rounded mound of hair. "It's embarrassing to sit out there, looking like this." She glanced down at her clothes.

Diane couldn't imagine what she was worried about. It was her scowl that people would notice. "Maybe they'll keep me for a while. Why don't you go ahead and leave."

"No. You rest a little more. If I have to, I'll call one of the other sisters in the ward. I'm sure your mother's going to feel terrible when she realizes she wasn't here when you needed her so much. But I guess that couldn't be helped."

Diane's defensiveness was building. "I didn't need anyone. The doctor gave me that shot and I hardly knew what was happening."

"Well . . . that's nice to know."

"No. I mean, thank you for staying with me. I didn't mean that. But I'm just saying, there was nothing anyone could do. Mom will be here as soon as she gets word."

"Fine. I'll wait out here a little longer. I hardly know whether it's worth it to go back to camp. I might just stay home. I hate to ask my husband to drive me all the way back up there."

Diane had no idea how to respond to that. She let it go. She shut her eyes and let Sister Hickcox walk away. What was lingering in her mind was the new information: that the doctor was likely to let her go right away. She hoped she would get to see him from time to time. Maybe she would have to come back to make sure everything was healing right.

An hour or so passed—quickly—and Diane drifted in and out of sleep the whole time. But then she heard her mother's distinctive voice, that out-of-breath, slightly husky quality that seemed to signal, so often, that Mom had a million things to do and was on the run again.

"She's right in here," a nurse was saying, and then, there was Mom, parting the curtain and stepping in. She looked disheveled, her fine hair having lost some of its curl, hanging limp, and her face red. She was wearing a pretty, box-pleated skirt, but she had been sitting in it too long, and it was badly wrinkled. She never seemed to bother with makeup anymore, either.

"Oh, honey, how are you?" she asked. "I came as soon as I could."

"I still feel a little sick," Diane said, and she knew that she had given her voice less "umph" than she had with Sister Hickcox.

"What happened? Did you fall?"

"Yes. Up on Ben Lomond. It took *forever* to get me down. They used a horse, but it shook my arm every time it took a step. I almost passed out."

"Oh, dear. That's rough."

But something in Mom's tone wasn't convincing. Diane wondered whether she even cared. "No one could find you, Mom."

"I know. It took a little while. I was in the library, and a girl from the English office came over and let me know. I took off right then—drove a little too fast, too."

"Was Dad down there?"

"I'm not sure. He said he might drive down today, but I had to be there earlier, so we each took our own cars."

"Didn't you look for him in the library after you found out?"

"No. I didn't want to take the time. I'm sorry I wasn't here sooner. Was it bad, getting it set and all?"

"It was the worst pain I think I've ever felt." She pronounced the words flatly, then looked away. Someone was playing a radio, on KNAK. Diane could hear Little Eva singing "Come on, baby, do the loco-motion." She wondered whether she would be able to dance now, with this heavy thing on her arm.

"So I guess you're mad at me for not being here."

Diane didn't answer. She knew she was being a little witch, but sometimes Mom needed to know. She made everyone else in the family adjust their lives to hers. It wasn't fair.

Bobbi touched Diane's forehead, pushed some loose hair back, and then stroked her head. "I broke my arm once when I was a kid," Bobbi said. "I know how much it hurts." She hesitated, and then she added, "but it gets better pretty fast. You'll be fine."

That was Mom's answer to everything. It would kill the woman to show a little pity for more than two seconds. "My friend told me that casts are awful. They itch like crazy."

"They do itch some. That's true."

"My summer's pretty well ruined now. I won't be able to swim or anything."

"Oh, come on, Diane. You'll play this to your advantage and get all sorts of attention from it. Most of the time you've just been sitting around this summer anyway."

Now Diane was furious. That was always her mother's attitude toward her. She really thought Diane ought to be scrubbing floors all day and getting dinner ready—just because *she* wasn't around to do her own job. Maybe the cast would be a good thing; Mom wouldn't ask so much from her all the time.

But Diane was hearing that mellow voice now, and suddenly she felt a lot better. She watched the curtain, avoiding her mother's eyes, and then he appeared. His dark hair was just a little messy, as though he didn't pay attention to himself, didn't have to worry about how he looked. Diane liked that. There was nothing very dangerous-looking about him, but she didn't mind.

"So, my friend, you're looking a little better. The color has come back into your cheeks."

"Thank you. And I must say, you look very nice yourself." She smiled at him.

He smiled too, taking notice of her, personally, for the first time. "So, what do you think? Can you sit up? Maybe take a ride in a wheelchair, out to your mother's car?"

He looked over at Mom.

"Hi. I'm Bobbi Hammond," she said.

"Don Markham," the doctor said. He didn't even use a title. Diane liked that too.

"I don't mind staying awhile, if you want to keep me," Diane said. "I kind of like it around here." She smiled again, fully.

"Well, my dear, you do light up this place. I'm sure we'd all like to keep you. But I think you're all right to go home."

"Do I get to come back and see you again?"

"I hope not. Not unless you break the other arm." Dr. Markham turned back to Bobbi. "Your own doctor can take things from here. I'd get her in before long. He'll want to get another X-ray and make sure things have stayed in place."

"Okay. I'll do that."

He looked back at Diane. "I'll tell them out front to release you. You can wear that lovely gown we gave you. It's going to be hard to get your blouse back on."

Diane was disappointed that he was sending her away. "Thanks for everything," she said. "You were so careful. It didn't hurt at all." She knew she was giving him a full dose of sweetness now. She also knew it was lost on the guy, who was probably more than twice her age, but she loved the way he smiled back.

Still, he left. And he had hardly walked out of hearing range before Mom said, "Diane, you're better at flirting than any fourteen-year-old girl ought to be. Where did you learn that?"

The fury was back. "I wasn't *flirting*. I was just trying to be nice."

"Oh, yes. And setting your arm didn't hurt a bit. That's not what you told me."

"Well, *you* wouldn't know, would you? Because you weren't anywhere around."

Diane heard her mother take a breath. She waited to see what kind of fireworks she might have ignited. "Diane, if you think I shouldn't be working on my Ph.D., tell me that—straight out. We can talk about it. We can decide what's best. But if you just take these little potshots at me—the way you do all the time—I don't know how to deal with that."

"I don't care whether you work on your doctorate, Mom. But don't come in here telling me how sorry you are that you were in Salt Lake. I know exactly what matters most to you."

"Come to think of it, maybe I like the potshots better." She laughed, softly, and then she sat down on the chair next to Diane's bed. "Apparently you're angrier about this than I realized. We really do need to talk."

"I'm not angry at all. I just know where I stand with you."

"Diane, don't do this. I haven't *abandoned* you. You're playing out this martyr role and it isn't fair. I work very hard around our home, and I usually leave my schoolwork until late at night. I don't get *half* the sleep you do, and you've never once missed a meal or come home to a dirty house. I do make these trips to Salt Lake, but most of the time I'm gone during the same hours that you're in school."

"Tell that to Maggie. She comes in from school and first thing says, 'Isn't Mom home yet?'"

"And how long is she usually there without me—if I'm not already there?"

Diane didn't answer. She was going to stop this. Mom could always make herself look like the Mother of the Year, but she had no idea how hard all this was on everyone else.

"Usually not more than half an hour," Bobbi said. "And that's almost always on Thursdays, which is my latest day."

But that was only one side of the story. Mom didn't know how tired she was a lot of times, how little she sat with the rest of the family and watched TV. She said she didn't do her schoolwork until late, but plenty of times she read things for school while Dad was the one in the family room with Diane and Maggie.

"Diane, you're going to understand all this someday. It's not easy to give up your personal goals. Finishing this degree has been something I've wanted to do for a long time. I know it's inconvenient, but can't you understand how much a woman needs something for herself? Is it so hard to give me just a little room for that? You don't even make your bed most mornings, but when you get home *someone* has done it."

Diane hated that accusation. She left her bed undone some mornings, but if Mom would just leave it alone, she would do it after school. Or what if it never did get made? Why was that such a big deal? Mom only did it so she could complain about it.

"Maybe you'll want a career someday, Diane, or maybe you'll have your own interests. Are you going to give up *everything* you care about, personally, once you get married?"

"I don't want a career. I want to stay home when I'm a mom."

"Are you sure of that?"

"Yes."

Bobbi laughed. "Well, if you love housework so much, maybe you could do a little more of it—just to get in practice."

But Diane wasn't going to respond to that. "I want to get out of here," she said.

There was silence for a good two minutes, but finally Bobbi said, "Diane, honey, I love you. And I'm sorry I wasn't here. I talked to Sister Hickcox outside, and she told me how well you handled everything. I wish I could have seen that. I missed out by not being here, and that's part of my choice, I know. But can't you understand a little how I feel?"

Diane wanted to be nice. She tried to think of something to say that would soften the bad feelings, but she couldn't bring herself to relent quite yet. "You have to do things your own way, I guess. And I'll do things my way. That's all there is to understand."

But when she looked at her mother and saw how devastated she was, Diane regretted the words. What she didn't know was how to get them back. "Mom, it's okay," she mumbled. "It didn't really matter that much." But she hadn't been able to say the words the way she was feeling them, and once again, she and her mom were at odds. She didn't know how that always happened.

CHAPTER 9

Hans was waiting. On the day after he had been confronted by *Direktor* Schreiter and Agent Meyer, his parents had been called in by the *Stasi*. The agents had questioned them, warned them, and told them the matter was not at an end, but since then, the Stoltzes had heard nothing. Berndt had been careful not to admit anything, just as Hans had been, and so the *Stasi* had no proof—but they didn't necessarily have to have. Local leaders would do what they chose to do. So every day Hans got out of bed wondering what the day would bring, and he could see in the eyes of his parents that they were waiting too. It was hard to think of anything else, hard to concentrate on school, on homework, on anything.

But weeks passed and nothing happened. In fact, Hans received notice that he had been accepted into *Oberschule* and would begin in the fall. Gradually he found himself believing that a miracle had occurred, that God had delivered him from danger. At breakfast one morning, that summer of 1962, Peter told the family, "I think, by now, the *Stasi* would have made its move. The Lord's looking out for you, Hans. I don't know how else to explain it."

Hans was usually skeptical about his father's seeing God in everything, but fear had humbled him lately, and it was hard not to conclude that Papa was right. Hans had found himself participating with his parents in their prayers, adding his own faith. As he got up from the table that morning, his mother asked, "Have you made your mind up about Youth Conference, Hans? We have to pay the money if you're going."

The summer holiday had just begun. School would be out for eight weeks. Every year, during the holiday, young Church members from all over the GDR gathered and had a chance to get acquainted. Hans had expressed his hesitancy when the conference was first announced. It would take place in Dresden this time, which sounded rather interesting—and a nice change—but such events might be watched by the *Stasi*. Church leaders had to file a request to hold the conference, and every speaker, every subject of discussion had to be described in advance and then reported afterward. The government always feared that such meetings could turn political, or that dangerous ideas, counter to Marxism, might be taught. What Hans feared was that his name would appear on the list of those who attended, and his participation might then be reported. He didn't need any new suspicions about his actions.

On the other hand, if the Lord really was looking out for him, he shouldn't turn his back on the Church. For the first time in Hans's life, he found himself thinking seriously about religion, really wishing that he could feel as much faith as his parents did. And every now and then he felt certain glimmerings—emotions that might have been prompted by the Spirit. His skeptical side still suspected that that kind of thinking was illogical, but he was equally skeptical about Marxism. His history teacher this last year had liked to speak of the "inevitability of the dialectic process." If religion was hocus-pocus to his teachers, he wondered how the same people could work so hard to make events of history fit their own interpretations. Still, he tried hard to be a good student, and he had been trained for a long time to see the world as explained by science. There was no room in it for creation stories and a God who cared about each individual and listened to prayers. One of his teachers had once laughed at the idea that some man was "living out there in the sky" somewhere, directing the world, listening to petty little prayers about the weather or somebody's sick friend. He called it a primitive myth, as meaningless as tribal stories of forest gods, or Greek myths about gods on Mount Olympus. "Fortunately," he had told the students, "only a few imbeciles in our society continue to believe such childishness these days. Once a people releases itself from superstition, man himself can step forward and make a better world."

Hans felt like a fool when he heard this kind of talk. He wondered how many of the students around him were thinking, "Hans is one of those imbeciles. He goes to that crazy American church." A number of boys had called it exactly that to his face. Believing, attending church, was bad enough to most of his friends, but an odd little sect, based in America—that was unthinkable. The other students were usually polite when they were around him, but sarcasm would often slip into their tone: "So, Stoltz, what are you doing this weekend? Ah, I guess you have church to attend. That must be nice for you."

Sometimes Hans would try to disconnect himself from the Church, hinting that it wasn't his choice so much as his parents'. And during those moments, when his embarrassment and estrangement were the worst, he would tell himself that he would stop going as soon as he was old enough to choose for himself. He didn't have to spend his whole life *trying* to believe something that wasn't easy to believe, cutting himself off from normal people.

And yet, here it was again. Another choice. And maybe there was something to this: God did seem to be helping him. Hans didn't like to think of some "man in the sky," but he had felt loved at times lately. He had prayed more sincerely than ever before, and the evil he had been waiting for hadn't struck.

"I guess I'll go," he told his parents.

"Oh, good," Peter said. "You'll have a good time. I saw what they're planning—some good meetings, but lots of fun, too."

Hans couldn't imagine that he would have much fun, but he would go. He would test this hint of faith he had felt lately, see if he could find out whether God really was with him.

As it turned out, he loved the train ride to Dresden. Berndt had decided not to attend. He, too, had been waiting for the ax to fall, and he thought it unwise to do anything to draw more attention to himself. But three others from the branch, all girls, were going. Hans had known them all his life, but they were older than he was, and he had never spent much time around them. On the train he found that they were entertaining—quite funny—and Hans was relieved to be taken away from his worries. He also enjoyed the first day of the conference in the Dresden chapel. He wasn't really moved all that much by the talks or the discussion sessions, but he was among young people who didn't think religion was stupid, and that was relaxing—not feeling like an outsider for a day. What he enjoyed even more was the evening that followed. The leaders got the young people involved in some games, which seemed rather childish at first—relay races, mostly—but Hans let himself go, entered into the mood of things, and he could hardly believe how much he liked the way he felt. Later, the leaders created smaller groups and introduced quieter activities: word games, guessing games. Hans liked the people he met, all different ages, many of them older than he was. He was good at the games and was soon the star player, the brightest personality, even among the older ones. He had never known anything like that. His ability in school had won him a certain respect, but socially, since leaving childhood behind, he had always felt himself on the edge of things, not really accepted. Here, he was not only an insider, he was liked.

The plan was for everyone to sleep in the church, the boys in the recreation hall and the girls in the classrooms. But a conversation had begun in Hans's group, and clearly some didn't want it to end. Instead of parting for their sleeping areas, several ended up in a little foyer, just outside the chapel. There were chairs there, but most sat on the floor. An older boy from East Berlin, Max Schwartz, was the one who voiced his thoughts most strongly, but Hans was also impressed by a couple of the girls, both a year or so older than he was: Uta, a girl from Freiberg, and Greta, from Leipzig. Uta was probably the more attractive of the two, with pretty long hair—light brown and silky—but Hans liked Greta's happiness, her cleverness, and he liked the way she treated him, as though he were as important as anyone else, even if he was younger. He liked her smile, too—the slyness of it, and what he thought was a hint of flirtation.

"I've quit apologizing for my religion," Max had announced. "I tell my friends at school that I go to church, and I tell them how much I like it."

But it was the quiet words of a girl named Erika that had set off the discussion: "I can't do that. My friends laugh at me." Almost everyone said they felt the same way.

Max was now stretched out across the floor. He was leaning on one arm, looking a bit mussed after the games. His hair kept drooping into his eyes. He would brush his fingers through it from time to time, but it always fell forward again. "You have to remember," he said, "most students come from believing families. I still think a lot more people believe in God than you might suspect. The majority, in fact. But no one dares say it. Some of the students who laugh at you at school probably go home and have prayers with their families."

Uta was sitting in one of the chairs. She was leaning forward, her elbows on her knees. "My friends admit that their families believe—some do—but they still think it's all foolishness."

"That's what they've been taught to think, taught to say," Max said, "but just wait until they need God sometime. See whether we look so foolish to them then."

Hans liked thinking that was true, and he liked Max's confidence in his own faith, but he also knew the realities. "Let me tell you what happened in Schwerin," he said. "A girl I know—a Mormon—was the best student in her school. Everyone knew it. But when the director gave the prize for being highest ranked, he gave it to someone else. And he didn't hide what he had done. He told the girl's mother that he couldn't give an award like that to a religious student."

Max rolled onto his back and put his hands behind his head. "You can't let that change anything," he said. "I am who I am. I can't try to be someone else just so the government gets what it wants."

Hans felt the tension. No one spoke. It was one thing to defend oneself, to claim faith, but it was quite another to say anything negative against the state. Everyone there had been trained never to let such words slip out, even accidentally. They had learned it in school, but even more, in all their Mormon homes. They were never to put themselves or their families in danger.

All the same, Hans admired Max for his brave statement. He wanted to tell Max what he had done, that he and Berndt had tried to escape. He wanted to know whether Max would ever consider trying it himself. But he didn't raise the topic and never would. It was important that no one know anything that could be used against him, not even these Church members. Who knew who might say something to the wrong people? Hans's father always warned him that Stasi spies had been known to infiltrate the Church by pretending to be interested in joining, or even by accepting baptism.

"I think," Greta said, "that if we do what we know is right, things will work out. Maybe we won't get to do some things we'd like to do, but at the end of our lives we'll be happy with ourselves. It's sort of like Jesus asking the apostles to stop fishing and follow him. They must have been thinking, 'How can I get by if I don't keep fishing?' but they went anyway, and I don't think they were sorry."

"Maybe they were sorry at times," a boy named Herbert said. "Or at least, discouraged. It's still what they had to do."

"But they must have known, for sure, that Christ was the Messiah," Hans said.

Greta turned toward Hans, who was next to her, sitting on the floor. "Maybe not, Hans. A lot of times they didn't even seem to understand Christ. I think maybe they felt something from him, and it was so good and right that they couldn't resist following. But it took time for them to become the strong men they were later on."

Hans didn't know about any of that. He had never read the scriptures carefully, never really studied the gospel. He had sat through hundreds of Sunday School lessons, mostly just wishing that the hour would soon end. He told himself, now, he needed to read the New Testament all the way through.

Max said, "That's how it is for me. When I read what Christ said—like during the Sermon on the Mount—I hear those words, and everything sounds exactly right to me. And true. So I tell myself, that's it, that's what I believe. Don't worry about the rest."

Hans was not prepared for the response he felt to Max's simple words. His chest filled up, as though inflated with warmth. Tears came to his eyes. He had never experienced this before, this power inside himself.

Hans wanted this. He wanted to hold onto this feeling; he wanted to be like Max. He had spent his whole life trying to meet others' expectations. His parents had wanted him to believe certain things, and his teachers at school, something else. What he had never done was probe his own heart. He knew he had to do that, not just rely on the strength of these new friends.

The next day, at the end of classes and activities, the entire conference met, more than seventy young people and many leaders, and time was allowed for testimonies. Hans had ended up sitting by Greta, and he wasn't sure whether that was an accident or whether she had made things work out that way. What he did know was that he had wanted to be around her again.

Max was one of the first to stand up. He told the others, "Last night some of us talked about how difficult things are at school, how silly the teachers and other students can make us feel. But I'm not ashamed of what I believe."

That seemed to set the theme for what others said. Greta's words touched Hans the most. He could see her skirt shake, and he knew that her knees were quivering. "Only once a year do I feel this happy," she told the group. "When I am with all of you, I know I am not wrong to trust in God. Christ seems to sit with us and put his arms around our shoulders, like a friend. I feel him here. And then I go back to my home and my school, and most of the time I feel alone. Without you, I could never make it. But all this next year I will remember the way I feel right now, and I will know that I can last for another year, until we see each other again."

Hans was crying by then. He wanted to stand up and say something similar, but he wasn't going to lie. He was feeling something happening to him, but he reminded himself these emotions would pass, and then he would have to think more carefully about all this. Maybe he was only feeling the momentary release from all the worry he had known these past few weeks. Maybe he was being overly influenced by this new companionship with Max and Uta and especially Greta. So he didn't stand up. But he cried so hard his body shook, and Greta put her hand on his arm. It was a simple thing, but it was something he would remember long after.

For the next few weeks, during the summer holiday, Hans continued to feel some of the emotions he had experienced at Youth Conference. Greta had written him three times, and even though the letters were anything but love letters, he felt that something good had happened to him, the two of them having met. What Hans also did was read the New Testament. He didn't want his parents to find out and to start making too much of this change in him. He wanted to do this on his own. But they did notice. He would read alone, in his bedroom, and put his Bible back in a drawer afterward, but his mother had seen him reading a few times, and his father had picked up on his change of tone. No one said, "We like what's happening to you, Hans," but one night his mother said, "Youth Conference was good for you, wasn't it?" and Hans, trying to sound noncommittal, had said, "Sure. I had a good time."

It was nothing much, but Hans could feel how pleased his parents were, and he liked the better feeling in his home. Little Inga told him one day, "Papa told Mama that you've grown up a lot since you went to that meeting in Dresden."

"What do you think? Have I changed?" Hans asked her.

"I don't know. You don't fight with Papa anymore. That's good."

"That's because I fight with you." He grabbed her, hoisted her into his arms, and pretended to put her in a wrestling hold.

Inga giggled, and then she hugged Hans, tight around the neck. He liked that.

"I'm glad you didn't go away, Hans," she told him, after he set her back down. "I didn't want you to go away."

Hans thought maybe he felt the same way now, even though he still thought a lot about America. What he feared was starting *Oberschule*. He had had virtually nothing to do with any of his school friends during summer holiday. He wondered how he would feel when he had to face the students and the atmosphere he had been so tense about in the past. On his way to school the first day back, he thought of Greta, of what she had said about surviving from one year to the next, and he already longed for Youth Conference next year.

But his day was routine, or at least it started out that way. In the afternoon, the head of the *Oberschule*, *Direktor* Knorr—a gray, emotionless little man—called an assembly, and it started the way these meetings always did. All the students and faculty stood to sing the "Internationale." Hans had feared this moment. He knew he had to make a decision. He sang the first two verses quietly, trying to call no attention to himself, but he had to decide, would he sing the third verse? There was a line that he had sung for years but always with a certain guilt. The whole song was about breaking free of superstition, but in the last verse, the claim was that "no savior from on high delivers." He had noticed other students, teachers, glancing at him when he sang the words. As he came to the line this time, he knew he couldn't sing it. He didn't want to make a show of it, but he also didn't want to hide the fact that he was refusing to sing those particular words. And so he merely shut his mouth, let the words pass by, and picked up again when he felt he could.

The meeting was nothing more than announcements and "orientation" to the fall schedule, and it didn't last long. *Direktor* Knorr gave a brief little speech about dedication and hard work, but it was all the usual stuff. What wasn't usual was that Hans had been back in his classroom only a few minutes when a student opened the door and said, "*Direktor* Knorr would like to see Hans Stoltz."

Hans came out of his chair quickly. He had been fearing a moment like this so long, it was almost a relief to face it finally. "Go ahead," his teacher said, and Hans hurried out of the room and down the hall.

But *Direktor* Knorr made him wait, and during the time in the outer office, Hans's nervousness mounted. By the time he finally entered the room and sat down before the director, a kind of despair had taken over. He expected the worst.

"*Herr* Stoltz," Knorr said sternly, "please be seated."

Hans sat down in front of the director's desk. The man was short, but he had a deep, strong voice, and a square, stolid face.

"I have received information about you—passed on to me by *Stasi* officials."

Hans nodded.

"I understand, during holiday, you attended a meeting with young people from your religion."

"Yes."

"Tell me what happened there."

Hans had not expected this. He didn't know how to describe it. "It's a religious meeting. We talk about our faith, about scriptures. And we have some fun: games and that sort of thing."

"Do you speak, in any way, about the German Democratic Republic?"

"No."

"Not at all?"

Hans wondered about the conversation with Max. Had someone reported some of that? What could he say? "Not in the meetings. Sometimes, we talk, as friends . . ." He wanted to be honest about this. There was nothing wrong with it. "It is not easy, *Direktor* Knorr, to be religious in a country that discourages religion. So sometimes—"

"That is not true. Were you not allowed to hold this meeting? Don't you have a church building? Don't you meet every Sunday here in Schwerin?"

"Yes, of course. But teachers tell us that religion is all falsehood."

"Stoltz, we place no restrictions on you. No one is required to believe any particular worldview, not in this free country."

"Yes. I understand what you're saying."

"But at this meeting, you sometimes, in a private way, criticize the government. Is that what you are saying?" He continued to stare at Hans.

"No. Not at all. We merely share our faith. But some of us did mention that having faith is not easy."

"In *this* country?" He leaned forward, waiting.

"In any country, I'm sure."

"But particularly, in this country. Is that right?"

"You know what I mean, *Direktor* Knorr. It's hard to hold onto faith when we're surrounded by so many people who don't share our beliefs."

"You didn't sing certain sections of the 'Internationale' today."

Direktor Knorr was watching Hans intently, his head forward, so he was looking through his bushy eyebrows. On the wall behind him was a sign, in red letters: "The German Democratic Republic: Center of Freedom and Democracy in Europe." Hans had seen such signs all over Schwerin for as long as he could remember. He rarely thought about them. But suddenly now, the absurdity of his situation struck him. He lived in a free country, all right. His opportunities were boundless so long as he did what he was told. "As I understand it," Hans said, "in this free country, no one is compelled to sing that song."

"That is true. No one is."

"I believe in a Savior, but the words of the song say that I don't. I couldn't sing them."

"Is that what you did at your last school?"

"No. I sang them. But I decided today that I couldn't do that any longer."

"And why is that?"

"I'm growing up, *Herr Direktor*. It's time to make up my mind about what I believe. I can't sing those words. For me, personally, they are wrong."

"And is that why you tried to escape our country?"

So the director knew that, too. Hans didn't know how to respond, but he doubted that it would do him any good to offer denials—nor did he want to lie.

"*Herr* Stoltz, do you own an air mattress?"

Hans was stunned. How did the man know about that? "No, I don't," he said, quickly but nervously.

"Did you own one at one time?"

Hans could see it all now. The border patrol had found the air mattress, out on the water, and the *Stasi* had somehow made the connection, maybe traced the sale of it. He knew this was the end game now, and he had no chance of winning. "Yes," he said.

"Did you use that air mattress to attempt an escape from our country?"

Hans nodded. "Yes," he said. "This free country."

"*Herr* Stoltz, let me give you some advice." Knorr waited, watching Hans carefully. "You are a bright young man. Great opportunities might have come your way. But in this country, as in any country, there are realities. Young people who refuse to embrace Marxist philosophy have limited possibilities. You must understand that. This is a state that is committed to certain social ideals. We cannot be led by those who reject those ideals. You do not lose your right to reject them, but you do lose the opportunity to lead and to work in certain careers. You were very fortunate to be admitted to *Oberschule*. Your grades were some of the lowest of the students who were accepted, and you have never participated in the Free German Youth. Your admittance to our school came before all these other matters were known to me, and now your actions have left me with no choice but to reverse that decision."

"I understand."

"No. You couldn't possibly understand, not at your age. You will have to seek training in a trade. You will have no opportunity to enter one of the professions that might have interested you much more." He leaned back in his chair. "You tried to leave this country. No one will ever trust you again."

Hans merely nodded.

"Well, then, collect your possessions, and leave the school immediately."

So Hans left. He had a few things in his desk—a notebook and some pencils—but he couldn't face the other students. So he walked from the office straight out the front doors and on home. When he reached his apartment, he found his father in the living room, already home from work. "Why are you here so early?" he asked.

"I was let go from my job this morning," Peter said.

"Let go? What will you do?"

"I've been assigned to work for the city, doing common labor. The pay is very low."

"It's because of me, Papa. I've been expelled from *Oberschule*."

Peter nodded, as though he had suspected as much. "I'm sorry, Son," he said, and he put his hand on Hans's shoulder.

"What will we do?"

"We'll get by somehow. We'll keep praying, and we'll hope that sooner or later—"

"It doesn't work, Papa. I've prayed so much this summer, and now, look at this."

Peter took hold of Hans's other shoulder, held him with both hands, and looked into his face. "Son, don't say that. Don't give up hope."

"We've got to get out of this country. That's the only hope we have now."

"No. We'll work things out, somehow. Let's bow down, Hans. I'll say a prayer for us, and then we'll—"

"No. I'm not praying anymore." Hans turned from his father and walked to his bedroom. What he felt was that he knew the truth, finally: There was no one "out there in the sky" answering prayers. He had tried so hard to be religious lately, to trust God, and now he could see what it had all come to.

CHAPTER 10

The football game was essentially over—nothing but "mop up" left. The coach had put in the second-team quarterback, and Gene was standing on the sidelines. Guys kept coming by to slap him on the back and tell him what a great game he had played, but Gene made a point of letting all his starters know that he "couldn't have done it without them." He glanced up at the crowd a couple of times, at the East fans in the Olympus High grandstands, and enjoyed watching the students celebrate now that the game was won. This was the clincher. East High had won the league championship and would be heading to the state play-offs. The score was 21 to 13, with only seconds left.

Gene kept thinking back to one great moment in the game. The score had been tied 7 to 7, and the East offense had been facing third down with a yard to go. Sometimes, in situations like that, the coach would send in a play, but this time he probably figured Gene would know what to call. It was obviously time for a fullback dive. But Gene had known the defense would stack in tight, looking for that dive, and he just couldn't resist. He called a play-action pass, made his fake, and then stood in the pocket with the ball on his hip, hidden. The defense had taken the fake all the way, and Greg Barkley, the big left end, had broken deep, wide open. Gene had fired a perfect pass, right into Barkley's hands, and he had gone all the way, taking those long strides of his, not moving very fast, but so far out in front that no one had touched him. Now, standing on the sidelines, Gene kept seeing that play in his mind, the football spiraling out toward Greg, spinning, spinning, catching the stadium lights, then resting gently into the big guy's hands. After the extra point, Gene had run off the field to his grinning coach. "It's good you got the ball to him," he had said. "I'd be all over you right now if you had called that play and it hadn't worked."

"I know. I was thinking about that when I made the call."

But Coach banged Gene's shoulder pad, looking the way his dad did sometimes, when he was so proud of Gene he could hardly stand it.

"Hey, can I play some defense?" Gene had asked.

"Not right now. Take a breath."

"I'm not tired."

"All right. Go in for Jerry. See if you can stop them from turning the corner on that sweep they keep running."

Gene had gone in and smashed his way through a blocker and dropped the Olympus halfback for a loss. Olympus had ended up going three and out, and then Gene had gone back on offense and led another drive, this time handing off a lot, but finally, when the defense was drawn in, rolling out to his right, looking to pass, and then breaking downfield himself, cutting back to break a tackle, spinning off another one, and loping the last ten yards into the end zone. The Leopards were up fourteen points, late in the third quarter. Olympus had scored a late touchdown, against East's second team defense, but the game had been out of reach by then.

When the game ended, Gene jogged off the field with the other players. He knew there was a victory dance scheduled back at the East High gym, but he didn't care so much about that for the moment. He just wanted to hang around with the guys for a while, savoring all this. The bus ride was wild, with everyone yelling and celebrating, and back at the locker room, every guy on the team, it seemed, wanted to talk to him for a few seconds. "You were *great* tonight, man," they kept saying.

The locker room was full of steam and the smell of sweaty equipment, and the noise was terrific, everyone bragging, recounting plays. Gene liked this better than anything else he knew: the winning, but also the reveling in the victory, sharing it with all these guys he liked so much. He sat down on a bench and pulled off his cleats and socks, but then he just sat there in his filthy uniform and talked with his friends.

"You got crazy out there on defense," Ben Swenson, one of the defensive tackles, told Gene. "Didn't anyone tell you that quarterbacks are supposed to be *pansies?*"

"I like to get a little *grass* in my teeth," Gene said. He growled, showing his teeth.

"You hit that big fullback and the guy didn't get up."

"He just twisted his knee or something."

"Maybe so. But you *nailed* him. I think you should play defense with us all the time."

"Tell the coach that. I'm always telling him I want to play both ways."

If the choice had been up to Gene, he would never come off the field. He was at his best when he didn't cool off, didn't stop to think, just played. There was a certain wildness that got into him sometimes, and when it did, he could crash around like a pool ball and feel no pain.

But his entire body was hurting now. His left knee—which he had strained early in the season—was getting stiff, and he was beginning to feel a bruise he had taken in the ribs. He had stayed in the pocket on one play, releasing a pass just as he had been hit, and the defender's helmet had banged him hard, just to the right of his sternum. There were scratches too, on his hands and ankles and calves, and his uniform was caked with dirt and lime.

Gene finally pulled off his jersey—with some help—and then dropped his shoulder pads onto the floor. He showered and dressed, and by then his left ankle was hurting a bit too, but he waited for Jeff Richards, and then the two walked out to the gym, where "Duke of Earl" was just beginning to play. "As I walk through this world, nothing can stop the Duke of Earl," Jeff began to sing with the record. Gene joined in with his own, deep "Duke, Duke, Duke . . . Duke of Earl."

No one was dancing yet. Most people were standing in groups, talking, but others were in motion, bouncing, letting the music reach their feet even if they hadn't found partners yet.

The kids who saw Gene first let out a cheer, and then a rumble went through the crowd. People surrounded him immediately. "Great game, Gene. Way to go." It was like a chant, coming from all directions, people reaching to slap him, pat him. He loved it, but he hated it too. It was embarrassing.

He didn't have a date exactly, but he had talked to Marsha Wimmer that day and asked her to come to the dance. She hadn't promised anything, but he had a feeling she would at least be there. He had taken her out twice now—once during the summer and once earlier in the fall. "Do you see Marsha anywhere?" he asked Jeff.

Jeff laughed. "I can't see a thing."

Gene knew what Jeff meant. People were still trying to get close enough to Gene to congratulate him. Gene had to thank another bunch of kids, one at a time, before he could tell Jeff, "She's supposed to be here."

"What's this thing you've got about her? You tell me you don't like her, but you keep asking her out."

"I didn't say I didn't like her. She doesn't like *me*."

"She doesn't like anyone. She's got her nose about ten feet in the air all the time."

Someone was tapping Gene on the shoulder, and he looked around. "Great game," a girl said—Jeniece Nelson. "Hey, just so you know, Marsha is over by the door, at the end of the gym. But she might not stay very long."

"Did she tell you to say something to me?"

"No. She told me *not* to tell you. Anyway, I was proud of you," Jeniece said. She slipped into the crowd, but others were coming, and Gene, for the first time, resented that a little.

Jeff leaned close to him and said, "Do you want me to get you to her?"

"Yeah. Block for me," Gene said.

"Okay, here goes. Just follow me."

And off the two went. Jeff kept saying, "Excuse me please. Hero coming through." Gene was saying, "Oh, thanks. I appreciate that." Or, "Hey, it wasn't just me. The whole team played great." But the important thing was, Gene never lost contact. He grabbed the back of Jeff's shirt a couple of times, just to be sure no one broke his momentum. And then, suddenly, they were out in the open, and from there Gene made a strong move down the court. He found Marsha near the back doors. He was pretty sure she had seen him coming but was pretending not to notice. "Hey, Marsha, I found you," he said. "Do you want to dance?"

"No one's dancing."

"That's okay. We'll start it."

She shook her head. "I don't want to be out there first."

"Why not?"

"Gene, that may be your style, but it's not mine."

"I don't know why. I'm a lousy dancer, but I don't care."

"That's my point."

Gene didn't take offense. He just smiled. He never understood people who stayed around the edges of dances—and everything else—hiding out. "Come on." He grabbed her hand, and they walked toward the middle of the hall. "Hey, let's dance," he called out. Neil Sedaka was singing "Breaking Up Is Hard to Do," a good slow number. Gene was glad of that. He wouldn't have to show everyone how bad he was at the Pony or the Frug. He was actually a little more self-conscious about his dancing than he wanted to admit.

Almost by command, the gym turned into a dance floor, with the group already out there beginning to dance, and then dozens more coming out from the crowds around the sides.

"They do whatever you tell them," Marsha said.

"It's not me. Everyone just wanted *someone* to make it happen."

"But who better than the *student-body president,* the *quarterback?*"

"You look really good, you know it?"

"Thank you. I only wish I were as pretty as you."

Gene laughed. "You still don't like me, do you?"

But that seemed to disarm her a little. She didn't know what to say. She was wearing a pretty tan shirt dress, and a tan ribbon in her dark hair. She had worn lipstick too, probably put it on after the game. It seemed to Gene that she had wanted to look good, and she had come at his request, after all. All of that seemed obvious, and yet she really *didn't* like him. He could feel it. So why had she bothered?

He moved away from her a little, trying to look at her face, but she was looking straight at his shoulder when she said, "I'm still trying to make up my mind whether I like you or not."

"I hope your decision won't be based on my dancing," he said.

She glanced into his eyes, and she laughed a little, as if to say, *You're right about that.*

Gene had learned a rather exaggerated dancing style as a sophomore. He would lean deeply to his left, then shuffle mostly sideways, stepping with his right foot behind his left. It had looked cool to him once, and it was what all the seniors did at the time, but he had noticed, this year, with so many fast dances taking over, that this "bent" look was passing away. His only problem was, he didn't know what else to do.

He was soon relieved of the worry. The junior-class president, a boy name Jerry Dobbs, stopped him to say what a fine game he had played, and once he was stopped, others gathered around him. For the rest of that record, Gene never got started again. And when the next record began, he saw people start to do the pony, in a line. That's the last thing he wanted.

"How about this? I'm so hungry, I could eat a tuna-fish casserole—and I *hate* tuna-fish casserole. What if we took off, and you didn't have to put up with my dancing anymore? We could go down to Dee's or somewhere and get a burger."

"That's fine, if you want. But I'm not hungry."

"How come girls are never hungry?"

"Do you say things like that just to irritate *me*, or is that the sort of thing you say to everyone?"

Gene was stopped. He had no idea what she was talking about. Had he insulted her?

But she seemed to see his confusion and said, "It's all right. Let's do get out of here."

And so they left, although not easily. They were stopped several times on the way to the door and twice in the parking lot. When he finally got into his car, he was relieved by the quiet. Now—if he could just say something to Marsha that wouldn't upset her. "Sorry about all that."

"Gene, I don't know what's wrong with people. In fact, I don't know what's wrong with *me*. The world's about to blow up, and we're holding football games and *victory* dances."

"What do you mean? I thought the Russians turned their ships around."

"Do you really think that's the end of it?"

Actually, Gene had thought so, but he didn't dare say it. On Monday evening, October 22, President Kennedy had gone on television and told the nation that the Russians had installed nuclear missiles in Cuba. Then he said he was setting up what he called a "quarantine" to block any Russian ships from carrying more weapons there. At first Khrushchev had announced that he was going to run the blockade, and there had been a lot of panicky talk about that for a couple of days. But on Wednesday the Russians had backed off and turned their ships around.

"Gene, those missiles are still in Cuba. There's talk that Kennedy will have to bomb the island, maybe even send troops in. If he does,

Khrushchev might try to take Berlin, or he might just fire his ICBMs. This whole world could go up in smoke, any minute now."

"We'd better get to Dee's fast, then. I need a last supper."

"I'm glad you think it's funny."

"I just don't think *anybody* is dumb enough to fire those rockets. Not Khrushchev, not even Kennedy. And he's messed up just about everything he's done so far."

"Look, why don't you just take me home?"

"No way. You promised to go. I'd look stupid down there after a game, all by myself."

Gene, of course, knew he had blown it again. It was a quiet ride downtown. He told himself he didn't care. This was definitely his final attempt with Marsha.

At Dee's he ordered two cheeseburgers, fries, and a chocolate milkshake—for himself. Marsha only wanted a Coke. He didn't try to convince her to eat anything more. On the way to their table, a white-haired man did stop them and ask, "Aren't you the Thomas boy?" Then he had to hear all about the game.

Gene and Marsha made it to a booth in a corner. He slid in on the vinyl seat, across from her. He was trying to think what to say. He never seemed to worry about that with anyone else.

"Why don't you take your letter jacket off?" Marsha said. "Then maybe people won't recognize you."

"Okay." He worked his way out of the coat, feeling the pain in his ribs again. "Does that bother you when people stop us like that?"

"No. It doesn't *bother* me. I just don't get it. It's like football is the most important thing in the world. I don't know why people *care* so much."

Gene was smiling again. No one else ever made him justify his life. But strangely, there was something rather interesting about doing that. "Everyone knows that football isn't *that* important," he said. "I mean, it's just a game. But it's great, you know. There's something about it that's . . . just . . . *great*."

"If you ask me, it's a caveman sport. You're all out there smashing into each other. I usually don't know where the ball is."

"See. That's why you don't like it. You need to understand the game."

"What's to understand? That one boy hikes the ball to you, and then you all start jumping on each other?"

Gene laughed. He watched her. Under the fluorescent light he could see the delicate fleece on her cheek. He watched her eyelids close for a moment, her dark eyelashes touch. He never seemed to notice those kinds of things with other girls—and he had no idea why he saw so much in her. "So, do you really think the world's about to blow up?" he asked.

"It could, Gene. I can't believe how casual you are about it."

"I was kind of worried until those ships turned back, but when they did, it said to me that the Russians didn't want to mess with us."

"Let's not talk about it, okay?"

"Okay. That's fine with me. But if you spot any bright lights in the sky, give me a heads up. We can duck and take cover under the table." She actually smiled a little, even though Gene could tell she didn't want to. He unwrapped one of his cheeseburgers and took a big bite. He also sucked in a gulp of his milkshake, chewed a little, and then asked, "Did you see that one pass I threw—the one for the touchdown?"

"I missed some of that. I was talking to Jeniece."

"You should have seen it. I threw a *perfect* pass."

"Oh, I know. I keep hearing how great you are."

"No. That's not what I'm saying." He swiped at his mouth with a napkin. "I throw hundreds of passes. We work on plays like that every day at practice. But that pass was perfect. I don't know anything else that feels like that."

"Feels like what?"

He didn't know how to tell her. "Do you play the piano or anything like that?" he asked.

"I took lessons for a while. I'm not very good."

"Well . . . you know how it feels when you do something . . . *exactly right*? When you try to do something for a long time, and then one time you just nail it?"

"I guess. Sure."

But that wasn't exactly the point. He tried to think. "When we're out on the field, under the lights, it's sort of strange—like we're all alone. You hear the crowd sometimes, but the sound seems miles away, and everything is just about you and the other team. It's like the game is the only thing going on in the world."

"I guess I don't get your point."

At least she seemed interested. "I know. I'm not saying it right. When I threw that pass, it was like I released it and it knew what it was supposed to do. It flew on this perfect line, and I could see it spinning under the lights—around and around, just hanging out there forever. Greg didn't have to *catch* it. He just put his hands out and the ball landed on them." Gene stopped for a moment. "I don't know how else to tell you. It was *beautiful* to watch—almost like someone else did it. And we were just out there, alone under those lights. Do you understand what I mean?"

"I don't know. I guess it's hard for me to imagine," she said. "But it's interesting to me to hear you talk about it." He could see the change that had come into her eyes.

"It seems to me like almost anything can be beautiful—if you know how to see it."

She seemed to think about that before she said, "I like that, Gene. I mean, I can think of all kinds of exceptions—and I guess I could argue the point—but I'm just sort of surprised to find out that you think about things like that."

Gene knew that wasn't exactly what she meant. She was really saying, *Maybe you aren't quite so stupid and superficial as I thought*.

"What do you like?"

"What?"

"Do you feel that way about anything—the way I do about football?" Gene went after his cheeseburger again, finishing off the first one in two more big bites. But as he chewed he watched. He could see that Marsha wasn't sure.

"I guess I love to read, more than anything else."

"But that's borrowing someone else's experience, isn't it? How do you get your own?"

"Maybe I don't."

"Oh, I didn't mean—"

"That's all right. It's a good point. Maybe I need something to *do* that would mean more to me. I write poetry, but that might be too much like reading. It's all in my mind."

"Poetry? Like what?"

"Not silly little rhymes."

"What then? Recite something for me."

"No."

She had hardly touched her Coke, but now she picked it up and took a tiny sip on her straw. It seemed more a way of avoiding his eyes than it was a genuine drink. There were very few people in the place now, and here in the corner, the two of them seemed quite alone. When Marsha set her cup down, he waited for her to look at him. "You need to drink more deeply," he said. "Suck the marrow out of life." He laughed.

"What's that from?"

"Thoreau. My English teacher made me read *Walden*. I hated it, but I liked that one idea: he wanted to sweep life into a corner and see what it was all about. And then I remember that line. He wanted to suck all the marrow out of life, or something like that."

"There's the difference between us. I loved that book. But when I read it, I kept thinking that I didn't really know how to live that way. When I read Thoreau, or especially Whitman, I find myself wishing that I could *relish* life, the way they do."

Gene could tell she was surprised by his perception about her. "I can't get into poetry at all," he said. "I don't understand it most of the time. Why do poets have to make everything so hard to figure out?"

"It isn't always hard. Sometimes you have to read a poem a few times, but when you get the idea, it's so compact that it hits you hard, like someone *socking* you." She doubled up her fist and made a little jab toward him—but not one that looked convincing.

"I don't think I've ever read a poem that had that effect on me. I listen to what teachers say, and I think, 'I guess so, if that's what you think,' but I don't get to the point where the light turns on—you know, inside *me*."

Something had happened to Marsha. She was leaning more toward the table, speaking without her usual aloofness. "The first poem I really loved was 'Dover Beach.'"

"Mrs. Branch had us read that. It's about the white cliffs of Dover, isn't it?"

"You have to listen to it, Gene. Arnold makes the sound of the waves with his words. It's just amazing."

"I didn't notice that. I never could figure out what the guy was so upset about."

"He's talking about faith. He says there was a time when faith was high and full, and now it's disappearing, going out like the tide."

"Why did he think that?"

"Well . . . I don't know exactly. I guess he felt like people didn't believe as much as they had at one time. He says that faith 'lay like the folds of a bright girdle furled.' Isn't that a great image? Like a sash, or something, in folds, just like the sea would look from above."

"It's no better than my football—spinning under the light."

"Is it really like that for you? That pretty to see?"

"It's perfect. I told you that."

"That's amazing. To me, it just seems like you guys are trying to hurt each other."

"Well, we sort of want to do that, too," Gene said, and he laughed. "But what happened to that poet guy to make him so disappointed with life?"

"Matthew Arnold? Well, it's not necessarily about him. But he says, 'Ah, love, let us be true to one another!' like that's the only answer he can see. He says the world looks pretty, but there's no peace, and no 'help for pain.' Then, in the last line, he says that the world is like a dark plain, 'Where ignorant armies clash by night.'"

"Man, that's depressing."

"No it isn't. Not to me. I feel so sorry for him, that he has so little hope, and he just wants to cling to his love and be true to her. It's sad but really romantic." She repeated the words softly, "'Ah, love, let us be true to one another.'"

"So it's kind of a romance story, in your mind."

She blushed, looking almost coy. "I guess. But not a stupid one."

"Is that what you want—a guy who would say something like that to you?"

For the first time, she was the one forced to explain herself. Her voice actually sounded younger than usual when she said, "Sure. I want to be in love someday—if that's what you mean."

"If a guy actually told you something like that, you'd laugh in his face."

"You don't know that."

Gene leaned back in his seat. He had never opened his second cheeseburger, had even decided that he didn't want it. He was still wondering about that last line. "Why did he say, 'ignorant armies'?"

"I think he was talking about people fighting each other and not even knowing why. What if someone pushes the button, Gene, and we all die? Would anyone know why?"

"Sure. We'd know exactly why. We can't let Communism take over the world."

"To me, that's just *talk*. The Russians are saying the same thing, and if we're not careful, we'll go to war over some 'ism' and destroy *everything*."

"I'll always stand up for my country. I'd feel like a coward if I didn't."

"Do you want to go to Vietnam and get killed?"

"I'm not exactly sure what that's all about. We just have advisors over there, don't we?"

"So you're ready to fight, and you don't know what it's about. That sounds like 'ignorant armies' to me."

"Our government knows what's going on. I hope we don't start fighting, but if it comes to that, I'll go."

"Gene, there are things that have no beauty at all—no matter *how* you see them. And war is one of them."

"There are also things you have to fight for—and those things *are* beautiful. I'll always stick with America, no matter what."

Marsha looked down at the table, waited for a time, and then said softly, "Gene, sometimes you're really quite interesting. But other times you say things that are so stupid, you're scary."

Gene smiled and leaned forward as she looked up. "Well, that did sound a little stupid when I said it." He laughed rather loudly. "I'm not saying our government can never be wrong. I'm just saying that I love what America stands for, and I'm willing to stand up for it."

"Fair enough. I don't disagree with that. But I hope you don't end up having to fight for 'wrong' instead of 'right.' And I hope we're all still alive when Christmas comes."

Gene felt the gravity in her voice, and he had to fight not to smile. Girls could be so dramatic. He just couldn't believe that the danger was all that great. "Well then—my love—let us be true to one another." He winked. She shook her head as if to show disgust, but she was blushing again. Suddenly, he thought he knew something. "You know what I think?"

"You think very little, so it's hard to guess."

"I think you're crazy in love with me, and you're mad at yourself for feeling that way."

"Oh, is that what you think?" But her blush was deepening, and she still wouldn't look at him.

"You keep telling yourself that you ought to be in love with Bryant Gibbs, but there's just nothing there."

"You are so stuck up," she said, but she was smiling, and she finally let her eyes engage his. He could definitely see something now.

"I'm sort of in the same boat," Gene said. "I like you, and I have no idea why."

But Marsha said, "Gene, I'm not dumb enough to fall for you. The only thing you like about me is that I don't drool all over you, the way most girls do."

"Maybe. But I sure like your eyes. And your lips. Every time I think I don't like you, I look at your lips, and I find myself thinking that I want to kiss you sometime."

"That is the stupidest thing you've *ever* said." But she was playing with him now, using those eyes, and he wanted to kiss her more than ever. Still, when he took her home, she retreated to her front door quickly, and Gene certainly didn't try any big moves. But he did want to go out with her again. He learned more about her, found a new level, every time he was with her. And there weren't many girls like that.

When Gene got home, he found his father sitting in the living room, alone. The two chatted about the game—the call Gene had made on third-and-one, his chance to play defense, and his aches and pains. But Dad just wasn't showing his usual enthusiasm.

"Did Mom go to bed?" Gene asked.

"Yes, she did."

"What are you doing?"

"I didn't have a chance to read the paper before the game. I was just sitting here . . ."

Gene could see that the paper was on the floor, and Dad had been sitting in his chair, a lamp on, but no television, no music. "Is something wrong?"

"Gene, I'm not entirely sure this world is going to make it through the next week—maybe the weekend. I've been trying to think what I should do for my family, and there's not one thing. Maybe we should have put in a bomb shelter a long time ago."

"Are you serious? Do you really think it could happen?"

"I think two men hold all our lives in their hands, and I'm not confident that either one is up to the task. I especially don't trust the people around them, on either side. If the generals make the decision, we may all be in trouble."

Gene felt a fluttering sort of vibration work its way into his chest. Marsha hadn't scared him, but Dad never just *talked*; he knew things. "God won't let it happen, Dad."

"I hope you're right. But I've seen war, and sometimes it seemed to me that God should have stepped in and said, 'Enough!' But he didn't."

"He won't let us blow everything up, though. That's not in his plan."

"That's what I keep telling myself, and I hope that's right." He looked up at Gene. "Pray for President Kennedy tonight. And pray for Khrushchev, too."

"All right." Gene wasn't sure what else to say. He thought of going off to his room, but he hated leaving his dad sitting there, looking so forlorn.

"One day, when I was fighting in the Ardennes, I saw a German boy lying dead in the snow," Alex said. He was looking across the room, not at Gene. "He had bled into the snow, and the blood had made a big half-circle, all the way around him. I got that picture into my head, and I started to dream about it. I would see that boy, and he would look so innocent—like Christ. It was as though we had killed Christ all over again. But lately, when I see that boy in my mind, I see *your* face. I don't want you to go to war—you or your brothers—and yet we keep getting into dangerous situations: Berlin and Vietnam, the Congo, and now this situation in Cuba. Maybe we'll be wise enough to avoid using our nukes, but I doubt we'll be wise enough to avoid war. It's my worst nightmare, to think of you boys doing what I had to do."

"I've thought a lot about that, Dad. I don't blame you for feeling that way, but I also know that each generation has to step up and do its part. I'll be ready if the time comes."

Alex finally looked up at Gene. He stared at him for a long time before he said, "Son, you have no idea what you're talking about—not the slightest idea."

CHAPTER 11

Diane and Maggie were sitting in the backseat of their family's Falcon station wagon. The two were far apart, looking out opposite windows. Bobbi was in the front seat, scrunched down a little, with her head leaning against the window. She seemed to be sleeping—or at least trying to sleep—but Diane knew she wasn't feeling well, hadn't been for the past few weeks. Only this morning, however, had Diane found out why: Mom was expecting a baby.

Bobbi and Richard had decided to try one more pregnancy, in spite of the doctor's concerns. That's what Mom had told Diane and Maggie that morning—Christmas morning of 1962—but the whole idea of it was embarrassing to Diane. She didn't want to hear about her parents "trying" to get a baby. From the time she had first known about such things, she had preferred not to think about her parents that way.

Everyone in the car was quiet now, and that was partly to let Bobbi rest, but feelings were not the best, either. It was a bad morning, even though it had started out well. Diane had gotten all the gifts she wanted: skis, poles and ski boots, and a great-looking pink ski outfit. She had picked everything out herself since she could never trust her parents with those kinds of decisions, but it was still fun to see it all again, and to call her friends and tell them that she was ready to hit the slopes. She had taken lessons the year before, at Snowbasin, but she had gotten by with rented skis and a childish-looking school coat. Now she was set. Her broken wrist had healed nicely and was getting strong again. She knew she was going to look good in that bright pink outfit. She had been letting her hair grow longer all year and now kept it straight. She could just see it, blowing in the wind, as she schussed down the mountain. She and a couple of her girlfriends would shop tomorrow—Wednesday—and they had already worked out a ride to Snowbasin for Thursday. Then, on Friday the plan was to ski Alta. Diane's cousin Joey, Uncle Alex and Aunt Anna's second son, had promised he would meet them and introduce them to some East High guys.

So everything had looked wonderful early in the morning, but then, just when Diane had been ready to take off to visit her friends and compare ski equipment, Bobbi had announced that Dad wanted to "hold a little meeting." That was irritating, but Diane tried to be nice about it. Dad talked about the "true spirit of Christmas," and there was nothing wrong with that, but then Mom had announced that she was pregnant. Diane was shocked at first, and then, gradually, angry. Mom was forty-three years old. How was she going to manage this? She was too busy as it was. Diane could guess already who was going to end up doing a lot of the baby-sitting.

Mom had made a little pitch about everyone pulling together and making the best of things, but Diane knew that the whole point was to get a boy, and she could imagine what a spoiled little brat the baby would be, if it *was* a boy. Still, Diane tried to be nice. She kissed her mom and congratulated her, and everything would have been okay. But then the subject came back to the Christmas presents everyone had gotten, and Mom had to make one of her sarcastic remarks: "Diane, I could see how excited you were about the books I gave you."

Diane knew she had only glanced at the books, but what was she supposed to do—pay no attention to her ski stuff and just start in reading some boring English novel? Mom always gave her the *worst* books to read. Diane tried to be nice about it, but the stories were always about some English "young lady" who loved a squire or an earl, or whatever those titles were. And then nothing would happen. Absolutely nothing.

"I'm *very* sorry," Diane had growled at her mother. "I'll go into my bedroom right now and read your books *all day*. Will that satisfy you?"

And then sparks had flown. Diane had ended up too angry to go see her friends and had actually stayed in her room most of the morning—although she hadn't opened the books. Dad had eventually come in and sat by Diane, with his arm around her shoulders. Diane had to be understanding right now, he had told her, because Mom had been so sick lately, and she was probably irritable. Diane could only think that her mother would be harder than ever to live with. Mom had finally finished her dissertation, and Diane had hoped that would ease the pressure on the family. But now, this.

Before the family had left for Salt Lake, Mom had finally come in to say she was sorry. "Honey, I don't know why I keep doing this to you," she had told Diane. "There are certain books I loved so much when I was growing up, and I always want you to have the same experiences. But I know we're different. I shouldn't try to force things on you that way."

Diane had hugged her mom and told her she was sorry too, but that hadn't changed the empty way she felt. She hardly cared about the annual trip to Grandma's house, even though all her cute East and Highland High cousins would be there. Still, she spent a long time on her hair, twisting it into a fancy French roll, and then trying on outfits until she settled on a winter sweater, white and deep green with a pattern of deer and snowflakes in the weave. And now they were finally on their way to Salt Lake, with light snow falling outside, and she was trying to raise her spirits so she could enjoy the day. But this old white car, with rust spots around the tire wells and the smell of sour milk from some spill long ago, was depressing, even embarrassing.

Her mood lifted rapidly, however, when she saw Gene and Joey getting out of Gene's car, having arrived at almost the same time. Gene was the better-looking of the two, but Joey was closer to her age, and wonderfully funny. He looked so "East High" in his ski parka with a lift tag hanging from the zipper, and then, when he got inside and took his coat off, in his sleeveless sweater and button-down-collar shirt. "Hey, Diane," he said, "are you still bringing your friends down to ski with us?"

"You know it. I can't wait."

Over the next hour or so, the family kept gathering. Diane spent some time talking to her cousin Kathy, and with Wayne, Kathy's little brother. Wayne was exactly her age—in ninth grade, still in junior high—and into skiing and swimming and tennis, all the things Diane liked. When they sat down for dinner, she was glad she ended up seated with Joey and Wayne, and with Sharon, Joey's sister, who was a year younger than Diane. The four sat at a card table in the entrance area of the house—the only place left with the dining room and living room so full. Diane was relieved that she hadn't been put with Douglas, Uncle Wally and Aunt Lorraine's retarded boy. He was a sweet kid, but Diane never knew what to say to him after a little while. This year Douglas was with his sister Kathy, and with some of the younger kids.

"So what's going on up in Ogden these days?" Wayne wanted to know.

"We're all *very* cool. Just a *little* cooler than you Salt Lake kids."

"Yeah, sure," Wayne said. Wayne was wearing a plaid shirt—a Madras "bleeder." Very cool.

Joey was quick to say, "Ogden High does have good-looking girls; I've got to admit that."

Diane didn't remind Joey that she was a year younger than he was—and not yet at the high school. "I'm glad you noticed," she said, and she patted his arm.

Grandma had cooked a turkey and also a ham, and she had filled the kitchen counters with bowls of food. Diane had tried not to take too much, but everything looked so good: mashed potatoes, enough to feed an army, with gravy; stuffing; peas and sweet corn; hot rolls with real butter; strawberry and raspberry jellies; candied yams; cranberry sauce; green salad, potato salad, and Jell-O salad with whipped cream; three kinds of pickles; black and green olives; carrot sticks and cheese-filled celery sticks; cucumber slices; and, on the table, big glasses of both ice water and apple juice.

The boys ate seriously, like men at work, and then they filled their plates again. Diane told herself she couldn't go back, so she ate slowly, enjoying every bite. But then she did give in and return for more of Grandma's special stuffing with mushrooms. While she ate, she talked to Joey and Wayne and listened to the laughter from the other rooms. All the uncles and aunts and Heinrich Stoltz, Anna's father, were sitting with Grandma and Grandpa at the big table.

"Why didn't Aunt LaRue come this year?" Diane asked. "I miss her. She's the funniest woman I know."

"I don't think she wanted to get in another big fight with Grandpa," Joey said. "Remember last year?"

"She was mad at your dad, too, wasn't she?"

"Not that much. She calls us once in a while. I don't think she's mad anymore, but Dad says she doesn't feel comfortable when she comes out here. I don't think she believes much in the Church anymore." Joey stuck his finger and thumb inside the buttoned-down front of his collar, pulling the two sides together. Diane loved the way he repeated that little motion, and she loved his easy way of talking. His hair was darker than Gene's, a rather ordinary brown, but it was cut in the same style, just long enough to part.

"I think Aunt LaRue's kind of gone off the deep end," Wayne said. "She's almost like a Communist, the way she talks."

"Maybe so," Diane said, "but I think my mom agrees with LaRue more than she does with Grandpa or either one of your dads. Last week, on the way home from sacrament meeting, she started into this big thing about Mormons worrying about poor people at Christmastime and then, the rest of the year, just calling them lazy bums on welfare."

"That's what most of them are," Wayne said.

Diane thought of some of the things her parents had said about poverty—how people got trapped and couldn't get out—but she didn't know whether she believed that, and she didn't want to disagree with her cousins, so she changed the subject to music.

But the four were soon in an argument about that. Diane and Sharon said that Johnny Mathis was the greatest singer *ever*. But Joey told them, "He's fine, if you're sitting with your arm around a girl. But if you want some real music, there's no one like the Beach Boys."

Wayne agreed with that, absolutely. But just when the argument was getting intense—if not very serious—Grandpa asked for everyone's attention. Diane couldn't see him from her table at the opposite end of the L-shaped set of rooms, but she could hear him without any problem. "I just have a couple of things I want to say. No meeting!"

Joey laughed. "Diane, do you have a family meeting after you open your presents on Christmas morning?"

"Oh, yes. Mom always says it's Dad's idea. But it's really hers."

"I know. It's a Thomas thing. My dad says it's a tradition from his growing-up years."

"Get this," Wayne said. "My dad always says that while he was away at the war, that's what he missed the most, those meetings with his family on Christmas morning."

All four of the cousins laughed, and Diane could only think that Uncle Wally must not have had much fun when he was a kid, if that's what he missed.

"I was just thinking," Grandpa Thomas said, "that Bea and I are about as blessed as two people can be."

Here he goes again, Diane was thinking.

"We have seventeen wonderful grandchildren, and this morning we have an announcement of another one coming—one I don't think any of you expected."

"Must be Aunt Beverly," Joey whispered. "She pops a baby out almost every year."

Diane ducked her head and laughed. "No, it's worse than that. You won't believe this."

In the living room, Wally's voice boomed out. "Mom, are you expecting?"

Everyone laughed, and Grandma Bea said, "I certainly am. I'm expecting a great-grandchild before too many more years. Then I expect a population explosion to follow. And I'm going to spoil every single one of those kids, no matter how many."

Grandpa was saying by then, "No, it's not Bea who's expecting—though she *is* a young woman still. Bobbi, do you want to tell them?"

This brought a gasp from the grownups, and then a round of cheers and clapping. Diane ducked her head and listened as her mother said, "I have no idea what caused this. Could someone explain that to me?"

Diane couldn't believe it. It was one thing to talk about babies but another to say something like that.

"I've got to tell you, I've had some second thoughts," Bobbi said. "I've been really sick, and the doctor says I have to be careful if I'm going to carry the baby to full term. But we've always hoped we'd get a boy sometime." She laughed. "We keep hoping it's easier to raise a boy than these girls we've got."

"Ooh, that's a cheap shot," Joey whispered to Diane.

"Shut up," Diane told him. But she was embarrassed. She knew her mother wasn't really kidding, no matter what everyone else thought. And Maggie was easy to raise. It was Diane Mom was talking about.

Grandpa took over after that. He talked a little about the family's great heritage, as he always did, and then he said, "On a day like this, I often think of those dismal days during World War II, when I wondered how things would turn out for us. The darkest time of all, of course, was the day we received the telegram and learned that we had lost Gene. I wondered then whether I could ever be happy again, and I think we all wondered that. To this day, when I think of Gene, I feel the old pain like it was yesterday, but you know, I am happy. I think all of us are. And part of that is knowing that Gene gave his life for something worthwhile, that he didn't die in vain—as it seemed possible he might have, at the time. I always feel too, that maybe he's with us on occasions like this."

Grandpa was getting emotional, as usual, and Diane hoped he didn't get too carried away.

"But anyway. That's enough said. I do wish that all the grandkids could have known Gene. I wish he were here today, with his kids—and Bea and I had a few more to gloat over. But at least we have his name-sake, our young Gene. And by the way, we sure are proud of him. I think you all know what a great football season he had this year. His team took region and made it to the semifinals for the state championship. Now he's the star of the East High basketball team. He also got very good grades again this fall, as busy as he is as student-body president. He's our oldest grandchild, and I've got to say, he's setting a standard for the rest of you to live up to. We have no doubt that you'll all do just as well."

Diane looked at Joey and rolled her eyes. He laughed, and then he whispered, "I'm going to be a juvenile delinquent, just to take the pressure off the rest of you."

"Yeah. Me too," Diane said.

"No, your family has done enough to break family tradition. They already moved to Ogden and started voting for Democrats."

Everyone was getting up from their tables. The big gift exchange was about to take place. Diane walked into the living room and sat on the floor, and she tried to act natural, but she was still feeling the sting of Joey's comment. She really did wish that her family fit in a little better with the Salt Lake cousins. Aunt Beverly's children were a lot younger than the rest, which separated them from the other cousins, but Diane always felt that Alex and Wally's kids were a step above her. Diane didn't know too much about family finances, but she did know that her mother got an annual payment from the family businesses, that she was considered a part owner. And because of that, her family did live better than a lot of the professors' families she knew. But Mom always gave away a lot of that money to charities. It was almost like the money embarrassed her. Diane dressed well, and she knew her cousins liked her, but she was never quite one of them. What irritated her was that she knew a lot of that had to do with her parents' attitudes—the difference they created between themselves and the rest of the family.

But at the moment, something else was bothering Diane even more. She kept looking across the room and seeing Gene—perfect Gene. Star of the family. Diane would never accomplish so much—or get those kind of grades. What Diane knew about herself was that boys watched her, hovered near her, lost some of their composure when she teased them. She also knew how much other girls envied her. But she was never satisfied by what she saw in the mirror. She hated her teeth—not as bright as she wanted them to be—and she wished that she were more willowy, like the models she saw in magazines. She did all right most of the time, had fun, and liked the attention she got, but when she was alone she was almost always unhappy.

Diane didn't say much during the gift giving. She appreciated the cute skirt she got from little Glenda in the gift exchange. Glenda had drawn her name, but of course Aunt Anna, who had wonderful taste, had bought the wool plaid skirt. She thought immediately of the blouses and sweaters she had that would go with it. She even planned when she would wear them next. But she just wasn't finding much fun in all the joking, the chatter she usually enjoyed each year.

Grandpa gave Grandma Bea a beautiful suede overcoat with a fur collar. Everyone teased him about spending so much, but he laughed and then claimed he had traded in a couple of books of Gold Strike stamps for it. He had also bought every one of the grandkids a transistor radio.

Later, Diane helped her aunts and girl cousins clean up in the kitchen. But when the women served pie to the men and kids and then went out to the other rooms to eat their own, Diane stayed behind with Grandma Bea. The two of them sat down at the kitchen table.

Diane had only a little sliver of pumpkin pie, with a tiny dab of whipped cream.

"Is that all you're going to eat?" Grandma asked.

"I've put on *so much* weight during the holidays," Diane said. "I keep eating fudge and divinity and . . . everything else. I'm starting a big diet *tomorrow*."

"It looks like you've started today."

"No. I've eaten like a pig. I shouldn't have any of this."

"Diane, you couldn't have gained any weight. You look perfect."

"I've gained three pounds, Grandma, and you know right where it all ends up."

"Oh, Diane, if I had ever looked as good as you—just one day of my life—I would have retired as the champion."

"Don't try to tell me that. I've seen those pictures of you when you were young. What a knockout. And you're still pretty."

Bea laughed. "Well, I'll tell you this much—I don't like getting old."

"Sometimes I wish I could," Diane said. She knew that would get a reaction, and maybe that's what she wanted. Grandma was easier to talk to than anyone else she knew.

"Why do you say that?" Bea had been eating a slice of cherry pie with ice cream. She slid it back now. "My eyes were too big," she said. "Why don't you at least eat the ice cream? It's Russell's—the best ice cream in the world."

Diane was touched by this little kindness. She always felt that no one in the world loved her quite so much as her Grandma Bea did. She used her fork, took a bit of the ice cream, and let it melt in her mouth.

"Grandma, I'm a big disappointment to my mom. I'm not at all what she wants. That's probably one of the reasons she wanted another baby."

"Diane! What a thing to say. How could *you* be a disappointment?"

"Mom wishes that I was brainy, like her. It about kills her that I don't like to read."

Grandma took a little more ice cream herself, and Diane watched her. She really did think that Grandma was pretty. She had dimples that made her look young, and her hair was a pretty mix of gray and white, almost as though she had had it colored that way. What Diane also liked was that Grandma didn't answer quickly, that she didn't just pass off Diane's words.

"Diane, Bobbi always loved her literature classes. It's just our nature that when we love something, we want the people we care about to share our pleasure."

"But why can't she accept the fact that I'm not like her? I like *different* things."

"Well . . . I don't know. She probably does. But it's hard not to live your kids' lives for them. I'm sure your mother remembers all the battles she fought with Al. He thought studying literature was a waste of time, and he—how should I say?—'encouraged her' to go to nursing school. That was not a pretty time. The two of them didn't get along very well."

"Was that when she almost married outside the Church?"

Bea laughed. "So you know about that?"

"Mom spoke to the girls at MIA one time, and she said she considered marrying a guy who wasn't LDS, and then she knew she couldn't do that. And now she's glad she didn't."

"Did you know the man she thought about marrying was a literature professor?"

"Yes." Diane laughed. "Maybe that explains her *love* of literature."

"No, the literature came first and then the professor. But the two loves were pretty mixed up with each other. I think Bobbi felt like she had found someone who was like her—who shared her deepest devotions—but he couldn't even honestly say he believed in God. It was a difficult choice—not one she handled easily, the way it sounds in a talk at MIA."

"So why did she marry my dad? Just because he was a member of the Church?"

"Oh, no. Bobbi met your dad in Hawaii. I guess you know all about that. He was a very handsome man—as he still is—and that got her attention first. But she found out what a good man he was, too. Don't ever think that she didn't fall in love. She did. Her professor friend, as it turned out, was killed in the war, but that wasn't why she chose your dad."

Diane didn't doubt that at all. She felt the love her parents had for each other. She took another little dab of ice cream. "Mom always says that Dad wouldn't talk about a lot of things when they first knew each other, and she had to force him to express himself more. She jokes about how she taught him to do that. But Dad still doesn't talk a lot—not an awful lot to me, anyway. What I can tell, though, is that he loves me. He doesn't try to change me. He'll look at me, and I can just see it in his eyes, that he likes me the way I am."

"Richard is like that. I think he feels that way about most people. He accepts us all, likes us, doesn't even ask himself whether we ought to be different. He's about as much at peace with himself as anyone I know. But he hasn't always been like that. He went through some bad days during the war, and afterward, too. I can remember when every day was an effort for him. He struggled with his burnt hands at first, but he also had to battle a lot of bad memories."

Diane had a hard time imagining that. "The war" was a story that hovered around her life. The Thomases almost never got together without someone saying, "Back during the war . . ." She knew her mom had been a nurse, that her father had been in the navy. And she knew what they said: that the war had a lot to do with the kind of people they were. But Diane couldn't think of her mother as a young woman, single, off in

Hawaii, where now the family sometimes vacationed and visited Mom's old friends.

"Let me tell you something you need to understand about your mother," Grandma said. "But finish that ice cream before it all melts."

"No. You finish it."

"Share."

"Okay." They each took a good-sized dab, and it was gone.

"Bobbi was never quite like other girls. She never cared as much as our other kids about 'things'—clothes and all that. She always loved to think about life, and talk."

"Maybe she shouldn't have had kids. Then she could be a professor, like Aunt LaRue—and do what she likes."

"Oh, Diane, don't say that. That's too harsh. You'll understand someday that every person who gets married—especially every woman—has to adjust. You can't do everything in this life, and once you become a mother, you give the major share of your life over to your children."

"But you worked for a long time."

"I did during the war, and then for a while after—when the kids were first raised. After I got back from our mission, though, I didn't really want to do that anymore. We still have our foundation, and I do a lot with that—try to use some of our money for good things. There are just different seasons in a life. You don't have to do everything at once. But any woman wants to hang on to some of those personal things she cares about. Maybe when you're a mother, you'll still want to ski."

"No problem. I'll take my kids."

"But what if you have a daughter who says, 'I don't want to ski. I just want to stay home and read a book'? Will you be understanding about that?"

"I think so. I know what it feels like when my mom won't let me be what I want to be."

"But won't you at least try to get that daughter out of the house and up on the slopes? Won't you tell her she needs some exercise, needs to get out a little, and not just read?"

"Maybe. But I won't force her to go."

"Does Bobbi force you to read those books she gives you?"

"No. Not exactly."

"Well, okay. I'll just say this. Bobbi isn't as good at mothering as she ought to be. But neither was I. And you know what? You won't be either. But you'll sure wish your kids could forgive you. Because you'll be trying your best."

Diane was nodding. She liked to think about it that way. "But Grandma, I can't help it that I *hate* those books. I've tried to like them, and I just can't."

"I know. But you know what? You're fourteen. You might be surprised by what you like at some other time in your life. I'm not at all the person I thought I was going to be when I was your age."

But that was something Diane couldn't imagine—either about herself or about her grandma. "What I wish," Diane said, "was that I could sit down just once and talk to my mom the way I talk to you."

"Try, Diane. Just tell her some of the same things, and I think she'll understand."

"I don't think so."

"Try. Okay?"

Diane said she would. But that night, after the family got home, Diane and Bobbi ended up, quite accidentally, alone in the kitchen. Diane knew this was her chance, but Mom looked tired, and Diane lost her nerve. She did kiss her mother and tell her goodnight, but then she went off to her own room. She did finally take a closer look at the books. One was called *Tess of the D'Urbervilles*. It was about England, of course, and it started out with some man walking down a road and then talking to a "parson," whatever that was. She couldn't even figure out what they were talking about. She read a few more pages but never did understand what the book was about, so she put it on her shelf with all the others.

⚬⚬⚬

Hans was sitting at the dinner table with his family. Grandma Schaller was with them, and it was thanks to her that they had a nice roast of pork to eat. Times had been hard for the Stoltzes. Hans was working as a laborer on a construction crew. He was supposed to be training for a trade, but he spent his days mixing mortar and carrying it to bricklayers, then cleaning up after them. It was work he hated, and work for which he received very little pay. Peter's work for the city was much the same. He helped repair roads, clean public facilities—whatever he was sent out to do. This was embarrassing to him, and he seemed depressed at night when he got home. Katrina still worked as a seamstress, but she never had been paid well—not compared to the high prices for food. The family was surviving only by dipping into their savings a little at a time. Peter kept saying that he hoped to find a better job eventually, but for now, he would have to settle for what he had.

But the Stoltzes had been careful not to talk about that today. Hans and Inga had both been in desperate need of shoes, and they had each received a new pair for Christmas. Inga was delighted, but Hans worried about the cost.

"I wonder what Aunt Anna and our cousins are doing today?" Little Inga asked.

It was an innocent question, but Hans saw the pain in his father's eyes. He said, quietly, "All the family gets together at their Grandpa Thomas's home."

"Is he *my* grandfather?" Inga asked.

"No. He's Aunt Anna's father-in-law. He's grandfather to your cousins. But your grandfather—my father—will be there today. He wrote to us about that."

"Grandma Stoltz died, didn't she?"

"Yes. A few weeks ago."

Hans knew how hard this was for his father: how much he had longed to see his mother one more time before she died, how much he still wanted to see his father.

"They're rich, aren't they?"

"Who? The Thomases?"

"Yes. And Grandpa Stoltz."

"Papa isn't rich. But he does fine," Peter said. "The Thomases are very well off."

"How do they celebrate Christmas?"

"Like us. They have a nice dinner."

But in better times Peter had sometimes described the way the Thomases lived: the big houses they had, the cars, the many gifts the children received for Christmas.

Grandma Schaller patted Inga on the shoulder. "We do have a fine dinner, don't we? Do you like the potato salad?"

"I love it."

"What about you, Hans?" Grandma Schaller asked.

Hans knew she had fixed the salad herself. "It's wonderful," he said. "And thanks for the shoes. I think you paid for those."

"I helped a little. I wish we could do more."

"We're fine, aren't we, Inga?" Hans said.

"Yes. But tell us about America, Papa," Inga said. "About all the presents."

"It was a long time ago, when I was there, Inga. But yes, they did have a lot of presents under the tree. They all gathered around and passed them out. It was very nice."

"I wish we could go to America and see our cousins—and have Christmas like that."

"Yes. That would be a joy to us," Peter said. "But we're blessed too.

We have a nice apartment and this good dinner. There are many people in the world not nearly so well off."

"I know."

Hans could hardly stand all this, but he didn't say a word. He knew the mess they were in was mostly his fault. He still felt resentment for the Church. It was the family's religion that lay behind so many of their problems. They would have left the country long ago if it hadn't been for Papa's loyalty to the Schwerin branch. Nonetheless, it was his attempted escape that had made things so much worse. Still, what could Hans do now? He brought in what little income he could to the family, and he went to church to keep some peace with his parents. He often thought of trying another escape. He and Berndt had even talked about the methods they might use. But that, too, would only hurt his family further. So he was left with nothing to look forward to but working six days a week at a job he didn't like and using the other day to attend a church he no longer believed in. At least he knew better than to pray. Hope was his enemy now. He was better off when he merely accepted his fate and went about it thoughtlessly.

CHAPTER 12

Kathy had never flown on an airplane, so she was excited. The only trouble was the turbulent ride over the Rocky Mountains, and Kathy's nervous stomach was put to the test. Twice she got out the airsick bag from the pocket on the back of the seat in front of her. She glanced at the man next to her, a businessman in a dark blue suit, and tried to look apologetic for what she was about to do. But both times the wave of nausea passed, and eventually the air smoothed out. She gradually felt much better.

She was sitting by the window, and she found it rather disappointing that so much of the nation was covered with clouds, but she did get a look at the Mississippi River and even saw where the Missouri dumped into it, near St. Louis. Then she saw the tall buildings of Chicago in the distance, as she landed at O'Hare. She was scared about locating her next airplane, but that turned out to be easy, and by the time she was in the air again, she was beginning to like this whole adventure. She was far away from home, and what was best, on her own.

She read a little this time, glancing out the window only once in a while. Then she chatted some with a woman next to her, and she felt no nausea at all. As her airplane approached Boston, she could see the city and the Atlantic shore, which she had never seen before.

Kathy did worry a little as she walked down the stairs from the airplane that once she was in the terminal Aunt LaRue wouldn't be there for some reason. But before she was inside, she could see her aunt standing at a window, waving. Kathy was amazed all over again at how beautiful Aunt LaRue was. She was wearing a pretty suit, simple and gray, very tailored, and she never wore much makeup, but she still seemed a splash of color, even from this distance. She had such a bright smile, pretty dark hair, and such lush coloring in her skin.

When Kathy got inside, she hurried to her aunt, who was waiting with her arms spread wide. "Oh, this is so fun," she was saying. "I've been excited for *weeks* to get you here. I'm going to show you *everything*."

"I'd like to see Boston some time, if—"

"Don't worry. We won't have time today, but we'll come back. And I'm also thinking we can drive to New York. I thought I'd try to get tickets to 'My Fair Lady' on Broadway."

It was the very thing Kathy had dreamed about, had even told her mother she would like to do. It was so like Aunt LaRue to know exactly what Kathy liked.

The two walked to the baggage area. "Aunt LaRue," Kathy said, "you can't believe how close I came to throwing up in one of those barf bags. This poor man sitting next to me kept leaning toward the aisle, like he wanted to get as far away from me as he could."

LaRue laughed in that wonderful, girlish way of hers, like a little drum roll, and then she leaned close to Kathy's ear and whispered, "I did it once. Don't ever tell anyone in the family. But coming out of Denver one time it was really rough, and I just lost it."

"But you fly so much."

"I know. I never thought I'd have any trouble. But I barely got the bag out in time. Even then, I splattered some on my shoes, and I stunk up the place like you wouldn't believe. The guy next to me was really cute, too. I didn't say another word to him all the way to Salt Lake."

Aunt LaRue could always make Kathy feel as though they were a couple of girlfriends gossiping and swapping secrets. She was ten years younger than Kathy's mom, but she seemed even younger, as though she were just a few years older than Kathy.

During the long drive to western Massachusetts, the two had a lot to tell each other. Kathy could often think of nothing to say to her mother, but she and LaRue shared everything, from Kathy's unsuccessful dating history to real ideas—important opinions—about President Kennedy, about problems in the world, about LaRue's research in economics.

Kathy also loved the New England countryside. She had never seen such luxuriant wooded areas. When they reached Northhampton, Aunt LaRue took Kathy to the Smith College campus first. They walked along the paths, in and around all the colonial red-brick buildings. "I want so much to come east to college, but *this* would be the perfect place. Do you think I could get in?"

"You've got the grades, Kathy, and you've done a lot of things, with all your volunteer work. It's just a matter of getting high enough scores on your College Boards."

"Does it help at all to have an aunt who teaches here?"

"I wasn't going to mention that, but the truth is, yes. I can put in a good word for you. To be honest, I don't think you'll have any trouble getting in."

Kathy was excited at the thought but a little afraid. School was out for the summer, but she saw some girls on campus, and they looked so much more sophisticated than she was. It was June now, 1963. The plan was for Kathy to stay for three weeks, mainly just to have this time with LaRue—who had invited her—but also to consider some of the places she might like to apply for college.

"So what are Wally and Lorraine saying about you coming here to school?" LaRue asked.

The two were walking under a huge old tree. *Northern red oak*, a sign at its base read. Underneath it the air was moist, and Kathy was beginning to understand what people meant when they spoke of the humidity in the east.

"My dad wants me to go to BYU. Mom's a little better about letting me do what I want, but I think it scares her."

"They're afraid you'll end up too much like me."

"Well . . . in a way. I think they worry that I'll get all wrapped up in school, and—you know—put that first in my life."

"That's a polite way of saying they're afraid you won't get married—that you'll end up an old maid like your Aunt LaRue."

"They still think you'll get married. Dad always says there's no way a woman as pretty as you won't get snapped up one of these days."

LaRue stopped and turned toward Kathy. "I hate that," she said. "That's what so many people think. If a woman gets married, it's first, because she's pretty, and second, because some man picks her out . . . from all *his* many choices. No one ever stops to think that I haven't found anyone *I* want. Do they think I haven't had any chances?"

"I'm sorry, Aunt LaRue. I didn't mean it that way."

"I know *you* didn't. But I get that every time I go home." She began to walk again.

"Mom told me that you came pretty close to getting married when you were in graduate school at Columbia."

"I guess that's true. At least I dated the same guy a lot. And *he* wanted to get married."

"Why didn't you marry him?"

"Well . . . first, I'll tell you the reason I gave myself. Then I'll tell you the real reason." She laughed at herself, and Kathy could feel that LaRue's anger was already gone. "I still had some things I wanted to do. I wanted to finish my Ph.D., and I didn't want a man to stop me. I also wanted to have a career. I'd done too much to get ready for it, just to throw it all away."

"Didn't he want you to work, once you were married?"

"Oh, I don't know. He said a lot of things. He claimed we could work it out. But he was possessive. He wanted a pretty wife, and I'm pretty. But I guess I'm a little tired of being valued for something I didn't earn. I wanted him to find *me* exciting, and I was never sure that he did. When he finished his degree, he would have found a job, and I would have had to figure out my life from there. That's how it works. Men do what they want, and women *accommodate*."

"But what else can we do, if we want to have families?"

"I don't know. I couldn't figure that out, and now it may be too late."

"Would you like to be married?"

"Sure I would. And I feel the loss a little more each year. I'm not in a panic about it, the way some women are, but I do feel that time is running out for me."

Kathy had wondered about all this, but Aunt LaRue had never been so open on the subject before. In Utah she was always making fun of all the eighteen- and nineteen-year-old brides. The two were walking through a botanical garden now. Some of the azaleas were still in blossom, bright pink.

"But I still haven't given you the *real* reason that I didn't marry him."

"Oh. I thought you were giving me the real reason first."

"At the time, I thought it was. But the biggest thing, however much I didn't want to admit it, was that he wasn't a member of the Church." She looked over at Kathy and waited a moment. "Does that surprise you?"

"I don't know. Not really, I guess."

"Well, it surprises me."

"Why?"

LaRue pointed to a bench across a little street under a giant sycamore, then walked to it and sat down. "I love the view here," she said. "It's a nice place to see the sunset. Watch how the colors deepen as the sun slips away." They were looking out across a pond with a thickly wooded little island in the center.

Kathy thought it was all very beautiful, the lawns, the grand trees, the atmosphere, but she wondered whether she would like to be so far from home. She had talked about coming east to school for years, but this was the first time she had realized how different everything would be.

"Part of it," LaRue said, "was that I knew how much I would cut myself off from my family if I married outside the Church. The rebellious side of me said that was *their* fault, not mine, but it was still something I feared."

"Do you think he would have joined the Church at some point?"

"No. And now we're finally to the *ultimate* reason—one step beyond the *real* reason." She laughed at herself but then said quietly, "The fact is, Jeff didn't believe in God. And I do."

"It'd be hard to raise kids that way, wouldn't it?"

"It's even more basic than that. It's *everything*. It affects your values, what you care about, what you choose to do with your life."

"I think my parents wonder whether you still believe in God."

"Sometimes I wonder myself. But rock bottom, I do. That's what I found out about myself. The only trouble is, every time I meet a man who's a member of the Church, I can't stand a lot of his other attitudes."

"Like what?"

"I don't fit any of the molds Mormon men are used to. I have too many opinions. I know how to make a living on my own. And I'm just too old. They all want to marry *girls*."

"There must be someone out there who's right for you."

"You would think so. That's what I keep telling myself, anyway. But how do I meet him? There just aren't that many Mormons back here." She pointed toward the west across the pond. "See what I mean about the colors? Look at the trees. And watch what starts happening to the sky."

"It sounds like you do a lot of this—watching the sun go down."

"Not really. I should do it more. What I do is spend way too much time alone, so I look for little pleasures like this." She laughed. "The truth is, a big family would drive me crazy after all these years I've been alone. But then, alone is driving me crazy too. So I guess it comes out the same in the end."

Kathy watched the pale yellow sky deepen toward orange. She could see the orange in the trees, too, reflecting off the leaves, shading the tones of green. She had never suspected that her aunt's life was less happy than it had always seemed, and the realization was not only sad to her but frightening. "Could I ask you a question?" she said.

"Sure. Anything. I've already told you more than I have anyone else in this world. Why not spill a few more things?"

"Why didn't you come home for Christmas this year?"

"Ah. Now you've gone right to the heart of things, my dear." She rested her arm on the back of the bench and put her hand on Kathy's shoulder. "I created such a furor the year before with my temper tantrum, and I wasn't sure I wouldn't do the same thing again, surrounded by my middle-class, Republican family."

"Hey, don't call *me* that. President Kennedy is my hero. And remember, Aunt Bobbi and Uncle Richard are Democrats."

"I know. But you know what I mean. I'm so different from my family now, that I feel like an enemy. I'm everything Alex is fighting against."

"I don't think so. Uncle Alex is more open-minded than you might think."

"More open-minded than Grandpa is what you mean."

"Well, yeah."

"I know he is. In fact, when Alex and I sit down and really talk, we can usually see each other's points of view. But when Dad and Alex and Wally get together, all I see is a line of soldiers with fixed bayonets—and I open up and start firing."

"So what did you do for Christmas?"

"Hated myself, and hated life. I tried to do some research and wasted most of my time, ate too much chocolate, and cried a lot—because I wasn't home. It was so stupid. Kathy, I love that house and my family more than anything in the world. I don't know how to be happy when I'm there anymore, but I made myself even more miserable by staying away."

"You should come back—maybe teach at the U."

"I know. I think about that all the time. But then I would really be surrounded. People in Utah all seem to think the same way. Even Richard and Bobbi make assumptions that no one else in the world does. I get mad every time I hear the way people talk—especially about Negroes."

"That's my big problem too. Mom and Dad think I walk around looking for a fight."

"I think what's hard for me is that so many Mormons don't even have opinions until the leaders of the Church tell them what to think. I can't be like that. Even when I was a little girl I just figured I could think things out for myself."

"That's how I am, Aunt LaRue. I get so mad when adults don't do what they ought to do, but Dad keeps telling me I have no right to challenge them—just because they *are* adults."

"I'll let you in on a little secret. Adults are just kids with a little more flesh wrapped around them." She smiled, but rather sadly. "Or at least that's how I feel. Maybe I'm just permanently stuck at about your age—destined never to grow up."

"I think maybe that's a good thing, Aunt LaRue."

"Then would you do me a favor?"

"Sure."

"Just call me LaRue. All this aunt stuff makes me feel like an old lady."

"Okay." And Kathy liked the idea.

The sun was almost gone. LaRue stood up. "Do you want to see my office?" she asked.

"Yes."

So the two walked across campus. They entered one of the stately old buildings and then walked down a rather dark hallway, their footsteps echoing on the hardwood. Kathy heard another set of footsteps thumping down a flight of stairs. A young woman leaped the last few steps and turned toward them. She seemed surprised that anyone was there. "Hey,

Dr. Thomas, are you going to the meeting?" she asked. She looked at Kathy, curious.

"What meeting?" LaRue asked.

"It's sponsored by Snick but it's for anyone who wants to get involved. A lot of guys from Amherst are coming over."

Kathy knew that "Snick" was slang for SNCC, the Student Nonviolent Coordinating Committee, an organization that worked for civil rights causes. She had thought it was mostly a Negro organization, but this girl was white.

"No, we weren't planning to go," LaRue said. "I heard about it, but my niece just got here from Utah. She's on a little vacation with me."

"You still ought to come. Both of you. We need more people. There aren't many around here this time of year."

This prim young woman hardly seemed the type to be fighting for causes. She was wearing a blue, oxford-cloth shirt and a tan skirt—all very "Ivy League." She had thick, black hair, which hung straight to her shoulders, and brown eyes that were amazingly intense.

"What exactly is the meeting about?" Kathy asked.

"We're trying to decide . . . my name's Norma Peterman, by the way." She stuck her hand out to Kathy.

"Kathy Thomas." Kathy shook her hand.

"We were going to drive to Birmingham, Alabama, to support the boycott down there. But that got settled. We may still go to Alabama. You saw what George Wallace did this week, didn't you? Or we could go to Mississippi—because of Medgar Evers."

Kathy certainly knew about both matters. Governor Wallace had tried to block two Negro students from registering at the University of Alabama. Under pressure from federal agents, he had stepped aside, but riots had been raging around the campus. That same night, Evers, an NAACP worker, had been killed by a sniper in Mississippi—shot in the back. "But what can you do down there?" Kathy asked.

"We might do the same thing the freedom riders did. We're thinking we'll drive down, maybe in a bus—Negroes and whites together. If those redneck sheriffs arrest us, we'll fill up some jails, and that could push the federal government to get more involved."

"If you do that, you're going to get hurt," LaRue said.

Kathy was surprised. LaRue sounded reticent. It was almost as though she were saying, "Things have to change slowly in the south," the way Grandpa Thomas would.

"We might get hurt. We know that. But if we get beat up we'll be on the news, and the world can see what the south is all about."

Kathy drew in her breath. She knew that Negro demonstrators were taking beatings rather than choosing to use violence. It was what the Reverend Martin Luther King preached. But this girl wasn't fighting for her own people. "I don't know if I could do something like that," Kathy said.

"Hey, we're scared. But that's okay. Sooner or later, someone has to say, 'I'm white, and if I don't do anything, that makes me responsible—right along with all those southerners.'"

"Norma, Kathy is sixteen. She's in high school. And I'm supposed to be looking out for her. So don't invite her along to get her brains knocked out—even if that's what you plan to do."

Norma smiled. "You gave me a C, Dr. Thomas. I probably don't have enough brains to worry about."

"You've got brains. But you don't study."

"There are too many other things to do." She glanced at Kathy. "And not enough people who care. Anyway, I've got to get going." She hurried past them and on down the hall.

Kathy actually wanted to go to the meeting so she could hear what the students were saying. She was so impressed with Norma. But LaRue clearly wasn't going. Instead, she led Kathy off campus, where they ate at a little café, and then they drove to LaRue's apartment, not far away. The place was spectacular. It was small, but LaRue had bought ultra-modern furniture, mostly in white, with black floor lamps, bent and running at odd angles, and she had spiced everything up with bright red throw pillows and picture frames. It was perfect, exactly the sort of thing Kathy would do if she were on her own.

Kathy unpacked and put her things away in LaRue's extra bedroom, the one she usually used for an office. Then she slipped on her pajamas and went out to the kitchen, where LaRue was heating water in a kettle for herbal tea. Kathy had never tried anything like that, and she thought of it as a little improper even though she knew it wasn't the kind of tea that was against the Word of Wisdom. But she liked it. She also liked the huge man's shirt LaRue had put on, and the rolled-up jeans. It made her look young. The two sat down in the living room on a big white couch in front of the television set, but LaRue didn't turn it on. She switched on her stereo and played a George Shearing album: "White Satin, Black Satin." It was a record Kathy had at home.

"So, have you been dating?" LaRue asked. "You never mention boys in your letters."

"That's because boys don't know I exist. I know I'm skinny, but sometimes I think I'm also *invisible*."

"You don't know any of the tricks, do you?"

"What tricks?"

"Oh, Kathy, maybe it's better that you *don't* know the wiles of women. But you could at least do something with your hair."

Kathy refused to get up before dawn to rat her hair and fuss with it for hours, or to sleep with those huge rollers so many girls used. Lately, she had been keeping her hair short, in a sort of "Dutch cut," with just a little curl. "Will you show me something to do with it—something that's simple but would look better?"

"Sure. But I'm surprised you care."

"I know. I never have that much. But . . ."

"But what? Is there some guy you like?"

"Oh, LaRue, it's pointless to talk about. He called me a *stick* the other day. He made a joke about using me for the pole vault."

LaRue laughed. "Hey, if he's teasing you, he's *seeing* you. My guess is, he can see how beautiful you're going to be."

"*Going to be?* When?"

"Some women are much prettier at thirty than anyone could have imagined when they were sixteen. You're all bones right now, sweetie, but your face, your teeth, are perfect—and you'll never be heavy. High-school boys can only see curves, but your lines are going to be so long and lovely, you'll drive the college boys wild."

"I thought you said that being pretty isn't important."

"No, I didn't. I said it's not something you earn, but still, it's a nice gift to have. So tell me about this boy? Is he worth the trouble?"

"Oh, LaRue, he's *so* superficial. He doesn't think about *anything,* doesn't read. There's not one good reason for me to like him."

"Except that he's *very* cute. Right?"

"'Cute' doesn't *start* to describe him. I actually went to a track meet this spring, just to see all his muscles. I couldn't take my eyes off him."

LaRue was leaning back, giggling like a teenager.

"His name is Val Norris, and he'll be a senior next year. He was in choir with me. He does want to go to college. Maybe he'll start reading by then."

"Why don't you drop by his house and teach him his ABCs? That might be a start."

"Hey, he's not that stupid." But Kathy was laughing now too.

LaRue sat up straight, trying to get her composure. "Kathy, I really thought you didn't care about boys," she said.

"I thought I didn't either." But that set them both off again. They leaned against each other and laughed for a long time. What Kathy felt was relief. She was glad to admit the truth to someone. She had never told a soul how much she liked this boy. *He* didn't even know.

"If you come back here, you'll miss your chance with him," LaRue said. "You need to think about that."

"I know. But it's nothing I'm serious about. I'm not going to worry about it."

Kathy tried to laugh at that, too, but LaRue seemed to take the idea seriously. "But why leave all those Mormon boys back in Utah? Do you really want to come here?"

"I want to make a difference, LaRue. I don't see how I can do that back home. Everyone thinks you're crazy if you stand up for things. I want to be like that Norma we met today."

"She's kind of a flake, if you want to know the truth."

"Maybe that's what it takes. If I come to Smith, maybe you and I could find the courage to fight for some things together."

"Or here's another thought." LaRue's tone had changed completely now. She sounded almost sad. "Do what I should have done. Stay home, go to the U—and marry a good man, one who respects the kind of person you are. The two of you could have a really good marriage, some kids, and you could—I don't know—run for Congress someday, after your children are raised. Something like that."

"Why do you say that? You know I've always wanted to come east to school."

"I know. And I'd love to have you here. But I'm not sure it's the best thing for you. I would think that seeing my life—understanding it, not romanticizing it the way you've always done—should raise some questions in your mind."

"LaRue, I'm surprised by some of the things you've told me today, but I'm like you, and I can't seem to help it. I just don't fit in back in Utah."

"Oh, Kathy, you're too young to know that. What I wish sometimes is that I had taken the safe route, that I'd stayed home and learned to fit in.

When I go home, and I look at Anna and Bobbi and your mom, even Bev, I tell myself, 'That's what I could have had. This is the good life, and I not only missed it, I don't know how to go back and get it.'"

Kathy thought about that, really was moved, and for the first time questioned what she had been dreaming of for such a long time. But she couldn't stand the thought of hiding away in a safe place, doing nothing, the way her mother and aunts had done. She couldn't help who she was any more than LaRue could.

CHAPTER 13

When Peter stepped into the apartment, he looked flushed, even excited—or maybe nervous. Hans was sitting in the living room, watching television, tired after a long day at work. "I need to talk to all of you," Peter said. "Where's Inga?"

She had gone to her room, and Hans was worried about her. It was September now, 1963, and for months Hans had watched the family worries weigh heavier and heavier on her. She had even lost her love for school.

Katrina went to get Inga and brought her back to the living room. Then everyone sat down. Dad walked to the television set and turned the sound a little louder. Then he sat down in the big chair, an old green overstuffed piece that was worn threadbare on the arms. He spoke softly. "I've been working on something for a while. I may have found a way for us to get out of the GDR. But it could be dangerous. I have to know what you think."

Hans felt a surge of excitement, but he also heard the fear in his father's voice.

"Peter, you've always told us that the Church needed us," Katrina said.

"I know that. And we've done our church work. But how can we stay in a country that wants to starve us? I don't see any other way out of this trouble we're in."

"How would we get out?"

Peter glanced toward the door. "That's what I want to talk to you about," he said, but so softly that Hans could hardly hear him. He got off the couch, moved closer, and sat on the floor.

"Papa, it scares me," Inga said.

"I know, little one," Peter said. "But I'll make sure it's safe. If it isn't, we won't do it."

"Whom have you been talking to, Peter?" Katrina asked.

Peter shifted forward in his seat. "I've made contact with people who can get false travel papers, visas, everything, so we can cross the border into Poland. That part isn't so difficult. Getting to a Western country is the hard part. But these people have a contact in Gdansk. They know some men who sneak people out on freight ships to Sweden. They've gotten quite a few out that way. They know what they're doing."

"They want money for this, I'm sure." Hans could hear that his mother was scared by all this, skeptical.

"Of course it costs money. But we have some savings left, and we have a few things we can sell. Maybe your mother could advance us a little. Once we get to Sweden, I can contact my father, in America. Or my sister. They'll help us. They'll pay for us to get to Salt Lake City. I can get work there. Then we could pay everyone back."

"If one thing goes wrong, we could—"

"Katrina, I know it's a gamble. But what else can we do?"

"I'm not saying we shouldn't do it. But I worry about trusting people. They might be men who take your money and then sell you back to the government."

"My contact doesn't even know my name at this point. He showed me the papers his people make. They're professionals. If they get caught, they're in bigger trouble than we are."

Inga had begun to cry. She tucked her head against her mother's side, and Katrina wrapped an arm around her. "If we're brave, we'll be all right," Peter told her. "And then, in America, things will be so much better."

"I don't know how to talk American," Inga said.

"We can learn," Katrina said. "Don't worry about that."

"Then you want to do it?" Peter asked.

"Yes. But move carefully," Katrina said. "Can you be sure it's not secret police trying to draw you in?"

"They're not police. I can promise you that. What they are is criminals."

"When can we go?" Hans wanted to know. He felt alive for the first time in months.

"Soon. But we need to pray about this and be certain we feel good about it."

Hans nodded, accepting that. He wanted now, with everything on the line, to let his father know he was with him.

The family knelt and prayed, and after, Peter asked the others if they wanted to go ahead with the plan. "I trust you to be careful, Peter," Katrina said. "I think it's what we have to do."

"I want to go. No question," Hans said.

"What about you, Inga?" Papa asked. "Can you be brave?"

She nodded, but she didn't look brave at all.

Almost a month went by before everything was worked out. But early in October the Stoltzes packed a few things—whatever they could carry in small suitcases—locked their apartment, and walked away. Hans did it without a second thought. His friend Greta hadn't written to him in months, probably because his own letters were full of discouragement. Besides, he hadn't attended Youth Conference this year, so there was little left of the friendship they had tried to create. But that was all right. In America life would be better. He could attend a university, and in Salt Lake City, most of the people were Mormons. No one would hate him for that.

So the four walked to the train station before the sun was up, and they boarded an eastbound train. The men who checked their papers hardly seemed interested. On the train, the Stoltzes sat in seats that faced each other, in an almost empty car. "This is all so much like what I did back during the war," Peter said. "It was the same. Four of us, a sister and brother."

He might have added: "The same danger." Hans thought of the way his father's family had been split up at the border, and all the trouble that had caused Peter. He knew his father had to be nervous now, even though he wasn't showing it.

"Remember," Peter whispered, "we can't seem worried or troubled by anything. We have to answer questions without hesitating, exactly the way we would if we were taking a little holiday. The minute we seem scared, that's when the border police will check us closely."

They had practiced all week. They had pretended they were sitting on a train, and Papa had first played the role of the conductor and then the border police. He would ask everyone where they were going, what they were doing, and each would take a turn answering.

"So let's talk about the weather, or the train ride, or not talk at all for now, so no one will hear us whispering. But when we reach the border, remember all the things we've practiced."

Hans nodded, then looked at his mother and Inga. Both seemed stiff. He hoped that someone who didn't know them wouldn't see that. He took some deep breaths and told himself to be relaxed. But his mouth was dry. He had brought a canteen full of water. He would take a drink before they reached the border so his tongue didn't stick to the roof of his mouth when he tried to speak.

"We can't pray together," Mother said. "But let's all say our own prayers."

"Yes. Of course," Peter said. "But don't think too much about everything. Better to read something or look out the window. We know what we're doing. We'll be fine."

The ride lasted into the afternoon but seemed much longer. When the train finally approached Gartz, where it would cross into Poland, the pressure increased. As the train slowed, the clacking of the tracks seemed to pound in Hans's ears. He looked at his family and saw how frightened everyone was. He smiled at Inga, nodded, but she couldn't bring herself to smile back.

The train had been stopped for a minute or two before a man stepped into the car. He was wearing a gray-green tunic and a poke cap: border police. As he approached, Hans could smell the tobacco on his clothes and noticed his cracked boots, badly in need of a shine. The man didn't seem careful, exacting; maybe he wouldn't be a problem. "Papers, please," he said.

Father had the identification and travel papers ready. He handed all of them to the guard. "Pretty day, isn't it?" he said.

The man didn't answer. He was a pudgy man, soft looking. His face showed no emotion, not even much attention. He glanced through the papers quickly. "Where is it you're going?"

"Gdansk."

"And what is the purpose of your journey?"

"We're visiting friends there."

He looked around at everyone but settled on Inga, who was next to her mother, across from Hans. "Where are you going from there, little girl?" he asked. "Will you leave Poland?"

Hans felt his chest grab and watched Inga. She hesitated, but by then Peter had said, "We'll spend the entire time in Gdansk." He laughed, as though he thought the guard had been joking.

The man was staring at Inga. "Who are these friends in Gdansk? Polish people?"

"No. They're—"

"I didn't ask you. I asked the little girl."

Hans saw Inga's eyes fill with tears. But she smiled and said politely, "They're from Schwerin, where we live. But they live in Poland now."

"How many children in this family?"

"Two, like us. They have a daughter my age. She's my best friend."

Hans finally took a breath. Inga had done well. The words had sounded rather memorized to Hans, but the guard seemed satisfied. He handed the papers back to Peter and mumbled, "You'll be cold up on the Baltic. Winter comes early there."

"Yes, I know. We wanted to leave sooner, but I couldn't get the time away from work."

The guard took a couple of steps away, and Hans thought it was over. But then the man turned. "What kind of work?"

"I'm a civil engineer. I work for the government."

The man nodded, seemed to consider for a moment, and then turned again and walked from the car.

When the door shut, Katrina whispered, "Was he suspicious?"

"I don't know. But don't whisper. Let's just be natural now, until the train starts again."

Hans was not sure this was over. The man had seemed dubious. What had he thought of Inga's answer? Katrina had hold of her now, and Inga was crying.

"You must not cry, Inga," her mother was whispering. "You must look quite normal."

But Inga was struggling, and Hans hoped the guard wouldn't come back.

Ten minutes passed, or maybe it was two and seemed like ten, but finally the train began to move. Hans watched his father breathe more steadily, saw him nod to Katrina. "Everything's fine now, Inga," she whispered. "You were brave. You answered exactly right."

Hans leaned toward her. "I'm proud of you," he said. "You said everything just right."

The train was picking up speed, and Hans wanted to scream for joy. He was on his way to America. He knew that this was an easy crossing, that the great danger was getting across the Baltic, but still, that was a matter of being smuggled. There would be no more questioning.

The train rattled on all afternoon and evening, and everyone was more relaxed—until they reached Gdansk. It was late when they arrived, so Peter paid for a taxi, and the driver took them to a small hotel near the docks. There, they were to register under their assumed names and wait for a contact. That would happen the next day, and the ship didn't depart until the day after that.

The family all slept in the same little hotel room, Inga on a couch and Hans on the floor with a couple of blankets under him. But he didn't sleep very much. He rolled around, never really getting comfortable. And the next day was tedious. They stayed in the room, trying to entertain themselves with Polish music on the radio. It was mid-afternoon when a knock came. Peter opened the door and a stocky little man stepped in. He was dressed in black, with big boots—like a dock worker. He stood near the door and said quietly, "Walk to the docks about an hour from now. Act as though you are taking a stroll. No baggage. When you walk past dock forty-two, you will see the *Ostsee* docked there. If I turn my back on you, walk on by. If I take off my hat, come on board. But don't draw attention to yourselves."

"Shouldn't we wait until after dark?"

"No. That's the worst time. That's when the docks are watched most carefully."

"Can't we bring our things? No one told us this," Katrina said.

"Do as I told you. Wear extra clothes if you want, but don't bundle up so much that you look strange."

"All right. In about an hour?"

The man raised his arm and pulled his coat sleeve back. "Yes. Four-thirty would be about right. And pay me now."

"No. I told them I would pay you on the ship, once we're on safely."

"Pay me half now."

"I'll pay you on the ship—as we agreed."

The man nodded. "It makes no difference," he said. But Hans had to wonder. Was this fellow trying to pull something?

The man left. But now so many things had to be left behind. Peter told the others to put extra clothes on, to stuff their coat pockets with stockings and underwear, but to leave the rest.

"Oh, Peter," Katrina said. "We'll have nothing."

"I know. I'll contact my sister when we get to Sweden. She can wire money to us. We'll buy a few new things for the trip to America. We can fly there, perhaps. How would that be, all of us in a big airplane, laughing at the GDR, free of the *Stasi* at last?"

Hans laughed, and Katrina and Inga got busy sorting through their clothes. But Hans didn't care about leaving things behind. He put on a sweater, then stuffed a pair of stockings in one pocket and some underwear in the other. That's all he needed. His clothes were old anyway.

Peter made sure there was nothing to identify them in the clothing left behind, and then he took the suitcases downstairs and left them out back with a pile of rubbish. Then he paid his bill at the hotel. When he came back upstairs, he said, "All right. It's time. Let's go."

So the four set out. They walked slowly to the docks. A cold wind was coming off the water, and the sun was already well down, not far from setting. Hans hoped the ship wouldn't be so cold. But mostly he wanted to be on board, hidden away somewhere. He wished the ship were departing that night instead of in the morning.

He tucked his hands into his coat pockets. It was an old coat, dark wool and worn, too small for him. It was one more thing he wanted to throw away. In America, he would buy nice clothes—the kind he had seen on West German television. He had seen a show called Maverick, about the West, about cowboys, and he had seen one about a family that lived in a beautiful house. The sons in the family wore what they wanted to school, had no uniforms. They went in jeans and plaid shirts, and their mother wore pretty dresses and pearls around her neck, every day. Maybe everything wasn't quite like that. Father said it wasn't so nice as that. But even he admitted that some families had more than one car. The Thomases did. And laborers earned more in a month than Peter had in a year, even before he had lost his office job.

The first time the family walked past the *Ostsee*, Peter told the others not to look for the contact man, that he would do it. But then he whispered, "He's not there."

They walked by, continued to the end of the dock, and then strolled back again. This time Hans spotted the man from some distance away. "He's on the upper deck," he told his father.

"I know. I see him." And then, as they drew close, "All right. He's taken his hat off. Don't walk any faster. Just turn and walk on board."

By the time they reached the ship and turned to walk on, the contact man was waiting on the main deck. He nodded, and then he motioned for them to step through an open door. Hans went first, his father last, and they followed the man down a ladder into the hold of the ship. He led them through a large, empty storage area, to the aft of the ship. He opened a hatch in a bulkhead there and stepped in first. Hans followed him into a little, dark area, nothing he would call a stateroom or even a storage area. It was just a small compartment with no furniture, only a few boxes. "Stay in here," the man said. "We'll bring you some blankets, but I can't promise you a pleasant night. It might be cold, and there's no light."

"None of that matters. It's just one night," Peter said.

"But now you'll pay me."

"Why not on the other side?"

"I have to have the money. I'm not taking you across only to learn that you have none."

"I'll show you. And I'll pay you half. Then we can—"

"Pay me now or get off the ship."

"Once you have my money, you could turn us in, or you could—"

"Why would I do that?"

"Why are you so worried about getting your money now?"

"That's how I do business." The little man stood with his feet set wide apart, his chest thrust forward.

Hans watched his father pause and consider, but there was no turning back now. He pulled a wad of bills from his coat pocket. He counted out the right amount. It was most of what he had. Hans half expected the man to demand more. But he didn't do that. He took the money, stuffed it into his coat pocket, and turned to leave.

"What about food?" Peter asked.

"We'll bring you something a little later. Just settle down now. Sometimes inspectors come by and walk through the ship. We pile boxes in front of this hatch, and they usually don't bother to move them. But there's no saying that they wouldn't do that."

"And what do we do if that happens?"

"Let's just hope it doesn't."

"But what if it does?"

"Then we're all caught." He walked out and shut the hatch. The only light was from a porthole, and the sun was almost gone. Hans felt something eerie about the whole thing, knowing how dark it would be all night. But he longed for the cover that the dark offered, and he knew he could wait out another night as long as the engines started in the morning and Sweden was the next stop.

Peter walked to the porthole and looked out. "Can you see the dock?" Katrina asked.

"Yes."

"Is anyone out there?"

"No."

"What's that sound?"

"He's stacking up the boxes, like he said he would."

"What about the food?"

"He said he'd bring it later. I'm glad he's putting up the boxes for now."

And then the room was quiet. Hans sat down on a box. He listened to the sound of the man bumping the boxes against the bulkhead. And then, over the next few minutes, the last of the light disappeared. Hans hated the smell of diesel fuel, the dank smell of decay. "Well, we made it this far," he said, all the same. "We're almost there."

But Inga said, "Why does it have to be dark?"

"Come here. Sit by me on this box," Hans said. "It's dark because we're going to watch a movie. It should be starting soon."

"There's no movie."

"That's what you think. It's a good one, too. It starts with a cartoon."

"No it doesn't."

"Just watch. You'll see it."

Inga laughed. "All I see is Papa's head. He's the movie."

"Yes, he's—"

"Be quiet. This doesn't look good," Peter said.

"What?"

"Two men are coming on board—men in suits."

Hans didn't want to believe this—not now, after coming this far.

"What are they doing?" Katrina asked. Hans could hear her panic.

"I don't know. I can't see them now."

Hans listened for sounds outside, but he heard nothing.

"What will they do to us?" Inga was whining.

"*Liebling*," Peter said, "listen to me. You must be quiet. We'll be all right. Just do what I tell you. For now, let's not say a word. We need to listen, and we must not be heard."

But Hans could see what his father was doing. He was struggling with the hatch on the porthole, trying to open it. Hans knew what that meant—that they all might need to go out that way. But doing that meant dropping into the water. Hans doubted that they could all manage that without someone drowning.

"Take your shoes off. Put them in your coat pockets," Peter said.

Inga was crying. Katrina was saying, "No, Peter, we can't do that."

"Let's hope we don't have to. Just listen now."

Hans was untying his shoes. He slipped them off, pulled out the socks and underwear, stuffed them in his pants, and then forced the shoes into his coat pockets. He could hear voices now, echoing through the hold of the ship.

"Don't leave anything if we go out," Peter whispered.

"Papa, I can't swim," Inga said.

"Be quiet now. Don't say another word. We'll take care of you. You must not cry."

Hans heard another little whimper and then nothing. But outside the hiding space, the voices were coming closer, speaking Polish.

Maybe the men would look about and then move on. But when it seemed that they had done just that, Hans heard a box move, heard it make a thump as it landed on the deck. They were coming in.

"Hans, go first," Peter whispered. "Hurry! I'll drop Inga down to you. I'll come last."

Hans scrambled for the porthole, stepped on a box, and poked his head through. His shoulders were a tight squeeze, but once through, he pulled himself the rest of the way. He felt the shoes in his pockets catch for a moment, then slip through, and he dropped head first. He banged his foot against the side of ship but didn't hit the dock, as he feared he might. Suddenly he was swallowed up in the water. He struggled to right himself but was able to swim upward until his head popped out. He wasn't sure he could catch his sister and stay up, not with his coat on, but he heard a little shriek and saw a dark object tumbling toward him. He caught Inga by the arm, and both of them went down. He was sinking, but he pulled Inga to him and paddled ferociously with his feet. All the quiet, the dark, seemed to be gripping him, holding onto his coat, pulling him down, but then his head broke through the water, and this time he got hold of one of the piles at the edge of the dock. He wrapped an arm around it, then jerked Inga higher and heard her gasp. He got a lung full of air himself just as his mother hit the water. She had fallen sideways, hit the water with her hip. But she hardly sank before he managed to get a leg under her. She wrapped her own legs around his and grabbed hold of his shoulder.

Hans was slipping, and then they were all under the water. For just a moment Hans thought he couldn't do it, that he would sink to the bottom. But he felt his mother break loose from his leg and rise, and he managed to come up again, still clinging to Inga. He grabbed for the pile and this time got hold of something. It cut into his hand, but he had a better hold. He pulled upward hard and got Inga up high again. "Mama," he gasped, "where are you?"

"Under the dock. I've got hold of something. Are you all right?"

Hans could feel something metallic cutting into the palm of his hand, but he wasn't letting go. Inga was clinging to him desperately, hurting his neck, but at least her head was above the water. What he knew now was that Papa should have dropped. He heard the tugging and struggling, up above. Papa was obviously fighting to get through the porthole but not making it. It was all like before, Hans thought, his father once again the one not to make it with his family.

"Where's Peter?" Katrina asked. "Is he coming?"

"He's caught, I think. He—"

But then something splashed on the water. It was Papa's coat. He had taken off the coat and dropped it, but time had to be running out. He heard his father grunt again, up above, and then he was tumbling down, slamming into the water.

There was a rush of motion, and the wave almost tore Hans loose from his grip. But he held on and kept hold of Inga, too, and then he felt his father next to him, breaking out of the water. "Swim under the dock, this way," Hans said. "Mama has hold of something back there."

"This way," Katrina was saying. "Come to me."

"Be quiet, everyone," Papa said. "We have to stay here for now."

For the first time Hans realized how cold the water was. He didn't know how long he could last, how long Inga could. She was still gripping him around the neck so tightly that he could hardly stand the pain—and his hand was being torn every time she moved.

"We're all right now," Papa was saying, but Hans knew that wasn't true.

CHAPTER 14

I t's all right. Come in here." Peter was whispering but motioning hard with his hand. Hans, by then, was shaking all over, chilled all the way through, and the pain in his hand was searing. He knew he was bleeding rather badly, but he still hadn't told anyone.

The four had not actually waited in the cold water a long time. They had worked their way under the dock to a ladder. "Listen to me," Peter had told them. "Those men must still be on the ship. We've got to get out of the water now, before they come back this way. Follow me up this ladder, and we'll find a place to hide."

Hans couldn't see his father, but he moved toward the sound, grasping a crossbeam above his head. He still had Inga. When he got hold of the ladder, he helped her take hold herself, and by then he could hear his mother fighting the water, grunting. He grabbed her coat and pulled her toward him. Then he helped her onto the ladder too. When she was gone, he finally pulled himself up, using one hand. Papa was there at the top to help him onto the dock.

"All right. Let's hurry. We've got to get inside somewhere, out of this breeze."

There were clouds overhead, with the moon glowing behind them, and well down the street was a single arc light. It wasn't much, but at least Hans could see where they were going. The trouble was, if the men came off the ship, they too would be able to see—and spot the Stoltzes.

But Peter had picked up Inga, and he was loping ahead, running in his wet stockings. Katrina was running to keep up. Hans kept looking back as he ran. He couldn't see anyone. When the family reached an alley, Peter turned. "Let's go this way," he called. As Hans made the turn, he glanced back one last time, still saw no one, and felt much better.

But after that it had taken some time to find this building—an empty warehouse with an open door. It was a chance to get out of the cold wind—but the building wasn't heated.

"We have to get our wet clothes off," Peter was saying. "Let me see what I can find. Maybe there's something we can wrap up in, to stay warm."

The place was black, and Hans had to wonder whether there was much hope in finding anything. He knelt and wrapped his arms around Inga. "Are you all right?"

"I'm cold," she said. She sounded frozen.

"I know. We're all cold. But we're all right now."

"No, we aren't."

"Yes, yes," Katrina was saying. "We're safe now. We'll be fine."

But Inga, of course, was right. They were anything but safe. Their money was mostly gone, so they had few options for travel or renting a room. Maybe the men on the ship had been border guards, merely making a random inspection, but it was just as likely that the family had been traced and were still being sought. Hans couldn't see a way out of this.

"Come this way," Peter whispered. "There are burlap sacks here. Get your wet clothes off and I'll pile them on you. Then I'll hang your clothes up to dry."

Hans took Inga by the hand and led her deeper into the darkness.

"Take off your coat, Inga," Mother said. "Your dress and everything. I'll hold you in my arms and get you warm. Papa can cover us up. You have to be brave again."

"I know," Inga said. Hans heard her drop her wet coat onto the floor and begin to pull at her dress. He took off his own coat and sweater. "Where can we hang things, Papa?" he said.

"I'm trying to find a place back here." Hans could hear him feeling around. After a time, Peter said, "All right. I've found some pallets. We can lean them against the wall and lay our clothes on them."

Hans reached with his good hand, hoisted a heavy load of clothes against himself, and then took the things to his father. Finally, he admitted the rest. "Papa, I cut my hand under the dock."

"Is it bad?"

"I don't know. But it hurts."

"All right. Let me cover your mother and sister. Then we'll try to do something with it."

Admitting to the injury seemed to increase the pain. Still, Hans waited. He listened as his father piled on the sacks. "Yes, that's good," his mother told him. "Keep some for yourselves."

"There are plenty. Make sure you're well covered."

"It scratches," Hans heard Inga say.

But Katrina told her, "It's all right. Lie still. You'll be warm in a minute."

Finally, Peter came back to Hans. "Here," he said. "I found something else—a piece of cloth. I think it's a flour sack. Wrap your hand tight in it."

Hans wrapped it around his hand as tightly as he could, but that only added to his pain.

"I'm sorry, Hans," Peter whispered.

Hans felt the agony in his father's voice and knew he meant more than just this wound. He was sorry for everything. "We were almost there," Hans said, and for the first time he thought not only of the trouble ahead, but of what he had lost: America.

"Get your clothes off. I'll cover you."

"What are we going to do?"

"I don't know. One thing at a time, I suppose. Get warm and dry—as best we can."

"How did they know? Did that man on the ship sell us out?"

"I don't think so. Why would he bother to stack the boxes if he knew they were coming?"

"Then who?"

"Maybe the guard. The one on the train, at the border. Maybe he suspected us and passed the word along to watch us."

"Then they might not know who we are."

"They shouldn't. I've never told anyone our real names."

"Maybe we can go home. Maybe that's the safest place."

"Yes. That's what I'm thinking too. We'll be caught if we stay in Poland. We have no resources, no place to stay—and no other connections to help us get to the West. But I don't know how we can get home."

It was more than Hans could think about. But at least there was one hope of safety—if they could return to Schwerin quickly, before the wrong people knew they were gone. Both he and his father had arranged to be away from their work for a week. They had done that to delay anyone from knowing they were gone, but now that arrangement could save them.

Hans unbuttoned his shirt with one hand, and then his father helped him pull it off. He dropped his pants to the floor, stepped out, and pulled off his socks.

"Lie down on some of the sacks," Father said. "I'll cover you."

Hans found a place close to his mother and sister, laid out a few sacks, and then lay down. Then he felt the bristly burlap begin to drop on top of him. "It takes a little while to get warm," his mother whispered. "But we're fine now. We're doing better."

Hans could feel air breathing through the burlap, but after a few minutes he also felt the warmth, and even though his hand was throbbing and the smell of the burlap was bothersome, he felt his exhaustion take over. He didn't think he could sleep, but he would rest, and think, maybe help his father get some answers.

The sun was not up yet, but Hans could hear sounds from somewhere, as though work was beginning on the docks. Hans realized that he had actually slept for quite some time. He moved enough to touch his left hand, the injured one. The wrap had loosened a little, but he could feel only caked blood on the outside. No blood was running now.

Hans heard someone moving inside the warehouse and was relieved when he heard his father's voice. "Hans," he whispered, "we've got to get dressed and get out of here. Our clothes aren't as dry as I'd like them to be, but there's nothing we can do about that."

Hans pushed back the sacks, stood up, and felt the cold air. He hurried to his father, who passed his clothes to him, still in the dark. Hans felt the dampness against his hips, on his shoulders, but still, he felt better to get dressed again. His sweater hadn't dried. He left it off, put on his coat, and then sat down to put on his socks and shoes. Both were damp, but he was glad his father had thought to have them keep their shoes. Only Papa had none, and no coat either.

When Hans was dressed, he helped his father bring clothes to his mother and sister. He heard them dressing in the dark, Mama encouraging Inga. "I'm hungry," Inga whispered.

"I know. We all are. Just be brave a little longer. Papa will figure something out for us."

"Yes, yes. We'll be fine," Peter told her. "I've got an idea about what we can do. Everyone stay here. I'll be back before long."

But he was gone longer than Hans liked, and he felt the worry in his mother's silence. At least some light was coming through the windows now. Mother finally saw the wrap on Hans's hand, all the blood that had soaked through. "How bad is it?" she asked him.

"It's nothing. Just a little cut."

"It's not little. You know it isn't."

She helped him tear the sack, using a nail in a wall to rip at it, and then tied the ends around to make the bandage more secure.

By the time Peter came back, the sun was shining. "Follow me," Peter called. "Hurry. Right now."

Hans grabbed Inga's hand, and he ran with her to his father, with his mother close behind. Then they trotted down the alley, toward the docks. "Now walk," Father said. "Don't look around. Just be natural."

Hans had no idea what his father had in mind. But he walked with Inga, letting his eyes survey the area. They were about to pass a truck when Peter suddenly stepped behind it. "Hurry, get in the back," he said.

It was a delivery truck. The back was open except for a heavy leather curtain. Papa jumped up quickly, then reached back for Inga. Hans helped her, using the wrapped hand without thinking, but he paid no attention to the pain. He helped his mother up the same way, and then he let his father pull him up. They closed the curtain behind them, then sat and waited.

"The truck is going to Warsaw. I heard the driver say so," Peter said. "It will be cold back here. But we'll be away from Gdansk, and that's what we need now."

The truck was mostly full of wooden crates, with only this small area empty at the back. It was a tight squeeze for them, hardly comfortable for such a long ride.

"How do you know there isn't more to pack in here?" Mother asked.

"I heard the driver talking with the men who helped him load. They're finished. He's gone in to sign the papers."

"Still, he could look back here for some reason."

"I know. But we had to take the chance. Let's be still now."

Time passed, and the man didn't return. Maybe he had gone for breakfast, for coffee, for something.

Finally, however, Hans heard steps, heard the door open up front, then heard it slam. He waited for the starter to sound, but time passed again, just a few seconds, and then the door opened. Hans held his breath, hoping the man was going back into the building for some reason. But suddenly the curtain rattled on its chains and slid back. A flood of light was in Hans's eyes, and in the middle was the figure of the man. He stepped back, and Hans saw his face, shocked.

He spoke in Polish, asking a question.

"I'm sorry. We speak German," Peter said. But then he did say a few words in Polish.

"What are you doing back here?" the man asked in German.

"I'm sorry," Peter said. "I'm sorry to frighten you. Could we ride back here? We have no money, and we need to get to Warsaw."

"I don't take passengers." But he was hesitating, and Hans saw in his face—his whiskered, mud-colored face—that he wasn't sure what he was going to do. "Why didn't you ask me, not frighten the life out of me that way?"

"We're desperate. We've had some bad luck, and—"

"You're East Germans—that's who you are. Men are looking for you. They've been going up and down the dock, asking questions, telling people to watch for you."

"We'll go now. Don't turn us in."

The man seemed to think that over. "It's going to be cold," he said. "I can't help that. You can push some of those crates to the back and get out of the air a little. That might help."

"Thank you."

"Yes, and if I get caught, what then?"

But he didn't wait for an answer. He pulled off his coat and tossed it to Peter. "Here's another coat, and I keep a blanket in the front. I'll get that." He pulled the curtain shut again. A few seconds later, he pulled back the curtain a little and tossed the blanket in. "Don't peek out. I'll keep moving, and we shouldn't have a problem. Have you eaten anything?"

"No."

"I can do something about that, in time. But make the best of things for now."

He returned to the cab of his truck, and Hans heard the door slam. Peter was up by then, sliding a crate back, helping Inga to a better seat. Then he put the blanket over her. By then the engine had started and the truck lurched forward.

It was a bumpy trip, and cold, but Hans was glad to be away from Gdansk, and he was glad that the driver knew they were back there. At least there wasn't the worry of being caught when the truck finally stopped. And maybe best of all, the driver kept his promise, stopping along the way to buy bread and cheese and bottles of water. Handing them the food, he said, "When I get to Warsaw, where can I leave you?"

"I'm not certain," Peter said.

The driver pulled the curtain open a little more. "Are you half frozen?"

"It's not so bad, and this food will help. I have a little money. I can pay you."

"It's all right. But what are you going to do? Do you have a place to go?"

Peter glanced at his wife, at Inga. "I'm thinking we might go back to our home, in East Germany. We have no place to go in Poland, no way to survive. But the secret police might be waiting for us at home. I don't know how they knew we were on that ship."

"I think I know. There are people paid to watch the docks. They report when they see someone like you get on board. Back a few months ago, many were getting out of your country this way, but things have tightened down. There are border guards around these docks all the time—watching, inspecting the ships."

"Then you don't think they know who we are?"

"I doubt it. Someone saw you go on board, but if they didn't see you well, I doubt you would have a problem, back in your country."

Peter looked at Katrina. "We could take the train back, using the same papers. If we get home quickly enough, the Stasi may have no idea we were gone."

"But Peter, we don't have enough money for train tickets," Katrina said.

"We have a little—just not enough." Peter looked back at the driver. "We spent the last of our money—almost the last—to get on that ship."

"But how did you get off?"

Peter hesitated, but then he said, "We jumped in the water."

"Even this little girl?"

Peter nodded.

"My goodness. You're brave, little sweetheart."

Hans watched Inga. He could see how frightened she still was. Her face was pale, her eyes still red. "It was cold," was all she said.

"I have two daughters," the man said. "And three sons. All grown. I'm getting grandchildren now. Five, and one more coming." He grinned, and Hans could see a gold tooth gleam from the side of his mouth. "I wouldn't want any of them jumping into such cold water."

"Are you German or Polish?" Peter asked.

"My mother's family was German. My father, Polish. I grew up mostly around Germans, though. I speak better German than Polish."

"Why weren't you forced out, after the war?"

"My father moved us from the German regions, to Warsaw. Since he was Polish, people didn't mind us so much."

"Have you ever heard of Mormons?" Peter asked. "In Warsaw, or any-where in Poland?"

"What is this? Mormons?"

"It's a church. A Christian church. The Church of Jesus Christ of Latter-day Saints."

"No. I never heard of this."

"We're members of this church. I'm only thinking that if I could find a member, maybe he would give us help. We could borrow enough money to buy train tickets."

The driver shook his head. "I know nothing of this. Mostly we are Catholic here. If you ask a priest, perhaps . . . but I don't know. There's not much money in the churches these days."

"Yes. I understand." Peter took a drink from a water bottle, then set it down, picked up the loaf of bread, and broke off a piece. "If you don't mind," he said, "take us to the train station—if it's not too far out of your way. I'll think some more. Maybe we can locate someone who knows where to find our church. It's all I can think of."

"All right. I'll take you there."

"Thanks so much for all your help," Katrina said. "I think God sent you to us. Not many men would have helped us."

"Some would. Many would. We don't like what's happened to our country either. Many would leave if they could." He smiled again. "Don't report me for saying so. All right?"

"We won't report you if you won't report us," Peter said. He laughed.

"All right. That's fair enough. When I stop at the train station, get out quickly."

"Yes. We don't want you to get in trouble."

The driver pulled the curtain closed again, and he drove on. And all along the way, Hans kept wondering what they could do. They needed money, immediately. The longer they were away from their apartment, the more likely someone would recognize that they had been gone. One idea did occur to him. He had heard of boys stealing from the men who sold newspapers and chocolate in the train stations. While one boy called his attention away from his money drawer, another reached in and grabbed the bills. He knew that Papa would never help him do such a thing, but maybe Hans could hang around a kiosk and watch. Perhaps a chance would come. There were times when things like that weren't really wrong.

"What are we going to do?" Katrina asked. "Can you think of anything, Peter?"

"I'm thinking. And I'm praying. Have you been praying?"

"Yes. Of course."

"Then something will open up to us. We'll find a way. When my family escaped from Germany during the war, we were caught once. But we got away. And I know it was because we prayed so hard, and God looked out for us."

Yes, and later you were left behind at the border, Hans thought. But he didn't say it, not in front of Inga.

Peter folded his arms. "Let's pray together," he said. And then he said the prayer himself. He got on his knees, even though the truck was rocking and jolting, and he asked that they could find a way to get some money. Or if there were some other answer, other than to take the train, that a way would be opened. Hans tried not to counteract the prayer with his own skepticism, but he had spent his hope on the escape, and that was gone. God had refused the one thing he really wanted. His only wish now was to get Inga home and safe.

The truck kept rolling, but eventually Hans heard more traffic, and when the truck stopped, Hans peeked out to see that they were now in the city and the driver had only stopped for a traffic light. "Keep watching," Peter told him. "When you see he's at the train station, let us know."

For quite some time the truck continued into the busy city. There were many stops but only for the traffic. Then, finally, the truck veered off and parked at a curb. Hans looked out and was getting up, sure this was the stop. But as he looked outside, he saw a police station. And he heard the driver call, "Don't get out. Stay inside for just a few more minutes."

Hans spun around, "Papa, it's a police station. He's turning us in."

Peter didn't answer. All was quiet for a moment.

"Come on. Let's get out—and make a run for it. He's tricked us all along." Hans pulled the curtain open and was about to jump out.

"No. No!"

Hans looked back.

"I trust him. He wouldn't do that. He could have turned us in back in Gdansk and he didn't. He's told us to wait for some reason. So wait."

"Papa, we're finished. We have to get out of here."

"No. Just wait."

For a moment, Hans thought of going by himself. He hated to accept what was coming, but something cynical in him said it probably didn't matter. They were finished anyway, whether they were dropped with the police or at a train station without any money—and with a father who thought he could pray his family home.

Hans sat back, waiting for what was coming. Ten minutes went by, maybe more, and then the driver was there, pulling back the curtain again. "I stopped at my bank," he said. "I want to give you this."

He reached out, handing Hans several bills. Hans held them for a moment, trying to believe what he was seeing. Then he handed them on to his father.

"We can't take this from you," Peter said.

"Of course you can. It's not so much."

"But I have no way to pay you back."

"That's fine. I'm blessed. I have a good job. I own my truck. Not many have so much as I do. I want this little girl to get home. I kept thinking about her, while I was driving, and I could only think what I would want for one of my grandchildren, in such a mess as this."

"Bless you," Katrina said.

"Yes, yes. I understand." He looked at Peter. "You must buy some shoes. I think I gave you enough for that too." He walked away quickly and got into his truck one more time. Then he drove to the station. There, the Stoltzes bought tickets, and nearby, Papa found a shoe store.

It was early the next morning when the family finally arrived in Schwerin, and nothing seemed disturbed at home. Hans's parents talked a lot on the train, and later, back in their apartment, about God's blessings. "We're supposed to stay here," Peter told everyone. "Our work is here. In the Church. The Lord has brought us back. That ought to be clear to us now."

Hans could hardly believe his father could say such a thing. Nothing had come of any of their prayers. Sure, the driver had been a kind man, and they had avoided jail—but that was all. What else did they have to hope for now? They had been dropped back in the same trouble they had been in, and now all their savings were gone. How was that a blessing?

CHAPTER 15

Diane was sitting in her Spanish class. She had just finished a vocabulary quiz, and now she was gazing out the window. She was on the second floor at Ogden High, in a room that allowed her to look out over the front lawn and across Harrison Boulevard. It was a pretty, bright November day in 1963. There had been snow the day before, over a foot in the mountains. She hoped that Snowbasin would open now, especially with the Thanksgiving break coming next week. It was Friday morning, almost noon, and she was glad to think the week was almost over. She could possibly even ski on Saturday if Mom didn't need help with little Ricky—Richard, Jr.—who had been born in the summer, on July 28. The truth was, as much as Diane had dreaded having a baby around the house, she was now nuts over the little guy and actually liked to tend him—but not as much as she liked to ski.

When she heard the little crackle of static come over the intercom, she wondered what was coming. She wished there were a pep assembly she had forgotten. "Teachers, I'm sorry to interrupt your classes, but I have an important announcement."

This was the principal himself, Dr. Connors. Diane wondered about the gravity of his voice.

"I'm sorry to have to tell you this . . . but President Kennedy has been shot."

Diane was stunned for a moment, and then, as the words sank in, frightened. How could that happen? Why would it happen?

"We have no official word yet on his condition, but the radio stations are saying that someone fired several shots at him, down in Dallas, Texas, and apparently he was struck in the head by at least one of the bullets. We're going to pipe this radio broadcast into your rooms at least for a few minutes and see whether we get definite word about his condition."

Suddenly the room was full of a broadcaster's voice, but the man was only repeating what Dr. Connors had just said. Kennedy had been rushed to a hospital. There was no word on his condition, but rumors were spreading through Dallas that President Kennedy was dead.

Mr. Galbraith, the Spanish teacher, walked to his desk and sat down. Diane could see that the color had left his face. "I can't believe this," he said. "Who would have done it?"

A boy in the back of the room said, "Maybe someone who loved America."

But there was an immediate reaction from most of the students. "Shut up!" a girl shouted at him. "What's wrong with you?"

Mr. Galbraith stood up so quickly he knocked his chair against the wall. "This is the president of the United States," he said. "I don't care whether you like him. He's our president."

Diane looked back to see the boy—a guy named Bruce Barker—grinning. He shrugged his shoulders as if to say, "I still don't care."

Diane knew that a lot of people didn't like Kennedy, but how could Bruce look so unconcerned? The president couldn't be murdered. What was there to depend on if things like that could happen?

Pictures started to come into Diane's mind: little John-John hiding under a desk in the White House; the president and Jackie entering a grand ball, looking so dazzling. She loved Jack Kennedy's smile, that shock of hair sweeping across his forehead, the way he tucked his tie into his coat as he walked, the way he smiled and waved to his supporters when he got off a plane. And Jackie had been so perfect, so beautiful, when she had conducted the nation on a tour through the remodeled White House, on TV. People like that shouldn't be shot at; certainly they couldn't die.

But the news reports were horrifying. One reporter, from Dallas, said, "I've talked to people now who were on the scene, who saw the actual shooting, and I have to tell you, this sounds very grave. A man told me he saw—and I hasten to say, this was only one man's observation—but he said he saw the president's head open up, saw blood fly. We're hearing, too, that Governor Connolly was also hit by a bullet, but so far we have no confirmation on that."

The girl sitting behind Diane had begun to cry. It was the thought of it, maybe, the president being hit in the head, his blood flying. But Diane still didn't want to believe that could happen—not to John Kennedy. He was too handsome for that, too young.

✧

The rumor circulated around Highland High during first lunch. When it got to Kathy's table, she left her food and ran to Mr. Taylor's classroom. She knew he had a TV and would have it on. But she had to push to get inside, a crowd having gathered already. Walter Cronkite, the CBS news anchor, was sitting at a desk, looking earnestly into the camera. He kept reassuring his audience that all the reports received, so far, were unofficial, but when he switched to a reporter in Dallas, the man said, "The word we have is that the president is dead. But we cannot say this for a fact." He promised to bring official word as soon as possible.

Kathy felt her knees buckle. This couldn't happen. She had loved John Kennedy since the first time she had seen him on TV. He was the only one she really trusted to fight for civil rights. He really *cared*.

"My dad hates Kennedy," a girl nearby said, "but he's going to feel bad about this. Everyone will."

"He's the president," another girl said. "How could someone shoot the president?"

Kathy wanted to scream at them to shut up. They weren't feeling enough anguish. She was crying, but she was trying not to go to pieces.

Maybe the reports were wrong, she kept telling herself. It was stupid to assume anything yet.

"Here's what we know for certain," Walter Cronkite would say. And then he would repeat the information: At approximately 12:30 P.M., President Kennedy had been driving with a convoy through Dallas when several shots had been fired; a Secret Service agent had rushed to the car and jumped on the back, and then the car had sped off; President Kennedy had been taken to Parkland Hospital; hospital officials had confirmed that both JFK and Governor John Connolly had been shot; their condition was still unknown.

Time kept passing, and the room kept getting more crowded. Kathy didn't speak to anyone; she knew she would fall apart if she did. But she could hardly stand what she was hearing. No one around her understood the depth of the tragedy. A couple of girls near the television were crying, but she heard them making comments about poor little John-John and Caroline. They didn't really get it.

Then the word came. Walter Cronkite spoke slowly: "From Dallas, Texas"—the flash apparently official—"President Kennedy died at 1:00 P.M., Central Standard Time." He glanced at the clock. "Some thirty-eight minutes ago." His voice pinched off for a moment. He took off his glasses and wiped his eyes. "Vice President Johnson has left the hospital . . ."

Kathy began to sob. She pushed her way out of the room, smashing people away with her shoulder, and broke out into the hallway. Then she ran. She ran outside, away from all these stupid kids, and then, not knowing what else to do, started to walk home. But she couldn't stop crying, couldn't get under control.

Lyndon Johnson would be president now. He was a southerner, a Texan; everyone knew that he and Jack Kennedy couldn't stand each other. What did he care about Negroes' rights?

What did anyone care? It was probably the Ku Klux Klan, or some other crazy white group, that had shot him. "We can't let them get away with this," she mumbled to herself. She kept walking fast, although she had nowhere to go. There was nothing at home that would change any of this, and try as her parents would to show concern, they didn't like the Kennedys. They made derisive comments about them all the time. Mom would see it as a tragedy that someone would kill the president, and Dad would talk about the world getting more evil all the time, but they wouldn't feel what she did. They never would.

Kathy kept walking up the hill toward her house. She wished she could leave for the south right now, do something to keep the civil rights work going—and show those rednecks they couldn't get away with this.

When she reached her house, she walked to the family room. Mom was already there, with the television on. She was sitting on the edge of the couch, listening carefully. "Oh, Kathy," she said, "this is so terrible. I just can't believe it."

Kathy couldn't talk to her, not about this. She listened for a few minutes to the rehashed accounts, people describing what they had seen, but she couldn't stand their descriptions. She decided to go to her room. But she was halfway there when the phone rang, and she was almost sure she knew who it was. She stopped in the hallway, waiting, and then her mother called, "Kathy, it's for you. It's your Aunt LaRue."

Kathy began to cry again. She ran to the phone and took it from her mother. "This can't happen," she said into the phone.

But she only heard crying on the other end. It was the first response that made sense.

"I want to go down there, LaRue. To the South. I want to keep the fight going."

"I know, I know. I've been thinking the same thing."

They didn't talk long, couldn't. And then Kathy went to her room and lay on her bed, her face in her pillow. What came to her mind was the talk Reverend King had given a few months before. Negroes from all across the country had marched on Washington—half a million people.

There had been great speeches that day, calling for change, but the climax had been Martin Luther King describing his dream. "I have a dream," he had repeated, over and over, and he had described the kind of America he longed for, ached for, where people would be judged for who they were, not by the color of their skin. "Free at last!" he had cried at the end. "Free at last! Thank God Almighty, we are free at last!" And it had seemed that day that it was going to happen. But now John Kennedy was gone. Did anyone else care enough about the dream?

❦

Gene had come out of the library and was walking across the University of Utah campus when he saw a friend of his from high school. "Hey, Mark," he said, but immediately he knew that something was wrong.

"They've shot President Kennedy," Mark said.

"What? Who has?"

"I don't know."

"Is he dead?"

"They're saying it's 'very grave'—stuff like that."

Gene hurried on to the Union Building, where lots of students had gathered in a lounge around a television set. But he could see immediately that the news was bad. People were crying, even some of the guys. Two girls were clinging to each other, sobbing.

Some guy Gene didn't know turned toward him and said, "He's dead."

"Who did it? Does anyone know?"

"No. Kennedy was in a convertible. And there were shots fired. They took him to a hospital, but he was hit in the head. There was nothing they could do for him."

Tears filled Gene's eyes. He hadn't liked Kennedy, but the man was the president, and someone had shot him. There was something so wrong with that.

"What's-his-name—that guy from Texas—will be the president now."

"Lyndon Johnson." Gene thought of that big, awkward man with the slow speech, the Texas drawl. However little Gene liked Kennedy, he was classy, with that great smile and those expensive suits. He also had a way of talking about America that could fire Gene up, almost in spite of himself. After his last State of the Union speech, Gene's dad had said, "I wish we had a Republican who could speak like that."

And Mom liked his good looks. "You don't know what I really did once I got inside that voting booth," she had told Alex. "What do you think a woman is going to do when she has to choose between him and Richard Nixon?"

Gene went home. He was finished with his classes for the day, but he heard, later, that all classes had been called off anyway. In fact, America was shutting down. Ball games and plays and concerts were being canceled—almost everything was. The nation was taking a collective breath, and in a strange way, people were turning to each other. No one talked of anything else. All the television networks stopped their programming, speaking only of "developments," "reactions," "funeral arrangements."

Gene sat with his mother and watched the news. The kids all came in, let out of school early, and they, too, were quiet and upset. Little Kenny, only seven, kept asking, "Why did somebody shoot him, Mom?" and when she couldn't give an answer, he would wait a while and then ask again.

Later in the afternoon the announcement came that a man had murdered a policeman in Dallas and then had been apprehended by the police, but now there was speculation that he was the assassin who had killed the president. Lee Harvey Oswald was his name, but no one knew anything about him. Was he a Communist? a psychotic?

When Dad came home, he sat down on the couch next to Gene and put his hand on Gene's shoulder. But he was listening to the latest information that was coming in on Oswald, and he didn't say anything.

When the report was over, Gene said, "I've been thinking all afternoon about this, Dad. It's a terrible thing, but maybe it's what was supposed to happen. Maybe he was taking us in the wrong direction, and—"

"Don't say that, Gene. Let's not do that."

"I just mean—"

"I know. But let's not do that. He's our president."

"Dad, I feel bad. I feel terrible. I'm not saying that. It's not like I'm celebrating. I'm just trying to find something good in it."

"Don't find anything good. We're sinking fast when people behave this way."

Mom said, from across the room, "It doesn't sound like this Oswald was doing this for an organization. He sounds like a loner."

Gene had dreamed so long about being president that he sometimes thought it was his destiny. And he wondered now how it would feel to know that every time he stepped out into the open, or rode in an open car, he would be in danger of being attacked by some nut.

"I made a decision today," Dad said quietly.

"What's that?" Gene asked.

"I'm going to run for Congress. I know I've talked about it for a long time. But today I decided. It just seems like nothing else is as important right now."

"Alex," Anna said, "that scares me. Our lives would change so much. I don't like the idea of taking our family to Washington."

"I know. And that's what we always say. But today it doesn't seem to matter whether it's the most convenient choice."

"You'll win, Dad," Gene said. "I know you will."

"I think I can. But it's going to be tough on our family. A campaign for Congress is ten times harder than what we've been through with these local campaigns."

Joey and Sharon and Kurt were all spread out on the floor in front of the TV. Joey, who was now sixteen, rolled over and looked at his dad. "I don't want to move," he said.

"I know. I don't blame you. But if I do win, we'll have some interesting experiences. There are nice places to live back there, outside Washington. You'd make plenty of friends."

"But there aren't any Mormons," Sharon said. "Would we even have MIA and stuff like that?"

"Oh, sure. Of course there are Mormons. We might have to drive a little farther to church, but that's all."

"I don't want to think about this right now," Anna said. "I feel bad enough already."

"I know. But I want you all to understand. I don't even want to be a congressman. I'd rather stay here. But good people have to do what they can to make this country work."

Gene thought about that for a time, and then he said, "We need more Republicans in Congress if we're ever going to stop some of this stuff that Kennedy wanted to do. He's the one who always thought the government ought to step into everyone's lives and take over."

Alex leaned back on the couch. The TV was still rumbling with the same news, repeated over and over, with only rare additions. "Well . . . yes," he said. "But I hate politics. I hate this whole business of having to fight for things you don't care about, or don't believe in, just because your party is behind it. I guess I should know better than to think I can be different, but I'd like to go to Washington and forget which party I belong to. I just want to do what's right for the country, and I'll tell you something: Kennedy started some things that *do* need to be finished."

"Like what?" Gene asked.

"I don't want to make a welfare state out of the country, but you know what? There are kids in this nation who don't get enough to eat. That's not right, to be as rich as we are, and to let kids go hungry."

"But if you start feeding people, they just—"

"Don't give me the party line, Gene. You know I don't want to see generations raised on welfare. We've already seen what happens to people who are brought up that way. But there's a minimum standard. Kids shouldn't have to pay for the sins of their parents."

"Now you sound like Kennedy."

"Thank you, Gene. I'm honored to hear you say that."

"Dad?"

"I mean it. I disagreed with the man about all kinds of things, but he did believe in fairness, and I'm afraid a lot of people in my own party only want to keep what they've got, not give a kid down in Mississippi a chance to be what he's capable of."

Gene was confused. He had learned certain principles—ideas he believed. He had heard them at Young Republican meetings on campus this year, and he had even heard his dad voice them at political rallies. Now his father was sounding almost like Aunt LaRue, or like Kathy. So what was right? Gene had been reading the newspaper much more lately, and U. S. News and World Report. He planned to sign up for a political science class next quarter. He knew he had to understand a lot of issues that hadn't really interested him until lately. But he hated to think how complex things were turning out to be. Maybe he wasn't smart enough to be president. Maybe no one was.

On television, a newsman was talking about Jackie Kennedy. She had flown on Air Force One back to Washington with her husband's body. Lyndon Johnson—who had already been sworn in as president—had flown with her. The newsman spoke of her stoicism, her grace. He mentioned the children and how this would affect their lives. John Kennedy had always been an abstraction to Gene, a principle he didn't believe in, but now—dead—the thought of his family made him seem a man. He had paid the ultimate price. His family would pay forever. Gene decided that his dad was right—this was no time to think about politics.

As Jackie got off the airplane, the scene was shown live, on television, and Gene watched with his family. President Kennedy's casket was carried to a waiting hearse, and then Jackie appeared, still wearing the suit she had been wearing when her husband had been shot. As she reached for the door handle of the hearse, Gene saw the stain. Her skirt, even her legs, were covered with her husband's blood. Gene looked at his mother, who was crying, with her hands over her face, and he too began to cry.

෴

All day Saturday and Sunday television programming was suspended. Everything was news of the tragedy: interviews with national and international leaders; tributes; details about Oswald; speculation about the future, about Lyndon Johnson as the president; and most painful, scenes from the young president's life. Some were clips from his speeches, his inauguration, his brightest moments, but there were also scenes with his family: at Hyannis, sailing; playing touch football with his brothers; walking with his children.

Kathy watched the TV clips all day. Then the next day, when she came home from Sunday School, she turned the TV on again only to hear the most improbable report she could imagine: there had been a murder on live television. Now all the channels were showing it, over and over. Some guy named Jack Ruby had shot Lee Harvey Oswald as he was being ushered from Dallas police headquarters, on his way to the county jail. Chaos seemed to have been let loose on the nation. Where would it all end?

But in Washington, Jackie Kennedy seemed to Kathy to represent the other side of America: grace under extraordinary pressure, resolution. She marched with her little children at her sides, to the sound of the muffled, black-draped drums. She led the procession to the Capitol Building, where her husband would lie in state. Inside the rotunda, President Johnson approached and silently bid farewell, and then Jackie walked gracefully to the casket, with little Caroline holding her hand. The two knelt by the casket, and Caroline looked up at her mother, as if for guidance. Then Jackie bent forward to kiss the flag-draped casket. Little Caroline reached to touch it. The scene was almost too much for Kathy.

For twenty-one hours, a broad line of mourners, at times forty blocks long, continued to enter the Capitol. Kathy watched them until fairly late and then got up the next morning to see that the line had never ended. A quarter of a million people, the television announcers said, had made their brief visit, passing by the closed casket and moving on.

On Monday schools were closed. Most everything was. Kathy and her family, with the entire nation, watched on television as six gray horses pulled the caisson, carrying President Kennedy's casket from the Capitol, down 17th Street, to St. Matthews Cathedral. Behind the caisson a dark horse, saddled but riderless, was led by a soldier. The boots in the stirrups were turned backward, to represent a fallen warrior. Then came Jacqueline—dressed in black, her face veiled—with Robert and Ted Kennedy at her sides in swallow-tailed coats. With them were dignitaries: Charles de Gaulle, president of France; Prince Phillip of England; Haile Selassie, Emperor of Ethiopia; Chancellor Ludwig Erhard of West Germany, and dozens more. It was a cold, bright day, and as the procession moved slowly forward, Kathy could see hundreds of thousands of people lining the streets.

Just before noon, the nation—and much of the world—paused for five minutes of silence. Kathy bowed her head during most of the time. She wanted to pray, but she felt too hopeless for that at the moment. When she finally looked up, however, the television cameras were showing people on the street, standing, head down, sorrowful, and she found a sense of unity in that. And then, after the silence, Cardinal Cushing performed the requiem mass.

After the funeral, the procession, to the sound of bagpipes, departed on its way across the Potomac to Arlington Cemetery. As the caisson carrying the president passed Jacqueline and her children, John-John—dressed in a little wool coat and short pants—raised his right hand to his dark hair and saluted his father, just the way the soldiers around him had done. Only a few minutes before, a television newsman had mentioned that it was the little boy's third birthday. Kathy had held up pretty well until then, but she sobbed at the sight of little John, and when she looked around, she could see that her whole family was crying. Douglas got up from where he had been sitting on the floor, and he came to Kathy. "It's okay," he said, and he patted Kathy on the shoulder. "President Kennedy's in heaven now. It's a very nice place."

"I know," Kathy told him, and she held him close.

The burial was all a little too formal for Kathy. She didn't like all the cannon and rifle salutes, and the fifty-jet fly-over, but she was touched when she watched Jackie light the eternal flame. Jackie's face was full of pain, but her movements were as dignified as ever. The final moment was in some ways the most painful—the mournful sound of taps resounding across the cemetery, the camera all the while watching Jackie and Bobby and Ted.

Kathy felt as though nothing would ever be the same in her life. But on Wednesday evening, the night before Thanksgiving, the new president spoke to a joint session of Congress and to the nation. He began, in his cumbersome style, addressing himself to his "fellow Americans," and Kathy cringed to hear how ungainly he was. But his words touched her: "All I have I would gladly have given not to be standing here today." He looked somber in his dark suit, and he sounded sincere as he expressed what so many were feeling—that the loss was almost too painful to bear. But his tone was also hopeful. He wanted to honor John Kennedy by carrying on his work. "No memorial or eulogy could more eloquently honor President Kennedy's memory," he said, "than the earliest possible passage of the civil rights bill for which he fought. We have talked for one hundred years or more. It is time now to write the next chapter and write it in the books of law." He spoke of education "for all our children," "jobs for all who seek them," and "equal rights for all Americans, whatever their race or color."

It sounded like the dream.

In the end, President Johnson reminded the nation of Kennedy's theme: "Let us begin." Then he announced his own: "Let us continue." He pronounced the word like the rural Texan he was—"contin-yuh"— but the sentiment was exactly right, and Kathy was moved. She wasn't going to give up either. She was going to keep fighting.

CHAPTER 16

W hat's the matter?" Gene asked Marsha. She glanced at him with that "you mean you really don't know?" look of hers, but she said nothing.

They were at the Sigma Chi Christmas party, where they had arrived rather late after going out to dinner with some of Gene's fraternity brothers and their dates. Marsha had been unusually quiet all night, and Gene could tell that she wasn't happy, but he had no idea why. They had eaten at the Hibachi, downtown, sitting on the floor in Japanese style. The food had been good, and the group of eight, in a partitioned little room of their own, had had a great time. Gene's friend Mark Waite was in unusually good style, making fun of the Beta boys and all the poor choices they had made for their new pledge class.

"Are you upset about something?"

"How could I be upset? I'm surrounded by all the *elite* of Salt Lake society."

Gene had no idea what to say. The fact was, he thought she was right. Sigma Chi was chock full of the sons of prominent people of the valley. Gene liked that—liked the kind of guys they were. They were young men with goals, going somewhere, but good guys too, who knew how to have fun. The business connections a guy could make in a fraternity like this had to be advantageous, and he liked being around guys who were a lot like himself. What was it with Marsha? She could find a problem with anything he did.

"Come on," he said. "Nobody thinks about being 'elite.' It's just a great group of guys."

"Let's see? How many in your fraternity come from working-class families?"

"I don't know what you call 'working-class,' but not everybody here is rich."

"You're right. I'm not. Now name someone else."

"I'm not going to name names. I'm just saying that you don't have to be rich to get into Sigma Chi."

"What do you have to be?"

"I don't even know what you mean. You can tell they pick guys who were good students in high school, and leaders, athletes—stuff like that. They just look for quality people."

"Of course. That's the whole point—collect 'the best' together, so you can look down on everyone else."

"It's not like that. It's just . . . I don't know. It's . . . fun."

Gene and Marsha were standing in the middle of the frat house living room. Music was playing on a stereo—"Moon River," a song Gene loved. He wondered whether anyone was going to dance. He would have liked to hold Marsha close and not get into another one of their "disputes." But Mark and his date, a girl named Madeleine Ferrell, walked over to them. "Hey, let's put on some *good* music," Mark said, "and do some *stompin'*." He started doing some rather awkward little bounce steps, with his arms held stiff in front of him.

Gene laughed. "You're a terrible dancer, Mark—worse than me."

"That's what I tell him," Madeleine said. "If he had done something like that at Olympus High, we would have kicked him out, just for looking so stupid."

Mark grinned. "You people just don't know sophistication when you see it. When I dance, I try to look like a butler holding a tray—and not spilling anything."

Madeleine laughed at that description. But then she began to dance. She was wearing a long dress with a straight skirt, but she knew how to do "the Swim," and she really got into it. All the while, she didn't take her eyes off Gene. She had short, snappy hair and brilliant eyes, big dimples. Gene found himself wishing he were with her—or at least someone like her.

"Marsha, do you know how to stomp?" Mark asked. "Or is that too silly for you?"

"Hey, she can really dance," Gene said for her.

"I thought she spent her whole life reading books."

"You ought to try a book sometime, Mark," Marsha said. "It's always that first one that's the most difficult."

"Ooh, oooh. She got you," Madeleine said. She stopped dancing and gave Mark a punch.

But Mark took it all in good humor. "You're wrong. I read a book already. It was that story about Dick and Jane. And Spot. There's a lot more to Spot than meets the eye, you know. I think he's a symbol of all that's wrong with our blemished world."

"Oh, brother," Madeleine said. She grabbed him and pulled him away. "Let's go see what they've got to drink."

Marsha turned toward Gene when they were gone, and he could see that she was steaming. "Would you rather not stay?" he asked her.

"How did you guess?"

Gene made up his mind. He would take her home, dump her off on her front porch, and never see her again. She didn't like his friends, his life, his choices. So what was the point?

Gene had to chase Mark down to tell him he was leaving, that the other six would have to ride home together in the same car. Mark said okay, and then, with a tone of understanding, "Hey, I'm sorry; I could tell things weren't going well." The only thing Gene felt bad about was that his evening was over, and he would rather have stayed for the party.

But Marsha surprised him a little as they walked out into the cold of the parking lot. "I'm sorry, Gene. I really am," she said.

"Sorry for what?"

"That I've ruined your night. Next time, take someone like Madeleine."

"You mean some *stupid* girl who doesn't know any better than to have a good time?"

Marsha didn't say anything. But after Gene opened the door for her and came around to get in on his side, he looked at Marsha and realized she was crying. He hadn't meant to hurt her. She was always slamming him; he had figured she could take a shot herself.

"I'm sorry, Marsha," Gene said. "I was just . . . I don't know." He couldn't think what he wanted to say. "But you really don't like Madeleine. I could see that. And I don't understand why. She's a nice girl."

"I'm sure she is."

Gene had no idea what else there was to say. He started the car and drove from the parking lot. Marsha didn't live very far away, and he decided to take her straight home. But as he was driving south on Thirteenth East, just approaching Westminster College, Marsha said, "Let's just go for a little ride, okay?"

"Why? What's the point?"

Gene had never treated Marsha this way, had never dared, but now that he had made up his mind about her, he saw no reason to prolong the evening.

"I just want to talk to you for a few minutes."

So Gene turned east and headed up toward Foothill Drive. Marsha didn't speak for a time, but Gene felt no need to help her out.

"Gene, don't you ever ask yourself whether there isn't something basically wrong with the idea of a fraternity or sorority?"

"No. I've wanted to be in Sigma Chi since I was in junior high. I was thrilled to get in."

"Tell the truth. You *knew* you would get in. You're exactly what Sigma Chi looks for."

"Thank you. That's a very nice thing to say."

"Why do people want to band together in groups and then look down their noses at everyone who's not 'good enough' for them?"

"What were you doing when you told Mark that he didn't read books? You were telling him, not very subtly, that you're better than he is because you're a reader."

"He started it. He was making fun of me because I *do* like books."

"He was just teasing. When you fired back at him, you hit way too hard. But he took it like a man. Mark's a very smart guy. He reads plenty. He just doesn't announce to the world that he's superior to everyone."

"Is that what I do?"

"Yes."

Marsha seemed to take that one "like a man" herself. She was quiet for a time. "I guess I do act like that," she eventually said. "But it's mostly when I'm around your friends. I get so tired of the whole scene. Everyone has money and straight teeth and beautiful clothes and nice cars, but no one seems to *care* about much of anything."

"Hey, what do you want us to do? Sit around and talk about 'world problems'?"

"Why not? You're *college students*, for crying out loud."

"Oh, come on, Marsha. On a Saturday night?"

"I'll tell you something that bothers me even more. We're almost all Mormons, but I don't hear anyone say a thing about that. The only mention is when some guy says he's going on his mission next year—almost as though it's something he *has* to do. Some of those guys who were drinking tonight—in the back of the room—are planning to go on missions next year."

"I don't drink. None of my close friends do."

"But you know the truth. Drinking is a big part of what fraternities are all about. How does that make sense for you Mormon guys to be involved with something like that?"

"Hey, there's a lot of drinking everywhere. In the business world, a guy will always be attending cocktail parties. That doesn't mean he has to do it himself."

"A lot of the drinking in the frat houses is by kids who are under age. And that's illegal. I would think you guys would have higher values than that."

Gene knew that was right. He had thought the same thing himself. But once again, Marsha always had to make a federal case out of everything. University people all knew there was plenty of underage drinking going on at frat parties, and no one ever said anything about it.

"Here's what I don't understand about you, Gene. I can't find anything you stand for. You're nice. You're fun. But the world's just a game to you. You know that you want to win, but you don't know what the prize is—or what the contest is all about."

"That's not true. Maybe I was mostly that way in high school, but I'm not anymore." The car heater was running warmer than necessary now, and Gene reached over and pushed the lever over.

"Tell me how you've changed, Gene. Because I don't see it. You read the paper once in a while—is that it?"

Gene felt some air go out of him. He had made a lot out of that, maybe, telling himself—and Marsha—that he was getting more involved with issues these days, when in truth, he didn't read all that much. But he knew he had changed in some ways. They were approaching the university again now, and he had planned to make the loop back to Marsha's house, but he did have some things he wanted to say, so he drove down the hill toward town. "I got recruited for sports a lot, Marsha, by a lot of colleges. My phone was ringing all the time there for a while. You were over at my house sometimes. You know what it was like."

"I'm sorry, but I don't understand what you're trying to say."

"It was tempting. I wanted to play. Dad and I had talked it over, and we had decided it was more important that I do well in school. But when everyone's after you to play, and all your buddies tell you that you should, it would have been easy to go for the glory one more time. But I didn't do it. I want to be a good student, and that's where I'm putting all my emphasis now."

"Okay. I respect that. But for you, doing well in school means getting good grades."

"What does it mean to you?"

"I thought it had something to do with learning."

"You're right. I'm evil. I ought to forget my grades and strive for a life of poverty."

"Gene, this isn't worth talking about. Why don't you just take me home? Then you can go back to the house and make eyes at Madeleine. I saw the way she was looking at you."

Gene just shook his head. He had no idea what that had to do with anything. At Nineteenth East he turned south. Now he really was going to take her home.

The two drove for at least a minute before Marsha finally said, "I shouldn't have said that. It was stupid. But I saw you two looking at each other when she was dancing, and it was obvious to me—as I'm sure it was to you—that you were with the wrong girl."

There was certainly an insult imbedded in that, even though Marsha probably didn't see it that way, but Gene was not going to fight back. He knew, at some basic level, that Marsha was right about him. He could also admit to himself that he didn't like some of the attitudes he noticed in his fraternity brothers. Sometimes he looked forward to his mission, to a time when the emphasis on clothes and coolness wasn't so important.

"Look, I know religion ought to play a bigger part in our lives," he finally said. "But everyone's still pretty young."

Marsha laughed, rather sadly. "I know exactly what you're telling me. It's what my dad always says—that I'm way too old for my age."

"Don't you think he has a point?"

Marsha didn't answer for a long time, but when she did, the words hit Gene hard. "I like to have fun, Gene. But somewhere along the line, I started listening to what they told us at church. I started reading my scriptures. I can't remember one time when Christ said that the important thing in life was to run around with the 'right' crowd. And when he talked about money, it was almost always to warn people how dangerous it was."

Gene had had it. He turned east, back up the hill toward Marsha's home. He didn't doubt that she was right about him, but what gave her the right to act so high and mighty? He was no different from his friends, and they were all good guys.

Gene walked Marsha to the door, and on the porch, he only said, "Well, I'll see you."

"Gene, I'm sorry," Marsha said. "I know you hate me now. And I don't blame you. I'm not a good enough person to criticize anyone else. It just seems like we all ought to be better than we are. The gospel ought to make more of a difference than it seems to."

"Maybe so. But people might look worse than they really are when you spend all your time standing back, watching for faults."

"I guess maybe that is what I do."

She was looking down, seeming crushed, and he was sorry. Too much of what she had said was right. But he had burned his bridges now, and he couldn't think what to do about it. "Well . . . I'll see you," he said, and he stepped off the porch. He heard the door open, glanced back to make sure she had gotten in safely, and then walked to his car. But he knew what he had heard, just before the door had shut. She was crying.

He thought of going back and knocking on the door. But he still didn't know what he could say, so he started his car and drove away. He headed for home, at first, but then he decided he didn't want to do that. He didn't want to come in early and have to explain to his parents what had happened. So he drove down to State Street and then out State all the way to Murray. He bought himself a cheeseburger and a cherry Coke at an Arctic Circle, and he sat in the car and ate all by himself.

❧

On Christmas Eve Katrina had bought a few extra things for Christmas dinner. She had had to save her money carefully and then stand in line for a long time. Hans got paid next to nothing, but he saved what he could, and he had bought his little sister a dress that she could wear to church. The family had returned from their failed attempt to escape the country with almost nothing. Inga had had to wear an old dress to church lately, one that was faded and worn and too small for her. She hadn't complained about it, but Hans knew how embarrassed she was. He had bought her a simple little blue dress, and he could hardly wait for her to see it. He hadn't gotten anything for his parents; they had told him not to. They also apologized that Hans would receive nothing, but everyone thought it most important that there be something for Inga.

But then Papa surprised everyone. He came home smiling. He looked excited, and he was holding a little bag, apparently having bought something. "Katrina, Inga, everyone come here," Papa called. "I have good news."

Inga and then Katrina appeared, pushing through the door from the kitchen. "What is it?" Katrina asked.

Papa smiled, but tears had begun to spill from his eyes. "Work," he said in a whisper. "I've found a better job."

It was impossible. Hans had resigned himself to the reality that Papa would never have respectable work again, and that Hans himself would never do anything but labor with his hands. But here was Papa, beaming, as though he had found a fine position.

Katrina ran to him and threw her arms around him. "Oh, Peter, what a Christmas gift! How did you find it?"

"It was Günther Knopf. I always knew he was my best hope."

"But how, Peter?"

"Sit down. Let me tell you."

Peter sat in his chair, and Inga and Katrina joined Hans on the couch across from him. "After those years that I worked with Günther, in the same office, he was moved upstairs to the accounting department. A few weeks ago, I heard that he had been made the manager of the office. I went by to talk to him, and at first he seemed interested in hiring me. But when I went back, he had changed entirely. I'm sure some government official had told him that he couldn't hire me. But we talked a little that day about religion. He told me that it was a mistake to identify oneself with a religion these days, and I merely told him that I couldn't deny what I believed. I didn't know what he thought about that. He was quite solemn, it seemed, and then he shook my hand and wished me good luck. I thought that was the end of it.

"But yesterday, when I went by the employment office after work, I found a notice for me to contact him. I went to see him, and he told me that he was still trying to get me approved. He must have told some of his leaders that I was a good man—or something of that sort. Or maybe he can't find anyone with the right sort of background. Sometimes the government looks the other way when a person is badly needed. All I know is that he asked me to come back this morning, and when I did, he told me I had the job. I can start on Monday. And then he said, 'I wanted to tell you today. I wanted you to have a nice Christmas.'"

"Is he religious himself?"

"I don't know. But I know he was raised in the *Evangelisch* church. I suspect he still believes in God, no matter what impression he gives his bosses."

"Oh, Peter, it's too good to be true." Katrina went to him again, knelt in front of him, and put her head on his knees.

"I bought a few little presents," he said. "I wanted to do that."

"But I have nothing for you."

"You have *everything* for me. You've put up with so much because of me."

"Papa, is it a good job?" Hans asked, and he wanted so badly to believe that the gift was complete, that his father would have a chance to better himself, finally, according to his talents.

But Peter said, "No, Hans. Not really. There's enough responsibility, that's certain, but the pay is poor, and it always will be. Günther assured me that I'll never have a chance to advance in the office, or to make much of a salary—but it's *much* better than what I've been receiving from the city."

"It's not fair."

"No. It's not. But it's better than what we've had. And it gives me a little pride back. I can't tell you how awful this last year has been."

"We know," Katrina said. "It's been hard for all of us, but hardest for you."

Peter looked over at Inga. "Things will be a little better for you now," he said. "We'll get you a new coat as soon as we can, and I know you need a better dress for school."

There was something a little cagey in Papa's look. He knew, of course, that Hans had bought a dress for Inga. But Inga seemed perfectly satisfied with the hope of a new dress before much longer.

"God's opened the way for us," Peter said. "And that's because we're doing what he wants us to do. We need to do everything we can to build his kingdom right here—even though we're so cut off from other members of the Church. A door has opened for us now; I just feel sure that if we keep our covenants with the Lord, other doors will also open."

Peter was looking at Hans, and Hans knew this was a speech for him. But Hans felt no confidence in any of it. He sat with the family for a time, but then he slipped away to his own room.

Papa had a dead-end job in an office. That was his "great" blessing. The pay would be better than he had been getting, but life would still be hard. And what of Hans's life? He had wanted a prestigious career, success he could take pride in. Without an *Oberschule* education, however, what chance would he ever have for that? Papa seemed to think that serving in the Church would make up for everything else. But Hans couldn't see it. He had told himself many times lately that he was going to stop going to church, but it was too late for a break like that with his family to do him any good in his career, and he knew how much pain it would cause his mother and father, even Inga. So he continued to attend, but he didn't feel "the Spirit" that Father always talked about, didn't enjoy all the long talks and the teary-eyed testimonies. The only thing in the Church that interested him a little was Greta, and he hadn't written to her in a long time. What could he tell her?

He lay back on his bed, and he looked, as he often did, at the scars on his right hand. The cuts he had received under the dock in Gdansk had never healed right. His palm was streaked with scar tissue, some of it still red. It was difficult for him to open his hand all the way. The scars were symbolic now—a lifetime reminder of what he had reached for, and what he had actually been allowed to grasp.

CHAPTER 17

Diane sat at the same table for lunch every day. She would try to get to the lunchroom as fast as she could when her third-period class let out, because the line was always long. She really wished she could leave the school, maybe walk down to Judy's Ice Cream for some sort of snack, but that wasn't allowed. Some high-school principals weren't so strict about that, but at Ogden High she had to buy lunch tickets every week, walk through the line, and get whatever the cafeteria was serving that day—no other choices. "Federal lunch," everyone called it, which she hadn't understood at first, but her dad said that the government provided money to the schools for the food, and that reduced the price to the student. But it wasn't *that* cheap—thirty-five cents—and the food, most of the time, was terrible. Teachers were assigned to monitor the room, mainly because food fights were always breaking out, but all the kids said that was only because the food was so sickening that they would rather throw it than eat it. Diane hated that kind of stupidity. She didn't want people throwing food on her clothes. Still, she dumped most of her lunch in the garbage every day.

Today was the worst. About once every two weeks the lunch ladies served pizza. But it was not anything like the stuff you could buy down at Rigo's on Washington Boulevard. This stuff was as thick as a casserole and tasted like rancid ketchup. Just the smell of it made Diane sick. She told the lunch lady she didn't want any, but she got a hunk of the stuff anyway. The only thing she could stand to eat was the slice of bread that came with it and the three carrot sticks. But that was all right. She was always trying to lose a pound or two, and it was easier to resist food when it was something she hated so much.

Diane and Becky Burton reached the table first, but they didn't have to worry about anyone grabbing it. All the students knew their own tables and pretty much sat in the same places every day. On the north side of the cafeteria, the third long table from the end, was where the popular sophomore girls sat. The girls at the table called themselves friends—that was all—and not one of them would have said that there was anything exclusive about the table, but everyone knew. It wasn't as though girls would get sent away if they tried to intrude, but Diane had seen some try to edge in, through a friend, or something of that sort, and after a while just give it up. It wasn't hard to tell who was really welcome and who wasn't. Just keeping up with the dress standards was tough enough, and some girls seemed to wilt under the pressure.

Diane was wearing a Scandinavian ski sweater on this cold February day, with a looping pattern in blues and gray from the shoulders across the front. With it she was wearing her dark blue box-pleated skirt, which picked up one of the colors in the sweater. She liked the way she looked with her hair down, but she hated how early she had to get up to wash her hair and get it dried.

"Diane, you look soooo cute today," Becky told her. "That new boy in English was watching you the whole hour."

"Oh, he was not."

"Don't tell me. I practically fell out of my seat trying to get him to look at me, but he was 'eyes right' the whole time."

"Really? I didn't notice that."

"Now tell me another lie."

Diane smiled and winked. "I can't believe how cute he is. Scott's his name—Scott Laughlin. I said hi to him this morning, and he gave me this little smile and said, 'Hey, how yuh doin,' and his head sort of wobbled." She tried to make the motion with her own head.

"I think he looks like that one Wilson brother, in the Beach Boys. His hair is kind of sun-bleached, don't you think?"

Carol Wyatt and Janet Torgeson sat down next to Diane and Becky. "I know who you're talking about," Carol said, "and I think he bleaches it. Guys from California do that. Everyone tries to *look* like a surfer, even the ones who don't go near the water."

"Scott does surf. He told me," Diane said.

"Where? In the Great Salt Lake?"

"No. I mean, he did surf—before he moved here. I asked him, and he said he did."

"What else is he going to say?"

"I'm not eating this stuff. It makes me sick," Becky said. She slid her metal tray away from her, toward Diane, and leaned her chin on her hands. "I'll tell you this much. I don't care whether he can surf or not. I'd sure like to see him in some swimming trunks."

"Becky!" Janet said. "You're bad."

But Diane whispered, "Me too." And then she added, "He's slender and everything, but if you look at his arms, you can see he's got muscles."

"You know what I love?" Becky said. "It's that little-boy smile of his. He's like the puppy who followed you home. He's just too adorable to send away."

"Are you going to *keep* him?" Janet asked. "Maybe he'll lick your face."

"Janet! You're the one who's being bad. Don't talk about me."

"I wouldn't be bad with him," Janet said. "But I sure would like to find out if he knows how to kiss."

"Like you know so much about it."

"You don't know how many guys I've kissed," Janet said. "I don't brag the way you do."

"I haven't kissed *anyone*," Diane said. "That's what I brag about."

Janet was the only one eating her pizza, even though she was the girl at the table who had told Diane, over and over, that she had to lose weight.

The table was filling up now as more and more girls arrived. Carol looked down the table and said, "Diane's bragging about never being kissed."

"Maybe no one's ever tried," someone from the other end of the table yelled.

From the next table, where an in-crowd of sophomore boys sat, a deep voice said, "Hey, Diane, if you want to get started, I'm available evenings—or all day on weekends."

Diane knew the voice: Clair Winkler, who played on the basketball team. He was a funny guy, and not awful looking—except for some serious complexion problems—but he wasn't anyone Diane wanted to waste her first kiss on. She ignored the remark and looked over at Janet. "You know what I love is the way his hair falls down in front. He flips it back every now and then, but it droops right back down again."

"Are you talking about *Clair?*"

"No. *Scott.* The new boy."

"Oh, I know. And I like how shy he is."

"Why did he move here anyway?" Carol asked. "Is he a Mormon?"

Diane shrugged. No one seemed to know. "If he's not, maybe I can do some missionary work," Diane said. She winked. "I think I might have the power of conversion in me."

"The way he was looking at you," Becky said, "I think he might eat from your hand."

The truth was, Diane had already thought about all that. She had a feeling that maybe he wasn't LDS, although she didn't know exactly why she thought so. She had hoped, from the first time he had shown up in her class, that she could go out with him sometime, but she had wondered whether it was a good idea to date a boy who might have values that weren't the same as hers. Still, her parents always talked about not judging people by whether they were Church members, and that seemed only fair. Maybe he didn't look all that much like James Dean, but there was something rather sly about that little smile.

"Remember," Janet was saying, "he's in my homeroom, and I saw him first. I even called 'dibs' on him."

"We'll see who *he* calls dibs on," Becky said. "I might trip and fall down in front of him, if I can't get him to look at me any other way." She shook her long hair the way models did in television ads. "Maybe he likes red hair."

But Diane didn't make any claims. She *had* felt him watching her today, long before Janet had mentioned it. She had a notion she might win this little contest.

A couple of days later Mrs. Mathis gave a pop quiz in English class. It was ten questions about *The Red Badge of Courage*. Diane had hated the book. It was all so slow and complicated to read. At the end of the quiz, Mrs. Mathis asked the students to exchange papers and mark the answers. The way she assigned rows, it worked out that Diane was exchanging with Scott.

Diane always did her homework, and she had read the book—as little as she liked it. She answered the questions easily. She wondered about Scott. Was he smart or not? As it turned out, his writing was neat, and his answers were pretty good. He had gotten eight out of ten. But the other two answers were clearly guesses. When the marking was finished, Diane turned to Scott. "Well, you missed a couple," she said.

"You didn't," he said. "You got every one."

"It was pretty easy."

That cute smile appeared. "I only read the Monarch Notes," he said. "It's harder to keep the plot straight when you only read an outline."

Diane laughed. There was something so carefree about the way he admitted to all that. "Don't you like to read?" she asked.

"I *love* to read. But not that kind of stuff."

"What do you read?"

"*Catcher in the Rye* is the best book ever written. I've read it about six times."

Diane hadn't read it, but she had heard about it. It had a lot of bad language in it, that was one thing she knew. "I don't read that much, myself," Diane said. "I like to go *do* things, not just hear about made-up people."

"Hey, I'm with you there," he said. "What do you like to do?"

His smile seemed downright suggestive, but she ignored that. "Ski," she said.

"Now that's something I want to start, but I haven't done it yet."

"Maybe I can show you how."

"How to what?" The smile had turned sly again.

"Ski."

"Oh, that too."

"I won't teach you if you're not nice."

"Oh, trust me. I'm very, very nice."

Mrs. Mathis was trying to get the students to be quiet now and turn their attention back to her. Diane whispered, as a parting shot, "My mother warned me about boys like you."

That was actually true. Diane had a feeling she had better let this go; he was a little too direct. But she knew she was blushing, and she didn't want him to see that. Maybe she wasn't going to date him, but she didn't want him to think she was a stupid little girl.

Mrs. Mathis was talking about Stephen Crane, about the meaning of the book. The only thing Diane was sure of was that Henry Fleming was scared to death when people started shooting at him. She didn't have to read a whole book to figure that out.

When class finally ended, Diane decided to play things a little cool. She turned toward Becky and said, "We'd better hurry to lunch before the line gets long."

That was nothing she needed to say. She and Becky always hurried to lunch. But it got her turned away from Scott. The only trouble was, she could see in Becky's eyes that someone was behind her, and then she felt the tap on her shoulder.

"So when are you going to teach me to ski?"

"Were you serious about that?"

"Sure I was."

"I'm no teacher. You probably ought to take some lessons from one of those professional guys up at Snowbasin."

"Just show me the basics and I'll catch on. I had no trouble learning to surf."

Suddenly Becky was next to her saying, "We could teach you. A lot of us go on Saturdays. You could rent skis and go with us."

"I'll buy equipment this week. My mom already told me I could. And I can drive, too. Diane, do you want to ride up with me and show me where to meet everyone?"

Diane wouldn't have agreed if Becky hadn't tried so hard to make her own move on the guy. It just felt good to show her which one he really wanted to be with. "Sure," she said.

"What time do you go?"

"We try to be up there by nine-thirty or so. Some people come later."

"Should I pick you up at nine?"

"Okay."

"Good." And then he unleashed that boyish smile of his. "Hey, it's a date. I'm excited."

He walked away, and Diane had forgotten about hurrying to lunch.

"Diane, why do boys *always* fall for you?" Becky asked. "It's like they see all that blonde hair of yours and they're blinded to anything else."

"All I'm going to do is show him how to ski. What are you talking about?" She smiled triumphantly.

By the time Diane got home that night, she wasn't feeling quite so satisfied about her little conquest. Her parents knew she skied most Saturdays, but they also knew the kids she went with. Most of her closest friends were still too young to drive, but there were enough older boys who could get their family cars that she usually had a ride. What Diane knew was that sometime between now and Saturday, her parents would want to know how she was getting to Snowbasin. They worried about who drove and whether it was someone who knew how to handle snow. Some of the sophomore girls were turning sixteen, getting their driver's licenses, but Mom and Dad didn't want some "new driver" negotiating the roads on a snowy morning.

Diane decided to take on the questions now and see what happened, but as it turned out, Dad had to stay at the college late for some sort of meeting, and Mom had papers she had to read. "Will you fix sandwiches—or something—for us?" Bobbi asked Diane. "If I don't get these papers read tonight, my students are going to shoot me."

Diane was a little annoyed by that. Mom hadn't taught during fall quarter, but she had taken on a couple of classes for winter term. It didn't make sense to Diane, not while Ricky was still so little. When Mom had finished her dissertation, Diane had thought the worst was over, but now she wouldn't even take a year or two off to be home. She was always trying to juggle her schedule around nursing the baby, running back and forth to the college, hiring baby-sitters—or recruiting Diane to take over. Diane worshiped little Ricky, but she didn't think her mother was being fair. Still, she figured it couldn't hurt her cause to be cooperative tonight. "Sure," she said, "I can figure something out. I've got my homework done already, so I have time."

Mom gave her an exaggerated glance as if to say, "What's with you tonight?" but what she said was, "If you make sandwiches, do a couple for your dad, too. I'm not sure when he'll be home." That first skeptical glance had irritated Diane, but she opened a can of tuna fish, mixed it up with some mayonnaise, and threw together some sandwiches. She also got out some chips and cut some carrot sticks, so Mom would see that she had made a bit of an effort.

Maggie only ate her potato chips and a bite or two of her sandwich and then took off, and Mom took a sandwich with her to her bedroom, where she was working on her papers. Diane watched Ricky, even though Mom hadn't really asked her to. He was in a happy mood, as usual, though, so she played with him on the living-room floor while she watched "Leave It to Beaver" and then "Have Gun, Will Travel." When her dad came home, he said he also had papers to grade, and he took his sandwiches and disappeared into his office in the basement. At that point, Diane gave up. After all her good efforts, this was turning out to be a bad night to say anything.

But a little later, when Ricky finally started to fuss, Mom came out of her bedroom and nursed him, and then she put him down for the night. When she returned, she said, "Honey, Maggie's going to bed now. Why don't you get your dad and we'll have family prayer."

Diane walked to the top of the stairs and yelled, "Dad. Family prayer!"

"Honey, I could have done that. You know he turns his music on and he can't hear a thing down there."

Diane didn't know why it was her job to hike down the stairs, but she did it without complaining, and then, after they had all gathered in the living room, knelt by the couch and had their prayer, she asked herself whether the time would be right after all. She was trying to think how to bring up the subject without making it seem like a big deal when Bobbi said, "Listen, I absolutely have to spend Saturday morning over at my office at the college. That's the only way I'm going to get these term papers read. I fell asleep tonight before I got the third one done. The baby kept me up half the night last night. I'm just dead."

Maggie headed off to bed, but Diane waited, stood facing her parents. "I'll be here," Dad said. "But I've got some projects around the house I wanted to work on. I wouldn't be much help with the baby. Are you going to be around, Di?"

"Well . . . I was planning to go skiing."

"That's fine," Bobbi said. "I already called Mrs. Long. She's going to take Ricky."

Diane was suddenly relieved, but she was still trying to think how to ask her question when Dad said, "Diane, do you have a ride up to Snowbasin?"

"Yeah. I do. No problem."

"Okay. Well, don't worry about it then, Bobbi. But I could pick Ricky up at noon and take care of him the rest of the day. That way you could spend the whole day at your office. If you could get those papers finished, it would take a lot of pressure off you."

Diane wondered what her dad was saying. Mom had been rather cranky lately, and Dad seemed almost scared of her. Diane hoped she would never put that kind of pressure on her husband when she got married. But Mom was saying she thought she could finish by noon, if she started early, and that seemed the end of the matter.

Diane was beginning to think she was home free when Dad asked, "Who's driving on Saturday, Diane?"

"Well . . . a lot of the kids are going. There are quite a few cars." She hesitated. "It looks like I'm going to ride with a new guy at our school. His name's Scott Laughlin."

"Who's he?"

"What do you mean?"

"Do we know his family?"

"No. Like I said, he's new." Diane took a couple of steps toward the hall to her bedroom. She was trying hard to seem casual about the whole thing.

But Bobbi was suddenly paying attention. "New from where?"

Diane stopped. She hated this kind of stuff. "California."

"Where do they live?"

"I don't know, Mom. But he's a nice boy. And he's got a driver's license."

"I'll bet he's never driven in snow," Dad said. He and Mom were standing next to each other now, shoulder to shoulder. They were like a rock wall.

"He's lived here for a while now, and he drives to school. We've had some storms."

"But you get on that curvy road to Snowbasin and you'd better know what you're doing."

"Dad, the weather's fine. The roads will be dry."

"What did you say his name was?" Bobbi asked.

"Scott Laughlin."

"What does his dad do?"

"Mom! How in the world would I know that?"

"Well, I just feel that you ought to know people before you start running around with them. Is this a date, or will there be other people with you?"

Diane glanced away. "If some other kids need a ride, they could go with us. I'm sure he wouldn't care."

"Diane, don't do that. It's a date, isn't it?"

Diane let her breath blow out, deciding not to fight back. She was losing this one fast. "He wants to learn how to ski. I told him I'd help him, and Becky told him the same thing. He just asked me to ride up with him, that's all."

"But he didn't ask Becky, did he?"

"No, Mom, he didn't."

"Is he LDS?"

"I don't know."

"Diane, what are you thinking? You ought to know a boy better than that before you agree to go out with him."

"Well, maybe some of the things you think I ought to know don't seem so important to me. Every time you went out in high school, did you know what the guy's dad did for a living?"

Bobbi smiled. "Probably not," she said. "But everyone knew everyone else in my neighborhood. Dad knew every family in Sugar House. The world just seemed a lot safer then."

"This boy is nice, Mom. I think you'd like him." The truth was, Diane wasn't at all sure of that. She just didn't want to be considered stupid.

Bobbi looked at Richard. "What do you think?" she asked.

He stood for a moment, the way he always did. It was not like Dad to reach any decision quickly. He seemed to ponder everything, from brands of toothpaste to what time it was. He would stare at his watch sometimes, as though he wanted the idea of the time to sink deep into his consciousness. "I think I trust Diane's judgment," he said.

It was an amazing answer, one Diane hadn't expected. But she was even more surprised when her mom said, "Well, I do too." Then she looked at Diane. "But honey, let's watch the weather this week. If it is snowy, it might be better to get him in a car with someone else. As far as that goes, you could do that anyway, couldn't you?"

"Maybe. I'm not sure. It depends on who else is driving."

"Why don't you at least check on that."

"Okay." Diane liked this trust, but she also felt some guilt. The boy just might be more dangerous than she was letting on. Maybe her parents were actually wrong to trust her judgment. But that's not what she said. "I think he might not be LDS," she said. "But I was thinking, if all of us are really nice to him, maybe we could get him interested."

Diane should have known when to stop. Mom wasn't buying that one. "I'm sure that's *exactly* what you had in mind when he asked you," she said, with one of her eyebrows cocked.

"Sort of. I mean, I did think about that."

"And tell me this. Does he happen to be *very* cute?"

"Extremely," Diane said, and she finally smiled.

"I thought so," Mom said. "You shouldn't let that enter your head, little girl. It's not important at all." She glanced toward Richard. "I married your dad because he's rock-solid and dependable—even though he's not much to look at."

Richard knew when to show off his own great smile.

"He's just the handsomest man in the world, that's all," Diane said.

Dad came over and kissed Diane on the head, but Mom was saying, "Just make sure he's also as *good* as your father. Then I won't worry about you."

Diane thought about that after she said her own prayer and went to bed. She didn't know much about Scott, but she worried a little about some of the hints he had dropped.

CHAPTER 18

Kathy had an appointment with her guidance counselor at Highland High on a Tuesday afternoon in May, 1964. Her junior year was almost over, and she wanted to find out all she could about scholarship opportunities. She would be applying to a number of eastern liberal arts colleges—and she knew they were expensive. Dad could afford to send her, no doubt, but she liked the idea of making her own way as much as possible.

But Mrs. Brittain had some bad news. "Here's the problem with that, honey," she said. "Those fancy schools use a different system from most colleges. First you have to prove you can get in—and then they find out how much money your parents make. If your family makes a lot, the way I imagine your dad does, they don't offer financial help—not much, anyway."

"I don't understand that," Kathy said. "It should be based on what *I* can do."

"Well, they don't look at it that way."

Kathy was irritated by a lot of attitudes she had run into. She wanted to apply to some of the Ivy League colleges, but those were all men's colleges. There were rumors that some of them might start opening up to women, but it hadn't happened yet. "What about Smith College?" Kathy asked. "Do they give scholarships, just for merit?"

"I doubt it, dear. They would probably consider your family income." Mrs. Brittain smiled. She was an older woman, very traditional, who wore ugly, clunky shoes and walked into school each morning in a black coat and hat. Her hair was gray in streaks, and she didn't pluck her eyebrows, which looked as snarled as a man's. She was leaning forward now with her arms folded under the weight of her expansive bosom. "Oh, honey, why do you want to bother with schools like that? What can you do once you graduate?"

"What do you mean? The same as I'd do after going to any college."

"Think about that, sweetheart. They don't have nursing programs or even give teaching certificates at a lot of them. And you certainly don't go there to go into secretarial work. Yet those three are the occupations open to women."

"Mrs. Brittain, I want to go to law school. All of those schools have pre-law programs. I've looked at their catalogs."

"Are you sure about that?" Mrs. Brittain leaned back in her chair, making it creak. "It's *very* hard for a girl to get into law school, and then even if you do, where are you going to work when you get out? Not many firms want to hire lady lawyers."

"I have some things I want to change in this world, and I think a law degree will help me. I don't care whether a bunch of old fogies want to hire me in their firm."

"What is it you want to *change?*"

"Lots of things. But right now I'm upset about what's happening to Negroes. Everyone says that Congress will pass President Johnson's civil rights law, but I read in *Time* magazine that southern states are already figuring out how to get around it. Southern mayors are saying they'll close their swimming pools rather than let Negroes swim with everyone else. And they—"

"Well, Kathy, you haven't been around Negroes. You might feel different if you'd been down there and seen the way those people live. I wouldn't want to get into a swimming pool with them either."

Kathy was speechless. She sputtered, trying to think what to say, and finally got out: "Who made them live in poverty? Who—"

"Oh, please. Negroes have been using those old excuses too long. The trouble with most of them is that they're too lazy to make a go of it."

"They work twelve hour-days down in Mississippi, picking cotton. How can you call that lazy?"

"No one forces them to pick cotton. They can move away from Mississippi and find a better job if they want to."

Kathy knew this was one of those times when she could explode if she wasn't careful. She let her eyes go shut for a moment, took a breath, and then said, in her most patient tone of voice, "They aren't given a decent education, Mrs. Brittain. Their schools are run-down old shacks. Half the time they don't even have textbooks. That just isn't fair. Can't you see that?"

Mrs. Brittain had crossed her arms over her chest. "That may be," she said. "But a lot of immigrants have come to this country, poor as church mice, and they've made something of themselves. Colored people can do the same thing if they really want to."

Kathy was still trying to breathe slowly and deeply. But her voice had a hard edge when she asked, "Is that what Negroes were, Mrs. Brittain? Immigrants? My history book said they were *property*. It was *illegal* for them to learn to read. Families were broken apart, and every door was closed to them once they got their so-called freedom. But then, I guess you're right. All that doesn't mean we should *swim* in the same pools with them, does it?"

"You get up and walk out of this office, young lady. I'm going to call your parents. You have no right to talk to me that way."

Kathy nodded, but then she said, as calmly as she could, "That's fine, Mrs. Brittain. Call my parents if you want. But I'm going to talk to them too, and to Dr. Doxey. I'm going to tell him what a great *guidance* counselor you are."

Mrs. Brittain was looking concerned now. She held up one hand, her palm forward. "Stop right there," she said. "We were just talking. I wasn't

forcing any of my opinions on you. I just don't happen to believe in socialism."

"Giving a person an even chance is not *socialism*, Mrs. Brittain."
Kathy stood up. "The last I heard, it was called the *American way*." She
walked out and shut the door, hard. But she was shaking, so angry she
could hardly control herself, and already she was thinking of all the other
things she wished she had said. But another thought was overriding everything else. If Mrs. Brittain did call her mom or dad, Kathy would be in for
it again. She would get another lecture about respect, about humility,
about controlling herself. Her parents might not agree with everything
Mrs. Brittain had said, but the maddening thing was, they probably came
closer to that old woman's position than to hers.

Kathy wanted to escape, just get away from school, but she had never
sluffed a class in her life, and she didn't dare start now. It was fourth
period, with only two classes to go; she could stick that out. But as she
neared her classroom, she met the last person in the world she wanted to
see at the moment. It was Val Norris, the boy she had liked for over a year
now, and he was with a friend of his, another senior, Bob Stowell.

"Hey, what's the matter?" Val asked. He stopped in front of her. "Are
you okay?"

Kathy was humiliated. She hadn't realized that she looked so upset.
Val already thought she was "way too intense," as he had told her once.
He had never let on that he knew Kathy had a crush on him, but she
could tell that he knew, and she hated that. It wouldn't be so bad if he
had asked her out, but he hadn't. "Nothing's wrong. I'm fine." She tried
to go on by.

Val took hold of her arm. "You don't sound okay." She loved his
voice, gentle but resonant, and she loved the fact that he was taller than
her, much taller. She felt so gawky around most boys.

"It's nothing. I just got in an argument with Mrs. Brittain."

Both boys, for some reason, thought that was wonderfully funny. They looked at each other and laughed.

Kathy felt the need to defend herself. They obviously thought she was upset over nothing. "I want to go to an eastern college, and she started telling me that I shouldn't. She thinks girls can only be teachers, nurses, or secretaries."

"What else *can* they be?" Bob asked, clearly baffled.

But Val spoke before Kathy could. "Kathy can be anything she wants. She'll probably be in charge of the United Nations or an ambassador, or something like that."

Kathy was touched by Val's confidence. She even liked the way he was looking at her, as though he held her in some special esteem. But then Bob said, "What are you, some big brain?"

"Yeah, she is," Val said. "She knows *everything*."

"No, I don't," Kathy said, and she hated to imagine what Val thought of her, really. What guy ever fell for a girl because she was "brainy"?

Val paid no attention to her denial. Instead, he said, "Hey, come with us. We've got a track meet this afternoon, over at South High."

"I can't do that."

"Sure you can. We have to go change, and then we're going to drive down there ourselves. We don't want to take the bus."

"Will they let you do that?"

"Hey, we're seniors. We're out of here in a couple of weeks. We do what we want." Val was smiling, and he obviously knew very well that Kathy's heart was palpitating, just at the thought of running off from school with him. She even thought she might do it.

"Yeah, come on," Bob said. "We'll let you be on the track team, just to show old Mrs. Brittain what you can do. You can be a lady shot putter, like those big Russian women."

"Shut up," Kathy said, but not with anger. What she felt was sadness. These guys would never understand her.

But Val still had hold of her arm, and he said, almost tenderly, "Don't let Mrs. Brittain get you down, Kathy. Someday she'll brag to people that she knew you when you were in high school." He waited just a moment and then asked again, "So do you want to go with us?"

"No. I'll see you later." And she walked away. She finally understood clearly what she had sensed from Val for quite some time. He liked her, even admired her, but not as a girl. Kathy hadn't revealed the more important subject she had discussed with Mrs. Brittain, and she knew why. Val, and especially Bob, wouldn't have known what she was so upset about.

Kathy walked on past her classroom without realizing she had made a decision. But she wasn't going to any more classes today. She just couldn't. She was hurting too much. She had become some sort of "weirdo," and she didn't know how it had happened. In elementary school she had had lots of friends; she had been very much in the center of things. But during junior high, when she had started to read so much, to think about so many things, she had begun to estrange herself from kids her age. Now, Val—and most everyone else—thought she was brilliant. But they were missing the point. It wasn't that she was smart; it was that she *cared*. Why didn't anyone else seem to care as much? Was it really so strange to feel the way she did? She had some girlfriends—mostly girls from the debate team—but the sad thing was, she was not that comfortable with that group, either. Those girls prided themselves on their intellect, their grades, their personal achievements, but they didn't concern themselves with the things Kathy thought were important.

She walked on down the hallway and then out to the parking lot. She had driven her mother's car that morning. She got in, started it, and then just drove. For fifteen minutes or so she felt sorry for herself, but something closer to disgust began to develop. After all, what had *she* done to change anything? There were horrible things going on right in her own city, and she had never taken a stand. She had talked and talked until people didn't want to hear her anymore, but she had never once joined the real fight.

Suddenly she knew what she wanted to do. She had been driving south on Highland Drive, nearing the Villa Theatre, but she pulled off to the side, made a U-turn, and headed back to Twenty-First South. She was going downtown. Maybe she couldn't pull off a sit-in, the way the brave Negro people were doing in the south, but she could certainly let someone know that not all whites approved of the discrimination that was going on in Salt Lake.

Kathy drove to the Midtown Theater, found a parking place on the street, and then walked to the ticket window. "I need to go inside. I'm not going to a movie. I want to see your manager."

She expected an argument, but the young woman in the booth merely said, "Go ahead. Tell the guy who takes tickets."

"Thank you." Kathy marched to the glass doors, opened them, and looked at a young man in a blue vest. "I want to see your manager."

"What about?"

"That doesn't concern you, sir. I have something I need to talk to him about."

The man grinned. "Well, *excuse* me. I can tell you have *important* business."

"Where do I find him?"

"In his office, I guess. Right down there."

Kathy wasn't at all sure where the man was pointing, but she didn't want to say another word to him. She walked past the candy counter and on to the end of the lobby. There was a door there, and she wasn't sure whether she should knock or just walk in—or whether the door might be a closet. She knew the ticket-taker was still watching her, and she didn't want to look like an idiot, knocking on a closet door, so she tried the doorknob and the door opened. Inside was a desk, where a secretary might have sat, but no one was there. A second door was off to the left of the desk. "Excuse me? Is anyone here?"

"Yeah. What's the trouble?"

Kathy walked to the inner door, but now she didn't know whether she should open this one or not. "I need to talk to you," she called out.

"Sure. Come on in."

Kathy opened the door and looked inside. A man of forty or so was sitting at a mahogany desk in a small but tidy office. He smiled. "Is it time for Girl Scout cookies again already?" he asked.

Kathy felt some resolution go out of her. She didn't look *that* young; he was teasing her. But his friendliness was disarming. He was a nice-looking man with a crew cut and a big, rectangular smile.

"I want to ask you about a policy I understand you . . . use . . . here at the theater."

"Okay. What's that?"

"I understand that you require Negroes to sit in the balcony, separate from other customers." Kathy was scared. She could hear her own voice quiver.

He was still smiling. "Actually, no. We don't have that policy."

Kathy couldn't think what to say for a moment. This wasn't possible. "What about the *practice* then. From what I've heard, that's where they sit."

"Sit down. Tell me your name. Is this a school assignment or something?"

"No, it isn't. My name is Kathy Thomas. I'm a . . . concerned citizen."

That brought the grin back. "My name is Laine Ritchey. Nice to meet you." He leaned forward, resting his elbows on his desk. "Okay, here's the story. We did have that policy for a long time, but we've dropped it now."

"That's because you know the law is going to change before long."

"Well, that might be part of it. I'm not sure. But last year a couple of Negro ministers came in and talked to my boss. They said it wasn't right to send coloreds upstairs, and I guess our owner agreed with them. He told me to stop telling them to go up there. A lot still do, but I guess that's because they're used to it."

"But do you tell them they can sit downstairs?"

"Not really. We just let people do whatever they want."

"Then you *let* the segregation happen. You just don't *make* it happen."

"I don't know about that, Kathy. There aren't all that many colored folks in Salt Lake, and I think the word has gotten around. Some of them would just rather stay with their own kind, and we can't tell them that they *have to* sit next to a white guy."

Kathy was stopped. All the way down to the theater she had thought of the arguments she would use, the accusations she would make. She didn't like the man saying "their own kind," as though people weren't all the same kind, but if some Negroes preferred to sit in a group, upstairs, what could she say about that? She finally thought to ask, "When Negroes sit downstairs, are they treated all right?"

"Mostly." He was wearing a sport shirt, with no tie, and his sleeves were rolled up. He absently rubbed his hand along his forearm, seeming to think about what he wanted to say. "We've had a few white people come out to the lobby and say they didn't like having coloreds next to them, but I only know of one time where a white guy said something to a Negro. He told a couple of young guys they were supposed to go to the balcony, and they told him they didn't have to and got a little angry about it. The guy came out here to my office and threw a fit, so I gave him his money back and he left. That was the end of that."

"And what did you tell him? That you were sorry to put him through such a terrible ordeal?"

Mr. Ritchey laughed. "I might have said something a little like that. You have to deal with all sorts of people in this job—you know, try to satisfy the customer."

Kathy felt some anger return. "Mr. Ritchey, I have a Negro friend. She goes to my school. She told me that when she was nine years old, she came to a Saturday afternoon movie at this theater. She was with two little white girls. She didn't know any better. She just thought kids were kids. But someone stopped her and told her she had to sit upstairs. She didn't understand, but she went up there all by herself. She was the only kid up there, and it was dark. She was scared to death. After all these years, she still cried about it when she told me. She was humiliated. She couldn't understand why someone did that to her."

"That *is* awful, Kathy. I'm really glad we don't do that anymore."

But Kathy could feel him trying to manipulate her—satisfy the customer—and her indignation was fired. "Do you know that Marian Anderson came to Salt Lake to perform, and the Hotel Utah let her have a room, but they made her use the freight elevator—so people wouldn't *see* her in the hotel?"

"I did hear about that." He nodded, solemnly.

"Most of the restaurants in town refuse to serve Negroes. Negroes can't dance in most of the dance halls or swim in the public pools. If the new civil rights law passes, that will have to stop, but why did *we* have to wait for a law? We're no better than Mississippi."

He leaned back, nodded sadly again, but then said what she knew was coming. "I can't answer for other places, but here, we're already trying to do the right thing."

"Oh, come on. I don't believe that for a minute. You just saw the writing on the wall and knew you'd have to change soon anyway."

Once again, he nodded, waited, and seemed to consider what she had said. She could feel that she had won this little battle of wits. But then he said, "Kathy, let me ask you something. This girl you were talking about—this Negro girl who's a friend of yours—have you ever gone to a show with her? Or gone on a double date—something like that?"

Kathy felt the question like a blow to the chest. It wasn't just that he had won the argument, after all; he had seen right through her. She knew already that she would never be exactly the same person again.

Mr. Ritchey didn't wait for an answer. He knew, of course. "Look, things *are* changing. Maybe they should have changed a lot more, a lot sooner. But I guess certain things seemed right to people, and now they don't. Maybe we'll all think a lot different someday."

Kathy nodded. She had no idea what to say.

"You've got a lot of guts. I admire you. I've got a daughter a little younger than you. The only thing she cares about is buying new record albums and nice clothes. She could take a page out of your book. I guess you're planning to go to college, aren't you?"

Again, she nodded.

"What do you want to take up?"

"I don't know."

"Well, you'll do very well, whatever you choose."

"Thank you." Kathy stood up. His good nature only added to her humiliation. "Well, anyway, I'm sorry I took your time."

"No problem. It was fun to talk to you. You're a great kid."

This last was just a little too condescending. Kathy didn't thank him again; she simply slipped out the door and shut it behind her. And when she passed the ticket-taker, she refused to look him in the eye even though he asked, "Did you find him?"

"Yes," she said, without looking, and she walked on out to the street. And then she went home. It was still too early, and her mother would want to know why she was there before school was out, but Kathy had other things on her mind—things she needed to give a lot of thought.

She did have one matter she had to deal with, however, and she decided she might as well take care of it immediately. So she parked the car in the garage, walked in through the kitchen entrance, and then looked until she found her mother downstairs in her utility room, ironing.

"Aren't you home early?" Lorraine asked.

Kathy admitted that she was, and then she unloaded the whole story—what she had said to Mrs. Brittain, the classes she had skipped, and her humiliation at the movie theater. By the time she was finished, she could sense that her mother understood, that she wasn't going to start with a reprimand about the things Kathy had said to Mrs. Brittain.

"So what are you thinking about all this now?" she asked. "What exactly do you think you've learned?"

"Mom, I talk so big, but I'm no different from anyone else. That's what makes me sick with myself. I should be a *real* friend to Verna. I talk to her, but I've never gone anywhere with her."

"Is that what you think you ought to do?"

"Yes. But it should have been a natural thing, if I'd thought about it right—not something I do now to make a point. She doesn't need my *zeal*, as you always call it. She just needed my friendship."

"People of different races don't get together a lot, honey. Most of us haven't even thought about it. But can't you start now?"

"I don't know. I'm not even sure she would like that. But I wish my motivation had been pure. Now I can't do it without knowing that it's another one of my causes—that I want everyone to see us together and admire *me* for it."

"The way I look at it, Verna's got to be lonely at Highland High. I wouldn't worry so much about all the subtleties. I'd just start being a closer friend to her—and then decide later how much time you want to spend together. My generation is going to drag its feet on things like that; you young people can change the world, just a little at a time."

Kathy had been angry about people telling her that change had to come slow, but it had never hit her that she had to start changing herself first. And maybe that wasn't something that happened in an instant.

"Let me ask you something else," Lorraine said. "Can you understand a little better how someone like Mrs. Brittain gets stuck in a way of seeing things that she was taught since she was a little girl?"

"Sure, Mom. But she can *try*. I don't see any sign that she's willing to ask herself whether she's wrong or not."

"I know it seems that way. But when people feel attacked they defend their position."

"I wasn't attacking, not when she started in on all that stuff about Negroes being dirty and lazy."

"I understand." Mom turned a shirt over, stretched a sleeve out straight, and then smoothed it with her hand. "But then you started accusing her, and she dug her heels in. Maybe a kinder approach would have worked better."

So it was back to that, after all. Mom had a point, of course, but people like Mrs. Brittain had no desire to see another point of view. "Mom, this is the woman who told me that I shouldn't try to be a 'lady lawyer'—and she's supposed to be my *guidance* counselor."

"But honey, she knows realities. It is tough for a woman to make it in a field like that."

"Just let anybody try to stop me."

Lorraine laughed. "I don't think anyone will, honey, but you may have to learn to fit into the system a little more as you work your way up."

Kathy hated that idea. Would she always be held back by people who thought she was "too intense"? She watched her mom iron, and the painstaking care troubled Kathy. It seemed such mindless work. "Mom, you've told me how you managed whole crews, even men, back when you were single. Don't you miss all that?"

"Those times were pretty exciting for me, Kath. I liked the responsibility. We were under a lot of pressure to get the work done, and we all had to push really hard together. So it was satisfying when we produced. And we felt like we were important to the war effort. But it was a lot of work, a lot of long hours. And I was lonely. I didn't know whether I'd ever see your dad again, or whether there was still anything between us. I got engaged to someone else and wasn't really sure about the man. It was just a very hard time. I wouldn't want to go back to it."

"But wouldn't you like to be *producing* something now? Don't you miss all that?"

"No, I don't. But honey, you have to understand how I feel. If you think I like to iron, I'm sorry, but I don't. I buy all the wash-and-wear stuff I can; I don't iron anything I don't have to. And you know me when it comes to cooking. I do the simplest things I can. I want some time for myself each day. I don't want to spend all afternoon cooking up a big dinner from scratch. But I ask myself what I really care about. And for me, it's my family. I love your dad and I love you kids. If I've *produced* anything, it's the five of you. I want to see you all through, and see you get your own families started. And then I want to be a grandma."

"Mom, I don't mean this the way it might sound. But your life seems *horrible* to me. It sounds like the only point is to *re*-produce—just make another generation."

Lorraine laughed. "Name me something that matters more. You kids are sealed to me and your dad. We get to stay connected forever. What else can you take with you from this world?"

"What you learn and experience. The person you become."

"Well, that's right. But some people look at a mountain and they're filled up by its beauty. That's enough for them. They don't have to go climb it in order to feel like they've done something."

Kathy liked that. It worked so well for Mom. She was a woman who had been collecting beauty all her life, storing it up inside herself. But Kathy wasn't at all sure she could be like that. She wanted to climb at least one mountain before she sat down and merely *looked* the rest of her life.

"I need to go, Mom," Kathy said. "I need to think. Maybe I need to reconsider some things in my life."

"You mean about law school?"

"No. Not that. But about Verna. And about myself."

"I know. You do that."

"But what do I do about missing school? I'll go on the sluff list in the morning."

"I'll write you a note. And I don't mind. It's not very often that a person learns as much as you did today."

"I didn't really learn anything. Mostly, I got myself confused."

"Kathy, that's what learning is all about. You have to know the right questions before you can get the right answers."

Kathy liked that, too.

CHAPTER 19

D ad, you're not going to believe this," Gene said. He was standing in the kitchen, talking with his dad over the phone. Anna was close to him, her hand on his shoulder.

Alex laughed, the sound a little muffled over the phone. "Believe what?"

"I got my call. Where do you think I'm going?"

"Germany?"

"Really? You thought that?"

"I've thought it all along. So where are you going?"

"South Germany. Headquarters in Stuttgart."

"That's terrific. The Black Forest is in your mission. That's really the prettiest part of Germany." Then he laughed. "Just don't plan to use any of the German you've learned in school—or from your mother. They speak a dialect down there that you'll never understand."

"But why did you think I was going to Germany? You didn't say anything to any of the Brethren, did you?"

"No. I wanted to, but I didn't. I just figured all along that with a German mom, and a dad who served in Germany—plus, you can speak a fair amount of the language already—it was the natural place to send you."

"I told the bishop that's where I wanted to go, but he said I wasn't allowed to request a mission anymore, the way people used to do."

"Gene, it's where God wants you to go. I feel sure of that."

"Do you think, somehow—like at the end of my mission—I could cross the border and have a chance to visit Hans and Uncle Peter?"

"I doubt it. They've really locked that place down now. Hardly any-one gets in or out. Even Church leaders are lucky to get in once in a while by going to Leipzig when they hold their big trade fair."

"Maybe by the time I'm finished, things will change."

"Well . . . I guess that's possible, but the government isn't showing much sign of loosening up. Germans are hard-headed people, Gene. Just like your mother." He laughed.

"Everyone says it's really hard to get any baptisms over there."

"It will be. I've got to tell you, this is going to be one of the hardest things you'll do in your life. I hope you're ready for it."

"I am, Dad. I've been thinking about it for a *long* time."

"I know you have. But I'm not sure you really understand what's so hard about it. It's something you have to experience for yourself."

"I think I have some idea—from talking to a lot of guys just getting back. But all of them tell me they're glad they went."

"I'll tell you what pleases me. That time over there will give you a connection to your mother's country—my country, too—in a way that nothing else could." He paused. "Listen, I'm going to button things up early tonight, and I'll come home. Maybe we can take the kids out for dinner or something. We need to celebrate."

"Okay. Do you want to talk to Mom?"

"No, that's all right. Tell her . . . or yeah. Let me talk to her just a sec-ond."

Gene handed the phone to his mother. She was still smiling, had been since he had opened the letter from President McKay. "*Ist Wunderbar, nicht?*" she said.

Gene had long noticed that his parents liked to use German as their personal language, the one they used when they were especially happy.

Gene could understand much of what his mother said, but he didn't speak the language as well as he wished he could. He had been doing a little better this last year, practicing for his German classes at the university, but when he was a little boy, he had gone through a time when he had been embarrassed that his mother spoke another language to him. It had made him feel different from other kids, so he had stopped answering her in German, and gradually they had spoken mostly English. Still, he knew more than most missionaries who were just starting out.

When Anna hung up the phone, she looked at Gene. "Your dad's really happy about this," she said.

"*Ja. Es ist sehr gut, Ich denke*," he told her, grinning. "And I get to go to the *pretty* part of Germany—not up there in Frankfurt, where you lived."

She punched him one in the middle. "If you come home speaking *Schwäbisch*, I'll wash your mouth out with soap, *mein Schätzele*."

Gene grabbed her and hugged her. "Mom, I'm so dang excited about this," he said. "I can't wait to get going."

"But your dad was telling you how it will be, wasn't he?"

"Yeah." Gene let go and looked at her. "But I need some hard things in my life. I've had it too easy."

"Yes, you certainly have. My little brother had been through *so much* by the time he was your age. I had, too, as far as that goes."

It was hard for Gene to imagine his mother as that girl who had escaped Germany during the war. Her past didn't fit with this beautiful house, the elegant furniture—the only kind of life he had ever known.

Gene walked over to the kitchen counter and sat down on one of the stools. "I feel like I need to have my faith tested," he said. "I believe in the Church, but I've never had any reason not to. It's just always seemed right to me."

Anna leaned against the cabinet and put her hands into her pockets. She wore dresses most days, even around the house, but she had been housecleaning that morning and had worn a faded pair of blue jeans. She still looked pretty, no matter what she wore. Sometimes Gene's high school friends would say, "Wow! That's your mom? She ought to be a movie star."

"There's nothing wrong with faith coming naturally, Gene. I fought the Spirit when I was young. I raised questions about everything—almost drove my mother crazy. But when my testimony came, everything changed. I still had questions, but they didn't matter in the same way. I had to sort out all the details, but I had the answer to the one question that mattered."

"Maybe I don't have a testimony, Mom. Maybe I just have a . . . habit."

"Don't underrate what you have, Gene. You're good. And you respond to goodness. When you were little, you were a stubborn little boy, and you would get into things. Sometimes I thought you were going to be a real handful. But I remember one time when you were about three or so. I told you that you were a bad boy, and you just melted. You cried and cried because I had called you that. And I've never said it again. Your little spirit just didn't want to be bad."

"Marsha says that I don't think enough, that I just accept everything."

"Do you still care what she thinks?"

It was an interesting question. Gene hadn't gone out with Marsha for months, not since the night of the Christmas party when he had taken her home early. He saw her now and then, and she was surprisingly cordial, which sometimes caused him to think of calling her, maybe trying again, but the idea always scared him. She had a knack for making him uncomfortable with himself, and he wasn't sure he wanted that. Still, it was strange how much she stayed in his mind, and curious how other girls he dated seemed lacking by comparison. But he answered his mother by saying, "I just think she makes a good point about me. I've never really had to stand up for what I believe, so I guess my commitment hasn't been very deep."

"When she says that about you, is she talking about your religious beliefs—or other things?"

"Everything, really." Gene looked through the family room, out in the backyard, which was full of afternoon light, the trees all intensely green. He tried to think what Marsha had said about him. It was late May, 1964, and a lot of time had passed, but he had never stopped thinking about the conversation they had had on their last date. "For one thing," he said, "she doesn't like fraternities. She says that we think we're better than other people. And I guess, as much as anything, she's accusing me of not worrying enough about things like that."

"Do you think she's right?"

Gene had actually hoped his mother might tell him Marsha was wrong, that Gene had more depth than she was giving him credit for. He didn't like having to answer for himself. "To some degree . . . yeah. I think that's kind of how I am. To me, being in a fraternity is just, you know, kind of cool. I like hanging around with the guys, and that's about as far as it goes with me. But I've noticed a lot lately how some of the members talk about guys who didn't make it into fraternities—stuff like that. It just sort of bothers me. Do you know what I mean?"

"I do know what you mean. I've never liked the idea of fraternities and sororities."

"Really? You've never said that."

"I know. Your dad told me they were fine, and I figured maybe the whole thing was fairly harmless. But for me, I wish people were friendly to everyone and not so exclusive about choosing friends."

"Good English, Mom. 'Exclusive.' That's a big word."

"See. You do think you're a big shot. You don't show respect to your mother."

She walked over to the kitchen table and sat down. He turned on the stool so he was looking at her again, but he had stopped his smirking. "Maybe that's what I like about Marsha. Maybe she's like you."

"I thought you *didn't* like Marsha. You've stopped going out with her, haven't you?"

"Yeah, I stopped asking her out. But . . . I don't know . . ." He wasn't sure what he wanted to admit. "I do keep thinking about her."

"Geney! What are you telling me?"

"Nothing. But it's strange. I've got to phone all my friends and tell them about my mission call, but the only one I really want to talk to is Marsha."

"I know why, too. She challenges you." Anna smiled. "And of course, she's *very* pretty."

"Do you really think so? I've gone with lots of girls who are better-looking than she is."

"Maybe. But Marsha has a look about her that I like. She doesn't work at being pretty. She has lovely skin tones, and her eyes are . . . luminous. Is that a word?"

"*Luminous?* Yeah, that's a word. It's a good word. Mom, have you been using those vocabulary-building cards I had to memorize back in sophomore English?"

"Be quiet. I know more English words than you, Buster Brown."

"Who's that? Busta Bwown?"

"I didn't say that."

Gene was laughing hard now. He got up and came to the table. "Anyway, I agree. I do like the way Marsha looks. But she has no idea how to be young. She needs to team up with Kathy, and they can go off to Africa and help Dr. Schweitzer—or something like that."

"So I guess that's that."

"What do you mean?"

"You don't like her and it's over."

Gene saw the point. Why was he talking about her then? "Honestly, it is, Mom. She has a low opinion of me. What else is there to say?"

"Only that it might be good for you not to be worshiped *all* the time."

Gene shook his head. "No one *worships* me."

"Go see her. Tell her your news."

"Are you serious?"

"She likes you much more than you know. It's killing her that you haven't called for so long. Don't you know that?"

"No. I don't know that."

"Well, trust me. My guess is, she's spent a lot of time lately wishing that she hadn't been quite so hard on you."

"I doubt it. She's had chances to tell me that, if that's how she felt."

"Gene, don't *ever* doubt your mother. That's the first rule around here. Now, change your pants, look a little more like a missionary, and go tell her before your dad gets home."

Half an hour later, Gene found himself standing on Marsha's front porch. He didn't even know whether she would be home yet. She worked on campus after her classes. But it was Marsha herself who opened the door, Marsha who looked surprised.

"I got my missionary call," Gene said. "I just wanted to tell you." He had thought about those words. It was a big enough reason to come over, and it didn't imply that he was trying to get anything started again. The last thing he wanted was to make some overture of that kind and get sent packing.

"Where are you going?" She didn't invite him in.

"South Germany. Stuttgart."

"Gene, that's great. That's where you wanted to go, wasn't it?"

"Yup. Dad even admits that it's the prettiest part of Germany."

"Where's your Mom from?"

"Frankfurt. That's kind of in the middle of Germany—not in my mission."

"So . . . are you excited?"

"I am." He didn't want to use a bunch of clichés with Marsha. "It's a hard mission. But maybe that'll be good for me."

Marsha smiled. Then she stepped out on the porch, walked toward the steps, and sat down. Gene sat down next to her. It was a pretty spot, with a full view of the valley. Gene could see the great smokestack out by Kennecott Copper and, north from there, Antelope Island, a gray spot in the blue-gray water of the Great Salt Lake. But he could also see downtown, the spires of the temple, the old Walker Bank sign.

"Gene, you're going to be a good missionary."

"Really? You think that?"

"Why does that surprise you?"

"Well . . . you know. You're—how shall I say?—well aware of my *deficiencies*."

"Gene, I'm sorry I've made you feel that way. That last time we went out, I was just so mad about the way some of those frat boys were preening themselves and talking like bigshots. I blamed you for everything they were doing. But when you get back from your mission, I think you'll be way beyond that kind of stuff. You're a good person—a lot better than I am."

"Better? You don't mean that, do you?"

"I do. I've thought about it a lot. You have this innocent goodwill. You like people. You think the best of them. I need to be more like that."

Gene could hardly think what to say. He wanted to deny all that, but he sensed that he would only sound false, so he merely said, "Well . . . anyway . . . it's a hard mission. The language should come pretty fast for me, and I don't have a hard time getting out of bed early. The only thing that scares me is trying to answer all the questions people probably have."

"You'll learn. You'll have a senior companion who'll know how to explain things."

"I'm going to study really hard between now and the time I go."

Gene watched an old green Ford pull into the driveway and stop in front of the garage. "That's my brother," Marsha said.

"Didn't he just get home from his mission?"

"Yeah. He was in France. He's been home about a month now." As her brother was getting out of his car, Marsha asked Gene, "So when do you leave?"

"I go into the Mission Home June 22. I leave for Germany June 29."

"Don't you go to the Language Training Mission?"

"No. It's not open for German yet. They sent one group through, just to try it, but I'll be going the full two and a half years."

"Wow. That's a long time. Does that bother you?"

"No. It's only three months shorter if you go to the LTM."

By now Marsha's brother was walking toward the front steps. Gene stood up to let him get by. "Robert, this is Gene Thomas," Marsha said.

"Oh, yeah. You're Alex Thomas's son, aren't you?"

"Yes." Gene shook Robert's hand.

"Gene got his mission call today," Marsha said.

"Oh, yeah? Where are you going?"

"Germany."

"Oh, man," he said, and Gene didn't know how to read that. "Well, I'm glad you're starting and I'm finished."

"Really?"

Robert laughed in a burst. He was a tall, thin fellow with arms that seemed to dangle from his sleeves as though they weren't hooked in quite right. "Yeah, really," he said. "It's hard over there in Europe. I'm glad I went, but I'm even happier to get back home. I've got to be honest with you about that."

"But it's a good experience, isn't it?"

"Sure. So's prison time, if you learn from it." His cackling laugh started again. "But hey, don't let me scare you. It's better to just go over there not knowing what you're getting into. If everybody knew what it was really like, half the guys probably wouldn't even go."

He walked up the steps, and Gene felt much more uneasy than he wanted to. "Are you serious?" he asked.

Robert turned around. "No. Not at all. I'm just putting you on. It was the happiest ten years of my life." He walked into the house, still laughing.

"Is he pulling my leg?" Gene asked Marsha.

"Sort of. But he really did find it hard. And he *is* glad to be home."

"A lot of guys say they wish they could have stayed longer."

"A lot of guys *say* a lot of things."

Gene was trying to sort all this out. He knew it would be hard, had been telling himself that all along, but he had heard so many returned missionaries get up at their homecoming meetings and say that they hated to come home because they were so happy in the mission field.

"Don't pay any attention to Robert. He loved his mission. He just likes to shock people."

Gene nodded. He figured it was a family trait. But still, there was something a little unnerving about the idea that he was so happy his mission was over. "Do you have a few minutes? Could we take a little ride?" Gene asked. He wanted to change the mood somehow, maybe see whether Mom could be right about Marsha. It almost seemed possible right now.

"Uh . . . sure. But I can only go for a few minutes, okay? I've got a paper due in three days, and I've left most of the research to the last minute."

"Marsha, that's the nicest thing you've ever said about yourself. I didn't think you did things the way I do."

"Oh, you don't know. Procrastination is my biggest problem."

They walked to the car, and Gene drove toward Hogle Zoo and then on up into Emigration Canyon, one of his favorite places in the world. The two talked about this and that, but mostly about his mission. But finally Gene said, "Marsha, I have this feeling that I met you at the wrong time. I don't think I was quite ready for you. Do you know what I mean?"

"Oh, Gene, no one was ready for me the way I've been the last couple of years. I'm the one who's done some growing up lately. I started that thing in high school of acting like such a young intellectual, challenging everyone and everything. This year of college has done wonders for me. It's rather humbling to find out I'm not as smart as I thought I was."

"Well, anyway, you've made me think about myself. That's been good for me." He hesitated, and then he added, "It was funny, but when I got my mission call, I thought of you right off. I wanted to talk to you. I haven't told anyone else yet, except my family."

"Really?"

"And I'll admit something else. I think I'm going to miss you more than anyone."

"Gene, that's just a little hard to believe. You haven't called me for *months.*"

"And you spent all that time waiting by the phone, didn't you?"

"No. But I felt bad. I was so *superior* that last time we went out, and I didn't blame you for hating me. I do like you, you know?"

"Every now and then I got that idea, just a little, but—"

"But then I'd treat you like I didn't."

"Well, yeah."

"That's because I *don't* like you sometimes. But I have missed you. That must mean something."

"I guess it doesn't mean you're going to wait for me while I'm gone."

"No, I guess it doesn't mean that. But you're not asking, either."

"I wouldn't ask anyone, Marsha, but I'd really like it if we wrote. And when I get back, I hope you're not married. I want to see how much I've grown, and see what you think of me."

"Don't put it that way. I need to grow just as much as you do."

"Well, I doubt that. But I would like to keep in touch during my mission."

He glanced over at her, trying to read the look on her face. She seemed genuinely pleased. "I'll write to you. But how many other girls are going to be doing the same thing, just hoping they can win the sweep-stakes?"

"I have some friends who might write, but no one I've said anything like this to."

"Really? Gene, that means more to me than you might think. No one like you has ever paid any attention to me."

Gene shot her another quick look. "I have a feeling I'd better not ask what 'someone like you' means. I don't think the description would be flattering."

"That's true. It wouldn't."

Gene laughed.

"But Gene, I like you more than I ought to. More than you think. You're so good to look at, for one thing. I try not to let that cloud my thinking, but it does."

"Well . . . just try to concentrate on all my bad traits. That should help."

"Gene, we probably aren't right for each other. I used to think it was your fault, and now I know it's probably more my fault than yours. But it would be interesting to see how much we both change in the next couple of years. Who knows? Maybe something could come of it."

Gene let that sink in for a time. He drove on up the canyon, glancing her way a few times and thinking how pretty she looked. "Would it be a good idea for us to spend some more time together before I leave?" he finally asked.

"I think it would be a very good idea," she said, and she smiled at him more generously than she ever had before.

"And what if I kissed you sometime? What kind of an idea would that be?"

"Well . . . I really don't know. Do you think we ought to try it once, just as a test case?"

"I think we ought to try it now."

"While you're driving?"

But Gene was already pulling off the road. In broad daylight, he pulled her toward him as she smiled. And when he kissed her, he was not at all surprised to find that he liked those rounded lips every bit as much as he thought he would.

CHAPTER 20

Diane was with Scott Laughlin. It was a warm Saturday night in early June. The two saw each other almost every day now. On week days he would stop by her house in the evenings, or they would take a ride in his Volkswagen, and every Friday and Saturday night they had a date of some sort. Tonight they had gone to a movie. Now they were just "dragging the Boulevard" a few times to see who was out and about. The routine was to drive north to Second Street, or even out to the old fountain that bubbled from a tree in North Ogden, and then to "flip a U-ie" and head back south to Thirty-Sixth Street or so. There were a lot of hangouts along the way. Guys without dates were always waving and yelling at cars packed with girls, talking back and forth while driving, but rarely did anyone ever seem to do more than chase around after each other. No self-respecting girl would climb out of her car into one filled with boys. Diane had seen fights on Washington Boulevard, and even some pick-ups, but that was mostly with the "greaser" types. Most kids just liked spotting friends, pulling over to talk, listening to music on KLO or KCPX, and enjoying the night air with all the windows down.

What Diane loved about Scott was that he was so much fun. He had a great little car—a bright yellow Volkswagen Bug that had been fixed up with cool seat covers—all rolled and pleated. Guys would pull up in their lowered GTOs or Plymouth Furies, stripped and leaded, their dual pipes rumbling, the car just quivering to go, and the drivers would look over and laugh at Scott in his little Bug. But Scott didn't care. It was a cool car, and he didn't need to prove anything. He never tried to look "bad," or fight, or hang out with all the guys who got drunk every weekend. He just liked being with Diane and maybe a few friends, and he always treated her great.

"Should we go out to Combe's?" he asked her tonight.

"Why don't we go up to the Blue Onion first and just see who's up there?"

He nodded and pulled into a turn lane so he could head east. He made the turn quickly before traffic reached him, and the fuzzy dice swung on his rearview mirror. The dice were a joke. Back in the fifties a lot of guys had hung those in their "hot" cars, but the things were out of date now, and they looked especially funny in a Volkswagen.

At the Blue Onion, Diane spotted her friend Carol Wyatt, who had been going out lately with a boy named Mike Frost. He was a senior, about to graduate, and this spring their romance had turned serious. Mike had been recruited by just about every college around, both for football and baseball. He had committed to Arizona State, but Carol had admitted to Diane that he was thinking about backing out. The two didn't want to be so far apart.

Carol and Mike were out of his car, leaning against the front fender, talking with another couple. The others were also from Ogden High but kids Diane knew only by name—Kitty Gibson and Boyd McEntire. Mike always drove a beat-up old Mercury station wagon. It was a heap, but it was part of his identity, like Scott's VW. "Let's go talk to Carol and Mike," Diane said.

"They're already talking to someone," Scott said.

"That's okay. I know them." But she knew what Scott was thinking. Carol was a sophomore, but the others were seniors, and Scott didn't know the guys. One thing Diane had learned about Scott was that he really was shy. He had never gotten to know an awful lot of people at Ogden High. He depended on Diane.

Diane got out of the car on her side, not waiting for Scott to come around, and she waved to Carol. Then she walked around, grabbed Scott's hand, and led him toward the group. "Hey, what's going on?" Mike said as the two approached. "Been out drag racing in that hot car of yours?"

"It'll beat that beast of yours off the line," Scott said, and he grinned.

"But the beast has more atmosphere," Mike said. "It's got the smell of sweat in it, from the whole football team stuffing into it."

Mike was a huge guy; he seemed to make two of Scott. He was probably six-four or five, and he had shoulders like the front haunches on a work horse. He was standing with his massive arms folded, his muscles showing under his Banlon knit shirt. Diane noticed the thick blond hair on his forearms, all the way down to his knuckles. The guy had always seemed a little too imposing to Diane, especially because of the power of his big voice.

"Where have you been, Diane?" Carol asked.

"We went to see *From Russia with Love*."

"Haven't you seen that before?"

"Sure, the last time it was here. We wanted to see it again."

"Can you believe how sexy Sean Connery is?"

"I think those shows are disgusting," Kitty said.

Diane turned toward her, surprised. "What?"

"The values in those James Bond shows are awful. He sleeps with every girl around."

Diane had sort of felt the same way, and her mom was adamant against them. But they were really popular, and the stunts were great. Diane didn't think she had to act like the women did in the movie just because they did those things. But it was Carol who said, "Oh, lighten up, Kitty. It's all just fun. No one takes it seriously."

Still, Diane was sort of impressed. Kitty was the only young person she had ever heard say something like that. It seemed like parents were always complaining about movies and music, but kids thought they had to like anything new just because it *was* new. Diane didn't have the nerve to say anything, but she did wonder about some of the movies she had seen lately.

"What do you think of the Beatles?" she asked Kitty. "I heard today they're coming back for a second tour later this summer."

But now Kitty rolled her eyes with delight. "I love the Beatles," she said.

"You mean you're not worried about their *long hair?*" Carol said. "My mom's just sure they're going to destroy us all. She thinks they're involved in some sort of Communist plot."

"I don't see what difference their hair makes," Kitty said. "There's nothing wrong with what they sing."

"You have to know my mom. She's still worried about Elvis Presley twisting his hips too much."

Diane glanced over to see that Scott was hanging back a little. She took hold of his hand and gradually pulled him in a little closer. But Mike and Boyd had begun to talk about baseball, and Scott was caught among the three girls. Carol was talking about the Animals, a new British group she liked. Diane wondered how to get out of the situation before too long; she knew Scott didn't like the way the two seniors were ignoring him. "Do you want to go inside?" she asked.

"Why don't we just take off?"

"Are you sure?"

"Yeah." He pulled her close and whispered into her ear, "I think I have an idea of something we could do." His breath in her ear sent tingling sensations down her neck and back. She knew what he meant, of course, and it was really what she wanted too. So Diane told everyone goodbye, and she and Scott went back to the car. And then he drove into the foothills, toward Beus's pond. It was a favorite place for kids to park, and a place she had been with Scott several times now. He stopped in a dark spot, where he could pull the car off among some oak brush, and then he reached for her. She let him pull her as close as possible with the gearshift between them. He kissed her, and now she felt the tingling spread all through her.

The kissing, the holding, continued in the pattern they had become accustomed to. She loved the way he kissed her neck, breathed into her ear, stroked her hair, her back. But tonight he seemed a little more urgent than usual. He kissed her with more fire, and she felt his hand working its way across her middle, each stroke a little higher. She liked the feel of it, but his hand kept pressing, rising, until she felt uncomfortable with how close he was coming, and she took hold of his wrist and pushed it down. He seemed to accept that, and she was relieved. She knew how much her parents worried about Scott, about the mistake she might be making by spending so much time with him, but he had always respected her values and never tried to do anything wrong. He had even stopped swearing when she had asked him, and he admitted that he had done some drinking in California, but he had stopped that too.

After a minute or two, however, she felt him grasp her rather roughly again, and his hand went back to her middle. Diane was a little frightened. "I think we'd better stop tonight," she said, and she pulled away from him.

"Come on, Diane. It's okay. We're not doing anything wrong." He reached for her again, got hold of her shoulders, and tried to pull her close.

Suddenly Diane was angry. She shoved hard and said, "Don't do that. I said I want to stop."

Scott dropped back into his seat. She could hear him breathing hard. "I don't *get* you, Diane. What kind of game are you playing with me?"

"Just take me home. I've told you I don't do things like that."

"Then why do you lead me on?"

"I'm not leading you on. I thought we were just kissing."

"A guy can't kiss forever, Diane. After a while, it drives him crazy."

"Then let's not kiss. Let's not go out anymore, either. I want to go home."

Scott didn't move. He was still breathing audibly, but she sensed that he was calming down. Finally, he said, "I'm sorry. Really, I am. I just got too excited."

"I did too, Scott. We can't do that kind of stuff anymore."

He leaned back against his door and seemed to think for a time. "Okay," he said. "But could you tell me why? My girlfriend in California didn't want to get herself in trouble, or something like that. But there was a lot of stuff we could do without that happening."

"I'm not like that, Scott. I'm not that kind of girl."

"What's that supposed to mean?"

"I have *values*. Those are things you only do after you get married. If I let you do things like that, I'd have to go see my bishop and tell him—so I could repent—and I'd almost die if I had to do that."

"Oh, brother."

"Scott, you won't ever understand me. You haven't been raised the way I have. Do you believe anything at all?"

"What do you mean?"

"What do you believe about religion?"

"I believe in God," Scott said, quickly, but Diane could see his face in dim outline, and his chin was set, his mouth. She didn't think the words meant much to him. "My family doesn't go to church, but my mom always taught me to say my prayers and stuff like that."

"What do you mean, say your prayers?"

"We say a blessing when we eat. And when I was little, I would always say that 'Now I lay me down to sleep' thing."

"What do you say now?"

"Nothing. But that doesn't mean I don't believe in God."

"So how do you decide what's right and wrong?"

Now he stirred a little and looked over at her. She couldn't see his face in the dark, but she knew he was softening, could hear in his voice that he wasn't so upset as he had been at first. "I don't know. Like most people, I know you're not supposed to lie or cheat or hurt people—stuff like that. How do you know?"

"There are commandments, Scott. And at church, my leaders talk about things we shouldn't do."

"Is that all your religion is? A bunch of stuff you shouldn't do?"

"No. There's all kinds of stuff we *should* do. Help people. Treat your family right. Pay your tithing. Go to church. All kinds of things."

He leaned back again, his head against the window. "Look, I don't have anything against Mormons. I think they're smart not to drink. My dad drank way too much, and he was mean when he did. That's why my mom divorced him. The only thing I don't like around here is that it seems like if you're not a Mormon, you're some kind of outcast."

"I thought you said your mom was a Mormon."

"She grew up that way, but she hasn't gone to church for a long time, and I never have gone."

"Didn't your mom ever talk to you about being baptized?"

"No. But then, you haven't either."

"What?"

"We see each other almost every day. But Sundays, you go to church, and you've never even invited me."

"I thought you'd think I was being pushy—trying to get you to join my church."

"Isn't that what you should want?"

"What do you mean?"

"Well, if we kept going together, and someday got really serious and everything, wouldn't you want me to be in your church?"

"I would *only* marry you if you joined the Church."

"How's that supposed to happen, if I don't even go?"

Diane was suddenly elated. Five minutes before she had concluded that this was their breakup, and now they were talking about his coming to church with her. Her parents had talked to her dozens of times now about being careful, not going steady at such a young age. And something inside Diane had always said that was actually right, that she probably should break up with him. But he was so cute, and so many girls envied her, that she just couldn't bring herself to make the break. Now she felt a whole new possibility. She could be a missionary. Her parents would have to be happy about that. She had told them all along that she wanted to bring him into the Church, but he was right: she had never invited him.

All the same, Diane said, "Scott, I don't know. I'm still thinking we should break up."

"I know what you're thinking: that I'll keep pushing you to do things you don't want to do." Now he leaned forward, found her hand, and held it in both of his. "But I promise you, right now, I won't do that."

"Scott, it wasn't all your fault. I'm just afraid we'll both get weak some night and make a really bad mistake."

"No. I won't let it happen. If I don't start things going that way, I know you won't. You're too sweet a girl to let that happen." For just an instant, Diane felt something uncomfortable in this—as though she were listening to a sales pitch. But then he said, "Could I go to church with you tomorrow?"

How could she turn down that request? "Sure," she said. "We could go to sacrament meeting, and you could see what it's like."

"Is that the meeting in the afternoon?"

She laughed. "Yes. You don't have to get up early, like I do."

"I'd get up. Do you want me to go to the morning meeting?"

But Diane wasn't sure she wanted to take him to Sunday School quite yet, although she wasn't sure why. Maybe she wondered what he might say there, in front of all the kids she had known all her life. "Let's start with sacrament meeting," she said.

"Okay. What time?"

"It starts at six. Do you want to come over for Sunday dinner with my family and then go to church with us?"

"I love that idea. I see all these families going to church every Sunday, and I've always wondered what that would be like. Mom and I just hang around all day. Mostly, I watch sports on TV, or something like that."

"Okay. Let me talk to Mom. And then I'll call you tomorrow and tell you what time."

"All right. Come here. Let me just give you one kiss."

She leaned toward him, and he held her face, then gently kissed her. This was so much better. Diane could hardly believe how happy she felt. Maybe it was good that all this had happened tonight.

The next afternoon Scott came over for dinner. He wore a white shirt, a nice sport coat, and a tie. And he was great fun. Maggie already knew him well and was in love with him herself. He seemed to know that, and he flirted with her, teased her, gave her a lot of attention. He even played with Ricky—bounced him on his knee until he laughed with delight. Mom was nice to Scott, if a little distant. Clearly she didn't quite trust him, and Diane thought that wasn't fair.

Diane couldn't believe it when Bobbi asked, "Scott, have you thought about what you might like to do when you get out of high school?"

"Well . . . not a lot. I'm sure I'll go to college."

"Here at Weber, or where?"

"I have no idea right now." He smiled. "You sound like my mom. She always tells me I need to keep my grades up so I can get a scholarship. She doesn't have a lot of money."

Bobbi smiled too, but she cocked her head to one side playfully and asked, "And do you listen to this wise mother of yours?"

Diane wanted to crawl under the table.

"I think I might have to work part-time while I'm in college," he said, and he laughed. "I don't think too many colleges are going to come chasing after me."

There was something disarming, charming about Scott's frankness. Diane knew Scott was no "big brain," but then, neither was she. And he certainly wasn't flunking any classes. But Diane knew what her parents were thinking, no matter how much Mom smiled.

"Have you thought what you might like to study in college?" Dad asked.

Diane knew her dad well enough to recognize that he was only making conversation, but he had still kept the pressure up, and Diane watched Scott shrug and squirm a little. "I'm not sure. I think maybe business or something like that. I know I don't want to *work* for a living."

Diane knew that was a joke, and she laughed harder than anyone else, but her parents let the subject drop, and that could only mean that they had concluded that Scott wasn't up to much. But Diane could hardly believe it. What did they expect a sixteen-year-old boy to say—that he had his whole life planned out?

Dinner ended with cherry pie and ice cream. Mom always joked about not being much of a cook, but she had made a real effort today, and Diane had helped. The pie was good—and Scott kept saying so—and then he and Dad slipped out to watch some baseball. That was something Scott knew pretty well, and Diane could hear him talking about Yogi Berra and someone named "Moose Skowron." Diane and Maggie helped Mom with the dishes, and then they went off to get ready for church. They had worn their Sunday dresses to dinner, but they disappeared into their bedrooms, fixed their hair a little, and then came out for the men. Dad drove the station wagon, and Diane was beginning to feel a little more relaxed about Scott being around the family. It was church that worried her. She didn't know what Scott would think of some of the things that happened there.

When they walked into the building, far too many people in the foyer and in the chapel wanted to shake Scott's hand and ask him whether he was Diane's "boyfriend." Old Brother Olsen had to say, "Laughlin? That's not a name I know. Who are your parents?"

"My mom's name is Marianne. My dad doesn't live here. My parents are divorced."

"Oh. I see," Brother Olsen said. And nothing more.

Diane gave Scott's hand a little squeeze to apologize. She walked into a pew and led Scott to the end, and Maggie made sure she got the chance to sit on the other side of him. By then Diane had noticed the priests getting the sacrament ready, and she decided she had better warn Scott about that. "They'll pass a tray around with broken bread on it, and then some little cups of water. Since you're not a member, just pass it on to me and then back."

"Can't I have any?"

Diane didn't know. "I don't think you're supposed to. Is that okay?"

"Sure."

The organist was playing prelude music, but Diane was embarrassed by how much noise was still going on. People were talking back and forth, shaking hands, laughing. A toddler ran down the aisle, and his big sister, in a satin dress, chased him down. She swept him up, tickled him, and carried him back as the little boy laughed wildly. But then, Ricky was as bad as any of the kids, already squirming and trying to get off his mom's lap.

Up in the front Diane saw Brother Smedley taking his seat across from the bishop. Diane's breath caught. Brother Smedley was on the high council, and apparently the speaker for today. He was a boring, long-winded man, and that was bad enough, but he was also fanatic about certain things. He was always talking about the last days—that the end was *very* near—and he liked to talk, more than anything, about having a year's supply of food. Would Scott think that had anything to do with religion?

Diane glanced at her dad, who smiled. They were both, undoubtedly, thinking about a family story. Brother Smedley had once called Dad and told him, "I'm just calling to remind you to get out and vote on Tuesday. If we church people don't get out, the Democrats are going to win a lot of these races. You know how this county is."

"Thank you very much," Dad had told him. "We Democrats need the reminder too."

There had been a long silence on the other end of the line, and then Brother Smedley had said, "You teach psychology up at Weber, don't you?" And when Dad had told him that he did, Brother Smedley had said, "I guess I should have known."

That was funny at the time, but now, here was the guy scheduled to speak. It was hard to say what he might get into.

For now, Diane had to deal with singing the opening hymn, "O Ye Mountains High." What would Scott think of that? Did he have any idea what "Zion" was? She held the hymn book and sang while he seemed to be reading the words. But after a time, he joined in a little. And then he got the idea that he was supposed to lower his head during the prayer that followed. Later, when the sacrament came, he passed the tray along, just like everyone else, and he seemed rather interested just to watch what was going on. Diane thought the ward was too irreverent, with so many crying babies and little kids, but when she whispered, "I'm sorry it's so noisy today," he shrugged, as though he hadn't really thought about it.

Then the sacrament was over, and it was time for Brother Smedley. He started with a lame joke about a man driving a car while singing a hymn, going faster and faster until he was stopped by the police. The punch line was something about being "Nearer to God," and Scott chuckled, even though Diane saw nothing funny in it. But Brother Smedley took up a new theme today. He wanted to talk about every member being a missionary. Diane practically froze.

"Brothers and Sisters, all around us are people who are wandering in darkness, without any direction in their lives. They don't understand the things of God. They worship the false god of our time: money. They are letting this land of promise sink into the depths of materialism and Communism, setting aside the holy principles this country was founded on. We need to have the courage to approach these people, ask them the golden questions, and then introduce them to our missionaries."

What followed was a long treatise on how members could find "golden contacts." People needed to befriend non-Mormons, get acquainted, and then watch for a chance to ask them how much they knew about the Church and whether they would like to know more. They might start by inviting these people into their homes for a nice evening, and after those people had seen the warmth and goodness in their homes, they would feel the Spirit, and there would be only one answer they could give: that they would love to know more.

All of that sounded a little too calculating, even tricky at times, but Brother Smedley emphasized the idea that President McKay had taught that every member must be a missionary because we had a great gift that the world needed. The motivation at least sounded right. But then he said, "Brothers and Sisters, let me add a warning. We need to go out to the world and draw the chosen people, those with open hearts, toward us, lead them to the truth. But it's a wicked world, and most people don't live as they should. In reaching out your hand don't get pulled toward them. This world is full of darkness, and so many people have no light at all within them. Those of us who've accepted God's truth must never try so hard to change the world that we get some of its scum upon us. I especially encourage our young people to be careful about the friends they make. Spend your time with wholesome, active members of the Church. You may think you can be friends with nonmembers and do some good, but all too often you're drawn away, and you end up taking on their behaviors."

Diane had felt herself tighten until she was almost rigid, and she felt Scott tense a little too. She whispered, "I'm sorry," but Scott didn't respond.

Brother Smedley spoke forever, as usual. The meeting was supposed to last an hour and a half, but he went past the closing time. By the time Diane got through some more handshaking, more questions about Scott, and got him out to the station wagon, she felt as though she had been through a marathon.

She and Scott got into the rear seat, and Mom climbed in and then took Ricky from her husband. The little guy had finally fallen asleep about an hour into the meeting. Bobbi turned around as best she could and said, "Scott, I hope you don't think that Mormons consider anyone who's not a member of our church a bad person."

"Oh, no. Not at all."

"Well, Brother Smedley is . . . how should I say? A little extreme."

"I kind of liked him." Silence filled the car. Diane couldn't have been more surprised. "Would it be possible for me to do something like that—you know, have missionaries come over to your house and teach me?"

"Sure it's possible," Mom said. "Would you like that?"

"I would. I've been thinking I might want to join. You know, since I live here in Utah now and everything. Mom was a Mormon once. Maybe I ought to be."

The silence lasted much longer this time. Dad started the car. Diane knew her parents had to be pleased, as she was, but they also had to be wondering whether Scott had any idea what he might be getting himself into.

CHAPTER 21

Gene's last few weeks at home had passed quickly. On the Sunday before he was to leave on his mission, in June, 1964, all the Thomases gathered at his home for dinner, and then, later in the day, Gene spoke at sacrament meeting. He felt good about the talk. He had tried out all his ideas on Marsha, and she had helped him give substance to what he wanted to say. Missionary work was not recruiting members just to add to the numbers of Church, he had said; it was taking a gift to the world, spreading the good news that members were blessed to have received. He told the story from Matthew of the young man who had come to Christ and asked what he should do to gain eternal life—the young man who was, as it turned out, unwilling to sell everything and give to the poor. Gene asked the members, and himself, whether they were willing to devote everything they had to the Church. But he didn't quote the passage about the difficulty of rich men entering the kingdom of God; that was a somewhat sensitive issue in his ward.

Almost everyone at the meeting shook hands with him before or after the service, and many of them put money in his hand or stuffed bills into his pocket. Gene was touched by that, and he was moved by the kind things everyone told him. He was going to be a *great* missionary, they kept saying, and Gene promised them he would do his best.

That night, after an open house, and after Grandma and Grandpa and all the uncles and aunts had finally left, Gene drove Marsha home. The two had been inseparable since the day he had received his call. They had dated every weekend, but more than that, they had spent almost all their long summer evenings together. Gene had spoken with her more openly than he had with anyone else he had ever known, and she had been just as candid with him. He had never known anyone so well, he felt, and he had never admitted so many of his own self-doubts, or discussed with anyone so many of his hopes.

Tonight, as he pulled into her driveway and stopped, he was feeling the reality as never before. He would soon be gone. This lovely interlude was almost over. "I was just thinking," he said, "how dumb I was to waste all those months when I stopped asking you out."

She turned toward him, leaning her back against the door on her side. "Not really," she said. "I don't think we were ready for each other until now."

Gene leaned back the same way, so they were facing one another but far away. A light on the garage shined into the car, but Marsha's face was mostly in shadows. "So what does that mean?" Gene asked. "It sounds almost like you're saying that you like me now."

"Don't do that, okay?"

"Don't do what?"

"You know I like you. But I think you want us to say something about the future, and I don't see how we can do that."

That was exactly what he had wanted. He should have known that Marsha couldn't be beguiled into a commitment. But as the days had grown short, Gene was beginning to feel some panic. Once he left, he didn't know what would happen to their relationship. He was almost desperate to reach some sort of understanding. Otherwise, how could they make it through two and a half years of separation?

"I love you, Marsha," he said. He had never said this before, but he knew it was true, and he wanted to hear the same words from her. It's what had to happen, he was sure, or he would lose her.

"Gene, please don't. We know what's happening between us, but let's not try to give it a name. Let's just write to each other and then find out who we are when you get back."

"I love you," he said again, simply.

She took hold of his hand and pulled him toward her. They kissed, and then she said into his ear, "Gene, I didn't know you until these last few weeks. Almost everything I thought about you was wrong. But we *are* very different. I don't know whether that can ever change."

"Maybe it doesn't have to."

"I don't know. But I know we've both changed a lot in the last two years. It's hard to say what will happen in the next two."

"We're both going to grow."

"Maybe we'll grow apart."

He pulled her tighter to him. "We don't have to. Not if we write and share everything that's happening to us."

"You can't force things like that, Gene. Let's just see where this goes."

Gene wanted to argue the point. But he knew Marsha better than that, and he also suspected she was right. So he kissed her again and then walked her to the door. But he was frightened. He knew that he loved her more than she loved him, and there was nothing he could do about that.

Hans was working outside one afternoon in late June when a steady rainfall turned into a torrent. He was in the rustic old section of Schwerin where he and a crew of men were digging up a cobblestone roadway that had fallen into disrepair. Hans hadn't really minded the rain so much. It had cooled the air and was a nice change. For days now the weather had been hot and humid. But when the rain had begun to fall in sheets, the work had become almost impossible, and the foreman, much to Hans's surprise, had finally said, "We can't continue in this. We might as well stop a little early today. Go on home."

It was more than a little early. It was only two o'clock in the afternoon, and Hans was elated to have this extra time. It opened up an opportunity he had been thinking about for a long time—one he had been rehearsing in his mind for weeks. He washed his hands, and then, still wearing his slicker and rain hat, he walked to his old school—the *oberschule* where he had once been admitted—a distance of well over a mile. When he reached the school, he took off his rain gear, rolled it up, and walked down the hall. Classes were in session, and he hoped he wouldn't bump into any students he knew. He was heading for the director's office.

He did see a group coming in from exercises, but no one he knew. He remembered the secretary, however, and he was humiliated to stand before her in his dirty work clothes, toting his rain gear. "I was hoping to speak to *Direktor* Knorr."

"Hans Stoltz. My goodness, you look five years older. I hardly knew you."

"Is the *Direktor* available?"

"I don't know. He's here. But I don't know whether he has time. Let me ask him."

"Tell him it's *very* important, and I almost never get a chance to come here. I'm off early today because of the rain."

"All right then."

She got up and walked into the director's office. She was gone longer than seemed necessary, but when she returned, she said, "He'll see you for just a moment. But he's very busy today."

"Thank you." Hans set his rain gear in a corner near the door and walked into the office. "*Herr Direktor*," he said. "I won't bother you long."

"What is it, Stoltz?" As always, the man seemed almost two-dimensional, as though nothing ever animated him.

"You once admitted me to this school. You must have thought I was capable of doing well here."

"Yes. But I didn't have all the facts at the time."

"What if I corrected my mistakes? Couldn't I re-enroll this fall and still prove myself? And wouldn't government officials be proud of you, if you could reform me?" Hans had thought about this little speech many times. He knew he had to make certain promises, and he wasn't even sure he meant them, but he couldn't bear to continue life as it was now.

"And how could you correct these errors? You can't change what you have done."

"I could stop going to my church. I'm ready to do that. I would join the Free German Youth. You told us all that we should commit to officer training school after our university studies, commit for a full three years, not just the compulsory year and a half. I'm willing to do that, too."

"I doubt that anyone would believe any of this, Stoltz. You tried to escape from this country, and you have always put your religion ahead of your commitment to the state."

"But I was young. I'm growing up now, and it's not fair that I be judged all my life by the things my parents taught me to do. A man can mature, finally choose for himself. Doesn't it show greater commitment when a young man chooses to support his government, even against the will of his family?"

"So you renounce your religion now, do you?"

Hans had thought so long about this. A hundred times he had told himself he could leave the Church behind. How likely was it that Joseph Smith had seen visions, seen God? Hans had prayed his heart out, just for the simple opportunity to leave this land, and there had been no help, no answer. All his life, Hans's parents had told him how evil and godless Communism was. But why not godless? Maybe it was better to build a system on sensible, scientific grounds, not on myths about gods. He didn't like the way government leaders told people what to think, all the propaganda signs on the streets, all the indoctrination in the schools, but was that so different from his parents, who fed him a steady diet of indoctrination about God and all his blessings, when in fact their only blessing seemed to be a meager, hard-earned existence?

Still, he hesitated. And Knorr seemed to see that.

"I will stop attending my church and leave it behind. It's what I plan to do anyway, sooner or later. I might as well face up to my parents now."

"You didn't say that you renounce your beliefs."

"Belief is nonsense. That's what I've come to see. My parents tell me to have faith, but what is that? It's only believing for no reason, just accepting things that have no proof."

"Why don't you want to say the words?"

"What words?"

"'I renounce my religion.'"

"I have said it. That's all behind me now."

Knorr nodded, but he said, "I fear it's too late for you, Stoltz."

"Could you talk to someone? Could you ask about my enrolling this fall and starting over with *Oberschule?*"

"Perhaps. It's something I need to think about. You made our schools—and especially *Direktor* Schreiter—look very bad to our superiors, Stoltz."

"This could take all that away, *Herr Direcktor.* You could tell your leaders that the teaching I received has finally paid off. I've overcome the pressure from my family, and now I'm ready to build the state in whatever way I can."

He nodded as though he were interested, but then he said again, "I will think about it. Don't come back again. Don't bother me about this. If anything happens, you will hear from us."

"Thank you." Hans stepped forward and offered his hand to Knorr, who gave it a quick shake without standing up. And then Hans left. Outside, the rain was still falling, but not as hard as it had earlier. Hans didn't bother to put on his rain gear. He let the rain pelt down on his hair and shoulders, soaking his old coveralls. He didn't hold out much hope. Knorr wasn't likely to stand up for him. He was a careful man, and he probably wouldn't take the chance. But worse, Hans felt dirty, felt as though he had overstated his case. He didn't like to go to church, and he suspected that his faith was dead, but he had come very close to renouncing his church altogether—had said as much—and that was more than he had been ready to do. He had the feeling that his decision was becoming inevitable, this break with his parents and with the Church, but it was going to hurt his mother and father. He hated the idea of facing them, of telling them what he had done.

But there was more than that. He had the eerie feeling that he had been heard, that the same God he had pleaded with for so long would now turn his back on him. He told himself that this was only a habit of mind, a way of thinking that he had learned from his parents. He had grown up asking God for the things he wanted. Now, more than any other time in his life, he wanted help getting out of the deep hole he felt he had fallen into, and sometimes, even lately, he had caught himself, in spite of all his doubts, asking for some kind of help. Now he was on his own. Surely he couldn't turn to God again. Religion was probably nothing more than superstition, but it was a form of hope that had kept him going at times. Now he had cut himself off from that, and if Knorr refused to help, he was absolutely without a resource.

Still, as he made the long walk home, he told himself that there was no going back now. His only hope was to separate himself from the Church and look for chances to prove to his government that he no longer wanted to leave, that he was willing to join the Free German Youth and, eventually, the party. He hadn't intended to put his faith in the state, but his actions had now brought him to that point, so he told himself that he would take his first step away from the choices his parents had always made for him; he wouldn't go to church that Sunday.

Hans said nothing all week, but when Sunday morning came he tried to do what he had to do without raising much fuss. He merely said, "Papa, I'm not feeling very well this morning. I'm not going to priesthood meeting." He was standing in front of Peter in the living room, still wearing his old cotton pajamas, the ones with the holes in the knees.

"You mean you're not coming to any of the meetings, or—"

"No, I'm not."

"Are you sick?"

"Not bad. But I guess I'm worn out. I just want to sleep this morning."

"Hans, you can't start that. You can make that excuse every week."

Hans didn't want to talk about other weeks. He didn't want a confrontation. He only wanted to take one step at a time. "I just don't feel like going this morning."

"Hans, what's happening? There's more to this than just not feeling well. I know how discouraged you are."

Hans felt some anger growing. His father had no right to make him feel guilty. He was sixteen now, and he could make his own choice to go to church or not. "I can't imagine why I would be discouraged, can you? Everything is going so well."

"Hans, things are going pretty well. Since I got a decent job we're much better off. We have that to be thankful for."

"Oh, yes, every morning, when I go out to tear up cobblestones or carry mortar, I think how lucky I am. I can do that fifty or sixty more years, and then I can die. The time will pass by quickly."

"Is that how life looks to you right now, Son?"

"It's not a matter of *looking*. It's the way things are."

Mom and Inga were in the final stages of getting ready, and then everyone would be setting out for their long walk. So Peter had little time, but still he sat down on his chair and motioned for Hans to sit down across from him. "Hans, I know how that must feel. But things never stay the same. God has given us one great blessing already. We thought I would never find a better job, but I did. It was nearly impossible, but it happened. Now, we have to find a better career for you. And it will happen, someway, somehow. I know it will."

Hans didn't believe that, but he didn't say so. He didn't want more speeches. He just wanted his family to leave, go off to church, and he wanted to sleep.

"Hans, sometimes it seems as though God isn't listening, but these are the tests we face in life. When we pass them, we see the blessings. When I was in the east, during the war, the days went on and on forever. And every day was agony. We were cold and hungry and sick. Every day I expected to die, and often I was disappointed when I woke up in the morning, still alive and facing nothing better than what I'd faced the day before. I told myself there was no God, or at least that he didn't care about me. I almost dared him to prove to me otherwise. I quit praying; I quit hoping; I let myself fall into despair. But God didn't give up on me, Hans. He not only saved my life; he led me home, back to my family. And he led me to your mother and all the good things that came of that—you and Inga, more than anything."

This was all so absurd. Peter had left out all the bad things that had happened: his mistake in coming back to the Russian Zone; the treatment he had received from the government; the failed escape. Father could always twist things around to make them look like blessings, but all of his choices had been wrong, and now he was raising a family with little more than enough to get by.

"I know how hard it is to be patient when it seems as though nothing is working out, but keep going to church, Hans, hold to your faith, and I promise you, God will open a way for you."

"I'm staying home this morning, Papa." Hans was not going to argue about any of this, but he had said the words firmly, with a touch of anger, and he could see his father's disappointment.

"That's all right, Hans. It's up to you, of course. But please don't give up on God; don't give up on the Church. Will you keep praying, and keep attending—even if you don't go today?"

So once again Hans had to answer, just as he had with *Direktor* Knorr.

He glanced downward, refusing to look into his father's eyes, and then he said, "I'm not going anymore, Papa."

"Not at all?"

"Not at all."

"Hans, you can't do that. You just can't. It's the greatest mistake you could make."

"I'm sorry. I know you don't agree with me. But it's my choice, and it's what I'm going to do."

"But why? Why give up so easily?"

Hans hadn't wanted this, but his father was giving him no choice. He decided he would have to take his stand. "I don't believe in God, Papa. I don't believe in the Church. So why should I lose everything for something you and Mama believe in? I'm going to see if I can get back into school, or at least get a better job. I'll join the Free German Youth, if that's what it takes. And I'll move away if that's the only way I can choose my own path without you forcing me every step of the way."

"Have we forced you, Hans?"

"Of course you have. You chose the Mormon Church for me, and now I have to live with that forever. It's ruined my life." Hans finally looked up, saw that tears were running down both his father's cheeks. Hans didn't want this. Why couldn't his father just let Hans go his own way and not make it all seem so personal? "Papa, we all make choices. You made yours. Now let me make mine."

"But Son, what kind of father would I be if I didn't warn you against making a choice that I see as bad for you?"

"You've warned me. I understand how you feel. But that doesn't change anything for me. I didn't set out to doubt the Church, or God; I've come to an honest decision. I simply don't believe any of that."

But now Hans realized that his mother had stepped into the living room, that she had heard at least this last sentence, and maybe more. She came to him and knelt down in front of him. "Oh, Hans, you're too young to make such a statement. You can't decide that forever—not at sixteen. You have so much more to experience in this life."

"Mama, that's fine. Maybe something will change my mind someday, but for now, it's how I feel, and it's very important that I do something. Maybe I still have a chance to have a decent life if I break with the things I've rejected in my mind anyway. If I keep on, just for you and Papa, I *know* I'll lose everything."

"Don't say that, Hans." But this was Inga, who had come into the room without Hans's realizing it. Now all the family pressure was on him. Inga could never understand what he was feeling, but it was she he hated most to disappoint.

"Let's wait a moment," Peter said. "Let's not force all these final conclusions. We have a lot to talk about. Here's all I ask of you, Hans. Keep an open mind for now. Maybe I can answer some of the questions you have."

But Hans wasn't going to do that. If he and his dad talked, they would only end up debating issues that could never be settled. "Papa, I want to do my own thinking," he said.

"Fine. But can't you trust me and your mother just a little? Can't you assume that we didn't come to our beliefs without some work, without some genuine spiritual experiences? Why not rely on our testimonies just a little for now, at least enough to keep an open mind?"

"I do have an open mind. But I'm going to do this my own way. I'm not going to church anymore. If you try to force me, I'll move away."

"How would you live, Son? You don't make enough to pay rent, or to—"

"I'll do what I have to do, Papa. But don't push me anymore."

That brought quiet to the room, except that Inga was whimpering. Both his parents were shedding tears, too, and Hans was sorry about that, but he could only tell himself that he hadn't intended to create this trouble. His father was the one who had forced the issue.

"We need to go," Peter finally said. "But Hans, this isn't the end of this. It can't be. I can't let you go this easily. I won't."

Hans hated the idea that his father was going to keep pressuring him, but he didn't say that, didn't say anything. At least he had taken his stand, and now the family was leaving, going to church, and he was not.

CHAPTER 22

Kathy was in LaRue's car, and they were heading south. The trip had started as another visit for Kathy with her aunt, but also with a plan to visit several colleges. Kathy was interested in some liberal arts schools in New England, and the College of William and Mary in Virginia. But on their way to Virginia, LaRue had told Kathy all about the student group that had left Smith a couple of weeks before, on their way to Mississippi. They were part of the "Summer Project," sponsored by COFO—the Council of Federated Organizations—an alliance of civil rights organizations, staffed primarily by SNCC people. The volunteers were mostly white students who would spend the summer registering Negro voters and setting up "freedom schools."

A few days before, on July 2, after a long filibuster, Lyndon Johnson had been able to sign civil rights legislation that was intended to stop some of the "separate but equal" laws of the South, but everyone knew that most of the changes in the law would be ignored by state and local governments. Literacy tests for voting, for instance, needed to be challenged in order to put pressure on the federal government to pass voting-rights legislation. If Negroes could register to vote in massive numbers, the power structure in the South would change rapidly. But that wasn't happening yet. The plan was to encourage Negroes to attempt registration. When they were turned away, a case could be brought in federal courts to demonstrate discrimination. The volunteers were also setting up summer schools that would aid Negro children who were not receiving adequate education. The schools would teach basic skills, but they would also discuss the history of slavery and of African people in America. The history books the children were currently using spoke of the "War of Northern Aggression" and the happy life of slaves in the Old South.

"Let's go," Kathy had said.

"Go where?"

"To Mississippi. That's more important than visiting colleges."

LaRue had glanced over at Kathy and laughed. "We can't do that. You're only supposed to be out here three weeks, and I need to get back to my research before long."

"Couldn't we help out for a couple of weeks? I'll bet they need all the help they can get."

"Kathy, no. There are all kinds of problems with that. For one thing, you're still seventeen, and the volunteers have to be at least eighteen."

"Don't squeal on me. I look eighteen."

"Actually you look *fourteen*, if you want to know the truth."

"Well, then, if they'll believe I'm seventeen and a half, eighteen isn't much of a stretch."

LaRue was shaking her head. "Kathy, Mississippi is a dangerous place right now. Three of the volunteers disappeared almost as soon as they got there."

"I know that. But we wouldn't have to do anything dangerous. Couldn't we just help out in an office?"

"*I* could. One of my students already wrote me and told me I ought to come down. But if I took you down there, can you imagine what your parents would say? They'd go nuts, and so would your grandpa."

Kathy sat for a long time after that, thinking it all over, trying to decide how she would make her case. Finally, she said, "Remember how we felt last fall, when President Kennedy was shot? We both said we had to do something."

"I know. I've thought about that many times."

"Nothing will ever change as long as good people do nothing. You know that. Next year I'll be eighteen, and I'm going to get involved.

When are *you* going to start?" What Kathy didn't say, but what she was thinking about, was her day of "protest" at the Midtown Theater. She had made a few attempts to draw a little closer to her friend Verna, but she had felt awkward about it, and not much had happened. She felt a nagging need to do something real for the cause.

"Look, I've thought about going ever since I got that letter from my student," LaRue said. "But I was sure I couldn't take you. If we did go, would you be careful, stay in the office, and do whatever work needs to be done?"

"Sure I would."

"What would we tell your parents?"

"We took a wrong turn in Virginia?"

"No. Really?"

"I'll tell them when I get home. They would just worry if we say something now, but they'll forgive me once they know it turned out all right."

"But will they forgive me?"

Both laughed, and Kathy loved LaRue more than ever. Maybe she was over thirty, but she was still the rebellious sister in the Thomas family.

They stopped by the campus at William and Mary, but then they kept going. They drove late into the night, stayed in a motel in South Carolina long enough to sleep a few hours, and then took turns driving through Atlanta and Birmingham. Roads became narrower, the going slower, but they made it to western Alabama before they slept again, and before noon the following day, they were in the town of Greenwood, Mississippi, where LaRue's friend was working.

By then, however, something was going on in Kathy. She felt as though she had left the United States. There was something new in the density of the forests, the vines, the drooping Spanish moss in the trees, and the suffocating humidity. But more than that, Kathy kept watching the towns they drove through. Negroes in Salt Lake were people like herself, with darker skin. Here, she saw what she wanted to call degradation but looked like something that ran deeper. She watched the brown-skinned men and women, bent in the fields, and saw nobility in that, but in the towns, she saw how deferential Negroes acted. The men walked about in tattered overalls and shabby shoes, stepping aside when whites came by, nodding without looking up. The children were energetic, but poverty was written all over them. Kathy heard their chatter and couldn't understand them. Most were wearing as little as possible—because of the heat—but she had never seen shoeless children, children dressed in such patched, ragged clothes.

Kathy was alarmed by what she felt. It was bad enough to see the way white men glared when they saw Massachusetts license plates on the car, and it was frightening to be tailed by a sheriff for no reason, but it was the Negroes Kathy felt uncomfortable about. They seemed foreign to her, dirty. She knew why. She knew the history of their people. But it didn't change her reaction: a kind of revulsion she was ashamed of. She thought of Mrs. Brittain's attitude.

By the time LaRue and Kathy walked into the new little library—built by SNCC the year before and now serving as an office for the COFO workers—Kathy knew what she wanted most: just to go home. The humidity alone was so sickening that she didn't know how she could last another day, and the smell of decay was in the air, even inside the new building, where fans whirred and worked their way back and forth.

LaRue's friend was sitting at a little wood desk upstairs, her long hair tied up in a loose clasp, sweat glistening on her skin. She looked as white as the ceramic swan Grandma kept on her knickknack shelf back in Salt Lake. She was wearing a slim little cotton dress, sleeveless but long. She stood up, wonderfully surprised. "Professor Thomas!" she said. "You did decide to come."

"But I'm not sure why," LaRue said. "How can you stand the heat?"

"You don't *stand* it. You capitulate to it. You just sweat and stink and live with it. You could take ten showers a day and still never feel like it did any good."

"We're dying. We've been driving through it for a couple of days." She motioned to Kathy. "This is my niece, Kathy, from Utah. We just wondered whether we could be of any help for—I don't know—a week, maybe two, if we can stick it out."

"I'll say, you can help." The young woman stepped to Kathy and shook her hand. "I'm Ellie Matson," she said. "I'm from Iowa, but I was in your aunt's economics class last year. She's the one who got me thinking about a lot of issues I'd never even worried about before. It's her fault I'm down here."

"She's had the same influence on me all my life," Kathy said.

"You're not a college student, are you?"

"Not yet. I will be soon." But Kathy was careful not to say that she still had another year of high school.

"What can we do?" LaRue asked.

"Sit down. Here, let me move some things." The office was littered with papers and pamphlets and boxes. Ellie moved a couple of boxes from a chair for LaRue and then pulled out a folding chair and opened it for Kathy. The fan continued to hum, and the moving air was wonderful. Kathy let her eyes go shut as it passed over her. She wondered what she could do that would actually matter. Something out there in this little town seemed to say, "We aren't about to change; we won't change; we don't even have the first idea how to change."

"We've got all kinds of paperwork to prepare," Ellie said. She made a futile attempt to push some of the loose hair away from her face. "We've been taking people down to the county courthouse every day. They try to register to vote, but Mrs. Lamb, the registrar, makes them take a literacy test. I swear, Dr. Thomas, *you* couldn't pass it."

"Just call me LaRue, Ellie. All this professor and doctor stuff isn't really necessary now."

"Well, anyway, she makes these people write an essay on the meaning of some part of the Constitution—and she chooses obscure passages that *no one* really understands. No one can pass it, but once in a while she registers someone, just to pretend she's being fair."

"Does everyone have to take the test, or just Negroes?" Kathy asked.

Ellie laughed. "If you asked Mrs. Lamb, she'd tell you the white citizens are able to pass the test, but that's a joke. The simple fact is, white people get to vote. Almost no Negroes do."

"How can they get away with that?"

Ellie laughed harder. "Oh, Kathy, you've got to stop thinking about this place as the United States. When people beat up on our workers, *we* get thrown in jail for inciting a riot."

"Is that happening?" LaRue asked. "Are project workers getting beaten up?"

"Oh, yes. You've got to be careful. But if you stay around here, in the office, or maybe teach at our Freedom School, you shouldn't have any trouble. It's the boys who go into the neighborhoods and work on voter registration, they're the ones who put their lives in danger."

"Have you done any of that?"

"Well, yes." She pulled at the neck of her dress, stretching the fabric off her wet skin. "I'd do it every day if I could. That's the most important work, as far as I'm concerned."

"Why doesn't the federal government do anything?" LaRue asked.

"We hope it will, sooner or later. We document every case. We're showing the pattern, demonstrating to the Justice Department how serious the discrimination is. We just hope that sooner or later the courts will enforce the law. The trouble is, the federal judges down here are southern boys, too, and President Johnson knows how much of his support comes from the South. He doesn't want to rock the boat *too* much."

"I wish we still had President Kennedy. He would have—"

"Kennedy gave some nice speeches, Kathy, but he did very little.

Lyndon Johnson at least got the new civil rights bill passed. But both of them have used the excuse that the courts have to enforce the law, and they don't want to interfere. That's supposed to keep all these states'-rights nuts down here from jumping the Democratic Party. What we have to do is keep showing the nation what's happening. I hate to say it, but I think COFO brought us white students down here, knowing that some of us would get beaten up, maybe even killed, and the nation would pay attention when white people got hurt. No one's ever worried about the Negroes who get murdered."

"And now those three workers are missing," LaRue said.

"They might not ever be found. But if two of them hadn't been white, you never would have heard about it."

"That makes me sick."

"I know." Ellie looked down at her desk. "I'm already disillusioned. I feel like I'm ten years older than I was a month ago. But listen, that's only one side of it. We're doing a lot of good through our schools, and I've never been so loved in my life. The Negroes here, most anyway, really appreciate what we're trying to do. You haven't really felt love until you go to one of our mass meetings, and we've got one going tonight. You need to be there."

"Okay," LaRue said. "But what should we do to get started? Is there someplace we can sleep, or do we need to take a motel room?"

"You don't want to do that. Once the white people know what you're doing here, you'll want to 'stay with your own kind.' Can you two sleep in the same bed?"

"Well . . . sure. I guess we can." LaRue looked at Kathy. Kathy nodded, but in this heat, she wondered what that would be like.

"Okay, I know where you can stay, then. Mrs. Morrow, one of our local supporters—a Negro woman—puts up some people for us. Two of our boys left for another assignment yesterday, so she has a room open.

Mrs. Morrow will feed you well. You just have to get used to a little different diet." She laughed. "Have you ever eaten grits?"

"No, but we're game," LaRue said. "We might as well have the full experience."

Before she had arrived here, Kathy probably would have agreed to all of this enthusiastically, but now she wondered what it would be like. She thought of the sharecroppers' shacks she had seen on the farms, thought of the Negro sections of town she had seen, where unpainted, ramshackle houses with sagging roofs seemed to be more common than not.

Ellie went with LaRue and Kathy in LaRue's car. They drove a couple of blocks through a shabby part of town, but the house they stopped at seemed nicely kept. There were climbing roses in front, growing on trellises over the porch, and a large, spreading magnolia tree shaded the front of the house. Kathy could smell a rich sweetness. "That's honeysuckle," Ellie said, "that and boxwood and chinaberry and a hundred other things that smell wonderful. That's the best thing I've found in the South."

Kathy carried her suitcase to the porch, then waited as Ellie told Mrs. Morrow, "We have two volunteers who are only going to be here a week or two. I thought they could maybe stay in the room where Charles and Michael were."

"Why, sure," Kathy heard the big woman say. But she was inside, where it was dark, and all Kathy could see was an expanse of faded gray fabric. She didn't expect what she got as she stepped inside. Suddenly the woman's big arms were around her. "Oh, thank you, deary. You jis nothin' but a chile yo'self. An' you come here to he'p wif the struggle. Now don' you worry one minute. I'm goin' to feed you good."

Kathy felt swallowed in the woman's softness, in the strange, lush smells in her apron, but her first impulse was to resist. She held stiff for a second or two, and then she gave way to what she began to feel, and she reached around the woman, tightening her own grip.

Then Mrs. Morrow went after LaRue and hugged her the same way.

When she stepped back, she said, "Why you two the prettiest ones we ever did have. Ellie, here, she's nice, but she not half as pretty as you. She way too white." She laughed in a deep, loose way, almost like a cough.

Kathy felt better. She was still leery about sleeping in a double bed with LaRue, and she worried that the heat would melt her, but she had found something that seemed more like a home than she ever could have expected. And that afternoon she learned a little about the paperwork she would be expected to process and file. She also met the kids from the freedom school, from little ones to high-school students, and they all treated her more deferentially than she liked but with wonderful acceptance.

That night she ate southern: fried chicken, cornbread, fried okra, turnip greens. She struggled a little with the greens, but she liked the rest, and she liked hearing Mrs. Morrow laugh with her children—five of them, from four to about thirteen—and with two volunteers, both white college boys, who also shared a bedroom. One was a Jewish boy from New York and Yale, Arthur Heller; and the other a Stanford student from Oregon named Jerome May. Jerome had taken to wearing overalls, as though to fit in with the local farmers, and Arthur had on jeans and a blue work shirt. They weren't handsome, but they were bright and funny. Arthur told a story about being harassed by the sheriff. "He drives up alongside us," he said, "and he leans out his car window. Then he says, 'You boys enjoying our nice July weather?' 'It's a little hot,' I told him. So he says, 'Well, now, I guess no one ask you to come down here. You coulda stayed back where it's cooler.' So I smile at him, big as I can, and I say, 'Yes, but I never would have known what southern hospitality was all about. Last week, for two nights, I got free board and room.' He started to laugh, like he really liked that one, and then his head jerked toward me, and he said, 'There's a lot more where that come from. You can count on that, Jew boy.'"

That seemed marvelously funny to Arthur and to all the rest. But

Kathy was amazed that a law officer could say something like that. "Have you really been in jail?" Kathy asked.

"We sure were." Arthur smiled. He was a slim boy with heavy, horn-rimmed glasses and the dark shadow of a thick beard.

"What for?"

"Loitering. We were waiting for some of our people to try to register."

"They can't do that."

There was a big laugh again. Kathy looked around at Mrs. Morrow's children and her husband. Everyone was crowded around a table not nearly big enough for such a large group. Kathy knew that a certain amount was paid to the Morrows for room and board, and Kathy and LaRue would now pay, but she doubted it could be enough to compensate Mrs. Morrow for all the food she had prepared.

"I think it's great you can laugh about something like that," Kathy said.

"How can you not laugh?" Jerome said. "If you don't, you just get angry. And the last thing you want to do is let those guys see that they're getting to you. They think, if they treat us badly enough, throw us in jail, call us names, harass us, we'll give up and go home."

"I'll tell you what, Miss Kathy," Mr. Morrow said. "We had enough. We had enough long ago. Ain't none of this funny—none at all. But change gon' to come. Real slow, but we see it a little now. That jis enough to give us some hope, so maybe now we *can* laugh."

"Don't see me laughing, do you now?" Carroll Lee said. Carroll Lee was the Morrows' fourteen-year-old daughter. "I don' see no big hope. I see more'n the same. My school 'bout fallin' down. Don't nobody fix it up. Don't nobody care. Us young'ns, we ain't goin' to wait so long. We fixin' to do somethin'."

"What?" LaRue asked.

"Slim Henderson, he gotta sto', right here in Colored Town. He makes all his money off'n us. Las' week when some people goin' down to regista', he grabs a colored woman, drags her by her hair clear 'cross the street. But somebody got a picture of it, and we got it put up all over town. Now we're sayin' don' shop at his sto,' and we gonna start holdin' up signs tellin' people to stay away. Now thas somethin' these white folks can understand, when they don' get none of our money no mo'."

"That's a good idea," Kathy said. "Look what the boycott did in Montgomery."

"It also got some heads broke," Mr. Morrow said. "And I've tol' Carroll Lee, I don' want her down at that sto'."

Carroll Lee didn't look up. She was eating, and she said to her plate, "Thas fine. For now. But I ain't gon' to be like old folks. I ain't puttin' up with all this."

"I don't blame you," Kathy said. "I feel the same way."

"Yah, sure. But what do you know? You white. You got yo' fancy clothes, yo' nice car out front. You come down here, be nice to colored folks for a few days, then drive back no'th, feelin' good about yo'self. I say, go on home. It's time colored people do it theirselves."

"But you love me and Jerome, don't you, Carroll Lee?" Arthur said. "You just can't help it. We're the best-looking white boys you've ever seen."

"You bof ugly, if you ax me."

"All right now," Mr. Morrow said, "you've had your say, Carroll Lee. Don't start talking like that."

Carroll Lee smiled. "All white boys ugly," she said. "They skin look like to'let paper."

Even Mr. Morrow laughed.

That night the Negro church was full, every seat taken and some people standing in the back. Project volunteers, with the help of Negro young people, had been handing out handbills and talking to people about coming out to the meeting. Some people liked to gather and hear what local preachers and SNCC leaders had to say, but they were hesitant to register for the vote. But if the workers could get people out to these meetings, build some confidence and excitement, often those who had held back before would get up the nerve to make that trip. So the mass meetings were held quite often, sometimes several nights in a row, and the Negro community thrived on the hope they engendered.

Kathy sat alongside LaRue, with Ellie on the other side, but there were only a handful of other white people in the congregation, all of them project volunteers. It was a strange feeling to be in such a minority, but Kathy was surprised that few of the Negroes held Carroll Lee's opinion. Most were more than welcoming, even too courteous. Kathy was still uncomfortable with the heat, her own sweat and everyone else's, even with the strange, sweet smells from outside blowing through the open windows. She could also hear the rattling hum of cicadas that made the night sound foreign to her. She wanted to like this, but she found herself longing for the meeting to pass quickly. Maybe the bed would be narrow for her and LaRue, but she was dead tired after all the traveling. Maybe the night would be a little cooler, eventually, and she could sleep.

But then the congregation began to sing. Kathy knew about "Negro spirituals." She had even sung them with her high-school choir. But she had never heard anything like this. Ellie told her that these were "freedom songs."

"It's that Freedom Train a-Comin'," they sang first. The minister would lead out, singing a line, and the congregation would come in before he finished, creating a kind of syncopation. The people sang full-voiced, full of spirit and joy. Kathy wondered if this was the only time the people felt really free, when they sang about freedom.

Then they sang "Ain't Gonna Turn Me 'Round," and for the first time Kathy felt hopeful. There was a force here that seemed undeniable.

Finally the Reverend—Ellie told them his name was Davis—stood at the pulpit. He laughed, saying how joyous the music was, how much he loved to be with the people. And then slowly, he began to draw in the crowd. "Here in Mississippi, there's a law for huntin' deer," he said. "They got a season for that. Can't no one shoot one any other time."

People laughed, and someone mumbled, "Sho' nuff. That's right." They seemed to see some humor that Kathy didn't get. Or maybe they knew what was coming.

"I think they even got laws 'gainst shootin' rabbits, if I got that right."

"Oh, you got it right," someone shouted. "They got that law."

"Thas right. I guess they do. And possums too. They got laws about shootin' a regular ol' possum. But what about Negroes? They got a law here in Mississippi 'gainst shootin' Negroes?"

"Not one," someone shouted. And others were picking up the idea. "No laws 'gainst that. Jis go ahead and shoot."

There was a rumble of laughter, a sardonic, knowing laugh. The whole congregation was nodding, mumbling. "Thas fer shore. Jis go ahead and shoot that colored man," Brother Davis was saying. "No one goin' to stop that."

The logic of his talk began to build. Some people thought it was possible to placate whites, to satisfy them by grinning and saying 'yassah' and 'nossah,' by ducking their heads, by accepting things the way they were. "But *change* gotta come," he suddenly shouted. "An' the white man ain't gonna hand it to us. We gotta stand up. We gotta face the man. We must not shake when he points his finger at us, calls us nigger, tells us what he's going to do. Maybe some of us even gotta git ourselves shot before it's th'ough. But change gotta come. And ain't nobody going to bring about that change but us people, right here, sittin' in this church here tonight."

"Some of you scared to go down and register. An' I don't blame you one bit. You sho' ought to be scared. I scared too. But I tell you what, brothers and sisters, ain't nobody goin' to turn me 'round." Without a signal, the congregation broke into song again. And this time Kathy realized she only thought she had heard the song earlier in the evening. This time, it seemed the roof might rattle loose and drop in on top of all of them.

And she was singing too, understanding when her line came in, when the odd rhythm took hold. She had never let herself go before, even though she had sung in choirs all her life. But here, the volume was so full and powerful, it was all she could do to mix some of her sound with the great chorus. She liked hearing her voice join with the others, and she liked the way the congregation was in motion, standing, sometimes waving, swaying from foot to foot, clapping hands. She had never felt like this in a Mormon church, never felt so in tune with everyone around her.

The freedom songs continued. And finally a prayer. Everyone joined in the prayer, too. "Yes, yes," they would voice, as the reverend would plead for courage, plead for more people to be ready to register in the morning. "Oh, yes. Lord, yes. Courage, Lord. Courage."

The Spirit was in the room, as surely as Kathy had ever felt it. She knew why she had come to Mississippi.

CHAPTER 23

A week passed, and Kathy could feel something happening to her. She still hated the heat and the dampness, but she slept well at night all the same. And part of the reason was that her days were long and busy. She liked the project workers. They were all students, not much older than herself, and different from her in their backgrounds. Most of them smoked—smoked a lot—and at night they would sometimes go to a local jive joint, order a pitcher of beer, and let their hair down. All that made it hard for Kathy to feel close to them at first, but what she kept seeing was their amazing commitment. Arthur and Jerome would come home at the end of a day and tell frightening stories. One day a car full of young men had pulled up next to them as they were walking on a lonely road, and a man in the backseat had stuck a rifle out the window. Arthur and Jerome had dived to the ground and rolled into the weeds, but all they had heard was laughing as the car sped away. When Kathy told them they ought to call the police, they both smiled. "We've had guys shoot in our direction twice. We reported it the first time, and the sheriff said, 'Them boys was probably jis shootin' at a rabbit. I can see where you two jis might look like a couple a' rabbits. There's a real likeness.'" Jerome imitated the dialect perfectly and even seemed to enjoy the sheriff's sense of humor. But all Kathy could think about was how amazed she was that they kept going out each day, even after that.

Ellie was a powerful example too. She handled everything. She taught at the freedom school, drove people down to the courthouse to register, waited with them, came back to stacks of paperwork, handled disputes among volunteers, was on the phone to headquarters—everything. What

Kathy felt best about was that she was taking a big part of Ellie's load just by processing papers that had stacked up since the program had started. LaRue got most involved with the school. She helped redesign some of the curriculum, and she taught a number of classes herself.

Kathy and LaRue both spent a good deal of time with the kids who came to the school each day. A lot of the classes were held in a local church, but others, by necessity, met on the lawn outside the library. Many of the kids would hang around all day, whether they were in class or not. They seemed to love Kathy, who was a little closer to their own age, and she could tell that some of the older boys clearly had crushes on her.

What surprised Kathy was how different she felt about these Negro kids she met at the school compared to the foreignness she had felt at first. It wasn't long until she didn't notice their clothing, ragged as some of it was. And she got so she could understand the dialect fairly well, most of the time. She was also surprised at the sophistication of the kids. They didn't show it in their grammar or in their learning, but she found it in their wisdom, their perceptions about their world, and she saw it in their recognition of what was going to be asked of them if change was ever going to take place. Like Carroll Lee, many of the kids were much angrier than Kathy had ever imagined. They watched their parents placate whites, saw their mothers work in white homes, and they told themselves they weren't going to be like that. They were going to stand up.

What impressed Kathy most was that such bravery seemed so fruitless. She kept telling herself that *some* of these whites must be willing to accept Negroes as their brothers and sisters. They all seemed to profess Christianity. But she saw no sign of any compromise at all. It wasn't just that whites considered Negroes inferior; they seemed to hate them, not even consider them human. Kathy could understand that, if they didn't live so close, work together, share a community. Kathy had learned in a week that the Negroes in town were as complicated as anyone else, and as varied. Some feared the movement but could barely communicate their worries. Others were articulate and amazingly full of love in spite of all they were living through. How could southern whites not know that, not accept the truth that Negroes were individuals, as varied as themselves?

During the second week Kathy and LaRue were in Greenwood, another mass meeting was scheduled. Kathy was excited to be there this time. Already, she knew most of the people, and many—especially the kids—beamed when they saw her. It was hard to imagine that she had become so much a part of things in only a week. Stokeley Carmichael was there this time, the national SNCC leader, and Robert Moses, who had started the movement in Mississippi. Carmichael was a handsome West Indian who didn't speak with a preacher's style. He articulated a logic for why the people needed to face their fears and go down to the courthouse to register. Moses spoke quietly but forcefully about the future that Negroes were fighting for. Afterward, Reverend Davis spoke again and got the congregation rocking. As before, the meeting ended with several "freedom songs," which seemed to mean so much to the people. They could enter those songs, believe for the moment that change really was possible. Kathy was just as moved this week as the time before, but she was a little more frightened. She could feel that the people, especially the kids, were growing restless. The speakers had expressed admiration for the young people, who on their own had begun the picketing and boycotting of Slim Henderson's store, but they had warned the children not to forget the vow of nonviolence. "If we try to fight the white man, the white man goin' to win," Reverend Davis told them. "He got the guns. He got the power. And that not the Christian way nohow. What we gotta do is love the man, and then we gotta be a man oursel's. We gotta look in his eye and say, 'I been down a long time, but now it's time I stan' up, and you and me, we talk man to man.' But it ain't right to hate the man. There's been way too much of that already."

Kathy loved those words, but she was hearing something different from some of the teenagers, even younger kids. "The whites ain't never gonna *give* us the vote," one of the boys had said. "We gotta take it. If he shoot one of us, we gotta shoot back. Tha's the only thing the white man ever goin' to un'erstan'."

What Kathy feared most was that the pressure was rising in Greenwood. The kids were making it difficult for Negroes to shop with Slim Henderson, but some had credit at the store and could get it nowhere else. When they were out of money, they felt they had to shop there, no matter how they felt about Mr. Henderson. But the kids on the picket line saw these people as traitors, and they were getting tougher— intimidating, shouting, even blocking the way. What was worse was the rising anger of white people, and of Slim Henderson himself. He had tried to placate his customers at first, but now he was becoming furious with the kids who surrounded his store. He had come out once and waved a pistol, demanding that the demonstrators move back. They hadn't moved far, and he hadn't fired the pistol, but Kathy wondered when he might.

Kathy was in the office on the morning after the mass meeting. She was typing up more notes for police reports. She was just rolling a new sheet of paper into her typewriter when LaRue hurried into her office. "The sheriff is arresting all the kids at the store. We're going over to see what we can do."

Kathy jumped up. A week before she would have said, "They can't be arrested for picketing," but she knew better now. She followed LaRue out the door and to her car. They drove the few blocks to the store. As they approached, Kathy could see a big bus, like a school bus, painted black. As they got closer, she could see that seven or eight men, some in uniform, some not, were walking the kids to the bus. The kids were going peacefully, and even though the sheriff's men were pushing them hard, she couldn't see that anyone was getting beaten.

But just as she stepped out of the car, she saw a boy go down. A policeman was standing over him, holding a long stick, screaming into the boy's face, and then he brought the club down hard across the boy's arms, which he had wrapped around his head. The policeman hit him twice, three times, and then threw a hard blow into the boy's back. By then Kathy was running. She heard LaRue yell for her to stop, but she couldn't let the man beat the boy like that. "Stop it! Stop it!" she was screaming.

She kept running and was almost to the boy when the policeman turned toward her. She saw the look of surprise in his face, and for just a moment, some satisfaction, it seemed, as though he were glad to be confronted, maybe glad that a project worker was giving him this opportunity. But he swung so hard, so suddenly, that Kathy didn't see the stick coming until it was almost there. Her arm shot up, but too late, and the stick cracked her across the side of the head. Pain shot through her brain—light flashed—and then a whirring pattern of black and white spun through her mind. She didn't know she was on the ground until she got her eyes to open and saw the man over her.

"Don't come at me like 'at," he said. And then he brought the club down again, this time with less force. But it caught her across the shoulder, sent a new pain shooting through her.

By then two more men—not policeman, or at least not in uniform—were there, hovering over her. One jerked the boy to his feet. The other grabbed Kathy by the wrist, pulled her to a sitting position, and then snapped her arm behind her back. Two men—the one who had first struck her and one of the new ones—hoisted her to her feet. "That's all for you, Missy. You're going to jail," the policeman said.

But LaRue was next to them by now. "Sir, listen to me. She wasn't trying to attack you. All she did was tell you, please, to stop. We care about these kids, and—"

"If you want a go to jail with her, jis keep it up," the policeman said. He was a big man, lean, and he was decent-looking, like someone Kathy might have known in her ward back home.

"But I don't understand that. I'm not threatening you. I'm trying to explain."

"You're a fine-looking woman, you know that? You gittin' some action from any of these niggah boys?"

"You're disgusting," LaRue shouted into his face. "You have no right to talk to me that way."

"Guess what? You jis bought yourself a ticket on this nice black bus. I hope you like these niggahs, 'cause you're gonna spend plenty of time with 'em in jail."

He still had hold of Kathy, but now he left her to the other man, a shorter fellow with a heavy middle hanging over his belt. The policeman grabbed LaRue hard, by the arm. As he did, he said something disgusting, obscene, and LaRue spun on him and slapped his face.

Kathy was being pulled away, but she glanced back to see LaRue on the ground. Ellie was down next to her, trying to help her. Kathy got jostled ahead, her arm still twisted painfully behind her back, but when she got a chance to look back again, just before she stepped onto the bus, she saw that the tall policeman was pulling LaRue to her feet, her face covered with blood. Another man had hold of Ellie.

Kathy couldn't believe the mess she had started, but she was still too angry to regret a thing. She just hoped she got a chance to go before a judge. She wanted to tell someone what was really going on.

The man who had hold of her tossed her into a seat at the front of the bus. Then he stepped back out the door. Kathy's head was still spinning and the pain was beginning to set in. She touched the side of her head, felt the sticky blood in her hair. One of the kids, a boy, reached forward, from the seat behind. He had some sort of cloth that he pressed against her head. She realized by then that it was his shirt, which he had pulled off. "Oh, thank you," she said. "You didn't have to do that."

But he kept it against her wound. "You brave," he said.

Kathy had begun to cry. It was the last thing she wanted to do, in front of the kids, but she was so frustrated, so upset with herself, and yet so touched by this little kindness.

LaRue was being pushed onto the bus by then, her dark hair a mess, blood running down her forehead, along her nose and into her eyes. Then came Ellie, her blouse torn, her bra showing, but at least no blood.

"You two niggah lovers sit down," the tall policeman said. "Don't try to resist again. You got enough 'gainst you already."

"When did I resist?" LaRue shouted back at the man. "You just like beating up on women. Aren't you *big* and *strong?*"

His answer was vile. He didn't strike at her again, but he repeated his accusations about her sleeping with Negroes, said it in the most disgusting language Kathy had ever heard.

"Shut your filthy mouth!" she yelled at him. "You aren't going to get away with this. You've beat up on the wrong woman this time."

But the policeman only laughed. "We'll see how much you like our jail," he said. "If you don't mind niggahs, maybe you don't mind rats neither." He walked off the bus.

Kathy heard Ellie say, "LaRue, you've had your say. Don't do it any more. It won't do any good. We'll get bailed out, and we'll report all this. But if you defy them, they'll just keep you in jail longer, and they'll pile on more fines."

Kathy couldn't believe that someone as young as Ellie was so under control, so willing to accept things as they were. But as she calmed down herself, she began to wonder what was coming next. She was thinking about those rats. Had he really meant that? And then the worst thought hit her: how would her parents react if they found out she was in a Mississippi jail?

A few more of the kids were brought onto the bus, and then a heavy fellow in coveralls got behind the wheel. The policeman stood next to him, facing the passengers. "All right now. Ever'one sit real still. Don't say nothin.' Don't do nothin.' You done enough already."

But almost instantly a deep voice in the back of the bus sang out, "Ain't goin' to let Chief Lary turn me round, turn me round, turn me round." All the kids picked it up immediately, some of them singing in syncopation, "Freedom, freedom, freedom, freedom."

Kathy had heard of Chief Lary, the chief of police, but she hadn't met up with him yet. What she knew was that these young people were amazingly resolute. She watched the policeman, but he didn't react. He sat in his seat and pretended that nothing was happening.

The bus bounced forward, jarring Kathy's aching head, but after a hesitation and a grinding of gears, it settled into a slow, rumbling motion. Kathy shut her eyes and held the shirt tight against her head. She hoped the cut wasn't too severe.

The ride was only a few blocks, and then everyone was ordered off. "Jis walk nice and slow, stay in single file. Anyone who breaks the line, or anythin' like 'at, you better be ready for what yer gonna git. And no more singin.' I heard 'bout 'nough of 'at."

Kathy managed to stand. LaRue stepped back to her and took her in her arms. "I'm so sorry I got you into this," she said. She was crying now, too.

"You didn't get me into it. I'm the one who started the trouble."

"I never should have brought you down here."

"We've got to move now," Ellie said. "Don't let them see you cry. Don't give them that satisfaction."

Kathy wiped her eyes with her free hand and continued to hold the shirt to her head with the other. LaRue had wiped some of the blood from her face, smeared it with her hand. Blood had dripped onto her blue shirt. She was taking deep breaths, obviously trying to get control. And then the three followed the line and stepped down from the bus. As they did, a group of people, mostly men who had gathered on the street, began to yell at them, "Hey, that's what you git. You come down here to agitate, and you got yerself agitated, didn't yuh?"

Most of the calls were more obscene, were mostly questions about white girls and "niggahs."

The kids were allowed to walk by themselves, in line, but policemen stepped out and grabbed hold of Kathy, Ellie, and LaRue. The tall policeman who had knocked Kathy down in the first place gripped her upper arm now, squeezing it hard, but Kathy didn't give him the satisfaction of knowing how much it hurt.

Inside the courthouse lobby, most of the kids were taken off to the left, but the policemen pushed the three white women through another door and then down a hallway. When they passed through the next door, Kathy saw a series of jail cells. There was no one inside. One of the men—the guy with the big stomach—fished a key from his pocket, fiddled with it until he found the one he wanted, and then opened a cell. He gave Ellie a push inside. "This here's our nicest room," he said. "I hope you don't mind bedbugs."

"I guess they'll get used to them after they sleep on them ol' mattresses for a couple of months," the second man, a little fellow with a missing front tooth, said. He pushed LaRue in.

The policeman who had hold of Kathy didn't say a word, but he walked to the door of the cell. He let go of her, and then, without warning, shoved her with all his force, both hands in the middle of her back. Kathy flew across the cell, fell forward, and then skidded into one of the bunkbeds, smacking her shoulder. She rolled up and fought the pain but said nothing.

"What's wrong with you?" LaRue shouted at the man.

But Ellie grabbed her. "That's enough," she said. "Don't bother."

"This here blondie, she understands," the policeman said. "I think she musta had a nice stay with us once before."

He shut the door and locked it, and then the three walked away. When they reached the outer door, the little one looked back and said,

"If you don't hear from no one for a few days, don't worry. We shore won't forget yer down here."

The other two laughed, and then they all walked out.

By then LaRue was helping Kathy up. Besides hitting her shoulder, she had slammed her ankle across the sharp edge of a bed leg and had cut it open. She could see already that the cut wasn't serious, but the bruise would be. Her ankle was beginning to swell.

"Just calm down now," Ellie said. "They'll probably let us sit overnight, but then they'll take us before the judge. Snick will get some lawyers here as soon as they can, and they'll get us out. But we could be in here a few hours or a few days, maybe even longer. The best thing to do is rest as best you can and not try to outguess them."

Kathy sat on a lower bunk and looked at the repulsive, stained mattress. LaRue sat down next to her. Her cut couldn't have been deep. The blood had dried on her forehead and wasn't running anymore.

"I'm going to write this all up," LaRue said. "I'm going to get it in the *New York Times* and on all the wire services. They aren't going to get away with this."

"It's all been in the papers before," Ellie said. "This isn't even a big story. If they had killed us, that would make a better article, but it wouldn't change anything. We've got three boys dead already, and all the FBI does is walk around, ask questions, and take notes. Too many of those guys are southerners themselves, and the ones who aren't don't want to make waves and get themselves shot."

"But people in the north don't really understand what it's like down here."

"LaRue, you're a lot older than I am. But I have to tell you, you sound like a child to me right now. Don't you know what the real truth is?"

"What truth?"

"People in the North love to talk about these terrible southerners and all the things they do to 'colored people,' but deep down, they don't care.

Northerners are as prejudiced as southerners. They just don't show their hatred in quite the same way. What we have is a racist nation, and nothing is going to happen until more people start to change how they think."

"So how do you do that? How can things ever change?"

"I don't know. I came down here because I thought we could make a difference, just a little at a time. But I'm starting to think that method would take a thousand years. Some of the Snick leaders are starting to say the only thing that will change this country is a revolution. Maybe Negroes have to go to war."

Kathy didn't want to believe that any of that was true, but she felt so powerless. Those men had done whatever they wanted to, and there was no one "out there" who could stop them, or maybe no one who cared enough to try. She wanted to believe that one call to Bobby Kennedy, and he would send federal troops to stop such a thing, but that obviously wasn't going to happen.

Kathy looked around. Two walls of the cell were formed by bars. At one end was a filthy, rust-stained toilet, sitting out where a person who used it would be in full view. Near that was a shower stall with no curtain. There were eight bunkbeds, hung from the wall by chains, but one of the upper bunks was broken and hanging at a crooked angle. There was a tiny barred window near the end where the toilet was, but little light came from it. The only other source was a bare bulb that hung just outside the cell. The concrete floor was caked with dirt and stains. Kathy thought of the rats the policeman had warned them about, and suddenly she wanted, more than anything, just to get out, to be home in her own bedroom.

"Will they notify my parents about this?" Kathy asked Ellie.

"I don't know. They might, after we're arraigned. Last time I was in, my parents didn't hear a thing. But sometimes parents are on the phone right away. You can never outguess these guys. They don't follow any one procedure. They just do whatever they feel like."

For the first time Kathy felt guilty. She knew that her parents had trusted that she was going to be traveling with Aunt LaRue. She couldn't blame them if they were upset about deceiving them. And certainly she knew they would be worried if they got a call or a letter telling them that she had been arrested. "Don't we get a phone call?" she asked.

Ellie only laughed.

It was a long night, and Kathy was in pain. The cut in her head had quit bleeding on its own, but her head throbbed. She was also feeling the huge bruise on her shoulder, and the one on her ankle. There was even a bruise on her arm where the policeman had gripped her so tight. But more than that, she hurt all over. She seemed to ache in her soul. The injustice kept running through her mind, keeping her awake and disturbed. The smell of the mattress, the absence of a pillow, of sheets, the fear that her cuts, unprotected, would become infected—all of it was just too awful. And she heard sounds—maybe the sound of rats; she didn't know. But the thought that rats might be near her, under her bed, never left her all night.

In the evening a meal had been brought in, but it was nothing that Kathy could stand to eat: rice with red sauce and lima beans. For breakfast, she and the others received fishcakes, grits, and cornbread. Kathy was much hungrier now; she ate the cornbread and a few bites of the grits, but that was all she could stand.

Most of the day passed while the three waited with nothing to do. Finally, late in the afternoon, more than twenty-four hours since they had entered the jail, a man came for them. "Okay, it's your turn before the judge," he said. "Follow me."

This man—the jailer or whatever he was—was a mild-mannered fellow, fairly young, the same man who had brought them their food that morning. He seemed entirely uninterested in his task. They followed him down the hallway, still in their rumpled clothes from the day before, still stained with blood. Once inside the little courtroom, in the same building, the glaring light seemed much too bright at first. A judge in black robes was sitting in front on a raised platform. "I'll take the little girl first," he said.

The jailer looked at Kathy. He opened a wooden gate and told her, "Walk up there in front of the judge."

So Kathy approached the judge, then stood and waited as he looked down at something in front of him, apparently something he was reading. "Name?" he finally said.

"Kathleen Beatrice Thomas."

"Where you from?"

"Salt Lake City, Utah."

"Age?"

She hesitated, because of Ellie, and then said, "Seventeen."

"Whatcha doin' down here, Kathleen?"

"My aunt and I came down to help with the summer project for a few days."

"What's the summer project?"

"We're here to help with the freedom school, and with paperwork and things."

"That's not what I asked you. What's this summer project? Would another good name for it be 'outside agitating'?"

"No, sir. People have a right to vote. All citizens over twenty-one have that right. We're helping people to register who haven't been allowed to vote in the past."

"And you think that's a good reason to incite a riot, resist arrest, use profanity in public, and assault an officer of the law?"

"I didn't do anything like that. That policeman was beating up on a boy, and I asked him to stop. Look what he did to me. He hit me in the head with his stick—for no reason."

"No reason, huh?"

"That's right."

"Listen, young lady, you've got a sharp tongue on you, and that's probably what got you in trouble, as much as anythin.' You're fined three hundred dollars, and you're lucky it's not more. When you leave our jail, I want you to get in your car, go back to Salt Lake City, and not bother us down here ever again."

"I am going to leave. I have to this time. But I'm coming back, if I can. We aren't going to stop fighting for what's right. A court like this—where you don't even listen to my side of the story—shouldn't even exist in America. People like you are going to be stopped, sooner or later."

"Is that all you got to say? Because if you want to say more, I shorely do want to hear it."

"I didn't assault anyone, sir. I didn't use bad language, but the policemen did. They said crude things to us. I didn't start a riot. I just asked that man to stop hitting a young boy. And how did I resist arrest? He knocked me down and hit me with his stick. There were plenty of witnesses out there. I can prove everything I've just said."

"All right now. I'm glad you told me your side of the story. Now that I understand a little better what happened, I'm going to change my decision. As I see it, you talked just about like that to an officer, showed him no respect whatsoever. And that's what brought all this on. So I'm changing that fine. *Five* hundred dollars!"

"What?"

"Now take this little girl back to her cell. Let her sit and think for a while. I shore do hope she's got five hundred—or her papa does—because if she don't, she might sit in that cell for a long time. Ninety days."

The little man opened the gate and motioned for Kathy. She was about to tell him that he couldn't get away with this, but she saw Ellie with her finger to her lips, and she decided not to.

Kathy followed the man back to the jail cell, and then she waited for the other two. They were both back in a few minutes. They had each received three-hundred-dollar fines. But they hadn't spoken back to the judge. Ellie had warned LaRue not to argue, and she had managed to do just that.

Ellie laughed when she told her own story. "When he asked for my plea, I said, 'I stand mute,' and the judge told me, "Well, good. I like a woman who knows how to keep her mouth shut. Ain't many like that.""

The day passed the way the previous one had, and then in the morning, a SNCC lawyer showed up. He had bailed them out. But he wasn't happy. He was a tall Negro, with a formal manner of speech acquired in some eastern law school. "Who are you two, anyway?" he asked.

"I'm a professor," LaRue said. "At Smith College. My niece and I came down to see whether we could help—just for a couple of weeks."

"Well, you helped, all right. Cost us eleven hundred dollars."

"You don't have to pay it. I'll pay you back."

"That's the best news I've had today. We're running out of money fast. The other thing you could do is head back to Smith. You might want to start today."

"Listen, we didn't do anything to deserve this. Kathy was only trying to stop that cop from beating up on a young boy."

He nodded, seeming to recognize his rudeness. "I know," he said. And then, after a moment, he added, "You're going to have to take a bus. Someone lit your car on fire."

Chapter 24

"G ood day," Elder Thomas said. "We are both missionaries of what is often called the Mormon Church. We are making a religious survey in the area. May we ask you a few questions?"

A woman in a black dress and a faded apron was staring at Gene. She glanced toward Elder Bentz and then back again. "I don't understand this, what you say."

"Good day," Gene started again, and he ran through his memorized lines. But he struggled with the pronunciation of some of the words. He couldn't say "religious"—*religiöse*—and he struggled to get the "ch" sound right in *Kirche*. Since he had arrived in Germany, just three weeks before, he had started to wonder whether he knew any German at all. The dialect in southern Germany sounded like a whole new language, and he was amazed at how often the people couldn't understand him.

But this time the woman had understood enough. "What are you? Mormons?"

"Yes. May we ask you—"

"*Nein, nein, nein.* I am Roman Catholic. What do I want with Mormons?"

She shut the door in his face. At least Gene had understood. Sometimes, when the people were friendly and tried to chat with him or even answer his questions, he had no idea what they were saying. The door approach involved showing a picture of the Swiss temple and asking people whether they recognized it. They didn't, of course, so then the missionary would tell the person being "surveyed" that it was a Mormon temple. The next question was, "How much do you know about the

Mormon Church—much, a little, or nothing at all?" And finally, "Wouldn't you like to know more?"

Gene was a little uneasy about the whole thing. Some people had gotten angry and told him that this wasn't a true survey. It was just another way for the Mormons to come around bothering people.

Of course, Gene had only understood the anger, not many of the words. He had been sent to Ulm, a town on the Danube River on the border of Bavaria. But it was in the heart of *Schwabenland*, an area that spoke one of the strongest dialects in Germany.

Elder Bentz was what Gene would have called, back at the University, a "good head." He was from Orem, Utah, a BYU student—and the two teased each other back and forth about the old Ute/Cougar rivalry—but Gene had already decided, quite confidently, that if Elder Bentz had been at the U, he very well might have made it into Sigma Chi. He didn't have the connections he might need, but he was the right sort of guy—funny, well dressed, and likeable. And he was smart. "He'll work you hard, but he'll show you the ropes as well as anyone," President Gardner had told Gene. "I couldn't give you a better first companion."

That was fine, but the description had made Elder Bentz sound a little like a slave driver. Gene had been relieved to find out he was also someone he would like so much. Elder Bentz was much shorter than Gene, with a barrel chest and short arms, but there was something classy about him, a friendly, confident style that everyone seemed to like. He spoke German extremely well, and he knew how to put people at ease. Gene would start a door approach in his halting German, and the door would sometimes start to close, but then Elder Bentz would begin to talk—casually, in his cordial way—and the door would come back open.

Of course, that didn't mean that people listened long. Most of them liked Americans, overall, and few were hostile. But they had "no time, no interest," as they always said, for Mormons. And that lack of interest—the closed doors—was taking more of a toll on Gene than he had expected. He had come out of the Mission Home in Salt Lake full of fire. Almost all the apostles had spoken to the missionaries during his week there. He had arrived in Germany expecting grand spiritual experiences, with occasional miracles, and so far all he had done was go from door to door all day and listen to people tell him that they didn't want to hear his message. Once in a while he and Elder Bentz had gotten inside long enough to give a little introduction to the Church, with the goal of setting up appointments for first lessons, but in almost three weeks of work, they had only given four actual lessons, and not one had gone well. Gene was still rather strained from all the changes in his life. He found himself bone weary by the time he got to bed each night.

But now it was Saturday, and for some reason that was really getting to Gene. The first Saturday in Ulm, when Gene had just arrived, Elder Bentz had had to take him shopping for a bicycle and an electric razor— since they didn't have hot water in their room. That had been fun, and new, and then attending church the next day in a nice little branch was exciting. The members had treated him well, teased him a little, and spoken some English with him, but they generally made him feel important. Then the next weekend, there had still been a certain excitement in the newness of what they were doing. But now, after knocking on doors another week, it was really hitting him that Saturday was like any other day, and so far there had been no sign that any particular day was much to look forward to.

Gene had always been willing to work hard, to do his schoolwork or his summer job, and all the while look forward to the weekend. Even when he had had to work on Saturdays at the dealership, he had still had the evening to enjoy. Now it was Saturday night and they were out tracting again, just as they had been every other evening so far.

Gene kept telling himself that missionary work was hard but one of these days a golden contact would come along. It wouldn't always be like this, with nothing but rejections. When he had been hit rather hard with homesickness, he had figured it was just the big change and all the adjustments he was making. He had eaten plenty of German food at home—that wasn't so much of a change—but the routine was more demanding than he had expected. They got up at six, studied before breakfast, ate mush prepared on a hot plate, and then were out by nine-thirty, on the doors all day and all evening. So far, he hadn't had a single one of those experiences that missionaries talked about: that one last house they tracted out, where someone was just waiting for them, or the person who had seen them ahead of time in a dream.

So Gene was struggling tonight. He had always loved summer at home, the lazy long evenings, the time with friends. He did like being in Germany—but he hadn't had a real chance to see anything. Ulm had a huge cathedral, with the highest steeple in the world. And down in the old part of town were narrow little cobblestone streets, buildings so old they listed to one side. Gene kept telling Elder Bentz, "I can't believe I'm really here. It's all so cool looking." But what he wanted was to buy a camera—which his mother had told him to purchase in Germany, where the prices were good—and then he wanted to wander these streets and take pictures. But with Elder Bentz, he wondered whether he would ever get the chance, even on Diversion Day. Their "days off," so far, had been filled with washing clothes and bathing. Gene had thought Elder Bentz was kidding when he said they would only get one bath a week—at a town bathhouse—and the rest of the time they would take "spit baths" at the sink in their room, but that was turning out to be true.

The elders walked from the apartment house, then turned and walked to the next building. It was an old place, squat, with probably only four apartments. At least the outside door was open. That meant they could climb the stairs and actually knock on the door. The newer, bigger apartments usually had a speaker by the downstairs door. When they rang the doorbell, they would hear a voice asking who they were. As soon as they got the word "missionary" out, the speaker usually clicked off.

Elder Bentz stepped inside, then started up the stairs ahead of Gene. "That last woman didn't understand a word I said," Gene said.

"She understood the second time," Elder Bentz told him. "You just tried to go a little too fast the first time."

"Say 'religious survey' for me again. I can't get that right."

"*Religiöse Umfrage,*" Elder Bentz said, and it sounded right.

Gene tried it a few times before Elder Bentz stopped in front of a door. Elder Bentz read the name off the doorbell and wrote it in his tracting book. This way, he could mark an "N" for "not home," a "CB" for "call back," or, more commonly, an "X." They didn't want to bother these people any more than they had to.

Elder Bentz rang the doorbell, waited for a time, rang again, got no response, and wrote down an "N," and the two stepped to the next door. He wrote the name again and rang again, and this time a woman showed up. She was young, maybe twenty or so, and pretty. She smiled. "Mormons, I think," she said.

"Yes." And then Elder Bentz asked a question—not one in the script—and laughed.

She laughed too, but she said, "I think not." *Ich denke nicht.* Gene got that. He also noticed that she was looking at him now—in fact, seeming to look him over. It was like being back at college. "Are you Americans?" she asked—Gene, not Elder Bentz.

"Yes."

"From where?"

"Utah," Elder Bentz said. "Both of us."

"Students?"

Gene finally said, "*Ja,*" since her eyes were still on him.

Elder Bentz asked another question, and she said, "No," then seemed to explain. Gene heard the word "religious." *Religiöse.* She said it beautifully. Her language wasn't Schwäbisch. It was clean, like Gene's mom's speech. And the girl was almost as pretty. She had blue eyes, big, and her hair was cut short, in a shag. What was tantalizing, though, was the way she kept eyeing Gene. He could feel that she was flirting. She and Elder Bentz talked for a few moments, and then they both laughed as she gave Gene a last glance and shut the door.

"What was that about?" Gene asked.

Elder Bentz headed down the stairs, still laughing. "Didn't you get any of it?"

"Not much."

"I told her that we just wanted to tell her something about our religion, but she said she wasn't religious. In fact, she called religion a swindle."

"So what was that, there at the end?"

"I told her we'd like to call back and talk to her whole family, so we could show them that our religion wasn't like that."

"She told me no, she didn't want that. But then, just before she shut the door, she said, 'But if you want to send your cute friend around some-time, I'd be happy to talk to him.'"

"Who, me?"

"You're the only 'cute friend' I've got, Elder. Didn't you see how she was checking you out?"

"Naw. I thought she was flirting with you."

"Oh, yeah, right. You're the tall, blond, Germanic type around here. You're going to have to be careful. You could cause some of these girls to have lustful thoughts."

Gene was laughing, but he was also surprisingly flattered by the girl's attention. As he stood before the next door, waiting for Elder Bentz to write down the name, he found himself feeling the nostalgia, with the thought of Salt Lake, back at the U, stronger than ever. The thought hit him again, and this time with ten times the force: this is *Saturday night*.

Elder Bentz rang the doorbell, and Gene got ready. But a little boy opened the door. Gene knew how to ask for the father, something a lot of new missionaries would not necessarily know. That was the sort of German he remembered from his growing-up years. The boy turned and yelled, "Daddy?"

After a rather long delay, a man appeared. He was wearing a white shirt, and he was half finished with tying his tie. It hung in front of him, looped but unknotted. The smell of aftershave was potent. "What is it?" he asked.

"Good evening," Gene said. He had noticed that Elder Bentz had said "evening," not "day," at the last door. "*Wir sind beide missionare—*"

"Oh, no. Please. We're going out tonight. I'm sorry." He pushed the door shut.

"Saturday night," Elder Bentz said. "Not the best time to tract." But he stepped to the next door, the one opposite, on the main landing. Gene had a hard time understanding why. If people were busy, in no mood to meet missionaries, why were they bothering? But Elder Bentz rang the doorbell, waited, and talked to a middle-aged woman. She was wearing black. Gene had never seen so many widows in his life, could hardly believe that they would still wear black so long after the war.

This woman was not kind. She spat out a response to Elder Bentz's question, said something that sounded harsh, and then shut the door.

"What was that?" Gene asked.

"It's something you don't hear very often, but some people say it: 'You Americans bombed our cities, killed our people, and now you come back to teach us religion?'"

"Wow. Don't they know who started the war?"

"I don't know. Most do. But I guess if you were in those cities, when the bombs were dropping, you end up hating the men in the bombers—no matter who started the war."

Elder Bentz entered the next building and hiked up the stairs—three flights this time. And they worked through the building. Three of the families—half—were not home. The others all gave the standard response. When the elders came to the last door, it was Gene's turn again. A teenaged boy answered the door. Gene asked him whether his mother or father were home, and he said no. Gene didn't know how to explain to the boy that they would stop by another time, and Elder Bentz was playing his cruel little game. He would let Gene stand and suffer until he thought of something to say. This was supposed to be all about learning how to manage without help, but Gene could think of nothing better to do than to recite the door approach. The boy was not about to try to identify the Swiss temple. He glanced at the picture and said, "No, I don't know what it is. But I don't have time for this. I'm going out."

Gene stood for a few seconds, trying to think of some logical response. Finally Elder Bentz took over. "Have a good time. We'll come back again sometime."

Gene understood every word. He wondered why he hadn't been able to come up with something like that. He knew the vocabulary; he just didn't know how to construct sentences. Still, there was something a little annoying about the way his companion would let him make a fool of himself and then suddenly come in and save him, like some kind of godsend.

The boy shut the door, and Gene walked outside ahead of Elder Bentz. Then he turned around. "When something different like that comes up, don't leave me standing there. I didn't know what to say."

Elder Bentz laughed. "That's how you learn."

"No, I don't. I just look like an idiot."

"Are you mad?"

"No. Of course not. I'm just saying . . . well, you know . . . what I said."

"I hated my first companion for doing that to me," Elder Bentz said. He grinned. "But I don't want to jump in too fast. If I take over every time, you'll depend on that. Do your best, but when I see it's a situation you haven't dealt with before, I'll try to get in a little quicker and just show you what I would do. You're going to be way ahead of me by the time you've been out here a year. You're already ahead of most guys, just coming out."

Gene nodded. And he felt a little better. The two walked to the next house, but now Gene could hear something. Music was playing, somewhere close, probably near the big cathedral. It sounded like a drum and bugle corps. "What's that?" Gene asked.

"I'm not sure," Elder Bentz said. "It sounds like they might be having some sort of festival down in the old part of town. I think what you're hearing are some of those medieval trumpets. That's probably where everyone is going tonight."

"What do they do—just listen to the music?"

"No. There's probably a lot of beer drinking, for one thing. I don't know exactly what's going on."

The two were still standing outside in front of another apartment building. "Why don't we walk over and have a look?" Gene asked. Suddenly there was something different, something really European to experience, and Gene felt a little excitement.

"No. We need to stay on the doors."

"Why? If most people aren't home, and the ones who are don't want us coming on a night like this, what's the point?"

"The point is, we don't have our hours in. We're probably going to end up a couple of hours below our goal, as it is."

"You mean, as hard as we've worked all week, we still don't have our hours in?"

"I set my number higher than the mission goal, but it's hard to work that many hours in a week unless you have lessons that run a little later. And this week we didn't have investigators at church, so we couldn't count those hours. That put us behind."

"So Sunday is considered a work day?"

"Of course—one of the best."

Gene stared at Elder Bentz, noticing for the first time that the button on one side of his collar was missing. There was something about these elders who had been out a year or more; they looked a little worse for wear sometimes. Elder Bentz was one of the sharpest of the missionaries, but his shoes were almost shot, with cracks in the leather where they bent, and his white shirts were turning yellow.

Gene didn't know what he was feeling, but it was something like resentment, and he was mad at himself for feeling it. But how could a person work every minute of every day—either that or study? He could be in Germany for two and a half years and never see a thing—except the inside of apartment houses.

"Can't we make street contacts over there, where the people are going?"

"No. Half the people will probably be drunk. If they don't want to be bothered at home, they sure don't want to be bothered when they're out having a good time."

"Do we just put hours in for the sake of hours—even if it doesn't do any good?"

"No. But the way I look at it, if I work hard the Lord will help me. And the more time I spend trying to find someone to teach, the bigger chance I have to find that one family that wants to hear what we have to say."

Gene nodded. He couldn't really argue with that, in theory, but he had also looked at the reality. These people didn't want to listen to any missionaries, and especially not Mormons. And more than ever, not on Saturday night.

Elder Bentz walked into another apartment house and up the stairs. He did his door approaches, laughed with the people, and was kind and patient even when they told him to get lost, and he was careful to jump in and help Gene a little sooner. But on they went, and Gene could tell that some people were annoyed.

What Gene was feeling by now was increasing gloom. For the first time, he let himself say it: "I don't know whether I can do this for two and a half years." But he didn't say it to Elder Bentz, only to himself. He had been so excited to come on this mission, but he had had no idea what the life was really like. He and Elder Bentz lived in a dingy room, sublet from an old widow. The bathroom was down the hall, but it wasn't a "bath" room at all. They weren't allowed to use the hot water it would take to bathe. That's why they had to take their trip to the bathhouse once a week. Food was cheap, so they ate lunch at a restaurant most days, but supper was cold cuts of meat and cheese, with bread, and breakfast was Elder Bentz's mush with apples and cinnamon—every day.

All that, Gene thought he could take. It was the tracting day and night he couldn't imagine himself doing—not for *thirty months*. What he really wanted was to turn around and go home. But how could he do that? What would everyone think of him? How could he face his parents?

Elder Bentz continued for another hour, and then finally, he said, "We are starting to upset people. I guess we'd better quit."

"What about the hours?"

"We made the mission goal. Next week we need to push a little harder, though. I want to make my goal—I mean *our* goal—of five hours over."

Never mind that Gene had had no part in setting that goal.

"What we need to do is build our pool of investigators so we can be in people's homes, really teaching them the gospel, instead of just going out tracting at night. But that'll come. We have to keep working this area until we get more going."

"But you've been working it for two months, haven't you?"

"Yeah. And we had some people coming along for a while. Then it seemed like a lot of them dropped out at the same time. That happens sometimes."

They walked back to their bikes, which they had locked up and left on a little side street. Gene wondered whether they would at least bike through the town, enough to see what was happening at the festival or whatever it was. But Elder Bentz took the direct route, went straight home, and when he got there, he got out his scriptures and got right into his study. Sometimes the two, when they were out on the doors, had talked about home, about life at BYU compared to the U, about Marsha, about Gene's high-school football and Elder Bentz's debate trips—all kinds of things. But when he was in the room, Elder Bentz really liked to study, and there was certainly little else to do.

Gene sat on his bed, took his shoes off, rubbed his feet for a minute, and then quietly slipped open the drawer on his little bed stand. He pulled out Marsha's letter—the only one that had reached him so far. He read it once again, trying to judge the nuances of her language. Did she seem to be waiting for him, or was she only sending a letter to a friend? But everything seemed carefully neutral, noncommittal. He did like that she ended with "love," however standard that was.

He also thought about all the things she described: the hot summer days in Salt Lake, her summer work. She had run into one of Gene's fraternity buddies, Barry Fletcher, who had been home from his mission a couple of years and was engaged now. Gene, for the first time, felt himself longing for that time, when all this was over. She also mentioned Gene's father's campaign for Congress, which was just getting going. She had seen his dad a couple of times on television, she said. "He should have no trouble winning," she told him, and Gene thought how much he would like to be there for that, to see his dad elected.

What struck him more forcefully than before was that he had ended his life—the one he had always known. He would live a new one here in Germany, and then he would return and create another one, but everything from his past was gone. He would come home a different person, and everything would be changed. Including Marsha.

He slipped the letter away, telling himself not to think that way, to get his head back into what he was doing. He had waited his whole life for this mission. This was the culmination of what he had promised himself he would do in his life. He picked up his German Book of Mormon, found where he had left off, and tried to read. But it didn't work. His vocabulary was too weak, and he didn't have the will to look up everything tonight. So he sat on his bed and stared at the page, even turned a page now and then, and then he finally put the book down and lay back with his arm over his eyes.

He let himself indulge in his one pleasure. He thought of Marsha. He tried to picture her, to remember their moments together. He thought of the last time he had kissed her, and he went over her words one more time. "I'm going to miss you more than I ever thought, Gene. You've become so much more to me than I thought you would." He tried to feel the vibrations that had come over him at that moment. He tried to think of her hand in his, at the movies, or her in his arms, dancing. But none of it would come back the way he wanted it.

Eventually Elder Bentz got up from the table, where he had been reading. "Why don't we just go to bed?" he said. "I'm really beat tonight."

"Okay."

So they each got ready for bed—put on their pajamas, walked to the bathroom and brushed their teeth, and then had prayers. Elder Bentz asked the Lord to bless their work, to bless the families who had shown some interest, and he asked a special blessing on "Elder Thomas, who is working so hard to learn the language and become a part of this work."

They each prayed then, silently, and when both were finished, they stood and shook hands. "You're getting there, brother," Elder Bentz said. "Just think how far you've come already."

Gene nodded, but he couldn't say anything. He unfolded his feather tick and slipped under it, and he was relieved when the light went out. He knew he had held out as long as he could. Tears began to slip from the corners of his eyes. He tried not to make a sound, tried to talk himself out of what he was feeling. But he was still seeing Marsha wearing one of those pretty summer dresses of hers.

Maybe he sniffed—he didn't know. Or maybe Elder Bentz had sensed it earlier. But after a time he said, "Elder Thomas, are you okay?"

"Sure."

"A mission is really hard at first. There are just so many adjustments for a while."

"I know."

"We should have just ridden our bikes over there to see what that music was all about. It wouldn't have hurt anything."

"That's okay."

Some time passed, and Gene hoped that was the end. But Elder Bentz said, "I'll tell you something that my first companion told me. I didn't want to hear it at the time, but it was still good advice—as I now know."

"What's that?"

"He told me to assume she won't wait. Just accept it, right from the beginning."

"Yeah. I guess that's right."

"It's easier to say than do; I know that. But it's still the best way to think."

Gene could hear Elder Bentz rolling over after that, getting himself comfortable. But Gene felt as though the breath had been knocked out of him.

CHAPTER 25

Brother Tippets was leaning forward, looking directly into Scott Laughlin's eyes. "Are you willing to commit, then, that you will pay a full tithe to the Lord?"

"Oh, sure. That's only fair. The Lord gives us everything. It seems only right to give back just a little."

Diane smiled when Scott glanced at her, but she felt uneasy, and she wasn't sure why.

Brother Ashworth, the other stake missionary, chuckled. "To me it's like paying your fire insurance," he said. "The Lord said somewhere—I think it's in the Old Testament, that if you pay your tithes and offerings, on the judgment day you won't be burned up." He leaned his head back and let out a laugh that vibrated the living room like a truck going by. He was a man of fifty or so, and in the ward's Seventies Quorum. He had come along with Brother Tippets, who was a younger man, a little more polished. But both of the men were beaming. This was the last of the six lessons, and Scott had gone through them like "Brother Brown," the mythical investigator who responded to all the questions in the missionary lesson manual.

What worried Diane was that he never seemed to raise any questions. He had listened to the lesson on the plan of salvation, heard about the three degrees of glory, nodded a lot, got most of the answers right, accepted corrections when he didn't, and never once raised an issue. Diane had sat there with her parents, in their living room, and she had thought of dozens of questions. Sometimes her dad, almost as though he saw the question Scott *ought* to be asking, would begin a little treatise on the nature of a spirit as compared to a mortal being, or on the difference between paradise and the spirit prison, and Scott would say, "Oh, I see," but that was all.

After that lesson, Diane had told him, "If anything doesn't make sense to you, just go ahead and ask. Now is the time to do that."

But Scott had said, "It all sounded about right to me."

"Some of it's different from what other Christians believe. You know that, don't you?"

"Like what?"

"Well, all that about a premortal life, for instance. We're the only ones who believe that."

Scott had nodded, thought for a moment, and then said, "Brother Tippets said that's the good thing about having a prophet. You get answers that the other churches don't have."

That was the right answer. Diane was impressed. He did seem to understand. Brother Tippets had told her that he was one of those people who was ready, prepared beforehand. When he heard the truth, it just seemed right to him.

That made sense to Diane, and she was happy that things were going so well. Certainly her parents would be happy to see Scott come into the Church. But Mom had said, after the first lesson, "He surely doesn't have much curiosity. Or skepticism. If someone told me some of that stuff for the first time, I think I'd be more likely to doubt it."

"It's not the first time he's heard some of it," Diane had told her mother. "He and I have already done some talking about the Church."

"Still, you'd think he'd at least want to know what happened to the gold plates. That's what people used to ask me when I was in the Navy."

"What did happen to them?"

Bobbi laughed. "Joseph Smith said he gave them back to the Angel Moroni. But when I was your age, I was all worried about that. Is this the first time you've thought about it?"

"I guess so."

"Maybe you and Scott deserve each other."

But that had stung. Diane trusted certain things. She believed in Joseph Smith, in the Book of Mormon. She didn't have to know every detail about how he got the plates, or what he did with them. Still, it did seem that Scott should have to wrestle with things a little more.

"Scott," Brother Tippets was saying now, "we originally set a date for your baptism for this coming Saturday. Should we plan to go forward with that schedule?"

"Oh, I don't know. That might not work."

"You are planning to be baptized, aren't you?"

"No question. But I doubt I can work it out for Saturday. I'm not sure what my parents would think about that."

"I thought your mother wanted you to join the Church."

"She does. But she talked to my dad, and you know, he's not religious or anything, and I guess he had some bad experiences with some Mormons he knew in California. He told Mom he didn't want me to join the Church, and she wants me to talk it out with him first. It's not like he would stop me, or anything like that, but she thinks I shouldn't do it until he feels a little better about it. I can keep coming and everything. We'll just wait for a while to do the baptism."

The living room was suddenly quiet. Scott and Diane were sitting on the couch, with Bobbi and Richard at either end, on chairs they had brought in from the kitchen. Ricky, thank goodness, was sleeping.

The missionaries were sitting on either side of the coffee table, with their flannel board set on top. They had been placing little symbols and reminders on the black flannel as they had explained the law of tithing. Diane was watching Brother Tippets, who was sitting in the chair that matched the couch, striped in gold and green. He was still leaning forward, nodding his head slowly. He was a quiet man and sort of delicate. Diane could see that he was coloring a little, showing red through his thin hair. "Scott, let me make a suggestion. You will understand much more, grow much faster, once you are baptized and receive the gift of the Holy Ghost."

"Yeah. I remember how you told about that. That's one thing I'm looking forward to."

"I think I would talk to your father right away, tell him what you believe, and what you're going to do. Then I would move ahead."

"Yeah. That's—"

"If you don't, the devil will be after you," Brother Ashworth said. "I've seen it happen. You put it off, and Satan knows that's his chance. He'll just work you over, make you doubt everything, lose your strength, even draw you into sin. If I was you, I'd call your dad tonight, get that taken care of, and we could still get you in the water by Saturday."

"That's a good point," Scott said. "I hadn't thought about that. But I was going to call my dad last night, and then my mom said that he was on a business trip. I think up in Northern Cal. And he won't be back until Sunday or Monday, something like that."

"Could you find out where he is and still call him?" Brother Tippets asked.

"I don't know. I don't think so. But I could ask my mom." His tone was remarkably offhanded, compared to what Diane was hearing from Brother Tippets. But then, Scott had shown up in Levi's with his cuffs rolled high, showing his white socks, and shortly after sitting down, he had kicked off his loafers and said he hated wearing shoes around the house. All the other men, even Richard, were wearing coats and ties.

"Will you try to reach him?"

"Sure."

"If Saturday won't work out, though, we could certainly do it the following week."

"Yeah. That might be all right. But the thing is, I don't want a lot of bad feelings with my dad. We're kind of on the outs anyway." Scott laughed. "And he's the one who says he'll pay for my college, if I'll go. So you know, I don't want to get him mad at me."

Diane was surprised by that. It was something that Scott had never mentioned to her.

"It's very important, Scott," Brother Tippets said with quiet calm, "that you do keep a good relationship with your father. But it's even more important that you build the proper relationship with your Father in Heaven. If your dad advises you against baptism, you may have to take your stand, tell him how much this means to you, and—"

"Oh, yeah. I can see that. I will." He cocked his foot over his knee. "But I've never been one of those guys who goes against his parents. You know what I mean? I want to do this and keep some peace in the family at the same time. I don't think it'll matter if I wait a little while." He looked over at Brother Ashworth and grinned. "I'll take the ol' devil on and give him a good fight." He made a boxer's motion, as though he were duking it out with Satan.

Brother Ashworth didn't look pleased. But Brother Tippets said, "Well, get in touch with your father. He might be just fine with everything, and we can go ahead. But if you want to wait a week or two, I think we should keep meeting. We can continue to answer your questions."

"I don't think I have too many questions. I pretty well understood what you told me."

"I know. But what we've given you is only the very basis of the gospel. There's a great deal more to understand and comprehend."

"That's for darn tootin'," Brother Ashworth said. "You can study this stuff all your life, and even then you're just scratching the surface. I learn something every week, in Church." He was wearing a tie at least four times wider than the narrow ones in style these days. He smoothed it out over his belly, as though he were very satisfied with what he had just said.

"Well, sure. If you have more to tell me, I'm glad to keep having these meetings."

"Good." Brother Tippets looked a little more at ease.

"I think we should seal this deal with some ice cream," Bobbi said, and she stood up. She had never lost all the weight she had gained during her pregnancy, and she still couldn't fit into some of her clothes. Diane was surprised she would eat ice cream.

"How nice," Brother Tippets said, "but maybe we should have a closing prayer first."

"Oh, excuse me. Of course." Mom sat back down, looking rather embarrassed. Dad said the prayer and pronounced a nice blessing on Scott, as well as the ice cream.

When Diane and Scott left, they drove for a while and talked. It was a pretty October evening, and Diane wanted to relax and enjoy herself. But she couldn't stop thinking about Scott's baptism. Finally she said, "I hope you don't feel like you have to get baptized—you know, because of me and my family and everything. If you don't want to, just tell them. Or if there are things you don't really believe, just tell me, and we can talk about it, or whatever."

"Hey, don't worry so much," Scott told her. He was driving with one hand, and he was turned in his seat so he could look at her. On the radio, Barbra Streisand began to sing about people needing people, and Scott mocked it, singing in an exaggerated, nasal tone. He made Diane nervous sometimes when he paid so little attention to his driving. But he stopped singing after a couple of lines and said, "I'm fine with everything. I'll get baptized, sooner or later."

"But you don't want to right away, do you?"

"I didn't say that."

"Sooner or later sounds like it could be, you know, a long time."

"Well . . . it *could* be, I guess. I don't want to get Dad all hopping mad. If I know him, he'll tell me to think it over for a while, not jump into something right away."

"But is it really your dad you're worried about? Or are you just not sure you want to?"

"I *do* want to, Diane. And I'm going to do it."

"Okay. But I won't ever pressure you. It's completely up to you."

"I know that. Don't make such a big deal out of it."

That seemed a strange thing to say. It was a huge deal. Didn't he understand that yet? Did he think he was signing up for membership in a club?

But that wasn't all that Diane was worried about. It had struck her after that first lesson, when Brother Tippets had tried to establish a possible baptismal date, that if Scott joined the Church, she was linked to him in a way that could be awkward. Was this a commitment for the future? At sixteen, was she agreeing to marry him someday? Or what if she got in an argument with him and they broke up? Would that mean that his interest in the Church was gone? She knew she would feel a lot better if she could sense a deeper commitment, or understanding, from him. She had asked him a number of times whether he was praying about things—the Book of Mormon and the truth of the Church. "Sure," he would say, and he had told Brother Tippets that too. And then, just as easily, he would answer, "Yeah. I feel like I am getting answers to my prayers." Why couldn't she feel more sense of importance in the tone of his voice?

"Scott, I've got an idea," Diane said. "Why don't we go to your house right now? Why don't we talk this over with your mother?"

"Why?"

Diane had just told him she didn't want to pressure him, but she found herself wondering what he had actually told his mother. "I don't know. Part of it is, I just want to get to know her better. We never seem to go over to your house, and you're at mine all the time. Don't you leave your mother alone too much?"

"She's not alone. My little sister's usually there."

"I know. But you're almost never home."

"She doesn't care. All she does when I'm home is complain about how loud my music is." He grinned. "She likes the peace when I'm not around."

"I know. But you just told the missionaries you're going to be baptized. It seems like we ought to tell her that. And then you can find out whether she knows where your dad is."

"Diane, I'm not calling my dad when he's out on the road. That makes too big a deal out of the whole thing, and he'll get his back up. It's better if I just bring it up sometime when he calls."

"Why didn't you tell Brother Tippets that?"

"You know how he is. He wouldn't understand something like that."

Diane had to think about that. Had he lied to Brother Tippets? What she finally asked, however, was, "How soon is that likely to happen—if you're never home?"

"Don't worry. I'll talk to him one of these days."

Diane was about to back off, but her instincts were making her nervous. "Scott, don't you want me to be around your mother? Are you ashamed of me or something?"

His head swung around. "Are you kidding? You're the nicest girl I've ever gone with. She thinks you're great."

"Then why don't we go there?"

"I don't know. There's not a lot of room. Your house is bigger. We can go downstairs and watch TV—instead of sitting there with my mom."

"You just want to get away from people so we can make out."

"You got that right." He grabbed her hand. "In fact, I could use a little right now."

Diane let the whole thing go. And Scott drove to their usual parking spot, where they did kiss for a while. But Diane was very careful these days. She stopped as soon as she could feel that he was getting excited. She thought she knew what Brother Ashworth had been talking about when he said that Satan would try to interfere with his progress. And the last thing she wanted was to do something that might compromise his righteousness.

But strangely, that was not the most pressing thing on her mind. Scott was cute, and he was funny, and she loved knowing that most of the girls at Ogden High would have gladly traded with her, but the truth was, she didn't know Scott. She was not any closer to him now than she had been after their first few dates. He liked to kiss her, and she liked that too, but it seemed the main point of their being together. And even though he no longer pressed her about doing "more," she felt sometimes as though he were still toying with the limits, hoping that one night she would be the one to let something else happen. Did he see any connection between that and all these lessons he had been taking?

"Scott, we'd better go," she said. "It isn't really good for us to come up here all the time—not when you're getting ready for baptism and everything."

"Hey, we haven't done anything—not one thing but kiss."

"I know. But President McKay always says that kids our age shouldn't spend a lot of time alone like this. It's too dangerous. Too many things *can* happen."

Scott pulled his arm out from behind her, turned, and started the car. "Are you upset with me?" she asked.

"No. Not at all. Let's go find some people. President McKay is probably right."

So they drove off the hill and south to the Blue Onion. But that worried Diane a little too. Scott was getting better acquainted and had gradually found some friends. That summer he had worked at the El Monte golf course. He had played a lot of golf in California, was pretty good from what Diane knew, and had hung around the clubhouse enough that he had finally talked the clubhouse manager into letting him work around the place. He did some maintenance for the superintendent—watering dry spots, moving hole placements, and that sort of thing. He had met a couple of guys from Ben Lomond High School and some others from Ogden—all guys who played golf a lot, and all pretty rich. Diane was not well acquainted with any of them but knew them all by reputation. They were playboys, had nice cars, did some drinking—even though most of them were LDS—and weren't known for sports or student government, or anything in particular, except that they were good-looking, dressed well, and were considered cool.

Scott wasn't spending a lot of time with them, but he saw them at the course, played with them at times, and sort of fit in with his good looks and easy manner. He didn't have as many clothes as they did, but he dressed well enough. He had begun to talk about those guys more all the time, and he had seemed to know ahead of time that they would be at the Blue Onion. He hadn't really said that, other than to say that they should "find some people," but the minute he walked through the door with Diane, he began looking around, and then he spotted them.

"Over here!" a guy yelled—a boy named Johnson. Diane didn't know what his actual first name was, but everyone called him "Chilly." He was sitting by a girl Diane didn't know, but across the booth were two Ogden High kids, Carl Fawson and Claudia Christensen. Scott took hold of Diane's hand and walked over to the table. "Hey, Carlo, Chilly, what's going on?"

"Sit down. Join us," Chilly said. "Do you know Margo?"

Scott slid in next to Margo and motioned for Diane to sit on the other side, next to Claudia. "No. Nice to meet you. This is Diane Hammond."

Carl and Claudia didn't seem to know Diane, which didn't surprise her. They were both seniors, and part of the rich crowd Diane was aware of but didn't have a whole lot to do with.

"Hey, Scotty, we're not playing for money with you anymore," Chilly said. "You're getting too much practice. How much do they let you play out there?"

"I can play free whenever I want," he said. "But I don't have a lot of time. Sometimes I play a few holes just before it gets dark, after most guys are off the course."

"Hey," Chilly said, looking at Margo, "the guy's not big, but he can *whack* that ball. He's got a *sweet* swing."

"I'm just trying to learn from you guys," Scott said. He used that sly smile of his.

"Yeah, sure," Carl said. "We're not giving you any handicap at all from now on. If you want to take our money, it's got to be straight up, stroke for stroke."

Diane didn't know what this was about. She didn't know that these guys played for money. Something about it bothered her. Couldn't he *lose* a lot of money? These guys had plenty to play with, but Scott didn't.

"Diane, has Scotty told you about the little business he has going?"

"No. I don't think so. What do you mean?"

"He picks up balls all over the place out there, and he sells them out in the parking lot from the trunk of his little bug. Everybody knows about it now, and he's cleaning up."

"Hey, I give 'em to you for two bucks a dozen. How much can I make at that?"

"Depends on how many dozen you sell. I think you're pulling them out of the pond—and those aren't supposed to be your balls."

"Finders keepers," Scott said, and he laughed.

"What a cool head you are," Chilly said. "No kidding. You're great. You're gonna be rich someday. I can see you playing the angles already."

Scott just smiled. "It's going to take a long time to get rich at two bucks a dozen."

"Not when you're also hustling guys into playing against you."

Scott looked at Diane. "I beat them *one* day, and suddenly I'm supposed to be a hustler."

But Diane was amazed by all of this. She had never heard a word about any of it. Why hadn't Scott said something?

"Be quiet a minute," Margo said. "This is my favorite song."

It was the new Beatles song, "And I Love Her." Margo let her head swing from side to side as she sang the words. She was a striking girl, with dark hair and pretty eyes—like light chocolate. "The Beatles are the best *ever*," she said, when the song ended. "They never make a bad song."

"*Wrong!*" Chilly said. "Half their songs are too *pretty*. The Rolling Stones are going to knock them clear off the charts. In five years no one will even remember the Beatles."

"What's wrong with pretty? You like me." Margo leaned in and kissed his neck. "Don't you think *I'm* pretty?"

"Don't start something you can't finish, little girl."

"I thought you *liked* the way we finish."

"I mean right here, right now."

"Try me."

"You're nasty, you know that?"

"Try me."

Diane couldn't believe any of this. She was not just shocked, she was aghast. She had never heard a girl talk like that. She knew that some girls had started to take "the pill" even before they were married, but she didn't think anyone she knew would ever be like that.

"I'll tell you the group I like," Carl said, ignoring all that, even though Chilly had started to nibble on Margo's ear and neck and she was making little moaning sounds.

Chilly raised his head. "Who's that? The *Osmond Brothers?*"

"Hey, they're cute," Diane said, and everyone laughed. But they were cute, and they had been on the Lawrence Welk Show. Who else from Ogden could say that?

"Listen to Paul Revere and the Raiders," Carl said. "They've got a great sound."

Diane thought she had heard them. But suddenly there were so many new groups, with all these British rock groups touring the country. And some of them did seem almost as bad as her bishop said they were—*especially* the Rolling Stones.

But on the talk went, and Diane knew she was out of this crowd's league. Claudia said something about the camping trip they had gone on, and Diane realized she meant these four, the two couples. How could high-school kids, guys and girls, go camping together? Did their parents know? And the other subject that they kept coming back to was alcohol. "Carl was so wasted last week," Chilly would say. Or Margo would tell Chilly, "How do you remember? You were so drunk, you didn't know where you were." She also teased him about losing his driver's license for going a hundred and ten in a forty-mile zone, on Harrison Boulevard. "It wasn't just because of that," he said. "It was my fifth ticket this year."

And yet, when everyone finally left, Chilly got in his car with Margo next to him, and the other two in the back seat, and he drove away himself.

Diane was frightened by then. "Scott, those aren't the right kind of people to hang around with—not if you want to join the Church."

"I think Chilly's a Mormon, isn't he? I know Carl and Claudia are."

"Not good ones."

"Oh, they're just having a little fun while they're young. Carl told me he'll probably go on a mission."

"Scott, that's all wrong. You can't drink and mess around like that, and then just quit and go on a mission."

"Carl told me a lot of guys do that."

"They shouldn't. I hope you don't think you can join the Church and then act like that."

"No, no. I wouldn't. But they're both good guys—that's all I'm saying."

"Scott, you shouldn't gamble with them."

"It's not gambling. It's playing for money. That's what professional athletes do."

Diane had to admit that might be true. But still the idea didn't sit right. "What about those balls? Should you take them from the golf course and sell them yourself?"

"Oh, Diane, it's no big deal. I just find a few balls, and I've sold some to Chilly and Carl and a few other guys I know. No one cares about that."

Diane wondered. Maybe she was way too strict about certain kinds of things. But she had the uneasy sense that she was in a situation she didn't know how to deal with.

"It's getting late, Scott. I'd better go home."

"Late? What time is it?"

"Almost eleven, and it's a week night."

"Oooh. We'd better hurry. I didn't realize it was the middle of the night."

He was laughing, but Diane didn't think it was all that funny.

CHAPTER 26

Hans was back in school. He had been reinstated as a student, and he was working extremely hard to prove himself. He was impressing all his teachers, and they told him so. He was especially strong in math, but he was good at all his subjects. In the past, other students had recognized him for being bright, but he was with a new class now, and these students had begun to speak of him as "the genius." He had spoken to his director a time or two, had told him that he had separated himself from his church entirely. "My parents still go, but I have no plans to attend. You don't have to worry about that. And notice my grades."

The director had reassured him that he had no question about his ability. All his teachers had mentioned how well Hans was doing. But the director could promise nothing about acceptance at a university.

At the end of the school day one afternoon, Hans's history teacher stopped him. "The *Direktor* has asked me to have you drop by his office today, before you leave school," he said.

"Thank you." Hans hurried down to the office. He felt good about this. He had worked hard, and he was almost certain that the director would be offering him some sort of encouragement.

When he entered *Direktor* Knorr's office, however, there was something more somber than usual in his demeanor. "Sit down, Stoltz," he said. "Thank you for coming by."

This all sounded wrong. The director didn't have to thank him. When he asked a student to appear in his office, the student knew there was no question that it was something he had to do. "I'm happy to speak with you, *Direktor* Knorr."

"I've talked to government officials about you since you returned. I've had several discussions. I've told them that I would like to see a path opened for you. You could very well graduate first in your class, and I believe you have grown in loyalty to your country."

"Yes. Certainly." Hans knew that wasn't exactly true. He had actually capitulated to his country. If he were granted his fondest wish, he would still leave it.

"I am afraid, however, that some of our leaders remain skeptical. The matter of your no longer attending your church doesn't matter much to them, they say. They consider you very fortunate to attend *Oberschule*, given your escape attempt. It gives you the opportunity for a clerical career, or something on that order, and it shows their willingness to work with someone who has been willing to reform."

Hans, of course, saw the rest of the logic. They weren't about to allow him to attend a university. "Do you doubt my loyalty, *Direktor* Knorr?"

"I cannot say, Stoltz. I'm not a mind reader. But I assured them that you are not only a fine student but a thoughtful young man. Your mistake occurred when you were very young. I told them you could be a great asset to our country."

"And my separation from my parents' church means nothing to them?"

"I wouldn't say that. I'm sure, from their point of view, it indicates some growth on your part. But the things we are taught as young people often sink rather deep into us. You cannot blame them for suspecting that this separation is only temporary, or even calculated for effect. You are the only one who knows how truly committed you are to your new course. You mentioned at one time that you planned to join the Free German Youth, but as far as I know, you haven't done that."

"I will, if you think it best."

"Don't you see? That's just the trouble. Why should you ask? It is this very thing that causes some doubt in your sincerity."

Direktor Knorr waited and watched Hans as though he wanted to find some sign of allegiance in his face. Hans looked him steadily in the eyes. "I wanted to believe in God. For a long time I tried. But finally, I could see that there was nothing to it. I told my parents so, and I stopped going to church. I no longer consider myself a Mormon."

"Yes. I understand. But the official tells me that universities should only remain open to the truest of our patriots. Even your intelligence is not of first importance. What he said, specifically, was, 'It's loyalty we want, more than anything—commitment to party principles. Intelligence gets too many people into trouble."

"Are you saying that my chances are lost, then?"

"I'm saying that it would be a mistake to offer you hope. There is no sign of any change. They are not opposed to your finishing here at our *Oberschule*, and that is a concession on their part. You know that I took you back without consulting them, and they have never been pleased about that. But still, they will offer you that much of an opportunity."

Hans felt something more like numbness than pain or disappointment. He had grown accustomed to the idea that life was not going to treat him well, and he had forced himself not to hope. "I understand," he said. "Thank you for the help you've offered me. I am grateful to be back in school."

"Don't let down on your studies, Stoltz. What you will have to carry with you, when you leave our school, is your distinguished record here. So keep up your strong work, and I won't give up entirely either. I'll bring up the subject with them later, after you've had a little more time to prove yourself."

"Yes, *Direktor* Knorr. I'll do my best." But Hans had no idea whether he could actually do that. At the moment he hardly felt that he had the heart. He stood and was about to go. "If I were you," the *Direktor* added, "I would not worry quite so much about others and their decisions. I would try to make the best of things. And above all, I would be true to my own convictions. This is more important, finally, than anything else in life."

"Yes. Thank you," Hans said, and he left the office. But as he walked home, he wondered what Knorr had meant. Hans didn't believe in Socialism, even though he could live with it. But now he was left with nothing to turn to. His government had more or less shut the door on his future, and before that his religion had seemed to ask the same sacrifice. What difference did it make? Everything turned out the same. He would end up in an office, as he always feared, living out his life as his father did, trudging off to a pointless job every day.

And now, here was Knorr, in that cold voice of his, telling him that he should be true to himself. True to what? He believed in nothing. His parents were the only ones who seemed to care about him, and he had defied them, created such a breach that there was no going back. He could pretend to believe in the Church, to satisfy them, but in the end, he wasn't going to be a part of all that, so what was the point in returning only to break with them again?

So there was nothing to hope for, nothing to believe in . . . nothing. *Direktor* Knorr wanted him to study hard, but for what? So he could get one of the better bad jobs?

Hans went home. He said hello to his mother but then slipped quickly away to his bedroom. This was his habit, since he had been working so hard in school, but he didn't open a book now. He lay on his bed and stared at the ceiling. The apartment house the Stoltzes lived in was relatively new—just a few years old—but the roof leaked already, and when hard rains came, the water would drip through cracks that had formed in the ceiling. What was left behind were rusty stains, in various patterns, from repeated storms. Hans stared at all those marks now, at the ugliness of everything in his plain, gray room. He might as well be in a prison, he told himself. Maybe he should try once again to escape, and if it meant a term in jail, what of it? Maybe they would shoot him, and if they did, would that be any worse than this?

Hans slipped off to sleep, but when he awoke, after an hour or so, he found that he couldn't stand the thought of showing up at school the next day unprepared. It was easier to study. So he got up and got out his books and went to work. And that's how the week passed. He went through the motions of life, seemed mostly unnoticed at school and at home. At least he didn't hope for anything, pray for anything. All that was over, and there was peace in that, knowing that he didn't have anything to fear. There was nothing more he could lose.

On Saturday afternoon his parents had to go over to the church for some reason, and they dressed up for that. They asked Hans to watch Inga, and he said he would, but then he went to his room again and left her to read by herself. He had taken to reading fiction these days, an escape that took his mind away from everything else. It was always easiest to obtain the great Russian novels from his library, and so he had been reading those: *Anna Karenina*, *Crime and Punishment*, and now *The Brothers Karamazov*. It was a book full of questions, full of things to think about, but he took little joy or even interest in that, simply plowing through the plot.

When his parents returned, his mother came to his room and knocked. "Hans, we need to talk to you," she said. "Come out to the living room for a moment."

He got up from his bed, where he had been lying with his book. He walked out to find his parents seated on the couch, with Inga between them. He sat down in the big chair, and he waited. "We wanted to tell you," Peter began, "that I have received a new calling in the Church. It will change our lives a good deal."

It crossed Hans's mind that it wouldn't make any real difference to him, but he was curious what this could be. His parents were both enlivened by something; he could see that in their faces. "I've been called to the branch presidency. It's a busy job. It will take me away from home a good deal."

"Papa, that's wonderful," Inga said. "You'll be so good."

Peter was still looking at Hans, but Hans could think of nothing to say. It would be hypocritical to congratulate him. It wasn't at all what he felt. But he didn't want any more bad feelings.

"He'll be sustained tomorrow," Katrina said. "And then set apart, right after the meeting. He's going to be ordained a high priest, too."

Hans nodded but still didn't speak.

"Hans, will you please come? You need to be there for this."

Hans's first thought was that it would be easiest to say yes, to make peace that way, and then slip back to his room. But he didn't want to offer that much hope to his parents and then have to deal with their expectations that he would go again the next week. So he said, "Papa, I know this means a lot to you. It's very nice. But I really can't go."

"Why?" Inga asked, her voice surprisingly strong.

Hans glanced at her, but he didn't feel he had to answer. He looked again at his father. "I've made my choice about this. Nothing has changed."

"That's fine," Peter said.

But his mother said, "No, it isn't fine. He should be there." She pointed her finger at Hans. "This is not just a matter of religion. It's one of respect. You need to show this much honor to your father on such an important day."

"What would it mean, Mama? I've told you that I don't believe in the Church."

"Is that what it is? Or are you afraid that someone might report that you were there? You worry what the government thinks more than anything these days. Will attending one week keep you from this all-important goal of yours—to attend a university?"

Hans took a breath. He hadn't told his parents anything about his conversation with *Direktor* Knorr. He rarely told them anything anymore. "Mama, I won't be admitted to a university. I've been told that now. So I don't worry about pleasing the government."

"Hans," Peter said. "Are you sure the decision is final?"

"*Direktor* Knorr told me that it was." That, of course, wasn't entirely true, but it was close enough.

"Son, I'm sorry. I know how much that means to you."

"No. I don't think you do. I don't think you and Mama understand much of anything about me." He stood up.

He was about to head for his room when Inga stood too and stepped in front of him. "What's wrong with you, Hans?"

"Wrong with me?"

"You're not nice anymore, like you used to be. You don't even talk to us. All you do is sit in your room and feel sorry for yourself."

For an instant, Hans was angry enough to shout at her, but he knew, just as quickly, that he couldn't bring himself to deny her accusation.

Katrina stood alongside Inga. "Hans, tell me this. If you have nothing to lose from the government now, why not come tomorrow—for your father's sake?" Her voice was as strong as Inga's, almost the same voice.

"Then what will be your next excuse to get me to go? I've told you, I'm not attending anymore. What difference does it make if Papa is being ordained? Don't you know that I wouldn't bring the proper *spirit* to the room? I don't have any spirit."

"That's not true, and you know it," Katrina said. "You used to be so close to God. I can remember when you were little and—"

"What did I know then? I only believed in what you told me. But I don't anymore. That's the end of it, and I don't want to be bothered about it. If you want me to move out, I will. There's no point in my finishing school now anyway."

He had told himself all week that he needed to finish, but now he wasn't sure. Maybe he should get away.

"Hans, no. We don't want that," Peter said. He stood with everyone else. "Let's all calm ourselves. I would love to have you there, but it's your decision, and now you have made it. So that's all there is to it." He was looking at Katrina, speaking to her more than to Hans.

But Katrina was not quite finished. "Inga is right, Hans. You aren't the same boy I've known since you were born. You've let the spirit go out of you. That's what you've done."

"Mama, don't talk about such myths. That's the trouble with this family. You've accepted all this superstition, and it's distorted everything. Now you want to pass the same heritage on to me."

Peter held up his hands to stop everyone. Then he said quietly, "Hans, I love the gospel—what it tells me about eternity, not just this life. I can live with a few difficulties when I know that mortality is only a moment in the vast spread of time."

"It's what you believe, and that's fine. It's not what I believe. Let's just leave it at that."

"Of course. But offer a little respect. I won't try to force my belief upon you, but don't call us fools. Don't tell us that what we believe is superstition."

"All right. I won't say that. I won't say anything about it. But don't force me into situations like this, where I have no choice but to defend myself."

"All right. That's only fair."

The matter seemed at an end, and Hans was relieved. He wanted to escape. But it was Inga who wasn't finished. "Hans, you're the one being foolish," she said, her voice full of tears. "We used to have a nice family. And now everything is terrible. And it's all your fault. You were the best brother in the whole world. Now you're a coward."

"That's not true, Inga. That's not fair." Hans had handled all the rest pretty well, but Inga's words hurt. She had always been precious to him.

"God gave you *everything*, Hans. And you won't even admit it."

It was something that Hans had once believed. The idea touched him. "I'm sorry, Inga," he said. "I'll try to be a better brother."

"Then go to church with us tomorrow."

But Hans couldn't do that, and he didn't know how to tell her. He had said all he had to say; now he wanted to go back to his room. He couldn't get there without tramping through everyone in the little living room, however, and so he took the other escape route. He walked to the door of the apartment and left. As he shut the door behind him, he heard his father say, "No, Hans. Come back." But he kept going—down the hall and then down the stairs and on outside.

It was a cool October day, and he had left without a coat, but he couldn't go back for that. He kept walking, heading down the sidewalk without any thought of where he might end up or how long he might stay away. He was angry, and he tried hard to build that part of his emotion. But what he felt most strongly was the estrangement. He had taken his stand, but in doing it he had cut himself off from everything he had always cared about. Inga had no idea how much he longed for the days when he had felt attached to her, to his family. There had been a time in life when he had had no idea that he could ever feel anything but that oneness with them. Now he had no one. He had lost his only friends at Church, had never really had close friends at school, and the people he wanted to feel close to, his parents and Inga, were unavailable. Every conversation, every moment with them, contained a subtext, as though everyone was thinking, without saying, "You're not part of us anymore. You've shamed us. You've reached the wrong conclusion. We can't think of you the same way we did—not unless you come back."

So what now? And again he looked into his future and saw nothing. Would he marry? Create his own family? Whenever he thought of that, the strange notion came with it that he didn't know how to build a family that was based on this nothingness he felt inside. His sense of purpose was based on what his parents had taught him. Living without that was like trying to stick something together without any glue. He knew their way of doing things, and he couldn't picture anything else. But it *was* superstition. He had tested this faith and prayer business, and it didn't work. He was almost embarrassed to think how silly it all was, these daily prayers to nothingness—this conviction that some "man" was out there in space somewhere, sending down directives, interfering with people's lives, listening to all these supplications, thinking them over and then dispensing "answers." How could that be true? How could his parents, intelligent people, believe in such things? Or was it only that they also knew of no other glue, and they settled for *something*, which was better than the nothingness he was feeling?

He kept walking. And today he saw his city differently, not as the place he had always known. It was a little gathering of humans, like an ant bed. People were moving in and out of their dwellings, busy enough, but living out an existence as important or unimportant as an insect's. Sometimes, when he prepared himself to step on a cockroach or a spider, he would hesitate and laugh to think how much he was like a god to the little creature. He could prolong the bug's existence for a few more seconds, let him go, pick him up and throw him out a window, or he could squash him without a second thought. And all the while, the insect was unaware that a giant was about to decide his fate. Were humans as stupid as that—just little life forms subject to the winds of chance? Sadly, yes. And yet here were all these people on the street, heading this way and that, all confident that their lives had more meaning than a cockroach's.

Schwerin was a beautiful city, surrounded with lakes. It had not been an industrial center until after the war, so its "old town" had been spared from bombing in World War II. Hans kept walking toward the old part of the city, where many of the buildings were hundreds of years old— beautiful, timbered structures. He could see the spire of the Schwerin Cathedral, the great red-brick gothic building that still attracted believers on Sunday. In spite of all the educational efforts and all the government control, religion persisted, and probably mostly because the fear of nothingness was greater than any other force.

It was strange to think that Schwerin might have been wiped out too, like most German cities. The great giant had gone about stamping his foot, squashing all the little bugs and their dwellings, but he hadn't bothered with Schwerin. Or was it the giant? What Hans knew about humans was that they professed religious beliefs, but they still liked to band together in groups and kill each other. They made beautiful things—edifices and art—and then they burned them, bombed them, or blew them apart with great artillery guns. And the giant only stood back and watched—apparently without enough concern to stop them.

Hans kept going, on through the old city to the edge of the Schweriner Sea—a great lake. It was one of his favorite spots, where beauty, for once, seemed to mean nothing more than itself. This lake had always been here, he supposed, or at least had been longer than anything made by humans. It was the earth itself that persisted, even though the insects might come and go. Even the great bombers from America and England couldn't touch something like this. He stood and watched the swans, dozens of them, that were swimming along the shore.

He tried to stop thinking, tried to take some pleasure in what he could see, but a new thought was coming to him. He told himself that Inga was right about him. Lately he had spent far too much time feeling sorry for himself. He wasn't going to do that anymore. Most of the humans who had lived on this planet had experienced a life far worse than his. Drudgery was the fate of most of them, and few had had the luxury to sit around and complain about it. He needed to accept the flow of things, to live his life. He wasn't ready to go back to Inga and be the brother she wanted him to be—not on her terms, anyway—but he would try to be nicer to her. He wouldn't indulge himself anymore.

He was still watching the swans. There were ten or twelve of them that were close, sitting placidly in the water. When they would move it would seem a sort of miracle—as though they willed themselves over the water—but he knew, of course, that they were paddling, working hard, in spite of their serene appearance. One departed from the others for no apparent reason and moved away, farther up the shore, on its own. As Hans watched the bird, wondering at its apparent will to separate itself, a powerful emotion began to build, filling him up. He felt as though something outside himself were working upon him, granting him something like consolation, reassurance. But he didn't explain that; he merely accepted. He told himself that he would get up each morning and do what he had to do, that he *could* do that. What he didn't understand was why tears were running down his cheeks.

CHAPTER 27

Elder Thomas and Elder Bentz were out "on the doors" once again. In some ways, Gene had come a long way. The door approach was no problem for him any longer. He even understood most of what people said back to him. Of course, they usually said more or less the same thing. He and Elder Bentz managed to give two or three first lessons most weeks, but so far, all those had gone nowhere. Since Gene had arrived, the elders had not gotten anyone past the third lesson.

It was all very discouraging. Gene had outlasted his initial homesickness, but he still found himself, all too often, counting the days. He wrote letters home that were full of enthusiasm, told Elder Bentz that things were "great," but he still woke up each morning thinking, *How can I do this again today?* He had never experienced anything quite so demoralizing as being told no all day, and often with resentment or even anger. He liked the members of the branch, and there had been a couple of activities that were fun. Once he and Elder Bentz had gone to an MIA party. They hadn't been able to dance, of course, but they had enjoyed the teenagers, and the members loved the elders. But normally they didn't attend such things: only when they were needed to help out in some way, or when they took an investigator.

Mostly they knocked on doors—all day, all evening, *every* day.

This morning Gene was struggling more than usual. It was November now, almost time for Thanksgiving. He kept thinking how much he would like to be home for that, to be with his family and see all his cousins. He and Elder Bentz tried to get inside buildings as often as they could, but much of the time that morning they had been out in a cutting wind. Gene's feet were freezing, and so were his hands. "If it's this cold already, what is winter like?" he asked Elder Bentz as they stood in front of an apartment house. Gene was writing down the names from the door-bells. He would like to have kept his hands in his coat pockets, but he couldn't when he was the one keeping the tracting book.

"It gets really bad sometimes," Elder Bentz said. "But not a lot worse than this—with the wind blowing so hard. We need to run home during lunch today and put on some more clothes."

But then, for no apparent reason, Elder Bentz started to laugh.

"What's so funny?"

"I was just thinking about something that happened last year. My first companion was from Southern Cal, and the cold about killed him. The guy would put on all the clothes he could. One time he left his flannel pajamas on, under his suit." Elder Bentz shook his head and grinned at the memory. "We were in a house, talking to some people. I happened to look down, and I noticed his pajamas hanging out from the bottom of his suit pants."

Gene laughed. "What color were they?"

"Blue. With some kind of little pattern." Elder Bentz had his head down, letting the brim of his hat protect his face from the wind, but now he looked up, and he laughed hard. "I looked over at the lady, and she was staring at his ankles like she was wondering what kind of new American style this must be."

"Did you say anything?"

"No. I couldn't. I just waited until we left, and then I told him. He about died."

Gene had finished recording the names. He pushed the button for one of the apartments on the top floor. "People over here must wonder about us sometimes," he said. "Elder Baker wears a suit that looks like he uses it for a tablecloth. The guy must never get anything cleaned."

Elder Baker was one of the other missionaries in Ulm. He was from

Northern California, from some little town Gene had never heard of. He was into the last few months of his mission.

"He can't afford much of anything," Elder Bentz said. "His parents can't send him the full eighty dollars. When the president raised it from seventy, he never told his family."

Gene had tried the bell a second time but had gotten no response, so he rang the other upstairs bell. "Wow. That's gotta be tough. I can see already that I'm lucky my relatives stick in five or ten bucks when they write."

Suddenly there was a crackling sound on the speaker by the door. "*Ja?*"

"*Guten Tag.* We are missionaries from the—"

"What? What are you?"

"We are missionaries from—"

"Missionaries?"

"Yes."

The door buzzed, and Elder Bentz pushed it open. The woman had answered from the third floor, so the two hiked the stairs quickly in their heavy coats. Gene was breathing fairly hard when he reached the third floor landing and faced the little woman, who was smiling. One tooth was missing from that big smile, and the woman looked old, but Gene didn't remember anyone being so happy to see them. Maybe she was a member.

"Come in. Come in," she said. "I'm so happy you've come. What can I do for you?"

She was walking ahead, directing them into her little kitchen, which was not just warm but hot. She motioned for the elders to sit down at the kitchen table. Gene unwound the muffler from his neck and unbuttoned his coat. He knew that he was going to be way too warm in a few minutes, but for now, the heat felt good.

Gene set his hat in his lap and said, "Frau Metz—is that your name?"

"Yes, yes."

"We visit families here in your neighborhood, to tell them about our church."

"Where are you from?" the woman asked, but the joy had gone out of her face. She looked confused.

"America," Gene said. "We're both from the state of Utah."

Again she asked, "But what can I do for you?"

"Not one thing. We just want to tell you about our church?"

"*Your* church? What church is this? Aren't you Catholic?"

"No. We're from The Church of Jesus Christ of Latter-day Saints. Sometimes people call us the Mormons."

Gene watched her confusion change to shock. "I thought you were *our* missionaries."

Gene couldn't think what to say. Elder Bentz jumped in. "Frau Metz, we have a wonderful message for you—a message about Jesus Christ."

"*Heraus!* Get out! I don't want Mormons. I am Roman Catholic. Always was, always will be."

"Of course. We didn't mean to—"

"Get out right now." She was standing up and waving her arms at them, as though she were shooing away a couple of bothersome dogs.

The elders were out of their chairs by then. Gene was backing away. But Elder Bentz made one last try. "We understand that you're Catholic. We only wanted—"

"Out! Out!" she was screaming, and then she grabbed for a broom that was leaning against the wall by her refrigerator. Elder Bentz caught up with Gene, and the two scooted out quickly. By the time they hit the stairs, she was in the hallway, holding her broom. "We don't want Mormons around here. You want more wives. That's what you're looking for."

Gene had expected to stop at the second landing, to continue their tracting through the building, but Frau Metz had come halfway down the first stairway, and she was still shouting.

"We'd better just clear out," Elder Bentz said.

As they reached the ground floor, a woman stuck her head out the door and looked at the elders with alarm. Frau Metz was still yelling, "We don't want you Mormons coming around."

"Good day," Gene said to the woman who was looking out at them, but nothing more. The elders hurried on outside and stuck their hats back on. Then they stopped and wrapped their mufflers back in place and buttoned up their coats. But now Frau Metz was yelling out the window, from way up above. "Keep going. Don't stay around here. No one on this street will talk to you."

Elder Bentz looked at Gene, and the two finally laughed. "Maybe it's time to go home and put some more clothes on," Elder Bentz said. He looked up at Frau Metz and said, "Thank you very much." And then under his breath, in English, "You *lovely* lady."

The elders walked on down the street as the woman continued to shout. "What a screechy voice," Gene finally said. "Everyone on this street can probably hear her."

"Hey, we need experiences like that," Elder Bentz said. "The old-time missionaries didn't deserve to have all the fun. You've got to admit, it's better than indifference."

And the strange part was, Gene *had* rather enjoyed himself. It was something of a change. At least they were going to break up the morning and ride back to their apartment to put their long johns on. But once on his bike, with the wind in his face, Gene felt the cold begin to penetrate again. And a thought struck him—one he had felt quite often the past few months. Why bother these people? Why not go home and live his religion and just leave this woman alone? If people over here didn't want to know about the Church, grant them their wish. Of course, Gene knew the answer to his own question, but at the moment, the thought of flying home was by far the most appealing idea in his head.

By the time the elders had added long underwear and sweaters under their coats, they felt a lot better. Elder Bentz suggested they try another section of their tracting area, just to avoid the street where they had been. "Maybe we can get into some of those big apartment houses on the edge of town. We can stay warmer in there."

That was fine with Gene, but he wondered what they would do when the weather got colder—if that was possible.

As they biked to the area, down a major street, with streetcars rattling by and a good deal of traffic, there was no chance to talk. Elder Bentz pedaled along in front, and Gene followed. But another familiar thought was in his head now. His father had come to Germany, converted his mother's family, and worked hard to establish branches. And when Gene had received his call, his dad had been so thrilled. That night they had talked about Gene picking up the work and carrying it on. Dad had had to cut his mission short because of the war, but Gene would return for him and help build the wards and branches further, continue the work of the kingdom. That had all sounded so great. But what if he never did? What he now knew was that some missionaries had been there two and a half years without baptizing a single person. Others had managed to bring a few into the Church, but no Germans among them. Some baptized American soldiers, or foreign workers from Italy. The branches were actually not growing much at all.

Gene told himself that if he worked hard and did his best, that was enough. And certainly, as long as he was with Elder Bentz, he would work hard. But in his own mind, he had always imagined himself a fine missionary, someone who would accomplish great things. His dad had been elected to Congress a couple of weeks before. He was an important man, and Gene had always expected to follow in his footsteps, but here Gene was, a missionary of the Lord, and he rarely felt anything spiritual. Most of the time, he was just dragging along behind Elder Bentz, wishing the day were over so he could get back to their apartment and lose himself in sleep. As he always did at such moments, he told himself to step forward, be more faithful, pray harder, improve his attitude, be patient. He just had to do a better job than he was doing, had to get his head and heart more completely into the work. He was doing well with the language, and now he just had to become the great, spiritual man his dad had been.

But tracting the rest of the morning went about the way it always did. An hour passed in the big apartment buildings, and the best they could get were a couple of weak "call backs": "You can come back in the evening sometime, if you want, and you can ask my husband if he's interested. But I can tell you right now that he isn't." Not exactly something to put in his next letter home.

But then a door came open, and a young man, maybe two or three years older than Gene, was standing in front of the elders. It was rare to find a young man home during the day. Elder Bentz gave the door approach, but the man had no interest in the "survey." "Are you from the States?" he asked, showing off his English.

"Ja. Wir sind—"

"You're Mormons, aren't you?" But now he spoke German.

"Yes. We would like to give you a message about Jesus Christ."

The man laughed. "I've heard enough about Jesus Christ lately—far too much."

For once Elder Bentz seemed unsure of what to say. He stammered for a moment and then said, "Would you like to tell me about that?"

"No. It would serve no purpose."

"It would be interesting to talk to you."

He shrugged. "It's all the same to me," he said. He stepped back from the door and motioned with his head for them to come in. Then he walked to a living room that was actually heated. These new apartment houses had central heating, with every room in an apartment about the same temperature. Older German homes didn't have that, and often only the kitchen was truly warm.

The house was nicely furnished, with mahogany furniture and plush carpets. The elders sat down on a couch together, and the young man moved a chair so he was more or less facing them. "What are your names?" he asked.

"I'm *Bruder* Bentz, and this is *Bruder* Thomas."

The man laughed. He was wearing an old shirt, with the sleeves left unbuttoned, and a pair of cotton pants, but no shoes or socks. His reddish hair was a mess. Clearly he hadn't been out of bed long. "Brethren, are you?" he asked. "Is this a church title?"

"Yes. We're sometimes called *Ältester*, but it sounds a little strange in German."

"Yes, you don't seem very elderly."

"What is your name, if you don't mind my asking?" Elder Bentz asked.

"Not at all. Werner Hausmann."

"*Herr* Hausmann, would you mind telling us what you meant before—when we were at the door?"

"Not at all. But call me Werner." He slumped sideways and tossed his leg over one arm of the chair, dangling his bare foot a little too close to Gene. "I was attending a theological seminary, training to be a Lutheran minister. Two weeks ago—no, I guess it's three weeks now—I quit. And I came home. Now I'm a lost soul. I have no idea what to do with my life. My parents are upset with me, but so far, they haven't sent me away."

"Why did you quit?"

"I don't know. I suppose I didn't have a good enough reason to be there. My parents told me I would be a good minister, and the idea seemed all right. I liked my minister when I was growing up. It looked to me like he didn't have to work too much." He laughed.

"But you said that you heard too much about Jesus Christ."

"Yes. Too much I didn't want to know." He glanced at Gene. "Don't you speak German?" he asked.

"I do. But not so well as Bruder Bentz. He has been in Germany much longer."

"How long have you been here?"

"Four months. Almost five."

"You do very well. You must have studied German in school."

"Yes. But my mother is German. We spoke some German at home." He smiled. "But not Schwäbish. She was from Frankfurt."

"My parents were from East Germany. They came here after the war. It broke their hearts when I learned dialect, as a boy. But I don't use it around them." He folded his arms across his chest. "I know Mormons believe in the Bible. But do they accept it literally?"

"Yes."

"You think that Jonah really was swallowed by a whale?"

"We assume that really happened. Yes."

He nodded, smiling. "I never thought about it, growing up. It was just a story, like so many other things. Noah and all those animals on the ark. Things like that. I shouldn't have gone to seminary without deciding what I believed about all that. I don't believe much of anything now. I'm not sure that's the best state of mind for a minister." He laughed again but not with any joy.

"Didn't your professors believe in those things?" Elder Bentz asked.

"No. And I guess that's all right. I doubt any of that happened. It was obvious to me, once I thought it all through. But I'm not sure now that Jesus did any of those things that are in the New Testament. The sources for the Bible are all so questionable."

Gene appreciated the clear German Werner spoke, but he heard, more than that, the controlled grief in his voice, and it touched him.

"We are aware that the Bible is not always translated correctly, but we believe it to be true otherwise," Elder Bentz said. "But we also have the Book of Mormon. It's another witness for Christ. It tells that Christ did live, and that he did the things we read about in the Bible."

"I know something about this. Joseph Smith—was that his name?"

"Yes."

"He got this book from an angel. Correct? And he translated it."

"Yes."

"How did he know how to do that?"

"God gave him the power."

"And you believe in all this?"

"I *know* it's true."

"What do you mean, you 'know'? How could you know?"

"I've read the Book of Mormon and the Bible, and I've prayed about them. God has answered my prayers and told me they are true."

"But what do you mean by true? Do you realize all the problems with the New Testament? The four gospels were all written later, after Christ, and the writers copied each other. It could all be tradition, as much as anything. How can you know what's true, what's partly true, and what is pure myth? If there was a man named Jesus—and I'm not sure there even was—how reliable are any of the accounts?"

"I told you what I believe," Elder Bentz said.

"No. You said you *knew* it. Have you ever studied any of these matters? Do you know about all these problems with the New Testament?"

"I've heard something about them. But it doesn't worry me. God has assured me that Christ is my brother, that he's the Son of God."

Werner swung his leg down, sat up straight, and looked Elder Bentz straight in the eye. "I'm sorry, but I doubt that. I think you've been raised to believe these things, and you never have questioned them. You're exactly like me, before I went off to the seminary. To tell the truth, I wish I could forget what I learned. I could have sat in church all my life and been happy with it. Now I don't what to think about any of it."

"I didn't just accept," Elder Bentz said. "I tested it for myself. I read the Book of Mormon, and as I read, I knelt often and prayed, until the Lord filled me with a testimony."

"No doubt about that?"

"No doubt. I can tell you that honestly, Werner. I know that God lives, that Jesus is his son, and that Joseph Smith was a prophet, called of God to translate the Book of Mormon and to restore the true church to the earth."

Werner nodded, but he was smiling just a bit. Gene wondered what he thought of Elder Bentz's testimony. He showed no sign of being touched by it.

And then Werner looked at Gene. "What about you?" he asked. "I suppose you feel the same way?"

Gene nodded and said yes, but even as he did, he felt a hint of hesitancy in his own voice, and he knew that Werner had heard it too.

"Did God answer your prayers the same way?"

Gene felt his eyes drift away from Werner's. "I'm a new missionary. My testimony may not be quite so strong as Elder Bentz's yet."

"What? You're out here gathering more to your flock—testifying—and you don't believe?"

"I do believe."

"But you aren't quite sure?"

"I didn't say that." Gene was looking at Werner's feet, the smooth white skin, with almost no hair.

"You said your conviction is not as strong. Shouldn't you *know*, like your friend here, before you start telling others?"

Gene thought for a time. And then he said, "I have read the Book of Mormon and prayed about it. I didn't feel any doubts. I . . ." He was struggling to find the right words now. "I knew, even when I was a little boy, that the Book of Mormon was true."

"Because your parents told you that it was?"

"I just knew it. I still know it."

Werner smiled, a really benevolent, kindly smile. "Bruder Thomas— is that your family name or your Christian name?"

"Family name."

"Bruder Thomas, I think maybe you are a little like me. You have accepted all this, like a child. But you need to *know*—like your friend here. I'm a skeptic. I think maybe he doesn't really know but only tells himself he does. But he can at least answer for himself. But you—you shouldn't be calling on people this way if you can't do the same."

Gene wanted to defend himself. He wanted to take back some of what he had said and profess a stronger testimony. But he had put himself into this mess, and now there was nothing to say.

"Werner," Elder Bentz said. "I think you should look at this the other way. Maybe you knew more when your faith was simple. There was a time when God gave you feelings of faith and acceptance. Someone has gotten you confused now, but that doesn't mean those early feelings weren't right. Bruder Thomas was taught the truth by good parents, and the truth went straight to his heart. There's nothing more reliable than that."

"Yes. And St. Nicholas visits every child in the world in one night. I once believed that, too."

"It's not the same."

"It isn't?"

"No. It's something magical, for little children. But when we get older, and we listen, we can hear God, feel his presence. I want to tell you again, God has filled me with his Spirit, has answered my prayers. I *know* that the things I told you before are true."

Werner nodded. He did seem impressed. "I envy you," he said. "But I'm sorry. I could never believe in such things."

"Would you like to read the Book of Mormon?"

"Actually, that might be interesting. Since I heard about it, I've wondered what was in it."

"Could we visit you again, give you a copy, and tell you more about it?"

"Yes. Of course. I have nothing to do. Drop by anytime. Just don't expect me to profess my faith and join your church."

"Could we stop by tomorrow?"

"Yes. But not so early. I can sleep until noon if I put my mind to it."

"All right then."

The three stood up. But Gene was in agony. He wanted to correct what he had said, to give a better impression.

"I'm sorry I was so hard on you," Werner said to Gene. "But you two ask for it when you call on people this way."

"It was no problem," Gene said. "I—" He stopped himself. He didn't want to get the whole thing started again.

But outside, he told Elder Bentz, "I'm sorry. I didn't handle that right. I should have just borne my testimony."

"That's all right. He was a tough customer. It was hard to know what to say."

"You said the right thing. Exactly."

"Well, that's how we learn out here."

Gene nodded, but he knew the issue was not quite that simple. It wasn't just that he needed to learn to *say* the right things.

"Let's go get some lunch," Elder Bentz said.

So the two rode to a little Gasthaus where they often bought themselves a cheap lunch, and then they went back to knocking on doors all afternoon. Late in the day, before suppertime, however, they were scheduled to come back for another hour of study. When they reached their room and took off their coats, Elder Bentz sat down at the table in the center of the room and took out his German scriptures. Gene got his lesson plan out. He usually used this time to keep his lessons fresh in his mind, since he had very few chances to give any yet.

"Let me make a suggestion," Elder Bentz said. "I know we read the Book of Mormon in German together, but a lot of times that turns into language study as much as anything. Why don't you spend this time for a while just reading the Book of Mormon in English?"

Gene nodded. He liked that idea. It was true that he had read the book, but he had done it sometimes with his family, and sometimes for high-school seminary. He had never poured himself into it the way he felt a need to do now.

"What I would do," Elder Bentz said, "is pray before you start to read, and then again after."

He didn't say, "So you'll get the testimony you need," but Gene knew that's what he meant.

Gene got his English Book of Mormon from the little nightstand by his bed. "Maybe that Werner guy was right," Gene said. "Maybe I shouldn't even be here."

"No. Don't listen to him about that. Read Alma 32 before you read anything else, and pray about that."

"Okay." But Gene wasn't sure what Alma 32 was about.

"Elder Thomas, you're like most of us when we first get here. What you told Werner was true. Your faith just isn't as strong as it needs to be. There's nothing wrong with that, but you're going to need something stronger to sustain you through everything you're going to face."

"Okay," Gene said again.

"Alma says truth is light, and it's good. When you taste the light, it's delicious, and you want more."

"Yeah. I remember that from seminary." Gene went to his bed, where he knelt and prayed. He told the Lord he was sorry he wasn't a better missionary, told him that he wanted to be much better, to not complain and think about home so much. "Lord," he said, "I do believe in the Book of Mormon. But I need to *know*."

After, when he sat down at the table and began to read, he told himself that he was ready to pour himself into the book like never before. But instead, his mind kept wandering. He had always been a kind of golden boy; he knew that. He had always, with little effort, managed to be good at the things he wanted to do. But this was not something he could control so easily.

Gene thought of Marsha, of what she had always said about him, that he needed more depth, that he didn't stand for anything. To have any chance with her, he had to go back a bigger man than he had been, a spiritual man. But this was much more important than merely pleasing Marsha. He had never failed at anything, and now he could fail at the only thing that mattered. He was scared.

CHAPTER 28

Kathy was at church. It was November now, and she was in her senior year at Highland High. But the past few months had not been easy. Wally and Lorraine were still upset with her. Not surprisingly, they believed that Kathy had had no business going off to Mississippi without their knowing, and they were especially upset with LaRue for taking her there. They kept saying that they were primarily concerned for Kathy's welfare, that they knew how easily she could have been killed, not just beaten. Kathy understood all that, even admitted it, and she had apologized, but she couldn't understand why they didn't have more concern about the *issue* she had been fighting for.

Change would come to the South, Dad would always say, as though he thought it would happen by magic, but Kathy saw little that made her hopeful. Lyndon Johnson had said all the right things, but she sometimes wondered how deep his commitment really was. What disillusioned her with the Democrats was that after a great deal of work that summer to elect Mississippi Negroes to the Freedom Party—a group that hoped to represent the state at the national convention—the party had rejected their claim and seated the old-guard, all-white Mississippi delegation. Lyndon Johnson hadn't had the courage, nor had anyone else, to offend the white voters. Sometimes it seemed that significant change would never come.

What Kathy felt most was her loneliness. She missed Aunt LaRue, missed the people she had gotten to know in those couple of weeks she had spent in Greenwood, and missed the college life she had glimpsed and now wanted to begin. She didn't think of herself as a loner, but the fact was, she didn't feel close to anyone at her high school. She grew weary of the empty-headed things people said, but she was also tired of arguing, and she felt she spent about half her life biting her tongue.

Kathy did like to go to church. She loved the hymns, and she liked taking the sacrament. She even enjoyed the good members she had known all her life—greeting them, chatting, sharing a sense of combined commitment. But why did they have to say so many things that drove Kathy crazy? She tried to have a good attitude—worked at it really hard—but people made such incredible leaps of logic. And they thought the world ended at the borders of Utah. The rest of the world was "the mission field"—which seemed to mean something like "outer space"—and there were too many mean-spirited stereotypes about people who weren't "members of the Church."

Kathy was sitting in her young-adult Sunday School class this morning, and Lynn Cutler—a returned missionary, about thirty, who had a little too much confidence in his own opinions—was expounding on one of his favorite doctrines. God's chosen children—the tribes of Israel—were scattered throughout the world, but they were the lambs who knew the shepherd's voice. They would be gathered in from the four corners of the earth and would build the kingdom in the last days. Kathy had heard that before, and she didn't disagree, but she wasn't sure it was a healthy thing to think of people that way: some chosen, some not.

"Brother Hadlock," Brother Cutler was saying now, "didn't you find in the mission field that some people were golden right from the beginning? The first time you taught them, they recognized the truth and embraced it?"

Ferrin Hadlock had returned that summer from a mission in Brazil. When he was a kid, he had always been very short, very quiet, but he had grown a few inches during his mission, and he seemed to have come out of his shell at the same time. "Yeah," he said. "That happened a lot of times."

"That's exactly what I experienced. Every missionary can tell you stories about—"

"The only thing is," Ferrin said, "when people went right through the lessons, no problem, and got baptized right away, sometimes they fell away real quick too—right after the missionaries who taught them got transferred. Or even before that."

Kathy watched Brother Cutler. Clearly, he didn't want realities thrust upon him. "A lot of times the members didn't do a good job fellowshipping," he said rather tersely. And then he turned toward the chalkboard.

But from the back of the room, Ferrin said, "Let me ask you about something else."

Brother Cutler turned around and waited, but he looked impatient.

"I know this is off the subject, but it fits a little bit with what we were just talking about, and it's something I just keep thinking about since I came home."

"What's that?" Brother Cutler asked. He folded his arms across his chest and didn't realize that he had run his chalk across one sleeve of his dark suit coat.

"One of the big problems we had in Brazil was knowing who was colored and who wasn't. You couldn't always tell just by looking at a guy. A lot of men accepted the gospel—just the way you were talking about— but then we had to check on their family background and decide if we could give them the priesthood. But most of the time, people didn't have records back very far. And it didn't prove anything anyway. You couldn't really tell by their names. Mostly, we just based it on how they looked. I'm sure we gave the priesthood to some guys who weren't supposed to get it."

Kathy felt a deeper quiet descend upon an already quiet room. Kathy was sitting next to her friend Cynthia Christofferson—who seemed to stiffen.

"And what was your question?" Brother Cutler asked. Kathy could see that the disruption was annoying to him.

"What's going to happen to men like that?"

"I'm sure the Lord will work that out. It isn't anything to worry about."

Brother Cutler turned to the board again. But Kathy was amazed by what she had just heard. She glanced around to see whether anyone else shared her concern. It was a big room, but people were spread out, mostly in little clusters. Some of them looked half asleep. Jerry North—a boy she had grown up with—had his arms crossed, and his head had fallen forward, onto his chest.

"What about the ones who maybe only looked colored and weren't?" Ferrin asked. "We might have kept the priesthood away from some guys who should have had it."

Brother Cutler turned around again and stared at Ferrin. Kathy thought she saw something like anger in the grip of his jaw. "I guess the Lord will sort that out too," he said.

"I hope so," Ferrin said. "It seemed like it put a lot of responsibility on us—you know, to decide something like that."

That seemed to be the end of the matter. Brother Cutler nodded but didn't respond. He picked up where he had left off, talking again about the tribes of Israel. But Kathy was appalled. She told herself for at least ten seconds not to say anything, but she couldn't resist. "Brother Cutler," she said. "Just a minute. What does that mean—God will sort things out?"

He hesitated, staring at Kathy for several seconds as if to say, *This is the last interruption I'm going to allow.* "Exactly that. The Lord will do the right thing, in all his wisdom."

"But how can we teach the doctrine that some people should get the priesthood and others shouldn't, and then have no sure way of knowing one from the other?"

The room had only *seemed* quiet before. Kathy glanced at Jerry North and noticed that his head had come up, but he wouldn't look at her.

"In most cases, we do know."

"Brother Cutler, I'm not trying to smart off. I'm really not. But that doesn't seem good enough to me. Did you know that in the early days of the Church, Joseph Smith ordained some Negroes to the priesthood?"

"Yes. I did know that. But Kathy, I'm not going to argue with you about this again. You always want to talk about this same issue."

"But this is something different. A man could live out his life without receiving a right—and a power—he deserved. Where's the justice in that? How can we let twenty-year-old guys, down in Brazil, make decisions like that and then say, 'Oh well, God will work it out?'"

Kathy had watched Brother Cutler's neck become splotched with red. "Why don't you ask your father that question?" he finally said. "We have other things to discuss today."

That, of course, was not a terribly subtle way for Brother Cutler to remind everyone that this troublemaker was none other than the bishop's daughter. But Kathy hadn't been angry. She hadn't argued. She had only asked. Was that so terrible?

Brother Cutler mumbled through the rest of the lesson, but he ended early, gathered his materials, and walked out first. "Kathy," Cynthia said, "why did you do that? He's going to go straight to your dad to tell him what you said."

"I didn't *say* anything. I just wondered about that whole thing. Doesn't it bother you?"

"I don't know. Not really, I guess. If people on the earth do things wrong, God *will* make it right, won't he?"

Kathy tried to think about that, to accept the idea, but it didn't sound right. "Cynthia, we send missionaries out preaching that we've got the pure doctrine. But this thing with Negroes and the priesthood just seems like such a big muddle to me. We've got this doctrine, and we don't even seem to know where it came from."

"Don't look at me, Kathy. I don't know anything about it."

Kathy watched everyone filing out of the class. Some glanced at her and then looked away, but no one said anything. She hadn't meant to make them uncomfortable. What she felt now, however, was how much she bothered them, how much they probably disliked her—and that bothered her much more than she wanted it to.

As Cynthia stood up, Kathy stood too and took hold of her arm. "Do you care?" she asked. "Does it matter to you whether Negroes receive the priesthood?"

"We don't have any in the Church, do we?" Cynthia asked.

"Yes, we do."

"Not many, I don't think."

"Does it matter how many?"

The room was empty now, except for Kathy and Cynthia. Cynthia looked into Kathy's eyes for a long time before she said, "Kathy, I don't know. You're smarter than me. You think about things I have no idea about."

"I don't do it to cause trouble. I really don't, Cynthia."

"I know."

"Is everyone always going to *hate* me?"

"Hate you?"

"Couldn't you see how people were looking at me?"

"They don't hate you—not the ones who really know you."

Kathy surprised herself with her own response. "But no one is ever going to marry me," she said. It was what she had thought so often lately. All last year she had liked Val Norris so much, and he had never once asked her out. Now there was a new guy in choir she would like to know, but the one time he had talked to her, she had disagreed with him about the elections. He had been wearing a Goldwater button that said, "In

Your Heart You Know He's Right." She had only teased a little, saying, "Yeah, *far* right," but that had set off an exchange that was rather heated. Afterward, she couldn't believe she had let it happen, not with a guy she thought she would actually like. He had never said a word to her since then.

Sometimes lately Kathy thought she knew her own future, and it looked like LaRue's. She told herself that she didn't have to measure her life by whether boys liked her, but she longed to meet a guy who shared at least some of her convictions.

"You'll get married, Kathy. You're pretty."

Kathy didn't think of herself as pretty—not at all—but she knew what Cynthia meant. Cynthia was painfully plain. Her face was like a ball, her cheeks thick and her nose too flat. But she was so good, better than Kathy would ever be. *Why wasn't the world fair?* she asked herself. It was the same question she had been asking for so long. She had first posed it when she was only ten or so, and she watched her little brother struggle to do things others did so easily. That had been bad enough, but when other kids had begun to tease him she had felt her first rage, and some of that had been burning in her ever since.

"I don't feel pretty," she told Cynthia.

Kathy walked home by herself, and then she went to her room. She knew her family was going to Grandpa and Grandma Thomas's for dinner today, but she wasn't sure she wanted to go. She would probably get into another argument with someone. What she didn't expect was the knock that came on her door, not ten minutes after she had changed into her jeans. "What?"

"It's Dad. Can I talk to you for a minute?"

"Sure. Come in."

He opened the door and stepped inside. He was wearing a dark gray suit and a narrow black tie. He reminded Kathy of some of the Negro ministers she had seen in Mississippi, always so correct in the way they dressed. He looked serious, too. But what he said was, "Honey, remember. We're going over to Mom and Dad's for dinner."

"Don't you have appointments?"

"Yes, a little later. But I promised Mom we'd try to make it for dinner first."

"Okay."

"You can't go dressed like that—not on a Sunday."

"Why not? I'll change back into my dress before we go to sacrament meeting."

"That's not the point. Grandma doesn't like us to show up in our old clothes—you know, on the Sabbath. You've noticed how she always dresses, haven't you?"

"Tell the truth, Dad. It's Grandpa who cares about things like that. Grandma Bea would probably put her own jeans on if it weren't for him."

Wally smiled. "That's probably true," he said. "But anyway, do it for me, okay?"

"All right."

"There was something else I needed to talk to you about."

"Brother Cutler must have talked to you."

"He did. And he was quite upset. He told me that you don't believe in the Church."

Kathy didn't want to get mad again, but she couldn't believe the guy would say something like that. "What he really means is that I don't believe in *him*, and he thinks he's the Church."

"Be nice."

Kathy walked to her bed and sat down, then stretched out on her back. "Dad, all I did was ask a couple of questions."

"Maybe so, but this thing about Negroes and the priesthood does bother you, doesn't it?"

"I don't understand it."

"I don't either."

Wally pulled Kathy's chair away from her little desk, turned it around, and sat down near the foot of her bed. But now she couldn't see him, so she sat up. "That's all I'd like to hear Brother Cutler say," Kathy said. "He acts like Negroes have committed some kind of sin—and don't deserve to have the priesthood. I don't see how that fits with anything else we believe."

"I don't either," Dad said. He was looking past Kathy at the picture of Christ she kept on the wall. "But you just said something important."

"What?"

"We believe."

"I do believe, Dad. I get mad at some of the members, but I don't doubt God. Aunt LaRue and I talked a lot about that. We both get impatient with the way a lot of Mormons do things, but we believe in Christ, and we want to live the way Christians really should."

"What about President McKay?"

"He's the most wonderful man on this earth, Dad. All I have to do is look at him and I know he's a prophet."

"If this practice of not granting the priesthood to Negroes were wrong, he would be the first to change it, don't you think?"

"I guess so."

"You sound a little unsure."

Kathy tried to think what she felt about that. She could see her dad watching her, waiting for the answer he expected. "Dad, sometimes I wonder if it's something that started back in the early days of the Church—when Negroes were still slaves, and all the churches were segregated—and it just keeps going because no one has questioned it."

"Is that what LaRue thinks?"

"She's talked about that. It's one of the things that she thinks is possible."

"But plenty of people are asking the question now, so I'm sure the Brethren are thinking about it—and asking the Lord."

"Maybe so. But maybe the members of the Church aren't ready. Maybe we're holding the Lord back because so many of us are prejudiced against Negroes."

"Another LaRue theory?"

"Yes."

"Well, I don't know. But I know there's a God, and I know he speaks through his prophets. And I know that God doesn't hate Negroes. So I just have to accept things the way they are."

"Would you say that if you were a Negro?"

"Probably not."

Kathy nodded. She loved her dad so much. She got irritated with him sometimes—because he was so strict about certain things. But he was honest. So was her mother. Kathy could trust them. And that's what she needed right now.

"Honey, I worry about you. But the truth is, you're way ahead of what I was when I was your age. All I could talk about was getting out of this valley. I wanted to get away from my dad, and I didn't think I would ever come back, once I did."

"What was the big problem between you and Grandpa, Dad?"

"I don't know. Mostly, I was just young and stupid. But he was not an easy man. He expected a lot from us, and he made his disappointment very clear. I thought he wanted another Alex, and I figured I was never going to make it. When I see Alex's name in the paper every night, I still feel like I'm the little brother who didn't amount to much."

That was amazing to Kathy. Her dad was the one who ran the family businesses—the car dealership, the plant that built parts for appliances, the land development company. And he was such a good bishop.

"Dad's softened a lot. He's a lot more easygoing with you kids than he was with us."

Kathy laughed. "I love Grandpa. I just disagree with almost everything he says."

"Kathy, you're some kid." He took hold of her bare foot, lifted it, and kissed her big toe. "Do you think you could be just a little easier on Brother Cutler? He doesn't have LaRue to tell him what's what in this world."

Kathy laughed. She threw her legs over the side of the bed and walked to her dad. He stood and she hugged him. "Dad, I know what you're saying," she said. "I need to be careful about letting Aunt LaRue do my thinking for me."

"Would I say that?"

"No. But you'd think it."

"I don't think you should let *anyone* do your thinking for you—including me."

"But you'd rather do it than leave it up to LaRue. Right?"

He stepped back and grinned. "Well . . . maybe so."

"Dad, I'm sorry I went to Mississippi. I mean . . . I'm not sorry I went. But I'm sorry I didn't call you."

"I wouldn't have let you go."

"I know. I was hoping you would forgive me after I did."

"Well, I guess it worked then." He smiled. Then he kissed her on the forehead. "Why don't you put that pretty green dress back on before we go. Okay?"

"Okay."

When Wally and Lorraine and the family arrived at Grandma's house, Kathy saw Alex's car already there, and as they walked inside, Alex was the first to greet them. "You're actually taking a day off?" Lorraine asked Alex.

Since Alex had won the election, he had been working nonstop to get ready to relocate to the East. He had local business affairs to close out, and he had been back and forth to Washington twice, setting things up for the move.

"Day of rest," he said, and he smiled. "And I needed it. At least I'm getting released from the stake presidency next week. That'll help."

Wally laughed. "You'll just get called to the presidency again, back in Washington, when you get there."

Alex rolled his eyes. "They wouldn't do that to me, would they?"

"Maybe not the first year."

President Thomas came into the room from the kitchen. He had an apron on. "No cracks!" he said, and he laughed.

"Are you actually fixing dinner?" Lorraine asked.

"No. I'm just peeling some carrots. Bea told me to put this on so I wouldn't get anything on me, but I don't know what carrot peels are going to do."

"Is Bobbi coming down?" Wally asked.

"No. They aren't going to make it today. Ricky's had some sniffles, and she doesn't want to take him out too much right now. But Bev is coming, with her kids. I thought they would be here by now."

Kathy liked Aunt Beverly, but she had nothing in common with her, and her kids were all little and rather wild. She liked Bobbi more than anyone else, and she liked to see Diane. Ricky was walking now—or actually running most of the time. He had become the new little star of the family. Kathy had hoped to see him as much as anyone.

"Give me that apron, Dad," Lorraine said. "I don't want you to hurt yourself peeling carrots."

"Gladly," Grandpa said, and he reached behind himself and undid the bow, then slipped the apron off and handed it to Lorraine.

"Where are the kids?" Wayne, Kathy's little brother, asked.

"Joey didn't come," Grandpa said. He pointed with his thumb. "But the rest of them are all upstairs." Wayne and Glenda and Shauna all hustled up the stairway. Douglas stood alongside Kathy, holding her hand.

Alex and Wally and Grandpa walked on into the living room from the front entry, and they sat down together. Kathy thought of going into the kitchen with the women, but she doubted they needed her, and she never felt all that comfortable around Aunt Anna. The woman was nice; she really was. But she was perfect. She was beautiful and serene and even smart, but she was everything Kathy wasn't. She was quiet and thoughtful, and she wasn't troubled by much of anything—not like Aunt Bobbi or LaRue.

Kathy took Douglas with her and had him sit at the end of the couch. Then she picked up a *Life* magazine from the coffee table. She began to thumb through it, searching for something that Douglas might like to look at.

"I saw the final vote totals in the paper," Wally told Alex. "You won by an even bigger margin than they announced at first."

"Yeah, I was surprised," Alex said. "I thought it was going to be a lot closer."

"The problem Welker had was that he thinks like Lyndon Johnson," Grandpa said. "He wanted to start another program to solve every problem in the world. He believes in all this Great Society business. That's not too hard to run against. People around here are sick of the federal government sticking its nose into everything."

Kathy rolled her eyes. But she wasn't going to say anything more today. She had found some pictures of a pair of great apes. Douglas laughed at that.

"That's probably right, Dad," Alex said. "But you can't just act like problems don't exist. Maybe the government can't do everything, but there are some things we *need* to do."

Kathy was turning pages again. She came to a picture of an American helicopter in Vietnam. Three American soldiers were jumping off, carrying automatic weapons. The caption on the picture said that the men were "advisers," but they looked like combat soldiers to Kathy. A comment came to mind, but she decided to keep it to herself.

"That's right. We need to leave people alone."

Kathy couldn't help herself. "Grandpa's right," she said. "There *are* times when our government does things it has no business doing."

All the men looked at her. She waited a second or two and then held the picture up. "I think we're fighting a war right now and pretending that we're not."

She knew, of course, that this would get a rise from Grandpa Thomas. "Well, now, that's a different matter," he said. "I'm thinking that's one place we have to take a stand. Goldwater probably would have sent ground troops in, and my guess is that Johnson will admit before long that it's something he's got to do."

"Why?"

"Honey, we've got to stop the Communists somewhere. If we back away from Vietnam, all of Indochina is going to drop right into Communist hands."

Kathy had been reading a lot about Vietnam lately, and it was another matter that she and LaRue had talked about. She didn't want to get into another argument, but she was sick of hearing how many people were ready to jump into another war. "Grandpa, the French lost over there because they didn't understand how much the Vietnamese people wanted to be free—and how long they would fight. In the peace treaty with the French, everyone agreed that free elections would be held, but now we're the ones who won't let the people vote—because we know the Communists would win."

"Of course they would win. Do you think that would be a fair election? Ho Chi Minh has his people infiltrating the whole country. The people out in the villages are scared to death."

"Grandpa, if people want to vote for a Communist government, we have no right to tell them that's not their right."

Grandpa was shaking his head, and something in his manner seemed to say, "Oh, little girl, what do you know?" Kathy hated that. But Grandpa was leaning forward now, and his voice sounded careful, reasonable, as he said, "Kathy, if we let Russia take over this world, one country at a time, what's going to happen to us in the end?"

"Russia has nothing to do with this."

"Oh, honey, don't be naive."

"Grandpa, it's a civil war. The Vietnamese hate the Chinese, and they have nothing to do with Russia. Ho Chi Minh is a nationalist. He's not going to let *anyone* run his country."

"Is that what you read in *Time* magazine, or where did you get that?"

She had read some things in *Time*, but she hated the way Grandpa pushed her argument aside without considering it. She saw her dad shake his head at her and scowl; she knew she had to stop. She was relieved when Alex said, "Dad, I think Kathy's got a good point about this. I don't think we can win a war in Vietnam—any more than the French could—and I really think we ought to stay out of there."

Grandpa turned toward Alex, pointing a finger at him. "Alex, that's the last thing in the world you ought to be saying. If you get a reputation for being soft on Communism, you'll *never* be reelected in this state."

"Look, I understand that. I was careful what I said during the campaign. But I don't want my sons over there, and I don't want to send anyone else's sons either."

"And you'll turn over the country to the Communists?"

Alex seemed ready to answer, but then he hesitated, as though he wasn't quite sure. Kathy took the chance to say, "Uncle Alex, how can we say we stand for freedom and then try to force our system on some country halfway around the world?"

"Look, I agree with that. But a lot of people feel the way Dad does. It's almost impossible to win an election these days if a man is accused of backing down to Communists."

"That's exactly right," Grandpa said.

"So is that what you're going to do in Washington, Uncle Alex? Say what people want to hear? Or are you going to stand up for what you believe?"

"Kathy, you're eighteen," Grandpa said. "To you, everything looks simple. But the world is a lot more complicated than you know."

Kathy was still looking at Uncle Alex, still waiting. Finally, he said, "You're right. There are things I need to stand up for. And Vietnam is one of them. I'm going to try to keep us out of there—whether I get reelected or not."

Grandpa let out a little moan, and then he started into his arguments again. But Kathy was paying no attention. She looked over at her Dad. He was smiling at her, looking pleased.

CHAPTER 29

Diane was with Scott, and they were driving up Ogden Canyon. The fall colors were mostly gone now, and the canyon looked dreary compared to what it had been just a couple of weeks before. But the two liked this ride and made it often. The Volkswagen was not a good car for sitting close, but they liked to talk and just spend time together, and this was the prettiest drive around Ogden.

The radio was also on, loud, and at the moment Manfred Mann was singing "Do Wah Diddy Diddy," the number one hit on the current charts. "Now we're together nearly every single day," Diane and Scott were singing with the music. "Singing do wah diddy diddy dum diddy do, singing do wah diddy diddy dum diddy do. We're so happy and that's how we're going to stay." They glanced at each other and smiled. Diane was snapping her fingers.

The next song was Roy Orbison's "Oh Pretty Woman." Scott pointed at Diane. "That's you," he said. "Pretty woman, walking down the street," he sang. "Pretty woman—the kind I'd like to meet."

Then came the Supremes singing "Baby Love," and after that Gene Pitney doing "It Hurts to Be in Love." Scott and Diane sang the words: "So you cry a little bit—to be in love—die a little bit—to be in love." And on the music went: Martha and the Vandellas singing "Dancing in the Street," the Beach Boys doing "When I Grow up to Be a Man," and the Rolling Stones knocking out "Time Is on My Side."

Between songs, Scott and Diane talked a little about this and that: people at school, Diane's trouble with algebra and Mrs. Davies, who, she was convinced, hated her.

"She might like you better if you got some of the answers right," Scott said, and he laughed.

"Well, I might like her better if she would just once explain something so I can understand it. I used to do all right in math until they started putting in all those X's and Y's and everything."

"You were a killer at long division, weren't you?"

"As a matter of fact, yes."

Scott cracked up. "I think we'd both better stay away from trig."

Scott took the South Fork turn, near Huntsville, and headed up into the next canyon. He drove on to the campgrounds where they had often come that summer for their own little picnics. "Should we go down and ride the bridge?" Diane asked.

"Of course. We can't get this close and not take a ride."

It was a little joke between them, something they had discovered that summer. They had been standing on the log footbridge that crossed the creek in the picnic area, and Diane had been staring down at the water when she suddenly felt a strange sensation. It had scared her, and she had looked up. But then she had tried it again. The rushing water had created an illusion, as though the water had stopped and the bridge were flying backward over the water at break-neck speed. She had told Scott, and he had tried it, and then the two had laughed together and "ridden the bridge" for a long time. It was a weird sensation, but Diane loved it, and she loved that she and Scott had shared the little pleasure all that summer.

So they walked from the parking lot down through the empty campground, and they stood on the bridge, watching the water. It was a cold day, and everything seemed colorless now with all the leaves off the trees, but the old bridge was always the same, and Diane found it sweet that Scott would enjoy coming back to "their place." Diane liked the sound of the running water and the silhouettes of the bare trees against the gray sky.

"The water's moving too slow," Diane said. "It hardly feels like the bridge is moving. Next spring, when the water is running high, it should be *wild*."

"Let's come back every spring—or at least every year—no matter where we ever live."

Diane looked over at him. "What do you mean, 'where *we* live'?"

Scott turned toward her. "Don't you want to stay together?"

"What do you mean? Get married?"

"Sure."

"What are you doing? Proposing?"

"Not exactly. But Diane, that's how I think about us. Don't you?"

"I don't know. I'm sixteen."

He reached out, pushed her hair aside, and then touched her neck with the tips of his fingers. "I love you, Diane. I've never told you that before, but I do. And I want to be with you forever. That's one of the great things about deciding to join the Church. Now I know that'll be possible."

Sometimes, lately, Diane had wished she could break up with Scott. She wondered whether there weren't other boys she would like, and yet she was spending all her time with him. She even wondered whether she knew him. She was hearing more things about him all the time. A girl who knew Chilly and his crowd told her that Scott was hanging out with those guys once in a while—that he had been drinking beer with them and making out with other girls. Diane had refused to believe that was true, but she had also hesitated to ask. Maybe she was afraid of what she might find out.

Still, she didn't want to think of any of that right now. He was so good-looking, so fun, and now he was touching her cheek so delicately that she found herself holding her breath.

"I know we're young," he said. "I'm not talking about getting married as soon as we get out of high school or anything like that. We both have things to do. But we can keep going together, and then—when the time is right—marry forever. That's what I want, Diane."

"I love you too," she found herself saying, and then he pulled her closer, holding her against his body. He was strong and solid, and she liked the feel of his body against hers. The autumn air was cold, and she loved the warmth she felt from him.

"Wow, you've never told me that, either."

"I know. But I do."

"Do you think about marrying me?"

"Sure. But let's just take things a little at a time. It's so far off before we could think about marriage."

"Sure. I know. But I'm going to keep thinking about it." He kissed the top of her head, then moved back a little and pushed her hair off her neck. He kissed her neck, then her ear, and she felt tingles run through her body. She was only going to do this for a minute or two and then stop. But now he was kissing her mouth, softly, his lips barely touching hers. Then again her neck, and this time, when he kissed her lips, it was with more intensity. She gripped him tight, and she felt his hands on her back, stroking.

Each kiss became more pressing, and now he was rubbing her back, lower and lower, and finally lower than he should. After a moment he moved his hand away without her telling him to, but the next kiss took on more heat. She couldn't let this happen much longer. She had to stop. But he was kissing her neck again, running his hands up her sides, touching her where he shouldn't. Now she was definitely going to stop, but he kissed her once again, and she let him leave his hands where they were for another few seconds.

But the next kiss was too hungry, a little frightening, and suddenly she pulled back. "Don't, Scott. We have to stop."

"No we don't. Why do we have to stop? We love each other." He was fighting to get close again, grabbing at her.

"Scott! Don't!"

But he wasn't letting her go. "You can't take me this far and stop now," he said, his voice harsh. "You're playing games with me, Diane." He had hold of her tight, wouldn't let go, and he was pulling at her sweater. Diane was terrified.

"Stop it, Scott. Stop it."

She twisted frantically, broke his hold, but before she could pull away he had her again. But now he was whispering, "Okay, okay. I'm sorry."

"You are not," she said, and she started to cry. "What do you think I am?"

"Diane, I'm sorry. I just get so excited."

"You don't love me. You just said that because of what you want to do."

"No. Honest. That's not true. I'm just crazy about you, and when we get started I don't want to stop."

"You were trying to force me, Scott. That's not right."

"I know. I know. I'm sorry."

She finally pulled away from him, and he let her go. "I don't trust you sometimes, Scott. I don't know when you're telling the truth. You say you want to join the Church, but then you find excuses not to. And you say you love me, and a minute later you're pawing me like that."

"Diane, you were kissing me the same way. I thought you liked it."

"I do like it. But you have to help me stop. You can't just go after whatever you can get. That's not fair."

"I know. I won't act like that again."

"That's what you said last time."

"I know I did. But let's not even get started like that from now on. Just a kiss goodnight, something like that. That's all we ought to do. I'm really sorry. I don't want to lose you." He ducked his head and closed his eyes, as though he were in pain.

"Scott, I need to know something. A friend of mine said you've been to some parties with Chilly and his friends. She said you were drinking and that you were after some girl named Eva. She told me you were 'all over her.'"

"What?" Scott stepped back.

"You heard me. You stand here and tell me you love me, but I don't think I can trust you."

"Diane, that's not true. A couple of times I've gone over to Chilly's house, after we play golf or something. Those guys drink, but I don't—not since I promised the missionaries I wouldn't. And Eva, she flirts with everyone, including me, but I don't even like her. No guy in his right mind would be dating the most beautiful girl at Ogden High and then mess around with that little tramp."

"Scott, don't say things like that. I'm not the most beautiful girl at Ogden High."

"Tell me anyone better-looking."

Diane wasn't going to get into that. That was not the point. But she found herself softening. She liked to think that he considered her that pretty. She didn't think he would lie, outright, and claim he hadn't had anything at all to drink if he really had. She knew how rumors got around, whether they were true or not.

"Diane, listen. My mom and I have talked a lot about my joining the Church. She has no problem with it at all. She wants me to join. When I brought it up with my dad, he said I should wait a while—until I get older—but he knew the choice was up to me. So Mom told me, to keep Dad from getting upset, I ought to wait until next year—something like that. But in the long run, she says I should do what I want to do. I just don't think there's a big hurry—when Dad's so much against it."

"Why haven't you told me any of this before?"

"Well . . . I did tell you that I felt like I had to get permission from my dad. I just didn't want to tell you that I might have to wait a year or so."

"Tell me everything, Scott. That's the only way we can have a good relationship. I don't want you going to parties at Chilly's house. If you're hanging around with guys like that, what kind of reputation is that going to give me?"

"I've thought of that. And golf is over for the year, so I won't even see those guys now. It's a good time to make a break. I just haven't had many friends around here."

"That's because we spend too much time together, Scott." She knew this was going to hurt him, so she stepped closer and took hold of his hand. "I think we need to cool it for a while—just not see each other so often. If you want to take someone else to the Christmas dance, or something like that, this might be a good time for that."

"No. I don't want to do that. Maybe I could think of someone else to take out sometime. But not to the Christmas dance. That's a night I want to be with you."

Actually, Diane felt the same way. There were a couple of boys who flirted with her sometimes, and they had hinted that they might like to take her out—but she knew they didn't ask because they assumed she was going steady. She really did want to go out with one of them—a guy named Brad Rasmussen—but she wanted to go to the Christmas dance with Scott.

"Do you forgive me?" Scott was asking now. He sounded repentant, but his tone seemed a little *too* strong, and Diane wondered whether she should trust him.

"Scott, it was my fault too. But I don't want it to happen again. If you ever come after me like that again, we're breaking up—forever."

"Okay. That's a deal. I think that's best for both of us." He took her in his arms and held her gently, carefully. Diane didn't mind that, but she wondered whether she hadn't missed her chance. Maybe she should have broken up with him while she was still angry.

When Diane got home that night, she chatted with her parents for a few minutes in the family room. Maggie was in bed, but Mom was sitting in her rocking chair, holding Ricky, who had fallen asleep. "This is when I love him the most," Bobbi said. "It's the only time I can keep up with him." He was like a little lump, his head back against Bobbi's arm, his mouth open.

Diane walked over and knelt down enough to kiss his cheek. "He's so cute," she said. "I think he was trying to say my name today. 'Di, Di,' he kept saying."

"That boy can carry on a whole conversation," Dad said. "You just have to understand his language." Diane could always tell how much her dad loved little Ricky, but it didn't bother her the way she once thought it would. She felt the same way about the little guy.

Diane sat down on the floor and then leaned against the chair that Mom was sitting in. Dad was sitting on the couch, at the end, with the reading lamp over his shoulder. He had a book in his hands—one that looked much too big and gray to be anything very interesting.

"So where have you and Scott been?" Mom asked.

"We just took a drive. And then we stopped at Farr's and got an ice cream cone."

"Oh, don't tell me that. I crave ice cream all the time, but I've vowed not to eat anything sweet until I get back down to fighting weight."

"You're down to Cassius Clay's fighting weight already," Dad said. "Just stick with that."

"Be quiet."

"Or how about Gene Fullmer? He's a middleweight. You can weigh one-sixty."

"Hush."

Diane twisted around and looked at her mother. She grinned as she said, "I had a double-decker—burnt almond fudge on top, raspberry swirl on the bottom. I almost got—"

"You hush up too. You're not funny."

"I know I'm not. I shouldn't have eaten so much. I can feel the fat, oozing its way down through my hips and into my thighs."

But Dad changed the subject. "What's Scott saying about the baptism?" he asked.

"His dad wants him to wait—like maybe a year. Scott is trying to decide whether he wants to go against his dad, or whether he should wait, so his dad won't be upset."

Dad nodded. "Well, we'll see what happens."

Diane wondered what that meant. She thought she heard some skepticism in her father's voice.

But Bobbi wasn't so indirect. "Are you sure he really wants to be baptized?" She shifted Ricky a little, pulling him against her chest.

Diane knew that her mother was getting ready to take Ricky off to bed. She wondered whether it was a good time to say some things to her parents that had been on her mind, but she didn't want to give them a bad impression of Scott. "He does, Mom. We talked about it again tonight." She hesitated. She could often sense how worried her parents were about her and Scott, so she gave them something that she knew would make them feel better. "We also decided that we were going to go out with other people sometimes."

"I think that's very wise," Dad said.

Bobbi was getting up. She gave Diane a curious look, as though she suspected there was more to what Diane was saying, but she didn't ask, and when she carried Ricky down the hall, Diane got up and went to her room. In a few minutes, however, Bobbi followed her there. She opened the door a crack and said, "Can I talk to you for a sec?"

"Sure. Come in." Diane had changed into her pajamas. Now she was hanging up her skirt.

"What's got into you lately? You've become so neat with your things."

"I've gotten so I don't like things to be messy." That was true, but she had lived with her own mess for a long time, and she wasn't sure herself why she had been taking better care of things lately. She did know that she had become aware of her mom lately, how hard she had to work to take care of a baby, and how tired she was. In the mornings, when she thought of leaving her bed unmade, it always worried her a little that Mom would come in and do it. Maybe she was tired of being blamed for leaving it, but she was surprised at how rarely her parents had asked her to baby-sit, and how good she felt when she did do some things around the house that needed to be done.

"That's a good trait, Di. Maybe you're more like me than you think. I just can't stand to live in a messy house."

Bobbi sat down on Diane's bed. Diane knew why she was there.

"So what's going on with you and Scott? Was this a little breakup tonight?"

"No, not really. I just told him we had to be careful about seeing each other too much." Diane knew what she was doing. Her answer would surely lead to another question, and in a way, she did want to talk to her mother about this.

"What do you mean, careful?"

"You know what they always tell us at MIA. You can be with a guy too much. It can get dangerous."

"Is it *getting* dangerous?"

Diane wasn't sure how much she could bring herself to say. She didn't want her mother to think she was terrible. So she said, "Mom, I think we've kissed too much. We haven't done anything *too* bad, but you know, sometimes it's hard not to. Do you know what I mean?"

Diane watched her mother. She looked worried, more than Diane wanted her to look. But Mom smiled, maybe forcing it a little. "Diane, this stuff has been hard for everyone, forever. It was hard for me, believe it or not. I may be your mom, but I actually know what you're talking about."

Diane didn't like to think about that. She couldn't imagine her mom

and dad kissing a lot and getting all excited the way Diane and Scott had
done tonight.

"Diane, I'm going to ask you something. If you don't want to answer,
don't."

"What?"

"What do you mean by 'anything *too* bad?'"

Driving down the canyon, and later at Farr's, Diane had felt the guilt
for what she had let Scott do. At first she had only been angry at him, but
what she knew was that she had been "in on it," all the way up to those
last few seconds. But Mom's question was almost too much for her. She
walked over to the bed and sat down next to her mother. Then she
ducked her head and let herself cry for a time. Mom began to stroke her
back. But still, it wasn't as bad as her mother was probably fearing.

"We just kissed a lot tonight, and Scott got really excited. He touched
me a little bit where he shouldn't. I stopped him. But not right off."

Bobbi put her arms all the way around Diane, pulling her close. She
was wearing a flannel robe that was soft and smelled of baby powder.
Diane felt something she hadn't known for a long time—this closeness to
her mom. She let her face nestle in the robe, her mother's gentleness, and
she cried hard.

Diane wanted to tell the rest—that he had gotten out of hand, had
begun to grab at her, but Mom would hit the ceiling if she heard that. She
would never trust Scott again. She hadn't heard him apologize, hadn't
heard him say how much he loved her. "Mom, if I quit going with him,
maybe he won't join the Church. He hangs around with some guys who
aren't good for him. And he might start spending even more time with
them. I hate to think what might happen."

"Then how much conviction does he have, if he can be influenced
that easily?"

"I don't know. But I think I've been a good influence on him. A lot of guys our age are doing all kinds of things they shouldn't. He might get pulled into that."

Mom didn't say anything for a time, and gradually Diane quit crying and sat up straight. When she did, Mom shifted so she was looking into Diane's face. "Di, tell me this. Do you trust Scott?"

"I guess so."

"I hate to tell you, honey, but that didn't sound very convincing."

Diane nodded, but she didn't say anything more to explain. What she wished right now was that Mom would make the decision for her—tell her never to go out with him again.

"If I were you, I'd do two things. I'd go to the bishop and have a good talk about what happened tonight. You need to take it seriously, not just tell yourself it was a little thing. And then I think you need to do a lot of praying about Scott and what's best for both of you."

"I already made up my mind I'd go see the bishop. And I do pray about all this stuff."

"Good. But honey, you've always told me what you wanted out of life: a good husband, a nice family. And I admire you for that. But you're playing with fire right now, and it could easily burn you—ruin some of your dreams."

"I know." Diane felt tears slipping over her cheekbones again.

Mom kissed her on the head and then got up and walked to the door.

"Mom?"

"Yes."

"Do you really admire me for my goals? I thought you wanted me to be more like you—to get a doctorate, or something like that."

"Oh, honey." Bobbi walked back, sat down by Diane, and hugged her again. "I'm sorry I've made you feel that way. I do admire you. You're you and I'm me, and we're not very much alike, but you're lovelier than I ever was, and you want the right things out of life. Just don't make mistakes that keep you from getting there."

"Should I break up with him?"

"I can't answer that for you, Diane. You have to make the decision. But thanks for talking to me about it. You didn't have to tell me any of this, and you did. That means a lot to me."

Diane liked that—liked the way she felt about her mother. But she also knew she hadn't admitted all her doubts about Scott. She still had a decision to make.

CHAPTER 30

Gene was riding his bike alongside his companion. They were heading back to the apartment. It was Christmas Eve, 1964, and Gene was glad to have some relaxing days ahead. The elders had not gone tracting that day. They had called on some inactive members, wished them a happy Christmas, and invited them to church. What Gene was excited about, however, was that he and Elder Bentz would spend the evening with a member family, and then, on Christmas day, they had another dinner appointment. Sister Pfeiffer was known for her wonderful cooking, and she would certainly outdo herself for the four missionaries that day. Then again on the Second Day of Christmas, another family had invited them. So the food would be great, and above all, there would be time to unwind and have fun, not feel that they had to produce so many proselyting hours.

Gene was trying hard to deal with the pressure he had felt all fall. There were times when he began to feel pretty good about his testimony, but then the doubts and worries would return. Germans were skeptics by nature, it seemed, and investigators had a way of raising questions that Gene had never thought of. Sometimes he wondered whether he weren't an impostor, serving as a missionary when he wasn't really ready, but his mom had told him that he had a good spirit, that he responded naturally to spiritual things. He tried to trust in that, and he tried to rely on his life-long faith, even if he couldn't answer all the questions. But that didn't always work, and he sometimes wondered whether he would ever feel the kind of testimony he needed.

Today another worry was also on his mind. He hadn't had a letter from Marsha for almost a month. She had written quite regularly the first four months he had been in Germany, but then, without explanation, the letters had stopped. Maybe it was finals time at the U. Maybe she was just busy with Christmas. Maybe . . . who knew? But he had a feeling that this was the beginning of the end. It was strange how quickly things changed when they couldn't see each other, couldn't talk. She seemed distant from him already, and surely it must be the same for her.

"So is today the day?" Elder Bentz asked.

"For what?"

"For you to get a letter from your girl. I watch you mope around every day after the mail comes and nothing's there."

Gene didn't know he had been so obvious. Elder Bentz had asked him a couple of times about the absence of letters, but Gene had tried to pass it off as though it weren't anything that concerned him. This time, however, he said, "This looks like a bad sign, doesn't it?"

"What do you mean?"

"I don't know. She never was all that excited about me. I guess it didn't take her long to lose interest." He didn't quite believe that, of course, but he knew it was one of the possibilities.

"I'm shocked," Elder Bentz said.

Gene was watching where he was going on his bike, staying fairly close to Elder Bentz, but now he looked over, and he saw that Elder Bentz was smiling. "Why are you shocked?"

"I've watched all these German girls practically faint when you walk by. I thought every unmarried girl on this planet was waiting in line in case you rejected this Marsha girl."

"Yeah, right." Gene ducked his head again, partly to keep the wind out of his face. It was actually a little warmer today than it had been, but a rather nasty little breeze was blowing. The two were heading down a broad street, not far from the Danube. When a car came along, traveling in the same direction, Gene dropped back for a moment and then pumped hard enough to pull up alongside Elder Bentz again.

"Elder Thomas, I'm serious. If I looked like you, I'd figure I had it made."

"Marsha would take you over me in a minute. You're what she's looking for—a guy with some depth to him."

"You're making this up, aren't you?"

"No. Not at all."

"So you think she's going to drop a 'Dear John' on you one of these days?"

"It's starting to look like it."

"Are you going to take it like a man?"

"What else can I do?"

Elder Bentz laughed. "When I got mine, it came like a bolt of lightning. She was writing all the time, putting little X's at the bottom of the letter—the whole bit—and then bang, one day she writes and says she's engaged. You know the line: It was 'just one of those things that happened.' She said it was the hardest letter she ever had to write. All that stuff. Why do they always say the same things?"

"I guess pretty much everyone gets one, sooner or later."

"No, not really. Only every guy who has a girl back home." Elder Bentz laughed again, his voice cracking high. "The smart guys don't have one in the first place."

Elder Bentz's bike was in a low gear. His short legs were working much faster than Gene's. "Do you know anyone who had a girl wait?"

"A couple. But that's kind of funny, too. After two and a half years, what those guys were worried about was that she *would* wait. They get to the end, they hardly know the girl anymore, and they start wondering whether they're *obligated* to marry her after that long. It's almost like they start to think that if guys are picking off most of the girls who are supposed to be waiting, why not mine? Didn't anyone want her?"

Gene laughed, but he said, "Marsha's not the kind of girl everyone would be interested in. She's nice-looking, but she's way too deep for a lot of guys."

"Well, I wouldn't worry about it too much. You'll hear one of these days. If it's a regular little letter, it'll be full of, 'I've just been so busy lately' kind of stuff. You only have to worry if it's fat. When they write you off, they think they can't do it in a page. They have to thank you for the memories and all that stuff. I guess they think it's letting you down easy, but it feels more like they want to put a knife between your ribs and turn it a few times."

"Was it that bad?"

"Not really. Not for me. I just figured I'd have a lot of fun looking around for someone new, once I got home."

"Yeah. That's the best way to think about it."

But as they neared their apartment house, Gene wasn't thinking that way. What he had to believe was that she would have sent him some sort of package or little gift, or at least a Christmas letter. Every day, lately, he had figured it would show up, and this was the last possible day. If he didn't hear today, that had to be a bad sign.

The elders parked their bikes out back and then came around the house to the mailboxes that were in the front hallway. Gene was a little nervous, as he had been every day lately. Elder Bentz used his key to open the mailbox. He pulled out much more mail than the two got at other times of the year. "Hey, my cards are paying off," he said. Elder Bentz had sent a lot of Christmas cards to relatives and people in his ward. When people sent a missionary a card, there was almost always a check in it, or maybe a five-dollar bill.

He began to fumble through the cards, but Gene had already spotted it: the off-white, crinkly stationery Marsha used. Elder Bentz handed Gene a couple of cards, one red, one green, and then he saw the letter.

"Oh, oh. Here it is," he said. "It's not fat—that's a good sign. But it's not exactly thin either."

Gene took the letter from Elder Bentz, then headed up the stairs. He used his key to get in, wasn't even sure how far his companion was behind him. He left the door open and walked to the table in the center of their little room. He sat down, then used his letter opener to slice the envelope open, neatly. He was trying to take his time, keep his control, not let himself get upset. He read the letter slowly, but he didn't have to read long before he understood:

> Dear Gene,
>
> I'm sorry I haven't written for such a long time. I've been trying hard to make a decision about what I should do. Those last few weeks with you, before you left, were so wonderful, and I let myself believe that something could come of our friendship. But your absence has given me time to think more objectively, and Gene, I can't imagine us ever ending up together. We're just too different. I can tell from your letters that you do want to think about a future together, and that really worries me. It seems to me that we're better off to make the break now. You'll concentrate better on your mission, and you won't be coming home to an awkward situation. So I'm not planning to write anymore, at least not on a regular basis. I hope you'll understand.
>
> I think I should tell you that I've been dating a boy named Merrill Dwyer quite regularly this fall. If you hear that from someone else, you might think that's why I'm writing this letter. But that's not true, Gene. I fully expect that I won't be married when you get back. And the problem with that is that you might interpret that to mean that I "waited for you." I just don't want to send you that message. One thing about dating

Merrill, whether I ever get serious with him or not, is that I have already seen that we're much more suited for each other. We think more alike and don't end up in the kind of conflicts that you and I sometimes experienced.

Gene, you're one of the nicest guys I've ever known. I started out very skeptical about you, as you know, but I gradually came to respect the kind of person you are. We had wonderful times together, and those are times I'll never forget. They'll always be part of my growing-up experience, and I hope that you'll hold onto good memories of me—and not just the awful ones when I wasn't very kind to you. One thing I know is that you'll have crowds of girls waiting for you when you get home. Half the girls at the U have you on their wish list, so you'll have your pick, and whomever you choose, she'll be a very lucky girl. I'm not just saying that, Gene; I mean it. Just because two people are not entirely suited for each other doesn't mean there's something wrong with either one. Certainly, most girls would say that I must have a crack in my head, just to think of stepping out of that long line of hopeful girls.

Gene, I just went back and read this letter through, and it sounds all wrong. That's because I don't really know what to say, or how to say it. I really like you, and this choice has been very, very hard for me. But honestly, Gene, I think it's the best thing for both of us. It's early in your mission, still, and you can get this behind you. When you get home, our friendship will be long behind you, and you can move ahead. I think we both knew this would have to happen someday. I'll still pray for you every day, as I have since you left, and above all, I hope this letter doesn't hurt your work. I'm so sorry it came at

Christmastime, but I felt like I had to let you know, and not just let you wonder why I wasn't writing.

May the Lord bless you, Elder Thomas. I know you'll be a great missionary, and I know you have a great future ahead of you, all through your life. I hope you can forgive me for this letter, and I hope we can remain friends forever. I may write a newsy letter now and then, just to keep you up on life on campus, if you would like me to do that, or if you would rather I didn't, just say so. I'll always hold you in a very special place in my heart. Please don't hate me. Give me a tiny space in your heart too.

Your friend,

Marsha

Elder Bentz had come in, somewhere back there. He had sat down at the table, across from Gene, and he was opening his cards. "I can hear you taking long, hard breaths, Elder," he said. "It must have been the dagger between the ribs."

"Yup."

"Really?"

"Afraid so."

"Well, at least it's over. You won't have to worry about it for two more years."

Gene tried to laugh. "I can't even get a girl to wait for me six months. That must be some kind of a record."

"Oh, no. I knew an elder who never got a single letter from his girl. He found out later she had a date the night he left, and she was engaged a couple of weeks after that."

Gene tried to laugh again. He was testing the pain inside, trying to decide how bad this was. He was a little surprised that the reality wasn't quite so terrible as the fear had been. "I always knew she would write a letter like this, sooner or later," he said.

"Then sooner is better than later."

"Yeah. I guess so."

"So are you going to be a man about it?"

"I am a man. You don't see me shedding any tears, do you? You probably bawled for three days."

"Not me. I chucked the letter aside and said, 'Well, that's that.' Didn't ever give it another thought."

"Was it really that easy?"

But now Elder Bentz hesitated, and when Gene finally got himself to look him straight on, he said, "No. It wasn't easy at all. But you know, you do what you have to do. You'll be okay."

"Yeah. It's just kind of a bad time to have it happen—you know, Christmas and everything." Gene looked away from his companion and glanced around the room. He had never quite gotten used to living in such a tiny space, with beds foot to foot and a small wardrobe on the opposite wall to hold their clothes. Something in the closeness of the little room reminded Gene how far from home he was, how strange it was to think that today was Christmas Eve.

"You're wrong about that," Elder Bentz said. "A guy might get a little homesick at Christmastime, but it's still the best time of the year for a missionary. The members feed you until you're stuffed—and then feed you more—and it's a nice time just to feel the Spirit and remember why we're here."

Gene wasn't sure that he felt much of what he would call the Spirit at the moment, but he was glad that he had some fun things to look forward to that night and the next few days. "How soon are we going over to the Schmidts' house?"

"I don't know. Sister Schmidt said to come as early as we wanted—or could. We could head over there now, if we wanted to."

The Schmidts had three little kids, who were fun to play with, and Gene had looked forward to that. But more than anything, he didn't want to think. He just wanted to get going, to keep himself busy. "Why don't we go now, then?"

"Okay. Let me finish opening these cards. I've picked up over forty dollars already. I'm making out like a bandit on those Christmas cards I sent. Look at your other mail and wash the tears off your face, and I'll be ready in a few minutes."

"Tears on my face—that'll be the day," Gene said. He opened up one of his cards and found a check for ten dollars inside and a nice note from Sister Michaels, an elderly woman in his ward at home. He ran his eyes over the words in the little note, but he had no idea what they said. He was still looking into himself, wondering when the pain was going to hit. What he actually felt was a sort of numbness, a disappointment that was hovering over him but hadn't quite settled into his chest, where he was expecting it any minute.

He was opening the second card when he heard a knock. Elder Bentz stepped over and opened the door. In the hallway, all bundled up in their winter coats, hats, and mufflers, were Elder Baker and Elder Davidson. "Hey, when are you going over to the Schmidts'?" Elder Davidson asked. Elder Baker was the senior companion, but he was a quiet guy; Elder Davidson usually did most of the talking. Elder Davidson had only been on his mission something like nine months, but he had studied a lot of German in high school, somewhere on the East Coast, and at BYU. His German was better than most, and he had a lot of confidence.

"We're going over right away. I'm just trying to count all the money I've been raking in today. Come on in."

The elders stepped in and began to loosen their coats. Elder Bentz sat down at the table again, and the two elders stood near the door—the only place there was to stand. "Elder Davidson's picked up almost eighty dollars so far," Elder Baker said. "I'm not getting nothing. Everyone must figure I'm almost finished and I don't need money now."

"I'll bet you didn't *send* cards," Elder Bentz said. "That's the key. People feel obligated to send cards to people they get cards from, right? And when it's a missionary, they decide they'd better drop a few bucks in the envelope."

"See—that's what I told you," Elder Davidson said. "I sent out a *bunch* of cards—as an investment. Baker wouldn't commit any capital, and as a result, he's getting no return."

"You guys really have the spirit of Christmas in you," Elder Baker mumbled, but he laughed.

"Hey, we're putting the money toward a great cause—our survival," Elder Davidson said. He was a tall, loose-jointed guy with a clown-like grin and wiry hair that seemed to do whatever it pleased. Gene had never known him to have a bad day. He was always happy.

He did have a point about survival in the mission, too. Getting by on eighty dollars a month was tough, and when members sent a little extra, it really helped. But it wasn't anything Gene could get himself to think about right now. He felt as though he couldn't quite connect to what was going on around him.

"Elder Thomas, have you picked up much?" Elder Davidson asked.

"A few dollars."

"Don't ask him right now," Elder Bentz said. "He's trying not to cry. He just got 'Dear Johned.' You're looking at a man in pain."

Gene smiled and shrugged. "I'm still up and running," he said. "It's going to take more than that to knock me down."

"You got the letter, just now?" Elder Davidson asked.

Gene nodded.

"You've got to be kidding. You got it after, what, four months?"

"No, five months—a little more than that."

Davidson was grinning. "Let me read it."

"No."

"Come on. I want to see what she says. I couldn't even get a girl to *go* with me back home. I'll never know the joy of a 'Dear John.'" He stepped to the table and held out his hand. "Come on, Elder, let me read it."

"No way."

"What a boob you are. I can see it in your eyes. You're about to start bawling."

"Not me."

"Prove it. Be a man. Let me read the letter out loud to these guys." He reached down and picked it up, and Gene didn't stop him. But he didn't want this.

Davidson didn't read it all. He scanned through it, laughing at some of the lines he liked, and then reading them out loud. "'So I'm not going to write anymore, at least not on a regular basis. I hope you understand.' Oh, sure." He mumbled as he continued to read to himself. "Oh, listen to this. 'I think I should tell you that I've been dating a boy named Merrill Dwyer quite regularly this fall.' Can you believe it? Ol' Elder Thomas, the congressman's kid, got shot down by some *goofball* named Merrill Dwyer. The guy's gotta be a loser."

Gene was surprised to find that he sort of liked this. The letter *was* pretty stupid. That became especially obvious when Elder Davidson read some of the other passages. "One thing about dating Merrill, whether I ever get serious with him or not, is that I have already seen that we're much more suited for each other," and, "But honestly, Gene, I think it's the best thing for both of us." Worst were the final lines: "I'll always hold you in a very special place in my heart. Please don't hate me. Give me a tiny space in your heart too." That got everyone laughing.

"Thomas, why did you ever go with this girl?" Elder Davidson asked. You're the king of the hill at the U. You could choose the homecoming queen, or anyone else you want. This is the luckiest day of your life to get rid of this chick."

Gene laughed, and he believed it, or wanted to. But more than anything, the laughing felt better than the despair he had thought he was going to experience. He could handle this. He would just write her off.

Elder Bentz had joined in by then. "Elder, that's a weak letter. I thought you said that girl had some brains."

"She does," Gene said. "She just—"

"Naw. Don't give us that," Elder Davidson said. "This is trash. You need to burn this letter and get over her, fast. You got any matches?"

"Hey, give me the letter."

"No. I can't do that. We've got to burn it and end this thing right here, right now."

Elder Bentz was laughing. "We can't burn it in the room," he said.

"Sure we can. Open that window. Give me that big bowl you use for mush in the morning. We can burn it in that, right there on the windowsill."

"I'm not burning it," Gene said. "Give it back to me." But he was laughing too.

"Oh, oh. You see the problem, don't you? He wants to read it over and over and bawl every time. He isn't over this girl."

"Just give me the letter."

"Are you a man or a crybaby? If you're a man, you'll let me burn it."

Suddenly it did seem like a good idea—the best thing in the world. This whole thing would be behind him, and he wouldn't be spending his days worrying. It really had been a stupid letter. Marsha had always treated him like he was some second-class suitor, just a guy she would keep around until she could find someone she liked better. It had turned out to be Merrill Dwyer, whoever that was. He was probably some philosophy major, with a minor in home economics. Marsha could have him. And good ol' Merrill could have her.

"Burn it," Gene said.

"Are you serious?"

"Never been more serious. Burn it to the ground."

"Okay, but we have to do a fire dance first. We have to drive out the evil spirits. Give me a match."

"We've got some down in the john. Just a minute." Elder Bentz got up and stepped out the door. He was back in a few seconds with a box of matches.

Elder Davidson said, "Okay, here's how the dance goes. It's something I learned in my many travels over the face of this earth."

But what he actually began was the Twist. Everyone laughed. Elder Bentz began to do a subdued version of the dance, as though he were not sure a missionary should be doing such a thing.

Elder Baker mumbled, "I can't do that." He was a quiet sort, probably more afraid of doing the dance wrong than breaking some rule. He always looked as though he were just recovering from a flu bug—pale and under-fed.

"Sure you can," Elder Davidson said. He began singing, to the tune of "Twist Again," "Hey, let's burn, like we did last summer. Let's burn again, like we did last fall. Let's light the fire a little bit higher. Let's give this girl to ol' Merrill Dwyer."

That got an enormous laugh, and by then Gene had joined in. He began twisting with more zest than he usually had at home. Baker wasn't twisting, but he was grinning at all this. Elder Bentz was getting into the spirit of the thing too. He got his bowl from off his trunk, in the corner, and handed it to Elder Davidson. Then as Davidson set the bowl on the windowsill, Elder Bentz brought a match. "Out, evil spirits," Davidson crowed, and the dancing stopped. He struck the match on the wooden sill, then held the letter over the bowl and lit one corner of the pages. As the paper began to burn, he separated the pages, letting them burn stronger, and then dropped them, one at a time, into the bowl. A pretty good flame began to grow, and a good deal of the smoke climbed to the ceiling and spread around the room. As soon as most of the flame had died down, Elder Bentz grabbed the bowl and walked it quickly to the sink at the opposite end of the room. He turned on the faucet and washed the smoldering ashes down the drain. There was a sizzle and more smoke, and then it was all over.

"You're a free man, Elder Thomas," Elder Davidson said. "Congratulations."

Gene laughed, but he didn't say anything. He sensed that they had gone too far. Elder Bentz had always been willing to laugh, to have a little fun, but this felt just a little over the line. They had laughed a little too hard, been a little too wild, there for a moment. And yet Gene did feel a kind of release. He would get back in a "missionary mood," get going hard in the work right after the holidays, but maybe the letter had come at a pretty good time, when he could shake the whole thing off and move ahead.

"Okay, Elders," Elder Bentz finally said. "We need to air this room out a little more and then get going."

But Gene understood what he was really saying: Let's ease up a little. We are missionaries, not a bunch of high-school boys.

Even Elder Davidson seemed to sense that it was time to end the thing. But he said to Gene, as he tried to wave some of the smoke away with an old *Der Stem* Church magazine, "You feel better now, don't you?"

"Actually, I do," Gene said. "It was just what I needed. She's gone now."

The elders had a nice evening with the Schmidts. They were a wonderful couple who had actually grown up in the Church—both of them—and met at a youth conference. There were not all that many second- or third-generation Mormons in Germany, but Gene could feel the difference in those who had that depth of background. Gene had fun with the Schmidts' kids—two little girls and a toddler boy—but he tried to keep them quiet at the same time. The spirit in the home was really nice. Eventually, after dinner, and after singing carols together, the Schmidts gave gifts to the elders: cans of food in a net—the kind Germans used when they went shopping. Gene rode home on his bike with the net in one hand, and for the first time it really hit him that it was now midday in Utah, Christmas Eve. He remembered running to the store for last-minute things that day, thought of Christmas Eve with his family, when the kids would act out the Christmas story while Dad read it from Luke.

He also thought of last Christmas when he had just broken up with Marsha, thought it was over then, too, and how much he had missed her. And then his mind skipped ahead to the summer, when the two had become so close. He thought of her birthday, when he had given her a pretty, powder-blue blouse. He remembered how she had looked in it, with her dark hair. He thought, too, of a ride they had taken together to their favorite spot in Emigration Canyon. They had gotten out of the car on a pretty summer night, with a bright moon shining. She had said how cold she was, and he had taken her in his arms. He had simply stood there, holding her, but he had realized how much he wanted to be near her forever. They had talked about his mission that night, about what it would be like to be gone so long and how exciting it would be to serve in Germany. What came back to him was that he had suspected even then, that night, that she wouldn't wait for him. And that had hurt him more than anything. But those final days before he had left, she had seemed to change. What had happened since then? Was it meeting this Dwyer guy? Was that the whole story? Or was it all about not being "suited" for each other? He had thought she had changed her mind about that.

But Gene didn't want to start running any more memories through his mind. It was not a smart thing to do. He would get a good night's sleep, get up in the morning for Christmas, have a nice day, spend it with the members, with the elders, laugh and sing, and eat well. All that would be fine. But he couldn't help thinking about Christmas morning at home, and Christmas dinner with all the family at Grandma and Grandpa Thomas's house.

By the time he settled down under his big feather tick, he was feeling way too much—feeling everything he didn't want to feel. He told himself not to, but he kept letting that summer night return to his mind, the touch of her against him. And he thought how different his mission had been from what he had expected, predicted, that night. He and Elder Bentz had worked hard, but they hadn't baptized anyone. And Gene had spent far too much of his time doubting himself, not enjoying his mission as much as he had assumed he would. All that had been piling up on him already, and now this. Marsha had chosen someone else over him, and she had done it quickly. It was humiliating.

He lay on his back, telling himself to let it all go, to sleep. He would find someone right for him someday. He just had to trust in that. But he kept seeing Marsha in that blue blouse and remembering how he had felt when he was with her, how pleased he had been when she had found "substance" in him finally. Suddenly, he wished he had the letter. He wished he hadn't let Elder Davidson burn it. He wanted to read it again, to remember exactly what she had said. Had she shut the door entirely? She hadn't said she was going to marry this guy. She even said she expected to be single when Gene got home. Was she just cooling off the direct tie—but still thinking that she could date him again when he got home? Or even if she wasn't expecting that, couldn't it happen? Maybe he would come home a better person than before, someone she could respect.

Gene had said a prayer with Elder Bentz, and by himself, but now, lying in bed, he began to pray again. He asked the Lord not to let all this end quite yet—to allow him some hope. But it was when he asked the Lord to help him become a stronger man, a better missionary, that he first felt a devastation that he couldn't bear.

Gene began to cry, the tears running down the sides of his face. And then he felt as though he were going to break. He rolled over in the bed, plunged his head into his pillow, and tried to stifle the sounds, but sobs were breaking from his chest. He was sure that Elder Bentz could hear him, but it didn't matter. He let himself cry.

When he finally turned back over, the crying finally under control but his breath coming hard, he heard from the dark, "Don't worry about it, Elder. I did the same thing when I got mine."

CHAPTER 31

Kathy was a little late arriving at Grandma and Grandpa Thomas's house on Christmas day. She had gotten a new book for Christmas—*Siddhartha*—that she had been dying to read, and she hadn't started getting ready when she should have. By the time her dad had prodded her a couple of times, she finally just said, "Go ahead. I'll drive the old car down in a few minutes."

"We don't need to take two cars. That's just wasteful."

"Dad, it's what? A mile? A mile and a half? It isn't that big of a deal."

He hadn't answered, but before long she had heard the big car—the Chrysler Imperial—pulling out of the driveway. And she had slowed down. She liked being at Grandma's house in some ways, but the noise and all the kids running around was sometimes more than she could easily tolerate. What she wished was that Gene were still around.

But when she finally parked up the street from her grandparents' house—behind all the cars—and then walked up the steps and on into the entry, she liked the rush of memories that came back to her. This was Christmas, here with all the relatives, the smell of turkey in the house and baking rolls, and even—in spite of what she had been telling herself—the noise. Uncle Alex grabbed her and hugged her. She was glad to see him again, home from Washington, where he and his family had recently moved so they could be settled in a little before he took office in January. They were keeping their house in Salt Lake, however, and had promised to be home as often as possible. "How's my *radical* little niece?" Alex asked her.

"Ready to take you on in the next election."

"Don't do it. You might win."

He gave her a fake poke to the chin, like a boxer, and said, "I could still beat you in a fist fight. So never mind that you're smarter than I am."

Kathy laughed, but she liked that, even though she knew that it wasn't true. Uncle Alex was a very bright guy. But it was nice of him to suggest that he thought she was smart. "So how is it back there? Have you met a lot of important people already?"

"How about President Johnson? Would you call him important?"

"Really? You met him already?"

"Just briefly. But he shook my hand and chatted with me for a minute or two. I think he was a lot more impressed with Anna than he was with me, though. He kept saying, 'My, my, Alex, you certainly found yourself a perty woman to marry. How'd you ever get so lucky?'"

"Yeah, I've wondered that for a long time myself."

Alex smiled and nodded, as if to say, "Me too." "We're going to miss Salt Lake," he said. "We found a house in Falls Church, and it's pretty nice, but our kids feel like they've moved to a foreign country. At school, they're the only members of the Church."

"I think I'll be in the East next fall, Uncle Alex. I'll come to see you."

"Do you know where you're going to be?"

"No. But Smith is my first choice. That's not very close, but I'll come down, and you can introduce me to Lyndon. I've got a few suggestions for him."

"I'll bet you do."

Anna came over then, and Kathy chatted with her. Then she worked her way through the living room and dining area, trying to talk to everyone for a minute. Aunt Beverly and Uncle Roger were there, on time for once, and their kids—Vickie, Julia, Alexander, and Suzanne—had joined up with Kenny and Pam, Uncle Alex's two younger kids. They were dashing about, yelling, and drawing lots of warnings from everyone—which they completely ignored. "How do you keep up with them?" Kathy asked Beverly.

Aunt Beverly looked rather bewildered when she said, "Oh, I don't. I just move in after the damage is done and try to make repairs where I can."

Kathy had the feeling that was probably true. But Aunt Beverly was an even tempered woman, always seeming satisfied with life. When Bobbi and LaRue wanted to talk about issues, Beverly listened, waited, but didn't comment, and then she would tell a little story about one of her kids, or tell them about a new movie she liked. And to her own surprise, Kathy liked that—liked that Beverly didn't seem to feel any need to sound as smart as her sisters.

Uncle Richard was in the dining room, helping to set out the silverware on the big table. But as always, he stopped and gave Kathy his attention. Kathy loved his quiet manner, and she thought he was about as handsome as any man she knew. "Are you really going to go away to college next year?" he asked her. "Diane says you're applying in the East."

"If I can get into a good place, that's what I plan to do."

"You could apply to Weber. I might be able to pull a few strings and get you admitted."

"Ogden's too dangerous. I don't dare go up there."

Richard just smiled.

Kathy walked on into the kitchen where she finally found the ones she was especially looking for: Aunt Bobbi and Aunt LaRue. Grandma was busy getting dinner ready, and Diane was helping. Bobbi and LaRue were probably supposed to be helping too, but they were standing in the middle of the kitchen, both wearing aprons, and busily talking. When LaRue saw Kathy, however, she spun and grabbed her. "Oh, Kathy, it's so good to see you," she said. "I've worried about you all fall."

"Why?"

"I don't know. I got you in such a mess, got your head cracked and everything else. Did you still go ahead and apply to Smith?"

Kathy had written to LaRue a couple of times that fall, reassuring her that the trip to Mississippi had been one of the most important experiences of her life and that she didn't regret it, no matter what had happened. But LaRue was a busy woman and not very good about answering letters. She had called a couple of times, right after Kathy had gotten home, but they hadn't talked since then. "Sure, I applied. I just finally got everything in."

"Honey, you did so well on your SATs, I'm sure you'll be admitted. I talked to one of the women in the admissions office, and she said a letter from a faculty member really does help a lot—so I lied like crazy in your letter and said you were as smart as me."

"That *is* a lie. I'm a lot smarter than that."

"Well," Bobbi said, "you two might be smarter than I am, but I have more experience."

"That just means she's *old*," LaRue told Kathy.

"Don't talk to me about age, little sister. You just crossed over the line. You're closer to forty than you are to thirty now."

"Yes. And someone I know is closer to fifty than to forty. You'll always be ten years older than me, old-timer, no matter how desperately you cling to your youth."

But Bobbi was remarkably young-looking for a woman in her midforties, and LaRue would always be stunning, no matter how old she got. Kathy loved these two aunts—loved their feistiness, their humor, their intelligence.

"You're both in the same category, if you ask me," Diane said. She was standing at the sink, where she had been mashing potatoes, but she had twisted around and was looking over her shoulder. "You're both *over the hill*. And Kathy is getting there pretty fast herself."

"I know. I feel that way. I turned eighteen this month."

That brought groans, of course, especially from Grandma. "You're all spring chickens," she said. "You don't know what it's like to get up in the morning and try to decide which ache you're going to complain about that day."

But the truth was, Grandma didn't complain very often about anything—except Grandpa, once in a while, and that was mostly in fun.

The family had its usual dinner and gift exchange. Grandpa had bought Grandma a color television, although everyone joked that he had really gotten it for himself. Uncle Wally had a new contraption himself: a Polaroid camera. He kept wandering about, taking pictures, and then showing off the prints as they became clear.

When things were settling into the low-key dessert time, with some of the little kids falling asleep and the older ones out playing in the snow, Diane said to Kathy, "Do you want to get out of this hot house for a while and take a little walk?"

"Sure," Kathy said. She had been talking to her cousins Joey and Sharon, who had been in the East only a couple of weeks before coming back for Christmas. They both seemed unhappy with the change in their lives, and Kathy was a little impatient with them. She thought it would be so interesting to live near Washington at their age, to meet congressmen and senators and see all the things there were to see in the city.

Outside, the cold was bracing. Diane had a snappy new ski parka, bright turquoise, and she looked spectacular with all her blonde hair streaming out from under her stocking cap. She even admitted that she had tried ironing her hair, the way girls were doing now, to get it perfectly straight. Kathy felt rather dowdy, by comparison, in her old green car coat. She had wrapped a scarf around her neck, but her ears were soon cold. She didn't want to be out very long.

The two walked down the hill under the big sycamores that lined the sidewalk. The sun was going down, but the last of an orange haze was still in the western sky. "So do you really think you'll get into Smith?" Diane asked.

"I don't know. But it can't hurt to have Aunt LaRue doing what she can for me."

"You probably wouldn't even need that; you're so smart."

"Not really. I work hard in school, but I'm not like those *gifted* people. One guy at our school got an almost perfect score on the SATs."

"I don't really want to go too far away to college," Diane said. "I think I might go down to BYU. I don't have to have high grades to get in there."

That kind of attitude was almost impossible for Kathy to understand, but she tried to be gentle by saying, "You might as well do your best. Your grades go with you all your life."

"You sound like my mom."

"Does she get upset with you about school?"

"Of course. I'm lazy, according to her. I could be as brilliant as she is if I would just try harder."

The two reached the first corner and, without consulting each other, turned toward the south and crossed the street. "She doesn't really say that, I'm sure."

"No. But that's what she means."

"Don't you get along very well with your mother, Diane?"

"It's not that so much. When I was younger, we really got into it sometimes. But lately, we just have this standoff. We know we're not the same, and we accept it. But Mom will always be disappointed with me. Deep down, she wishes I was more like her."

"I'd love to be like Bobbi. I'm proud of her for finishing her doctorate while she's still raising a family."

"I'm just glad it's finally finished."

"Yeah, I guess it was hard. But it's something I worry about. How can a woman be married and still do the things *she* wants to do? Maybe it's better to be like LaRue."

"All alone?" Diane asked. "Don't you want to get married?"

"I do. But I'm just saying that women get cheated. They have to give up everything to raise children. Men get to keep right on going with what they want to do."

"I don't agree with that at all, Kathy. I'll tell you the person in our family I admire more than anyone."

"Who?"

"Your mom. She always seems so peaceful. Your dad makes a good living, and she keeps the home running. To me, that's how it's supposed to be. And that's what I want. If I could be in my forties, and still as pretty as Aunt Lorraine, and have such a nice house and such a nice family, I can't think what else I would want. No one checks your high-school grades to see if you qualify to be a good mother."

Kathy wasn't surprised by any of this; she had heard Diane say similar things before. But it struck her more than ever how different she and Diane were. She walked for a time, hunched her shoulders, and tried to wrap her scarf higher to cover her ears. "The only thing is, Diane," she said, "maybe my mom is satisfied with things in her life. But I don't know if that's how a person ought to be. When I was in Mississippi this summer, I saw such terrible poverty that I was ashamed to come home to our big house and all our comfort. We could cut up our house and give about ten families better living conditions than they've ever had in their lives."

"Now you sound *exactly* like my mom. And I guess that's right. But I don't know how to solve all those problems. I just want a nice life."

Kathy wasn't going to push this. It would only cause hard feelings. But she had little patience for Diane's attitude. "You know what's stupid," Kathy said. "If my mom had you for a daughter, she would be so much happier. You're just what she wants."

"And I drive my own mother crazy," Diane said. "She wants me to be more like you." Both girls laughed. "Do you think our mothers could make a trade? We might all four be happier."

"Maybe so. But Diane, you really ought to respect your mother for the way she keeps herself so alive and interested in everything. Too many women get married and then don't care about the rest of the world."

"I know what you're saying. I wish I could be more like my mom, but that's just not me. The other night I sat down with my parents and started watching the news. I've been trying to do that lately. So my dad says, 'What's gotten into you lately, Diane? I didn't think you liked the news.' Before I could even say anything, Mom says, 'She just likes to look at Dick Nourse, this new newscaster. She thinks he's cute.'"

"Oh, wow. That was a cheap shot. Weren't you furious?"

Diane laughed. "Kind of," she said. "Except we both knew she was right. That is mostly why I've been watching."

Both girls laughed, and Kathy said, "Oh, I know. I switched channels just because of him."

The girls had walked a couple of blocks south now, and Kathy pointed to the east when they reached the next corner. "Let's loop back around," she said. "I'm freezing."

Diane didn't say anything, but she followed Kathy's lead. "I guess we have to be ourselves," she said. "We can't be something we're not."

"Don't you ever wonder who you really are, though? You just said you're not smart, and I don't think that's true. But if you say it enough, maybe it becomes true. We get an image, and then we end up fitting it, whether it's really us or not."

"I don't know, Kathy. That's probably true, but it shows you're smart to think of it. I just don't think about things as much as you do."

"And I think way *too* much; I have no idea why."

As they walked up the hill, they came to a place where the sidewalk was icy. Diane had on a pair of after-ski boots, and she was able to get better traction. She took Kathy's hand and helped steady her until they got back to dry pavement, but they were careful until they made it to the next corner and turned toward the north again. "There's something I need to make a decision about, Kathy," Diane said.

Kathy had the feeling that whatever Diane was about to say was the reason she had wanted to go for this walk. "What's that?" Kathy asked.

"I need to decide whether I should break up with Scott."

"Why do you think you might want to?"

Diane didn't answer right away. It was as though she hadn't formulated that answer for herself and had to find words for her feelings. When she finally spoke, her voice sounded careful. "I have a feeling that he isn't being honest with me."

"Honest about what?"

Again, some time passed. The two were walking rather slowly, and the sun was gone now. In the twilight, Kathy could see the steam from her own breath blowing back into her face. She could hear the squeak of Diane's boots, the scrape of her own shoes, and somewhere in the neighborhood a sad dog was barking, as though it was unhappy to be left outside.

"I think Scott has been doing some drinking with his friends."

"He's not LDS, is he?"

"No. But he's taken the lessons, and he says he wants to join the Church. He always tells me that he doesn't drink, but people have been telling me that he does."

"Have you told him that—what you're hearing?"

"Yes. And he says that he's been to some parties where other guys are drinking, so kids assume he is too, but he's not."

"But you must have some feeling whether he's telling you the truth or not."

"I think he's lying, Kathy. And I think he's lying about some other things. He says he wants us to stay together and get married someday. But he keeps trying things with me—you know what I mean?—and it's like he's trying to wear me down—like if he tells me he loves me, I'll finally give him his way."

"You mean he's trying to have sex with you?"

Kathy could feel that she had embarrassed Diane with the bluntness of her question. But Diane said, "I guess so. At least he wants to do things I've told him I won't do."

"Does he keep trying, even after you've told him that?"

"He's only really pushed it a couple of times. But after the first time, he said it would never happen again. Then it did. He says he's sorry, that he just can't help himself—stuff like that—but I wonder when it will happen again."

Kathy knew what Diane needed to do, but she was sure Diane knew too. She wondered whether it would do any good to tell her. "Have you talked to your mom about this?"

"Sort of. But this one time, he started grabbing at me really hard. I just couldn't tell my mom about that. Would you tell your mother?"

Kathy laughed. "Well, first off, I don't inspire such passion in any of the boys I know—who mostly consider me their *buddy*. But if I were in a situation like that, no, I probably wouldn't talk to my mom." She laughed again. "But I think I could talk to yours."

"Would your mom get really upset with you?"

Kathy had to think that one over. "No," she finally said. "But I think she'd be shocked. She trusts everyone."

"So what would you do, if you were in my shoes?"

"Diane, there isn't even anything to think about. Get rid of the guy. He's just trying to manipulate you until he can get your skirt over your head. At best you're playing with fire, and at worst, he's out to burn you."

"I know."

"So?"

"What if he really does want to join the Church? If I break up with him, he never will."

"I think he would be joining for all the wrong reasons."

"But if we break up, I won't have anyone. I like to be with him and everything—except when he's like that. And it's not all his fault. I like to kiss him, too, and sometimes I've probably given him the wrong idea."

"Diane, this is a mess just waiting to turn into a bigger mess. Get out before it gets any worse."

"Yeah. That's what I've been thinking." The steam escaped from her mouth in a long stream. "I just have to get up the nerve to tell him."

"I'll tell you what he's going to do. I know people like this. First, he'll act like he's destroyed and try to get your pity, and then, when he knows you mean it, he'll get really ugly and tell you that he can't stand you."

"I don't think so. I think he really does care about me."

"Maybe I'm wrong. But he sounds like that kind of guy. And I should know. I'm very experienced. I've had three dates in my life, two of which were sort of group things where the guy, in each case, acted like he didn't know he was with me."

Both girls laughed, but then Diane said, "Remember that time—on Christmas day—when Gene wanted to know what our goals were?"

"Sure."

"I said I wanted to find a guy who looked sort of dangerous."

Kathy laughed. "Yeah. I remember that."

"That's sort of how Scott is. But I've changed my mind now. I just want to find a really good guy—someone I know I can trust."

"Maybe so, Diane. But maybe you've been in too much of a hurry."

"I know. I don't want to go steady with anyone again—not for a long time."

"So you're going to dump Scott?"

"I think so." She walked for a time, and then she added, "No. I'm going to do it."

"Good," Kathy said, but she wondered. She hoped Diane really had the nerve to make the break.

"Just before Gram died, I sat with her one night," Diane said. "She told me never to let a guy run my life. I kind of think that's what Scott is trying to do. He's just tricky about how he does it."

"You've *got* to break up with him, Diane."

"Yeah. I know."

That evening Diane and her family drove back to Ogden. Maggie fell asleep before they had gotten out of town, and Ricky was sleeping too. Bobbi was holding him and talking softly to Richard, but Diane was paying little attention to what they were saying. She was thinking about her own "mess," as Kathy had called it. She knew what she had to do, but every time she thought of actually carrying out her decision, she feared the moment. She wished she could take Kathy with her to help her think straight when Scott tried to change her mind. Or maybe her mom.

She spoke before she was even sure she had made up her mind to do so. "Mom and Dad, I want to talk to you about something."

"What's that?" Dad asked.

"I think I want to break up with Scott. Do you think that's what I should do?"

"Why do you want to?" Richard asked.

"Lots of reasons, I guess," Diane said. But then, after a few seconds, she added, "I think he's been telling me lies."

"Well then, you have your answer."

"Diane," Bobbi said, "we've hoped you would break up with Scott for a long time. I didn't trust that boy, even when he was taking the lessons. I just didn't believe he was sincere about the Church, and I didn't like the excuses he came up with for not being baptized."

"Why didn't you tell me that?"

"We can't run your life, honey. We want you to do the right thing, but you can't do it just because we say so."

"But maybe you should have at least told me what you thought."

"Maybe. But Diane, Grandpa always tried to tell me what to do, and

I resented it. Sometimes I even did things just to show I could be independent. I vowed when I was growing up that I wouldn't be like that. I would let my kids think for themselves."

"But Mom, I needed some advice."

"You think so now, but I doubt you would have listened."

There was only the steady humming of the tires after that. Diane had her answer, of course. Her parents had figured Scott out long before she had. But she was angry now. They shouldn't have left her on her own like that.

⌇

Kathy couldn't stop thinking about the things she and Diane had said. When she got home that night, she went back to her book, but her mind wasn't on it now, and after a time she put it down and walked to the kitchen. She found her mother there, sitting at the table, drinking a cup of hot chocolate. "Oh, wow, that smells so good," Kathy said.

"There's still some warm milk in the pan. Just put some chocolate in it."

So Kathy made herself a cup, and then she sat down at the table with her mom, something she normally didn't do. Kathy saw her mother's little look of surprise. "Reading tonight?" Mom asked.

"Yeah. But I sort of lost interest."

"Really? I didn't think you ever did that."

Kathy wondered what that meant. Was it just a little censure—a reminder of Kathy's image? "I'm tired," Kathy said. She held her cup close and blew on the hot chocolate. "Mom, Diane and I went for a walk today. She told me something interesting. She said she'd rather be like you than anyone else in our family. She loves how peaceful you are."

"That was nice of her," Lorraine said, but then she smiled. "Did you set her straight?"

"Why would you say that? You know that's how you are."

"Sometimes. Sometimes not. But didn't you say, 'Diane, that's the very thing that drives me nuts about my mother?'"

Kathy was "found out," and she knew it. She felt the heat in her face. "Something like that," she finally admitted. "But I also told her that I wished I could be more like you."

"Kathy, now come on. It's not nice to lie to your dear old mother."

"I'm not." Kathy watched her mother. She could see in her eyes that she wasn't upset but clearly disappointed by the tension that had existed between them for so long. "I spend too much of my life all riled up about things."

Lorraine sipped at her hot chocolate, then set her cup down. "Kathy, I'm kind of a quiet person. And I don't fly off the handle about most things. So I guess people see that, and they think I'm more satisfied than I am. I have my struggles, the same as anyone. And sometimes I feel anything but 'peaceful.'"

"I know. But it's still the feeling you give people. It's what everyone loves about you."

"Kathy, I don't think it does a lot of good to think of each other in such simplified ways. I don't know anyone in this world more lovely than you when you're dealing with Douglas. He loves you more than all the rest of us put together, and that boy has perfect instincts about people. Still, how many people know that side of you?"

"But Mom," Kathy said, "it's the way I feel about him that makes me get so mad at people who don't take good care of him. Down in Mississippi I fell in love with those Negro kids who just wanted a little fairness in their lives. That's why I got so furious with that policeman who was beating up on one of our boys."

"I know. I understand all that." Again, she took a sip of her chocolate. "But honey, that policeman is probably nice to his kids. There's probably a side to him that is totally different from anything you've seen."

"That's hard for me to accept, Mom. He can't claim to be a Christian and then beat up on Negroes—out of pure hatred."

"People get sick ideas into their heads. But it doesn't mean they're worthless. God loves them, too. They're also his children."

"I don't know how to think that way, Mom. I watched people with the veins standing out in their necks, screaming 'Nigger lover!' at me, like I was doing something hideous, just to help teach some kids. There's something wrong with people like that. I can't forgive them as easily as you do."

Lorraine was holding her cup in both hands, as though she were taking pleasure from the warmth. There was something so amazing about her in that regard, how many things she found joy in. "When I was in Seattle during the war," she said, "I got to know a young Negro man who worked on my crew. He was home from the war after he had been wounded really badly, shot in the stomach, over in Europe. He thought he had proved something by fighting for his country, and he really expected things to be different when he came home. But he told me, 'People are still afraid I might move in next door to them, or come calling on their daughters. Nothing has changed in this country.' It broke my heart, but I've never known what to do about it. It's just not in me to go out and try to change things. The only thing I've tried to do is change my own heart. If everyone did that, we wouldn't have to worry."

"But most people aren't willing to see that they've been wrong. Sometimes you have to challenge them, force them to think in ways they never will on their own."

"Sometimes *you* do. I don't think I could." She waited for a moment and then added, "Is it okay if we aren't the same about this?"

"Sure, Mom. But can you understand how much it matters to me to try to do something—to not sit by and let things continue the way they are?"

"Of course I can. I just fear for you. I don't want you to get hurt—physically *or* emotionally. Those fights take so much out of a person."

"I know. I wonder about that too."

"I also worry that you'll resent me all my life because I don't get involved in the fight myself."

"Mom, I don't feel that way. Sometimes I wish you and Dad would fight harder for Douglas, or wouldn't get so down on me for what I try to do, but I did tell Diane tonight that I wish I was more like you. And I meant it. I like you a lot better than I like me. I'm not a nice person when I get angry."

Lorraine laughed. "I'm proud of you, Kathy. You understand so much; you care about things; you stand up for things that are right. But honey, you scare me to death. I'm so afraid you're going to end up dissatisfied with life. At some point, I want you to have what I have: a family. I'm just afraid you'll never be satisfied with that."

Kathy knew what she meant. She wasn't sure either. But it was the other worry that plagued her more. "Mom, I'm afraid no one will ever love me enough to *want* me for a wife."

"Someone will know you well someday—will know your whole heart—and then he'll love you."

"I don't let anyone get that close."

"You will."

Kathy had begun to cry. She wasn't sure she believed her mother's words, but she liked hearing them so much. "Mom, I love you," she said. "I'm sorry I cause you so many worries."

"Honey, I don't think you can even imagine how much I love you. You were my first baby. You came to me from God, for Christmas. It's just so hard to watch you become a woman and not seem really happy."

Kathy couldn't think what to say. She wondered herself. Would she ever be satisfied with her own life? But this was not the time to say that.

She reached across the table and took hold of her mother's hand, and they sat for a long time that way.

※

Diane went straight to her bedroom when she got home. She got ready for bed, but she still felt empty. She would talk to Scott as soon as she got up the nerve—maybe tomorrow—but she knew she would miss him, no matter how sure she was about her decision. She got into bed, but she just sat there, without turning out her light. She tried to think what she would say to him.

After a time, there was a little tap on her door. "Diane, are you awake?"

"Yes. Come in."

Bobbi opened the door and stepped inside. She shut the door behind her and leaned against it. "I saw that your light was still on."

"Did Ricky settle down?"

"Yes. But he fell asleep too early. He'll be up with the chickens in the morning."

"You're tired, aren't you, Mom."

"Yes, I am. And I'm sorry."

"What about?"

"Di, you were right. I should have talked to you. I should have told you what I thought of Scott. I was afraid of interfering, but you needed me, and I wasn't there."

Diane watched her mother, saw the tears begin to drip onto her cheeks. "Oh, Mom, don't worry about it. You're probably right; I wouldn't have listened."

Bobbi walked over and sat down on the bed. She rested her hand on the blanket, touching Diane's knee. "Honey, your instincts are so right— better than mine most of the time. I just couldn't imagine you doing anything but what was right, if we gave you some time."

"I'm not as good as you think I am, Mom." The words cost Diane. She began to cry.

"Oh yes you are. I may not be the mother I ought to be, but there are some things I know. You've always understood goodness."

"Then why does danger look so good to me?"

"I don't know. We all want to toy with it. It seems so exciting."

They looked at each other, and Diane thought she could see in her mother's face the young girl she had once been—someone who had had to deal with all the same stuff Diane was worrying about now. "Maybe we're not so different as we seem," she said.

Bobbi scooted up and took Diane in her arms. "Maybe we're not," she said.

CHAPTER 32

H ans used his key to open the apartment when he got home from school on a cold February day in 1965. His mother and Inga were not home, as they usually were by now. For a time, after he had first learned that he would not be admitted to a university, he had gone about his studies with little enthusiasm. But he couldn't do that for long. He had gotten used to doing his best in school, and he liked the way he felt when he was proving himself. His reaction was to go to the other extreme, to work harder than anyone else, to do all he could to graduate as the best in his class. Maybe that would make the government look foolish. Hans still wasn't going to church, but his motivation was different from when he had made his first break with his family on that issue. He had merely put the Church behind him now. He didn't believe in God or the things he had been taught in church, but he no longer felt defiant. He had resolved to go his own way but not to cause tension in the family if he could help it. Lately, he had felt a new strength sustaining him, and what he liked most about that was that it seemed to be coming from inside. He wasn't just reacting to everyone else, as he had done when he was younger.

Hans went to the kitchen, found himself the heel of a loaf of bread, spread a little margarine on it, and sat down at the table. He decided to work on his calculus first—the subject he liked best and found easiest. He would read his European history text later. He hated the Marxist interpretation in all the history books. He didn't believe half of what he read.

He had been working on his calculus for most of an hour and was almost finished when he heard a key in the lock. In a moment he heard his mother's voice, but also his father's. This was a little early for Papa, and Hans wondered what was going on. But he waited until his parents came to the kitchen. Hans had fallen into the habit of avoiding his family, especially his father, as much as he could. Conversations usually started out innocently enough, but it wasn't long until Peter would bring up the Church, in one way or another, and several times he had asked Hans please to come back, to give the Church one more try. Hans hated that kind of pressure, even though he found it easy enough to resist.

Now Hans could hear Inga's voice, heard her say, "They can't make me do it, Papa. Can they?"

"No. They can't."

Katrina opened the door to the kitchen. "Oh, here you are," she said.

"Where have you been?" Hans asked.

"Inga had some troubles at school. We were called in by *Direktor* Schreiter."

Inga had come in now, and Peter. Hans could see that Inga had been crying. She didn't look as tidy as usual, either. One of her braids was coming loose, and there was a smudge across her cheek where she had wiped her tears away. "What kind of trouble?" he asked.

"The other children called me names at school. They said I was crazy. Jürgen Perle told me I should be sent to an insane asylum." But she wasn't crying now. She sounded angry.

"Why? What's this all about?"

Katrina sat down at the table, across from Hans. "Yesterday they were singing the "Internationale" in school. The teacher noticed that Inga wasn't singing the third verse."

"I *never* sing it," Inga said.

"The teacher must not have noticed before. She asked Inga why she wasn't singing—thought she hadn't sung any of it, I guess. But Inga said—"

"Let Inga tell him," Peter said. He stepped up next to Inga at the end of the table, and he put his hand on her shoulder. "Tell your brother what you told your teacher."

"I said, 'I won't sing those words.' So the teacher said, 'Why?' And I said, 'Because I believe in the Savior. My brother wouldn't sing the words and I won't either.'"

Hans glanced up at his father. He didn't like this. He knew why Papa had wanted Inga to tell the story. It was to shame him. That annoyed Hans, and yet, he did feel some shame. He hated to think of Inga taking abuse from the other kids, hated to think it had happened because she thought she had to live up to something he had once done. The worst thing was, he now regretted the stand he had taken. It had been the cause of so many of his problems.

"That all happened yesterday," Katrina said. "But today the children started in on her. When they were outside for their sports activity, some of them told her that only mental cases believed in God. Inga told them to leave her alone, so one of the boys—this Jürgen Perle—pushed her and knocked her down. But the teacher sent *Inga* to the director's office, not the boy."

"Tell Hans what you told *Direktor* Shreiter," Peter said.

"I told him I wasn't crazy. And no one should call me that. I can believe in Jesus if I want to."

"Yes. But tell him what you said about the Church."

"I told him that my family went to church every Sunday. And we love Jesus. Then I said that I would *never* sing those words about there being no God."

Hans wanted to shout at his father, to tell him that this was his fault. Inga was going to suffer just the way Hans had. *Direktor* Schreiter would report all this, and Papa's job could be in jeopardy again. Why couldn't his father see that? And why did he think that he could use Inga this way to embarrass Hans?

Hans noticed that Inga's big eyes had filled with tears. He pulled her to him. Then he wrapped his arm around her shoulders and said, "Don't be upset. It's all right now."

But Inga's response was not what Hans had expected. "I wish you would come to church with us, Hans," she said. "You told them before—about the song. Now you don't even come to church."

Hans let go of Inga. He leaned over and put his elbows on the table. He couldn't think what to say to her. She would never understand him. "Don't let the children bother you," was all he said. "Just pay no attention to them."

"*Direktor* Schreiter said he wouldn't allow anyone to hurt Inga," Katrina said, "but he thinks it would be best if Inga sang the whole song, no matter what she believes. We told him she wouldn't do that, that it was blasphemy against the Lord to sing such words."

Hans wasn't going to be drawn into the conversation, but he did say, "Schreiter can't stop the teasing. He probably doesn't even want to. It will go on and on now, every day." What Hans meant, of course, was that his parents shouldn't put Inga through this, that she might as well just sing the song.

But that's not what Inga seemed to hear. "It's all right. I won't cry again. I don't care what they say to me. I have friends at church. I don't need the children at school to like me."

That meant she would always be the strange Mormon child, the religious fanatic, just as he had been. Why couldn't his parents see what they were forcing her into?

"I wish you could have heard her." Katrina reached across the table and touched Hans's hand. "When she told the *Direktor* she loved Jesus, I could see his face soften. So many people still believe in God, but they're afraid to say they do. I feel sure he admired her for being so strong."

Hans looked at his little sister. She was so beautiful, so innocent. He remembered those days when he had felt just as sure and strong. He actually liked that self—the one he remembered—better than the one he lived with now, and in some ways he wished he could go back and be that boy again. He wished he could give his parents what they wanted and be the kind of big brother Inga longed for. But it wasn't in him now to pretend he was something he simply wasn't.

"Hans," Peter said, "I told Inga that I would give her a father's blessing—to give her strength to face the heckling she still might face. I would like you to be with us for that. Let's go into the living room."

Hans was caught, and once again, angry. His father was finding another way to include him in something he didn't believe in. But what could Hans say? He had to show his little sister that much support. So he merely nodded, and then he walked into the living room with the others. Peter brought one of the kitchen chairs with him, and he had Inga sit down on it. Hans and his mother sat down on the couch. "Katrina, would you say a prayer first—to invite the Spirit?" Peter asked.

Hans bowed his head with the others, but he paid little attention to the words. His mother asked that they all might be filled with the Spirit, and that Peter might be guided in what he said. Hans looked up as his mother closed her prayer, saw his father step closer to Inga and then wait for a moment, as though allowing time for the Spirit to touch him before he put his hands on Inga's head. There was something impressive in that, how seriously Papa took this ritual. It certainly was real to him, and that softened Hans a little. He sometimes thought he saw a certain falseness in religious expression, as though people were pretending to be moved more than they really were. But he had never seen that in his parents. They did believe.

Papa placed his hands on Inga's head, touched her pretty hair. Hans closed his eyes again.

"Inga Stoltz," Peter said, and then he invoked the name of Christ and the holy Melchizedek Priesthood. "You have been brave and strong, and you have stood up for the things we believe." Hans felt the "we," felt how long he had been missing that connection in his life, but he wasn't going to let his father manipulate him this way. He wasn't going to slip into an emotional state and forget all the things he had been wrestling with these past few months.

"Inga, you are a pure spirit. God has blessed you with great faith for one so young. What is right and good rings true to you. You cling to those truths, and you are not afraid to speak out for them."

Hans felt the truth of that. He knew that his father was right. There was something extraordinarily good about his little sister. She possessed more love than anyone else he knew. The words did touch Hans—and the beauty of his little sister's goodness.

"I bless you with added strength, Inga. I bless you with the confidence to withstand whatever insults you may have to face. And I promise you that if you will do that, the Lord will fill you with power—power that the other children will feel and understand. They will find no pleasure in hurting you. They will respect you for who you are."

Inga had begun to cry. And it was perhaps that that released something in Hans. He had to struggle not to shed tears himself. He hated the thought of what Inga might have to face, but the blessing seemed real to him, and he found himself thinking that Inga would be helped by it, that the children really would feel her power.

When the blessing ended, Inga stood up and then stepped around the chair to hug Papa. He held her for a time, patting her back softly, and then she stepped to Mama, who hugged her too. Hans could see how much this all meant to her, what comfort she was receiving from this tie to her family. When she stepped to Hans, he slipped off the couch, bent a little, and took her in his arms. "Thank you for being here, Hans," she said, and he felt tears fill his eyes. But now he wanted to get away. All this was hurting too much.

But Peter asked, "Hans, could I also bless you?"

Hans straightened and looked at his father. He was about to say no, when Inga said, "Oh, yes, Hans. It will help you so much."

"Please," his mother said. "You need this, Hans."

It was easier to say yes than no, with everyone wanting this, but Hans was frightened as he sat down in the chair. He was afraid they would expect too much of him now. They would all pressure him to go back to church. And yet, when he felt the press of his father's hands on his head, he remembered these blessings, felt his father's love. "Hans Heinrich Stoltz, my dear son," Peter said, and he began to cry.

Hans didn't want to give way to this. He fought the emotion. His father needed to do this, but Hans would not allow his emotions to control his reason.

"Hans," Peter said, once he could speak again, and once he had invoked Christ's power, "You are a good young man. You're honest, and you want to do what is right. I know that you are trying to find answers to your many questions. I bless you with the Lord's Spirit, to grant you the assurance that goes beyond questions to the knowledge that God is with you at all times, that he is real."

Hans took a breath as he felt some kind of calm come over him. He didn't think to trust it or to doubt it; he merely felt the relief.

"Hans, I bless you that you will feel the touch of your Heavenly Father in the touch of my—your earthly father's—hands."

A vibration moved through Hans, worked its way from his head into his chest, sent tingling sensations all through him. He felt for a moment as though he were rising, floating above the chair, as though his father were hoisting him with his touch. Hans didn't think; he merely knew, and he began to cry. He wasn't sure what else he heard after that, but he felt something familiar inside, as though he had returned to himself.

When the blessing was over, he was still sobbing, although trying not to. He didn't know exactly what the knowledge meant, but he knew he had taken a step back toward his family, and he knew they knew. He stood, and they all came to him, wrapped their arms around him. The four stood, Inga with her arms all the way around Hans, her head against his middle, and Mama and Papa, each on one side, reaching around Inga and around him.

Hans didn't say so, but he knew he was going to go to church that Sunday. He wasn't sure how he would feel in another day or two—or even in a few minutes—but he knew that he had to try again. He had to stay close to Inga, and he knew he wanted to see whether there was something in his father's hands that he had been discounting.

Everyone was wise enough, even Inga, to know better than to ask Hans what his tears meant. Hans didn't commit to anything either, afraid that he might change his mind. But on Sunday morning he got up early and got his best clothes on. His father had already left for an early branch presidency meeting, but when Hans walked out to the kitchen, his mother was fixing a quick breakfast, as she usually did on Sunday mornings, just some mush and toast. She saw him in his white shirt and tie, and she didn't say a word. She only came to him and put her arms around him. But when Inga came in, she was joyous. "I knew you would go with us today," she said. "I knew it."

"I want to be as brave as you," he said. It was more than he was sure he meant, but she needed this right now, and part of why he was going was for her.

But the best was arriving at the little meetinghouse. As he had ridden the streetcar to church, Hans had dreaded the moment, thinking that people might make too much fuss over his arrival. But when he stepped through the doors, he was surprised at how much like home the place felt. He had grown up here, with these people, and everyone seemed pleased to see him. They didn't remind him that he hadn't been there, but they shook his hand, hugged him, welcomed him in a way that he had never felt before. And when he walked into the chapel, he saw his father up front, sitting on the stand. He only nodded, nothing more, but Hans could see what this meant to him, saw him swallowing, saw how hard he was trying not to cry.

Hans still didn't know what he believed, not for certain, but he knew there was something right about this place, this family. And during the meeting, when the speaker was as boring as all the others he remembered, he spent his time thinking about what he wanted to do. What struck him was that he wanted to be as good as his sister—and if there was something to what his parents believed, maybe he would find out.

So on the following morning, before school started, he went to *Direktor* Knorr's office and asked for permission to speak to him. This was a step that he felt he had to take.

"Let me ask him," she said. She walked to the door, stepped in, and then shut it behind her. When she came out, she said, "You can go in. But don't take long."

Hans stepped inside. He was holding his heavy wool cap in his hands and was still dressed in his big winter coat. "*Direktor* Knorr, there was merely something I wanted to tell you."

"Yes?"

"I told you once that I was no longer attending my church. You said that you would continue your effort to see whether I could enter a university when I finish *Oberschule*."

"Yes. I remember."

"I just wanted to tell you, there's no use pursuing that now. I've begun to go to church again with my family."

"Sit down, Stoltz."

Hans was surprised by this response. He had expected to be dismissed immediately once he had made his little statement. But he sat down and unbuttoned his coat.

"Why is this? Why have you returned to your church?"

Hans wasn't sure he knew that, entirely. And he didn't want to make any false claims. "My family goes. It makes everyone happier if we all go together."

"And that's the only reason? You told me before that you had given up your beliefs."

"I know."

"So what is it? Do you believe in religion or don't you?" *Direktor* Knorr was holding a pencil in his hand. He had obviously been writing something before Hans had come in, but now he began to tap the pencil against the thumb of his other hand, a nervous little gesture that made him seem impatient, maybe even out of sorts with Hans.

Hans wanted to be succinct—and quick—but he didn't know the answer. "I don't know," he finally said. "I believed in God when I was young. And then I began to doubt all those things. Now, I'm not sure. But I want to attend the meetings with my family and discover what I feel."

"You realize what this could mean about your future, don't you?"

"Yes. But it probably doesn't matter. You told me last time I talked with you that there was little chance for me anyway."

"But you're willing to turn this small chance into no chance?"

"Yes. I think so."

"Why?"

It was strange for Hans to realize that he hadn't thought these matters through very carefully. "I think there might be a God," he finally said. "My father and mother believe very strongly, and so does my little sister."

"Stoltz, I'm sorry, but that doesn't make a lot of sense. You knew all this when you talked to me last time."

"I know." But then Hans took the chance of revealing too much, looking like a fool. "My father holds the priesthood in our church. He's in the leadership of our church here in Schwerin. This week he gave me a blessing. It seemed real to me. I don't know how to explain it other than that. It seemed that God was part of what we were doing. I know that sounds like a lot of silliness to you, but I don't feel I can put that all aside. I want to find out what it means."

"You don't know what I believe, Hans. You don't know what is silliness to me and what isn't. I don't discuss those matters with anyone."

Hans didn't know what that meant, and he didn't dare ask. What Hans did see in the man's eyes was a new familiarity. The director had called him Hans, something he had never done before.

"Let me ask you a different question."

Hans nodded.

"Would you be interested in becoming an engineer?"

"I don't know. I've never thought about it."

"It's not so different from what you told me you wanted. You said you wished to be an architect."

"Yes. It's one of the things I've thought about."

"An engineer works with architects. Some engineers—depending on the type of engineering you get involved in—do almost the same work."

Hans didn't understand what was happening. What was the man trying to say to him? "Yes. It might be something I would like."

"You're good at math. You like science. I think you would do very well as an engineer."

"Yes. I suppose."

"I spoke with one of our city officials last week. He told me that more engineers are needed, and he wanted a list of our best math students. I put your name on it. I put it at the very top."

"But what about my religion?"

"Would you give it up, make the same commitment you did before, if I try to keep your name on that list? They'll surely ask about your religion, once the list is reviewed."

Hans had felt a surge of excitement, and now he thought he saw what the director was up to. The disappointment struck him, and suddenly he wondered—maybe he should agree to this. He hadn't promised his family anything. He had only gone to church that once. Still, he knew, even as the thought came to him, that he couldn't do that. "No," he said. "You can take my name off the list. I'm going to keep going to church, at least for now."

"But this chance won't come again."

"I know."

Direktor Knorr smiled, looking pleased, and now Hans was confused. The man seemed to be playing some sort of game with him. "I'm going to leave your name on top of the list, Hans. And I think they might be willing to overlook the religious matter if I reassure them that you'll be an excellent engineer and a trustworthy employee. These government men are practical people. They discourage religion, but they're sometimes willing to forget all that when their needs demand it."

"But what about the other matter—my attempt to leave the country?"

"Thousands and thousands left this country. These men know that many more would have gone, if they could have. But they still need engineers."

"I would like that so much, *Direktor* Knorr. All I want is a chance to do something interesting with my life. I wouldn't be a problem to anyone."

"I know that. But I can't promise anything, either. One other thing about our leaders is that they are not predictable. There's no guessing how they might react to a situation. They may take my list, hand it on, and never give it a second thought. Or, they might check out every name, very carefully. In any case, you will be with us awhile yet. Who knows what might change by the time you graduate? But I will keep your name on the list."

Hans stood up. He stepped to the desk and shook the director's hand. "Thank you," he said. "It's not clear to me why you're doing this."

"Hans, you have worked harder than anyone else in this school. You've done yourself proud. I want my best students to succeed."

"But you're taking a chance to support me. You wouldn't have to do that."

Direktor Knorr stood up. "I told you, Hans," he said, "you don't know what I believe. No one does."

Hans nodded, feeling a flood of warmth running through him—almost the same sensation he had received from his father's hands.

CHAPTER 33

Kathy was home on a Sunday evening, March 7, 1965. *Judgment at Nuremberg* was showing on television for the first time that night, and Kathy and her parents wanted to watch it. Wally had always been interested in programs about World War II, and Kathy had inherited some of that fascination. It was a movie about justice being administered to the Nazis, and that was something Kathy had already read about. Now she wanted to see how well the trial was portrayed.

The only trouble was, Douglas wanted Kathy's attention. She tried to get him involved with a coloring book, but he wanted her to color too. So she sat on the floor next to him, colored, and tried to watch at the same time. Wayne had gone off to his room, uninterested, and Glenda and little Shauna were rather annoyed that the "grown-ups" wanted to watch something so boring. They had gone to Glenda's room, but they were playing her record player, with the door open, and the sound of the Supremes was rather distracting.

Kathy had just stood up to walk down the hall from the family room and shut Glenda's door when the movie was suddenly interrupted. Frank Reynolds, one of the ABC newsmen, announced that a "brutal clash" had taken place in Selma, Alabama, that afternoon between Negro protest marchers and Alabama state troopers, led by the infamous Sheriff Jim Clark. And then films of the clash began to roll. The first image was horrifying. State troopers, in uniform, wearing hard hats, were charging into a double line of people, mostly Negroes, who cringed but didn't run. The protestors were flattened, knocked down by the charge, but then the troopers began to pound the people on the ground, using long clubs. "Oh, no!" Kathy screeched. "That's John Lewis. I know him." He was at the front of the line in a light-colored rain coat. A trooper had him down on the ground, grasping his arm with one hand and pounding him over and over with a stick. Lewis sank to the ground, grasping his head, but he didn't fight back.

Somewhere behind the scenes, in the chaos of sounds, a voice cried out, "Get 'em. Get the niggers!"

The camera cut to another angle. Horses were charging into the people. Some of the protestors were running back across a bridge; others were being rolled over, trampled under the hooves of the horses. And in the foreground, the beatings were going on and on, the subdued men, down on the road, still receiving blow after blow.

It was all horrible to watch, but the images continued, just kept coming and coming as the camera focused on one beating after another. In the middle of it all, a big, male voice was shouting shocking profanities and saying, "Get those niggers. And get those *white* niggers!"

Wayne had apparently heard his sister's screech. He had hurried down the hall, and then Glenda and Shauna had shown up. The little girls were shocked. "What are they doing?" Glenda wailed. "Why don't they stop?"

Shauna seemed more worried about Kathy. She grabbed her around the legs. Kathy bent down and held her, but she was crying now. It was all so familiar. She knew how it felt to be hit with those sticks, to be hated so much.

The scenes continued unrelentingly: fifteen minutes, Kathy later learned, but it seemed to last an hour. Eventually there was tear gas and marchers running to get away. But even then the troopers didn't stop. They chased the people on foot and on horseback. They clubbed them even as they ran away. Frank Reynolds said little but let the footage speak for itself. At the end, he only announced, again, that this had been Alabama's response to a peaceful, nonviolent protest march against injustice to Negroes.

"All they want to do is *vote*," Kathy cried. "They want their children to be able to play in the same park with white kids and have decent schools. What's wrong with people?"

Mom had gotten up from her chair, come to Kathy, and put her arms around her. "Who was that man you knew?" she asked.

"John Lewis. He's the leader of Snick now. When I was in Mississippi, he was at the headquarters in Greenwood sometimes. He's just a young guy, barely out of college, but Mom, he's like Jesus. He's this quiet, good, sweet young man, and he would never hurt anyone. He *believes* in non-violence. He's been beaten up and jailed, over and over, and he never lifts a finger to defend himself."

"Something's going to happen now," Wally said. "People have seen this, all over the country. They won't put up with this stuff anymore."

It was the strongest statement Wally had ever made about the racism in the south. He was always so soft-spoken himself, as gentle as John Lewis, but Kathy knew he had his own memories. He had been part of that horrible march in the Bataan Peninsula; he understood injustice.

"I'd fight back if someone started pounding on me like that," Wayne said.

"But that's just the point, Wayne," Kathy said. "If you fight back, you keep the violence going. Negroes are trying to be like Gandhi was, in India. They meet violence with love—and look at what that says to the victor, and to the rest of us. It shows up evil for what it is. If they had fought back they would have lost. This way, they won."

"I've never seen anything so sickening," Lorraine said.

"But Mom, that's what's been going on *forever* in the south. A white man can kill a Negro for no reason, just out of hatred, and the courts let him off, every time. No one will pay for killing Medgar Evers. No one will pay for killing Emmett Till. Most white people in this country don't even know who they are."

Judgment at Nuremburg had come back on. Douglas was still sitting on the floor, looking up at Kathy. "It's okay, Kathy," he said. "It was just a show. They're all right now."

And that's what scared her. Maybe people would see it on TV almost as though it were just another show. Somehow, someone had to do something.

That night, when Kathy went to bed, she lay awake for a long time. She kept wondering what she could do. A lot of people were going to be shocked by what they had seen on television that night, the way her parents had been, but most would *do* nothing specific. They would wait for the government, the courts, *someone* to solve the problem. Maybe their attitudes would change a little, and that was good, but change needed to come now, not ten or twenty or fifty years later. People who cared needed to show that they did. What she wanted to do was head for Selma, be part of the next protest if there was one. But that was probably not something she could pull off. She had enough money in savings to buy a bus ticket, but her parents would never allow it, and she couldn't just run off from school.

For the next few days she followed the accounts in the newspaper and on television. Lots of people *were* heading to Selma. Famous people were gathering there—movie stars and performers, Negro and white, along with the best known of the civil rights leaders: Martin Luther King, Jr.; Andrew Young; James Farmer. Kathy saw footage on the news of a vigil at a Negro church in Selma, a mass meeting where the people were singing freedom songs. Kathy longed to be there, to add her support, but she told herself over and over that she couldn't do it.

During that same week ground troops—two divisions of American soldiers—began to land in Vietnam. Until now, the only Americans had been "advisers," and even though rumors were spreading that these troops had participated in more than an advisory role, now, for the first time, fighting troops were being sent. Kathy knew what everyone was saying, that the Communists had to be stopped, but she wondered. Some very smart people, including Uncle Alex, seemed to think the United States was getting itself involved in a civil war, supporting the side with the least commitment to the battle. Kathy worried how deeply involved the U.S. might become, but she also saw an irony that bothered her even more. Why would the country send its boys halfway around the world to "ensure the freedom" of the South Vietnamese, when no such freedom was being guaranteed American Negroes?

On Monday, March 15, President Johnson appeared on television in a broadcast to the nation. He told America: "At times history and fate meet at a single time in a single place to shape a turning point in man's unending search for freedom. So it was at Lexington and Concord. So it was a century ago at Appomattox. So it was last week in Selma, Alabama." He announced that he would move ahead rapidly to pass a Voting Rights Bill. He called upon Congress to stop delaying and get the bill to his desk. He wanted voting rights extended to every American. He wanted a bill that would end the so-called literacy tests and poll taxes that kept Negroes from voting in many states. He ended by saying, "Their cause must be our cause too. Because it is not just Negroes, but really it is all of us who must overcome the crippling legacy of bigotry and injustice. And we *shall* overcome."

Kathy thought of the times she had sung the song with her friends in Mississippi: "We shall overcome someday." But she didn't believe any law would change things as fast as was needed. Someone had to *enforce* the law, and George Wallace, governor of Alabama, had already announced that he would defy any further laws the federal government tried to pass. Such laws were unconstitutional, he claimed, and would destroy the "southern way of life." It was Communists who were stirring up the "nigras," according to him. Colored people had always been happy in the South until "outside agitators" had started causing so much trouble.

What Kathy also followed each day was the progress of a request Negro leaders had made in Alabama. They wanted to start the march over—walk from Selma to Montgomery, the state capital, just as they had planned to do before. And this time they wanted protection. A brave Alabama judge had not only granted that protection but had denounced the tactics of the governor and his state troopers during the last attempt. The new march was set for March 21, and Kathy felt that people who cared should be there, should join the others, should make this march so immense that no one would ever forget it. She was still telling herself she couldn't go, but one afternoon, as she was walking home from school, a terrible idea struck her: what if no one from Utah was there? People were gathering from all across the country, but she had not heard that any representatives would be there from Utah. Maybe there wouldn't be a single Mormon in the march, and what did that say about her own people, if no one cared enough about this to do something? Suddenly she felt she *had* to go.

Kathy thought she could leave on Thursday and get there in time. The march was going to take four days, so she would have to miss the next week of school, but she could be back by the following Monday, at the latest. She might have to travel all night on buses, getting little sleep, but she would miss seven days of school, and that was something she had never done in her life. She could take her books with her and get a lot of studying done on the bus. What she knew she had to do was convince her father, and do so by making a reasonable, quiet case for her going, without seeming overwrought and upset. So she waited until that night, after Douglas and the girls had gone to bed and Wayne was in his room. Dad was in his little office off the family room, and Mom was watching television and ironing. Kathy stepped to her dad's door, so nervous she was shaking, and said, "Dad, could you come out here for just a minute? I need to talk to you and Mom about something."

"Sure. Just a minute," Wally said.

Kathy turned around. "Do you care if I turn the TV off for just a minute?" she asked her mother.

"Not at all. I wasn't really paying much attention."

"Seventy-Seven Sunset Strip" was just coming on, and Kathy knew how stupid her parents considered the show. She walked over and switched off the set. By then Dad had come out. He dropped into his favorite chair, smiled, and said, "What's up?" Mom was still ironing.

"You know there's going to be another march to Montgomery on Sunday, I guess."

"Yes. It sounds like that judge has approved it now."

"That's right. I doubt there will be any violence this time. The marchers are going to have federal protection."

"I hope you're right. But it's a long march, and it sounds like a lot of people are going to be down there. You string that many people out over a lot of miles, and I'm not sure there's any way to assure everyone's safety."

Did he suspect something? Or was he just giving his opinion? "Do you think anyone from Utah will be down there? Or any Mormons at all?"

"I don't know. I haven't read anything about anyone from here going."

"Don't you think *someone* from our church should be there?"

"Not necessarily. Marches bring a lot of attention to a cause, but the main thing is, a lot of people need to change their attitudes. I think that's happening around here. Most of us grew up not even thinking much about the way Negroes were treated down south. Now, we're finally hearing about it."

"It's not just in the South."

"I know. We have our problems here in Utah. I doubt that colored people always get a fair shake when they apply for jobs, for one thing."

Kathy nodded. She glanced at her mother, who was peering up from her ironing and looking curious, at least, maybe even concerned.

"Dad . . ." And Kathy thought to add, "Mom. I've been in the South. I only know of one other person from Utah who was in Mississippi during Freedom Summer. He was there longer than I was—the whole summer—but still, the two of us are about the only ones I'm aware of who have tried to be part of the civil rights movement. I've been thinking that I ought to be in Selma this Sunday. I could show the people down there that people from out here do care about them, and we're willing to stand with them."

Wally smiled. "Honey, I do appreciate your devotion to these things, but no. Absolutely not. You can't be taking off from high school, and—"

"I've hardly ever missed school, and it's my senior year. How much could it hurt? People take time off to go on vacations with their families, or to—"

"Yes. *With* their families. But you're talking about going down there alone. How would you even get there?"

"On a bus. I could keep up with my school work during all those hours I'd be traveling. And I have enough money of my own to pay the fare."

"No. Kathy, there's no way a responsible father is going to let an eighteen-year-old girl travel all by herself on a bus to Alabama and let her take a chance at getting her head knocked in. Again! I still get angry every time I think of what LaRue got you into last summer."

"LaRue didn't get me into it. I wanted to go."

"But she should have had the good sense to know better."

"But Dad—"

"Honey, think about it," Mom said. "There's nothing to debate here. It's not even something we would consider." She had stopped ironing and was standing with her arms folded.

Kathy stood for a time, caught between the two of them. She looked from one to the other. "Then go with me. We could fly down there together. Maybe we could just march the first day and then come back. Someone needs to go. Why shouldn't it be us?"

"Why *should* it be us?"

"I told you. I'm part of the movement. I've had my head cut open. I've been in jail. I'm involved in this, Dad, and I ought to be down there. If you believe what you say you believe, how can you, in good conscience, just sit here and ignore what's happening? Good people have to stand up and be counted. Those marchers are all our Christian brothers and sisters. I can't tell you how inspiring it would be to both of you to attend one of their meetings and listen to the people sing their hearts out."

"I don't doubt that for a minute, Kathy, but most of this nation will not, cannot, be there. Some will march, and the rest of us can support them in our own way."

Kathy walked over to the couch, crashed onto it, and folded her arms. She had come close to crying when she had thought of the meetings she had attended, the powerful singing, but now she was angry. "Dad, that's just an excuse. You say your heart is with them, but if a Negro came walking into your dealership, would you hire him?"

"If he could do the work, sure."

"So how many have you hired?"

"How many have applied? We have some Negroes in the parts plant."

"I just think it's really easy to sit up here in Utah and say, 'Oh, those terrible southerners—they make Negroes ride in the back of the bus,' and then do nothing of any kind to change the way things are here. Do you think almost all the Negroes in Salt Lake live in the same area because they happen to *prefer* the west side of town? Or do people suddenly raise the prices on homes when Negroes start looking around the other neighborhoods? I've heard people say it a thousand times: If 'they' start moving onto our street, the property values will all go down. Our legislature *finally* passed a civil rights bill, but they took all the teeth out of it. There's nothing in it to stop discrimination in housing."

Wally didn't speak for a time. He waited for her to look at him. "So what are you saying? That I'm like that?"

"I don't know. Would you want a Negro family to move in next door?"

"I wouldn't mind—not if they were decent people."

"What does that mean? You wouldn't say that about white people."

"Of course I would."

"Not in the same way. You immediately respond that way because you think that a Negro family probably *wouldn't* be decent."

"Not at all. I didn't say that."

He hadn't said it, but Kathy knew how people thought. She had heard so much of that kind of stuff. Utahns weren't beating up Negroes, but a lot of restaurants and hotels and dance halls had only started admitting Negroes last year, after the first civil rights act had passed. And she had heard all the stereotypes about laziness and dirtiness. She knew that most people in Utah wanted change in Alabama, but at the same time they resisted any change here at home.

"I'm going," Kathy suddenly said. "I'm eighteen, I've made my decision, and I'm going."

"No you're not."

"You're not," Mom added. "We're still your parents. I don't care how old you are."

"I'll be leaving for college this fall, and I'll be making all my own decisions."

"Not all of them," Dad said. "You won't even be going away to college if you don't start showing more responsibility."

Kathy stood up and pointed at her dad. "*Responsibility?* What are you talking about? That's all I've ever shown, my whole life. While other kids are messing around, I'm always studying. I'm the one who gets the good grades, looks after Douglas, tends the kids, does everything you ever ask of me. If anyone is irresponsible, it's the two of you. The irresponsible thing is *not* to go to Alabama."

Dad stood up. "Honey, now wait a minute. Listen to me. I shouldn't have said that. You have been responsible about most things. But it would be irresponsible, for us, to allow you to put yourself in danger."

"Dad, what do you think all those marchers are doing all the time? The only way to challenge this nation is to force the issue. Those Snick workers walk into the teeth of the enemy every single day. Schwerner and Goodman and Chaney *died* for this cause. You were willing to put your own life on the line for your country once, when you were my age. And that's all I want to do—fight for my country. President Johnson said that none of us will be free until we all are."

Dad was listening; she could see it in his eyes. He slipped his hands into his pockets and looked at the floor for a time. But then he said, "Honey, I can't let you go. You're just too precious to me. You may think you're grown up, but you're still my little daughter. You can't travel all the way across this nation all by yourself on some old bus. I just can't let you do that."

"Dad, I told you. I'm going."

"I'll send the police after you, Kathy. I'll have them pull you off the bus and bring you home."

"I'll find another way. I'm going."

"No. Look at me, Kathy. I'm your father, and I say to you, no. You are *not* going."

"I've never defied you. Maybe I went to Mississippi without getting your permission, but I've never done something that you told me directly not to do. But I'm doing this. And I'm doing it because I have to. It's wrong to stay home when I feel the way I do. When your father tells you to do something that you know is wrong, it's time to defy him."

Kathy turned then and walked to her room. She locked the door, and she didn't answer when her mother came down later, knocked, and said, "Honey, let me come in. We need to settle this in a better way."

But what did that mean? They only wanted to talk her out of it. So Kathy said nothing, and she packed a little suitcase. She put in walking shoes and a waterproof jacket—in case of rain. But she didn't need a lot of clothes. She could wear the same jeans every day. That's what the other marchers would do. She packed her books. She didn't want to ruin her grades. That's what her father didn't understand about her. She *did* take responsibility for her own life. She didn't just study to satisfy him and mom.

What she knew was that her parents had decided to leave her alone for the night. But they would be back the next morning, and they would try to talk her out of this. So Kathy waited until they had gone to bed, waited an hour after that, and then opened her bedroom window, climbed out and shut it, then walked around the house. A dog barked next door, but she didn't see any lights come on. So she walked on up the driveway. She hadn't quite figured out how she was going to pull this off, but she was on her way to Selma.

∽

Kathy waited until Sunday evening before she finally called home. But she had decided to call her grandma, not her parents. Grandma Bea was the one person she thought she could talk to. Fortunately, it was she who answered the phone, not Grandpa, and she accepted the collect charges. Then she said, "Kathy, is it you? Are you all right?"

"Sure I am, Grandma. I'm fine."

"Oh, honey, we've been so worried about you. Why didn't you get in touch sooner?"

"Dad told me he would call the police. I was afraid they'd be looking for me."

"He didn't do it, Kathy. But he's worried to death about you. We all are."

"There's nothing to worry about, Grandma. The first day of the march was perfect. There were three thousand people. Did you see it on TV?"

"Of course we did. We all watched to see if we could spot you, but we couldn't."

"I wasn't important. I was just someone in the crowd."

"Not to us."

"Grandma, I've felt rotten since I left. I know it was a bad thing to do, but today, out there with all those people, I never felt so happy in my life. I feel like I'm supposed to be here. And there's no danger. They have federal troops down here, helicopters flying around, and everything."

"I know. But things can happen when people get so angry."

"Not this time. I saw my friend John Lewis today. He's marching anyway, even after they cracked his head open two weeks ago. He told me a lot of movie stars and singers and people like that will be here by the end of the march. Quite a few are here already. No one would dare hurt famous people like that."

"Do you have to stay the whole time? We could buy you an airplane ticket, and—"

"I can't do that, Grandma. I want to use my own money, and I want to stay for the whole march. The road is narrow tomorrow, so most of us are taking buses to the next stop. Then we'll walk two more days after that. At the end, they're going to have a giant mass meeting, and thousands and thousands of people will be here by then. Martin Luther King is going to speak. I don't want to miss that."

"I heard it's cold down there. Where are you going to sleep?"

"It is kind of cold tonight. But I'm okay. I bought a blanket, since I didn't have a sleeping bag. But listen, Grandma, there's a line of people waiting for this phone. I have to go. Call my parents, okay? Tell them I'm all right. I wasn't running away or anything like that. This was just something I had to do. Tell them I'll be back by Saturday or Sunday, depending on the bus schedule. And I really am fine—just fine."

"Listen, honey, Grandpa's right here. He wants to talk to you."

"No, Grandma, I—"

"Kathy?" It was Grandpa.

"Yes."

"I want you to come home now. Let me wire you some money, and you can catch a plane in the morning."

"No, Grandpa. I'm going to complete the march."

"You shouldn't have run off like this, honey. Your father told you not to go."

Kathy didn't answer. There was no way to explain all this—not in any way that he would accept.

"It looks like this voting rights law will get passed now. That's good. The rest of this march is just for show. There's no real point in staying. You don't know what some of these Ku Klux Klan boys might do. If they can catch one of you outsiders away from the main group, or—"

"Grandpa, I've got to go. I won't wander off alone. I'll be fine. I'll start home as soon as the march is over."

"Listen to me, Kathy. Don't hang up."

She stopped, waited.

"Honey, you're tearing your family apart. Can't you see that? I'm glad you care about the Negro people, but there are right ways to do things and there are wrong ways. Defying your parents was wrong. You have to know that."

"Grandpa, I'm eighteen. I have to think for myself."

"Think all you want, honey, but don't defy. You just can't do that. Can't you see what's happening to us? LaRue has gone off, torn herself away from the rest of us, and half the time I can't talk to Bobbi. She thinks she knows everything. This family has gotten through some hard times, but we did it by sticking together, not by splitting apart."

Kathy stood in the smelly old phone booth. She glanced back through the glass door to see the impatience in the faces of the people waiting outside. What could she say?

And then she realized that Grandpa was crying. "Come home, honey," he said. "Please. Just come home now."

"Grandpa, you always told us about your great-grandpa—the one who lost his little boy and still got up the next morning and did what he had to do. Thomases believe in what's good and what's right, and they stand up for those things. They don't quit when things get hard."

"But this is different. This is . . . just different."

"No, Grandpa. This is exactly the same. I'm here because of all the things you and Grandma and Dad and Mom have taught me. I wish you were here too—you four and all my uncles and aunts and cousins. That would be the best thing I can imagine. There's so much love here, Grandpa."

Grandpa Thomas didn't speak for a long time, and Kathy was getting nervous about the people outside. "I've got to go," she finally said again.

But Grandpa said, "I love you, Kathy. Be careful. And when you get home, let's sit down and talk about all this."

"Grandpa, you'll just—"

"No I won't. I'll listen."

"Okay. Tell Mom and Dad I love them. I've been homesick all week. It's been hard for me, Grandpa. Really hard. I *will* talk to you when I get back, okay?"

"Okay."

"Goodbye." She hung up the phone and stepped from the phone booth. A woman pushed past her, in a hurry to get in. Kathy walked a few steps, but then she stopped, unable to keep control any longer. She began to cry, hard. She had been wrong to leave the way she had. She knew that, had known it all week. But she was also right to be where she was. She didn't doubt that either. Grandpa was afraid the family was tearing apart, but that wasn't true. The family would be all right. It was Kathy who was in the middle, and she was being ripped in half.

CHAPTER 34

G ene was on a train; he had been transferred. He had checked in his big trunk full of clothes and belongings to the baggage car, loaded his bike, and now was sitting by a window, watching the countryside go by. He had actually seen very little of Germany so far. Right after Christmas he had been transferred to Ravensburg, south of Ulm, not far from Switzerland, and now he was on his way back through Ulm and on to Stuttgart, traveling the same route, going back the way he had come. Gene would be a senior companion now, and his new companion, Elder Johns, was a "greenie," right out of the states. The District Leader in Stuttgart was going to pick Elder Johns up at the mission home and look after him until Gene arrived later in the day.

It was all quite amazing. No one Gene had talked to had ever heard of such a young elder being made a senior to a new missionary. Elder Hafen, his senior in Ravensburg, teased him about being a "wonder boy," of being President Fetzer's—the new mission president's—"fair-haired boy." But Gene suspected that it was his German, as much as anything, that had brought this about. He told Elder Hafen, "You're the one the president thinks so highly of—you and Elder Bentz. He figures any missionary trained by you two has to be good."

And actually, there was something to that. Elder Bentz had taught Gene to work hard, to be diligent and serious about the work, to pray and study—all the things a missionary needed to do—and Elder Hafen had been the same way. Something else important had also happened. Gene and Elder Hafen had finally baptized someone—an impressive young couple with a little daughter—the Schönfelds. It had been a remarkable experience for Gene. After tracting for so many months, meeting no one who was really interested, the Schönfelds had seemed ready and waiting. They had known a Mormon family in town, had always admired them, and one cold evening when the elders had shown up at their door, they had invited them in, mostly because of those good associations. They had agreed to hear the lessons, and their acceptance had been almost instantaneous. Everything had made sense to them, and they had taken the time to read the Book of Mormon. Both had come away believing that it was a genuine scripture.

Gene had extracted faith from the Schönfelds as though he were being converted with them. It was as if he were hearing the gospel for the first time. The plan of salvation had always been part of his thinking, but now it took on a profound rightness as he listened to Karl and Erika express their wonder and satisfaction with a plan that explained life's meaning. They wanted their daughter sealed to them, and for the first time Gene comprehended what it meant to be linked to his own ancestors, and to his posterity. He wasn't sure that God had filled his heart with all the conviction he wanted, but he had felt real stirrings, felt a power affirm the truth of crucial principles. That had moved him miles ahead. He felt now that it wasn't wrong for him to bear testimony, that he did have a deep enough faith to express. What he wanted, however, was the power he had seen in his two seniors, the power he knew his father possessed.

What worried Gene most was that he wouldn't be up to this next challenge. He had to teach a new missionary, just as Elder Bentz had done, and he needed to impart the same commitment to the work. He thought about the hard days this new guy would face. Maybe he wouldn't be as homesick, as disheartened as Gene had been, but if he was like Gene, he wouldn't express his inner struggles, and Gene needed to be sensitive to all that. One thing he hoped was that the new elder didn't have a girl back home.

Riding on the train this March day, looking out across the plowed soil and budding trees, he tested himself a little by letting his mind run back to Marsha. He had told himself a thousand times that they really weren't meant for each other. He believed that was probably true, but when he thought of her, he still felt pain. Was it only that he had wanted something and hadn't gotten it? Was it his ego that was hurt? Or was his other thought right, that he would never find anyone who meant quite so much to him? If he never dated her again, he was at least thankful for the questions she had left in his mind. And those questions brought him back to the crucial issue: his missionary work. He either carried the Spirit with him or he didn't. The people who heard his testimony didn't know he had played sports, had been a big wheel in his school, and they wouldn't have cared if they had known. Most of them only wanted him to leave them alone. But those few who did listen wanted to feel something, and Gene knew he had to lift himself to another level now. He wouldn't have a senior companion to rely on.

And so Gene spent part of his trip saying silent prayers, returning time and again to the same request: "Lord, help me to do this. I can't let this new elder down. I have to take another step up. I have to be stronger. Please, Lord, help me."

A man was sitting across from Gene, facing him, so that he was riding backward but looking out the same window. He had gotten on the train in Ravensburg with Gene, but he had made his way on crutches since he was missing his right leg. He was a man about Gene's father's age, or maybe a little older—maybe fifty or so. Gene had exchanged a few pleasantries at first, and then afterward, they had slipped into their own reveries. Gene wondered whether he shouldn't try to open up a conversation about the Church, but the man had engrossed himself in a book, and Gene had decided to leave him alone, at least for the present. He hoped a conversation would start naturally, sooner or later.

Now, as Gene was lost in his own world, the man finally said, "So, are you going very far today?"

"To Ulm, and then on to Stuttgart."

"Do you live in Ravensburg?"

"I've lived there for a few months, but I'm actually from America. Salt Lake City, in the West."

"You're not German?"

Gene smiled. "Half German. My mother was from Frankfurt."

"*Ach.* I see. That's why you speak our language so well."

"Yes. But I've had to work at it. I didn't speak German at home very much."

The man nodded, and the conversation might have ended, but Gene felt he really needed to say something about the church. "I'm here as a missionary," he said.

The man nodded. "From the Mormons, I suppose."

It wasn't a hard guess. People knew these young men who came to their doors in dark suits. And of course, Gene had mentioned Salt Lake. "Yes. Have you been visited by Mormon missionaries?"

"All too often," the man said, and he laughed. "They won't leave me alone."

"That's because we have an important message for you," Gene said.

"Yes, yes. But don't start. I'm not a religious man."

Gene laughed. He knew he could think of a comeback and find a way to approach the man, but that would be awkward, with the two facing each other for another hour or so. And so he let it go.

"How did your father meet a German girl? Was he a soldier here?"

"He was a soldier here, but that's not how he met her. He came here before the war—also as a missionary." Gene had never been comfortable about telling Germans that his father had fought in the war. Most Germans liked Americans now, and Gene never mentioned the war unless someone brought it up. He just thought it was better left alone.

"Your father was a missionary here, and then a soldier? That must have been strange for him. Difficult, I would think."

Gene had known the story since he was a little boy. He had heard his father say that it was hard to serve in Germany and then return during the war. But never before had the idea struck Gene with such force. He had been here long enough to understand now. He couldn't imagine himself leaving and then returning to do battle. How could he think of the Schönfelds as his enemy, or all the good members in Ulm or Ravensburg? How had his father ever managed it? "It was the worst thing he ever had to do. He's told me that."

"Where did he fight? Do you know?"

The man seemed comfortable with all this, wanted to know, so Gene said. "He jumped from airplanes. I don't know the word for that in German."

"*Fallschirmtruppen.*"

A *Fallshirm* had to be a parachute. The word made sense. "Yes. He was in Normandy."

"On D-Day?" He said the word in English.

"Yes. And then he jumped into Holland. I know that. And he was in the Ardennes." There were other stories. His dad had dropped behind the enemy lines to help with the crossing of the Rhine. But Gene hesitated to tell that.

The man was nodding. He was a nice-looking man with graying hair and clear blue eyes. He looked powerful, sitting down, with large shoulders and big hands. He had handled his crutches with ease as he had made his way to the seat. "In case you're worried, he wasn't the one who blew my leg off," he said. "That was a Russian. I fought in the east."

Gene didn't know what to say. The man seemed good-natured about the loss, but Gene didn't want to ask about it.

"So your father, after being a missionary and a soldier, does he still believe in God?"

"Yes. He's been a leader in our church. And now he's *Mitglied der amerikanischen gesetzgebende Versammlung*." It was the complicated German way of saying "a member of congress." Gene had told very few Germans about this—partly because it had taken him a long time to learn to say it, but mostly because he didn't want to seem prideful. But his companions had told some people, especially Church members, and everyone who had heard it had been impressed. Gene saw the same reaction in this man, and he was immediately sorry he had said anything. He knew he had been bragging.

"A war hero. A religious leader. And now a national leader. You must be proud of him."

"To me, he's just my father."

"Yes, of course. But you must feel some need to live up to him—to be as great as he is. That's not easy for a young man."

"I'll never be such an important man, I'm certain. I don't worry about that."

The man smiled. "Be careful. A missionary shouldn't lie."

Gene was surprised by the man's perception, and embarrassed. He felt the heat in his face. "My father is also a *good* man," he finally said. "I hope I can be like him in that way."

"I'm certain you're that already," the man said, obviously aware that he had unnerved Gene a little. "But it's not easy, this whole matter of living up to our parents' wishes and still satisfying our own desires. My father was a minister, and he wanted me to follow him into the Lutheran Church. But I came home from the war without a glimmer of faith left in me. I've been a great disappointment to my family."

"They must admire your courage, all the same."

"Everyone says that, but I have no idea why. It takes no courage to walk on one leg. It's merely what I have to do. The courage is to live with all the bad memories, the terrible dreams. That's what I had to fight my way through. What about your father? Did he suffer with nightmares?"

"I don't know. I don't think so."

"You don't know because men don't like to talk about it. They come home from war, and they're crazy inside, but they don't want anyone to know. So they live with it, and they make the best of things. But they never forget. What I don't understand is anyone who has fought in a war, seen the worst of mankind, discovered his own animal nature, and then found a way to believe in God. There's the courage. Or the falseness. Some men go about their lives claiming belief, when inside they know how things are—the same as I do."

"My father honestly believes. I have no doubt of that."

"I suppose. But I'll tell you this, there is so much more going on inside any of us than we admit to others. Jesus Christ would have us love one another, as ourselves. But it's not possible. It's a lie, if you ask me. When I faced death, I preferred to kill. That's what I know." He smiled rather benevolently. "That's my religious message for you. What do you say to that?"

Gene hesitated, trying to think what he could say that would match this man's honesty—and yet refute his conclusions. "I think it's very difficult to love someone so much, but I've felt that kind of love when the Holy Ghost was with me. I think that's the only way we can do it."

The man had listened. He watched Gene's eyes for a long time, and Gene tried hard not to look away but to let him see inside. "You *are* a good young man," he said. "But I don't know whether you will always believe in such things. Life can change a person."

Gene accepted that and didn't argue. What he hoped was that he would learn to love more, not less.

The man finally went back to his book. He never told Gene his name, but he left Gene with a lot to think about. As Gene waited for his next train, at the station in Ulm, he found himself wondering about his father. Had he come home from the war full of confusion and doubt? Had he had bad dreams? It didn't seem possible. His father was always about three rungs above the rest of humanity. Gene thought of him as almost perfect. He had fought in the war so valiantly that his leaders had commissioned him an officer, right in the field. Grandpa had told Gene that, and even though Gene had never seen his father's medals, he knew that he had won them for valor, putting his life in danger to knock out four giant artillery guns. He had faced an enemy that had outnumbered his own troops several times. Then he had returned to serve as a bishop and counselor to the stake president. He had done everything right.

Gene had to wonder at himself. He struggled to be away from home, to spend his days knocking on doors, even to face questions that he couldn't readily answer. Where was he heading, compared to his father? It was all deeply disappointing. Marsha had been right about him. He didn't have the substance to be the great man his father was. When he thought of his one-time goal, to become president of the United States, he had to laugh at himself.

When Gene boarded the next train, he dug into his briefcase for some stationery, and he wrote a letter:

Dear Mom and Dad:

I wanted to let you know that I'm transferring today. I'm on my way to Stuttgart. But you won't believe what's happened. I've been made a senior companion, and my new companion is a greenie. I just hope I can get him off to a good start. I haven't been a very good missionary so far, and I've got to do a lot better now. I'll have to admit, I'm pretty scared.

I can't imagine loving anyone, outside my family, as much as I love the members of the Church over here, and especially the Schönfelds. What I can't imagine is how I could leave and then return to face these people as an enemy. Dad, I just didn't understand before I came here what it was you had to do, and now that I do understand, I admire you more than ever. I've always known what a great man you are, but what you did was just an idea to me. Now I've been here and I *know*. I could never be the man you are.

And Mom, I've been thinking about you, too. You gave up your country, your language, almost everything. You must have been so homesick at first. I think about you being in England when I was born, and Dad in danger, in the war. I didn't understand homesickness until I came here. I think I can imagine now how much you must have missed Dad, and Grandpa Stoltz too. I've never been tested the way you two were, and I hope I never will be.

I'll write again as soon as I can. I'll let you know all about my companion and our place in Stuttgart. I hope everything is well at "home"—if you can call Virginia that. I miss you and the kids so much. I have the strange feeling that I've always loved you but not understood you nearly enough, but my respect for both of you has gone up another notch.

Love,
Gene

When Gene arrived in Stuttgart, three elders were at the train station waiting for him. One was a tall blond fellow from Salt Lake named Elder Bates. He shook hands with Gene first and said he was the district leader. Gene happened to know that he had been in Sigma Chi, back at the U, but he decided to wait until later to talk to him about that. The second was a husky, older-looking fellow named Elder Lawson, who was the district leaders's junior companion. And the third was a clean-cut missionary in a shiny new suit and a short haircut, Elder Darrell Johns. "This is your new companion," Elder Bates said.

"Where are you from, Elder Johns?" Gene asked.

"Preston, Idaho."

"And you just got in—when?—yesterday?"

"The day before. We were at the mission home yesterday. They kind of filled us in on everything."

"Are you still pretty tired?"

"Not right now. But I sure had a hard time staying awake yesterday."

The other three elders laughed. Certainly, they all remembered. "Well, we'll need to get you set up with a few things. Have you bought a bike?"

"No. Not yet."

"We'll need to take care of that, and then we've got to hit the ground running." Gene glanced at Elder Bates. "We won't be able to get all our hours in this week, but we will every week after this."

"That's what I like to hear," Elder Bates said.

For the next three weeks Gene pushed hard all the time. He knew that Elder Johns was dragging sometimes, but it was crucial that he get the idea, right from the start, that missionaries worked long hours and didn't mess around. Elder Johns had gone through the new German program at the Language Training Mission in Provo, so he knew some German, but he admitted that he had put off his mission a year so that he could ski one more season and make up his mind whether or not he really wanted to go. Gene understood the impulse, but he also knew that priorities had to change now, and he wanted to make that clear. The fact was, Gene hated all the hours of tracting they were putting in, but he had to build a pool of contacts so they could spend more time teaching.

At least Elder Johns didn't complain, and he certainly had the legs for biking. Some new elders couldn't keep up when they first arrived. That was never true of Elder Johns, and added to that, he had a sense of humor. He didn't show it much the first few days, but gradually he and Gene were enjoying each other, and they had met some people on the doors who were willing to accept at least one lesson.

Something about all this absorption in the work, and becoming a senior, seemed to rid Gene of many of the concerns he had felt when he had first arrived in the mission field. He needed the Lord, and the Lord was there. And home was so far away that it didn't press in on him the way it had at first. He still found the work hard, and he still counted up the months to think how long he had to go, but he was looking ahead, not back.

The Stuttgart ward met in a nice old building, which also served as the stake center. Stuttgart was a big city, but it was full of parks and trees, and now that spring was coming on, all the flowering trees were in bloom. It was not the greatest place to use a bike, with all the busy streets, so he and Elder Johns often used streetcars when they had no other choice.

One day the two came back to their apartment for their afternoon study and found that they each had letters. Gene sat down at the little desk in his room and read the letter from his parents. They had finally gotten Gene's letter—the one he had written on the train. Most of the letters from home were written by Mom, but this one was from Dad:

> Dear Elder Thomas:
>
> I call you that because you are sounding more like the real thing all the time. What a joy your last letter was. I suppose there is no way a child can ever understand his own parents— know who they once were and what life has cost them—but your letter was as close as we will ever come to that in this life, and it meant a great deal to both of us.
>
> But son, you overestimate me. You've heard the story about the time when I was a missionary and blessed your mother. You know that she was healed and that had a lot to do with the whole family coming into the Church. Here's what you don't know. On that day, after I blessed your mom, I was terrified. I felt certain at the time of the blessing that the Lord was in those promises, that they weren't just mine. But almost

as soon as I got outside, I began to doubt. I was young, and it seemed unimaginable to me that through a power I possessed, a healing could occur. I wondered whether I had really felt the Lord's Spirit, or whether I only imagined that I had. No one was more surprised than I was when Grandpa Stoltz came to tell us that your mother was getting better.

Maybe you wonder why I would tell you that. But I want you to know that I was no super missionary. I was a guy like you, trying to do my best. We all start in the same place, Son. We all have to grow. And growth isn't very steady. Just when we think we're almost "there," we can slip back again. When I returned from the war I was a wreck. But I had your mom, and I had you, and I just had to do the best I could. It was several years after the war before I started to feel something like myself. I didn't do anything "great." I just managed to survive a tough situation.

Gene, I love you. I'm proud of you. You have always put yourself into every task with full enthusiasm, and you do virtually everything well. You're growing up a little, facing some tests, and that's all you've ever needed to become the man you want to be. Trust in the Lord and keep working hard. Don't worry about the rest. I think you have it in your head that you have to live up to some set of credentials that you imagine I have. But that has nothing to do with what matters in this life. Just be yourself, and that's more than enough.

Your mom sends her love. She said she'll write in the next day or two. Everyone is fine here—except that Joey and Sharon and Kurt would all rather be home in Salt lake, and they never stop telling me so. I guess they'll get used to things here. You keep your mind on your business and teach that junior of yours all the things Elder Bentz and Elder Hafen taught you.

Love,

Dad

Gene wiped some tears from his face. He felt as though he could breathe deeper, as though nine months worth of tension had been released from his chest. He waited for a time and then turned around and looked at Elder Johns. "Another letter from your girl?" he asked. "Already?"

"It's not easy to live without *me*," Elder Johns said, and he grinned.

"So do you think she's going to wait for you?"

"She says so." He nodded confidently, still smiling.

"Maybe she will," Gene said, but then he added seriously, "Elder Bentz always told me that it was best to assume she won't. That way, you don't get knocked down so hard when you get the Dear John."

"That's what you did, right? And your Dear John didn't bother you a bit."

Now Gene was smiling. "Something like that," he said.

"How was it, really?"

Elder Johns was sitting at the table in the middle of the room. It was an overcast day, and the elders hadn't turned any lights on. The gray light from the two big windows seemed to draw away all the color. Elder Johns, tan as he actually was, looked as drab as his gray suit. Gene looked at him for a time before he decided to tell him the truth. "It was pretty bad. And then it got worse. At first I thought I had handled it, but I think it bothers me more now, the longer I don't hear from her."

"Is she getting married?"

"I don't know. I don't think so. Not for a while, anyway."

"Maybe you'll get another shot."

"Maybe. But it's not very helpful to think that way. I'm better off if I just assume she's gone and I'll have fun looking around again when I get back."

"Yeah. I can see that."

"Well . . . we'd better get to our studies."

Gene turned around in his chair and reached for his German Bible, but he heard from behind him, "Elder Thomas?"

"Yeah." Gene twisted in his chair again.

"There's something I need to talk to you about."

Gene stood up enough to turn his chair so that when he sat down again, he was facing his companion. "What's that?" he asked.

Elder Johns was leaning over the table with his arms crossed and his weight on his elbows. He was looking down. "I grew up in the Church, you know, just like you. And my parents always talked to me about going on a mission. It was never something I got excited about doing on my own."

"But you made up your own mind to go, didn't you?"

"I don't know. I put it off for a while. But all my buddies were gone by then. My bishop kept after me all the time, and my family. I finally gave in, as much as anything."

Elder Johns continued to look at the table, and Gene thought he knew what he was feeling. "Elder, it's really hard when you first get here. Everything is different from home, and knocking on doors all day just isn't a lot of fun."

"I don't mind that so much."

"Really? So what's on your mind?"

"I'm not like you, Elder Thomas. I don't have much of a testimony. I've just sort of gone along with things, without thinking much, and now I feel like I'm out here just faking it."

Gene thought for quite some time. There were things he could have admitted, but he wasn't certain that would help. "Here's what I'd do," he said. "I'd get out your English Book of Mormon. When we study together, in German, we end up talking more about language than we do about the gospel. But I'd kneel down and pray before you read, and then again after, and I'd ask the Lord for a testimony of the Book of Mormon. That's kind of the crux of everything."

"Have you done that?"

"I have, Elder, and it made all the difference. That book is real. I know it is."

"I thought when you got out here a lot of stuff would happen. You know, miracles and everything."

"I know. And you'll see some stuff. I've had some experiences that have really helped me. But there's nothing automatic about getting a testimony, just because you're here."

"Yeah. I can see that."

"Why don't you go ahead and have a prayer by yourself. And then study. We can do that every day during these afternoon study periods."

"Okay. Thanks. I've known for a long time I've needed to do that."

Gene nodded, and then he turned his chair back to his desk. He picked up his Bible, but he didn't open it yet. He bowed his head and said his own prayer. He thanked the Lord for how far he had come. His mission still looked long, but he was sure now that he could make it. He had never understood when he was younger how hard a mission would be, but it was encouraging to feel that he was growing into the job.

He glanced back to see Elder Johns kneeling at his bed, and he remembered.

ABOUT THE AUTHOR

Dean Hughes has published more than ninety books and numerous stories and poems for all ages—children, young adults, and adults.

Dr. Hughes received his B.A. from Weber State University in Ogden, Utah, and his M.A. and Ph.D. from the University of Washington. He has attended post-doctoral seminars at Stanford and Yale Universities and has taught English at Central Missouri State University and Brigham Young University.

He has also served in many callings, including that of a bishop, in The Church of Jesus Christ of Latter-day Saints. He and his wife, Kathleen Hurst Hughes, who has served in the Relief Society general presidency, have three children and nine grandchildren. They live in Midway, Utah.

If you liked this book, you'll love the *Children of the Promise* series by Dean Hughes!

What was life like during World War II? How did the war affect the lives of those who fought and those who kept the home fires burning? Find out in *Children of the Promise*, the carefully researched and beautifully written story of a family living through those turbulent years from 1939 to 1947. Meet the characters readers have come to love: Alex, who served a mission to Germany and returned to fight those among whom he had preached; Bobbi, a Navy nurse with a divided heart; Wally, a young rebel who finds his true path in the trials of a prisoner-of-war camp; and many others. *Children of the Promise* will touch your heart in an unforgettable way!

Volume 1: *Rumors of War*

Volume 2: *Since You Went Away*

Volume 3: *Far from Home*

Volume 4: *When We Meet Again*

Volume 5: *As Long as I Have You*